The Burning Pen

The Burning Pen

Sex Writers on Sex Writing

Edited by M. Christian

alyson books
los angeles | new york

MANUFACTURED IN THE UNITED STATES OF AMERICA.

THIS TRADE PAPERBACK ORIGINAL IS PUBLISHED BY ALYSON PUBLICATIONS, P.O. BOX 4371, LOS ANGELES, CALIFORNIA 90078-4371.
DISTRIBUTION IN THE UNITED KINGDOM BY
TURNAROUND PUBLISHER SERVICES LTD.,
UNIT 3, OLYMPIA TRADING ESTATE, COBURG ROAD, WOOD GREEN,
LONDON N22 6TZ ENGLAND.

FIRST EDITION: NOVEMBER 2001

01 02 03 04 05 a 10 9 8 7 6 5 4 3 2 1

ISBN 1-55583-615-1

LIBRARY OF CONGRESS CATALOGING-IN-PUBLICATION DATA
THE BURNING PEN : SEX WRITERS ON SEX WRITING / EDITED
BY M. CHRISTIAN—1ST ED.
ISBN 1-55583-615-1
1. EROTIC STORIES—AUTHORSHIP. 2. EROTIC STORIES, AMERICAN.
3. GAY EROTIC LITERATURE. I. CHRISTIAN, M.
PN3377.5.E76 B87 2001
808.3—DC21   2001035770

COVER PHOTOGRAPHY BY PHOTODISC INC.

Acknowledgments

Books, especially anthologies, are never orphans—and this book has had many wonderful parents: the fantastic Scott Brassart and Angela Brown at Alyson Books, who believed in me and this project; Martha, for her caring and support; and all the very special writers (and friends who are also writers) who have written such marvelous stories and who were willing to share with us the people behind the literary magic: Laura Antoniou, Scott Brassart, Patrick Califia-Rice, Jack Fritscher, R.J. March, Lesléa Newman, Felice Picano, Carol Queen, Shar Rednour, Thomas S. Roche, Simon Sheppard, Cecilia Tan, and Lucy Taylor. Take a bow: You all deserve it.

—M. Christian

Contents

Show and Tell

There's an old maxim in the theater: Don't let the wheels show. Don't reveal the mechanisms, don't expose the papier mâché, hide the cue cards. Preserve the magic. Keep the mystique and illusions safe and sacred behind an asbestos curtain.

I'm romantic enough to comprehend the sentiment. Sometimes knowing that Peter Pan was on wires, King Kong was only six inches high, or that Audrey Hepburn didn't sing in *My Fair Lady* takes something important away. The illusion crumbles and the show becomes nothing but a grand lie.

Authors don't escape the urge for carefully guarded privacy, but regarding the written word, there is not so much a need to keep the mechanisms secret as there is a fear on the part of readers. Writing is singular, and the stakes are higher. Peter Pan is one character in a delightful play, Kong is still wonderful for the magic that brought him to life, and Audrey Hepburn is still adorable as Eliza. But a writer is one person, and the writer's work is the creation of one will. When writers' illusions are revealed, the fall is potentially much farther: Their whole body of work can be soured.

In the case of the authors I present here, it is what they write that prompted me to put together this book. More than any other fiction, sexual or erotic fiction (and nonfiction) raises profound issues for the reader. Without knowing the authors and why they write what they write, suspicions and prejudices can do more damage than any peek behind the curtains. Projections fly fast and furious. Most of us understand that horror writers don't hack people up for research, but if you write something sexually imaginative, everyone looks at you with suspicion or addresses you with supposition. Erotica writers are often seen as the living embodiment of their fiction. This is inaccurate at best, dangerous at worst.

I assembled this book because these suppositions and suspicions reminded me of something else too many people are ignorant of—something basic, life affirming, and yet in these days potentially fatal: sex and sexual orientation.

The Burning Pen is a grand tour behind the scenes with some of America's greatest sex writers. If this book succeeds—and I truly believe it has—then the curtains have been parted, the wires made visible, the author proudly revealed.

There are already too many myths and fallacies around sexuality without allowing the creative writing of sex to add to it. As everyone knows, sex has lost its innocence (if it was ever innocent to begin with): We can no longer afford to keep our eyes shaded closed to against sexual truth. It's time to take sex writing out of the closet, look at it, understand it, and—in the case of these authors—play with it, enjoy it with literary flair.

To that end, I put together this book. With the invaluable help of Scott Brassart and Angela Brown of Alyson Books, I contacted writers who I believe are at the literary forefront of sex writing, inviting them to step onto the stage and show us, warts and all, themselves: the writer exposed. The authors presented here have all written a personal essay on about their craft—why they write what they write, how they came to explore sex and sensuality in their fiction and nonfiction, what connection (if any) their sexual history has to what they write, and other important questions. Some are funny, others are melancholy, and all are true. Through these essays, each writer proudly proclaims him- or herself as a writer of sex and sensuality. To further demonstrate both their style and talent, the writers, at my request, have contributed one of their favorite stories—a fictional complement to their factual revelations.

Some of these essays might change the way you look at a particular writer's fiction—and sex—while others will add a dimension otherwise unseen. I applaud everyone involved in this project, not just for their unarguable talent as writers but also for the bravery mustered to help me dispel illusions, reveal secrets, and show the real faces behind the literary masks. As I said, I understand the fear of doing this—it threatens to tear away the veil between fiction and reality, and it can confuse the author with their works. But it's much more important not to add to the lies and misconceptions of sex and sex writing.

When ignorance can be the difference between life and death, between prejudice and understanding, it's important that that the curtain be parted, the actors drop their roles, and the writers write about themselves.

There is indeed something more important than not letting the wheels show—especially for the show of sex: The truth is always more important than any fiction.

—M. Christian
San Francisco

Smut Writer

By Lesl a Newman

From a very early age, I knew I would grow up to be a writer. I didn't know I would grow up to be a smut writer. Nor did I know I would grow up to be a lesbian writer. But that's a different story. Or then again, perhaps it's the same story.

I started writing poetry at a very early age. When I think about that now, it puzzles me. No one ever read poetry to me, and when I was old enough to read, I did not read poetry to myself. Yet, on some intuitive level, I knew I needed to take pen to paper (or, at that time, crayon to black-and-white composition notebook) and express myself through verse. My writing has always been my alpha dog, my teacher, my top. When my writing is kind enough to show up, take me by the hand, and lead me somewhere, it is always in my best interest to follow.

I did not come out, even to myself, until I was 27. But looking back at the poems I wrote in my teens and early 20s, I am amazed at how "pre-lesbian" they are. I have always said I write not in order to be understood but in order to understand. Clearly my writing had a perfect understanding of what was going on inside me, but I was unable to learn what it was so desperately trying to teach me for years and years and years.

Consider the following poem, written in 1975, when I was 19 years old. It was the days of the "sexual revolution," and I was an active heterosexual—or so I thought—participant.

When We Were Seven

When we were seven
Vicki and I put on
our feet pajamas
and slept
in her big sister's double bed
without touching.
She was the best lover
I've ever had.

When I read that poem now, all I can think is "Duh!" I was slow to learn, though my writing continued trying to teach me. Two years later, in 1977, many boyfriends and no female lovers later, I wrote this poem:

A Long Time Coming

Woman, beware of the creature
with subway rumblings in his voice,
with dark hair sprouting from his chin and cheeks.
He will admire your velvet fur.
Beware of the danger between his legs.

He will treat your heart like a pin-cushion
and turn your sisters against you.
Your eyes will grow black like the night
when he will try to steal your name.

Woman, throw your birth control pills
to the pigeons of City Hall,
dangle Dalkon Shields from your ears,
Plant morning glories in your diaphragm.
We will find new ways to multiply.

Double duh! Not only was I trying to tell myself I was a dyke, but I was already prophesying the lesbian turkey-baster baby boom!

Another sign that clearly shows there was a raging bull dyke inside me just dying to get out was the number of poems I wrote in those early years that mentioned breasts. In high school my creative writing teacher told the class to pick our favorite poet and write a poem imitating that poet's style. This untitled poem, written in the style of Anne Sexton, was penned in 1972:

preparing for your hands
to read my body
like a poem
I put on the gypsy scarf
you love to frolic in.

tonight you soared so high
above willows and breasts
you didn't even notice the gypsy scarf
huddled on the ground
among your hyacinths

Another poem, written five years later:

THE GIFT

Here is a shell
I found this afternoon
over by the rocks.
Take it home
to tuck away
in a drawer among your scarves,
and when you find it again
remember this night:
when the moon rose high
on your cheekbones
and my breasts fell
like two tears
into your hands.

My first response in rereading these two poems is: *What's with all the scarves?* And my second response is amusement as I realize that, since I had yet to touch another woman's breasts, I inserted my own into as many poems as I could. (In fact, a male poetry teacher I had in college told me I had "too many breasts" in my poems.) In all the love poems I wrote to men, which mostly recounted experiences of love, loss, pain, anger, and occasionally revenge, I never once mentioned that certain body part my lovers had that I didn't.

The first woman I slept with was, not surprisingly, a poet. We both wrote poems about the momentous occasion, and both our poems mentioned breasts. I spoke of "the moon casting shadows of light across my breasts and belly." (Still mentioning my own breasts, I see.) My lover wrote of "dark nights lightened by a lover's nipple" and "a breast beckon(ing) beneath a sweater." Our affair did not last long, mostly because I panicked and ran from her and from my confusion. It took another three years before I had the courage to come out to myself and to the world. And a strange thing happened when I embraced my lesbian self. I started writing prose in addition to poetry. Prose about being a lesbian. Prose that detailed what lesbians do. With each other. In bed.

My first published book of prose, written in 1985, was your basic proverbial thinly disguised autobiographical first novel. What's interesting to me about *Good Enough to Eat* is that it is told in two parts: The first part ends with a heterosexual love scene, the second part ends with a lesbian love scene.

In the first part of the novel, the protagonist, Liza Goldberg, finds herself in bed with her boyfriend, Michael. In the midst of giving him a blow job, her mind wanders: "One, two, buckle my shoe. Three, four, shut the door. Five, six, bite those pricks." Clearly Liza is not enjoying herself. Luckily for her, Harvey, her gay roommate, walks in and knows what's going on because he and Liza have had many frank discussions about her less-than-satisfying relationship with Michael as well as her growing attraction to other women. Harvey comes to Liza's rescue by asking her what a lesbian is doing in such an uncompromising position. Michael, stunned, asks Liza if she really is a lesbian. Liza's response is, "If you had the choice of having some jerk stick his big smelly prick into your mouth every two minutes or holding a sweet soft woman in your arms, which would you pick?" Liza's words teach her who she is, just as my words taught me. At the end of the book, after an explicit sex scene, Liza falls asleep with Anemone's breast in her mouth, "dreaming the dreams of one who is at peace, one who, at least for the moment, has everything she wants."

The reason I ended my first novel with a graphic lesbian sex scene was that I simply didn't know any better. I didn't know I was doing something radical, revolutionary, and potentially controversial. I was simply being true to my characters and writing a story. And since I have always used writing to explore all aspects of my experience—family relations, childhood memories, my eating disorder, etc.—it never occurred to me *not* to write about this new, exciting, wonderful part of my life.

After the novel, I continued writing both poetry and prose, and I began to create in another form: the short story. The short story had the terseness and intensity of poetry, and the luxurious elbow room of a novel. I wrote four books of short stories between 1988 and 1999: *A Letter to Harvey Milk, Secrets, Every Woman's Dream,* and *Girls Will Be Girls.* The difference between the short stories and the autobiographical novels (in 1990 I wrote *In Every Laugh a Tear,* another novel whose plot closely follows my life) is that the stories contain a myriad of characters engaging in a myriad of activities, both sexual and otherwise. The challenge of writing over 60 short stories in about a decade was to use my imagination to create a variety of characters and situations, some of which were based on my life, but most of which were not. Ironically, in 1988, I met the love of my life and began an exclusive sexual relationship, which continues to this day. Learning to be creative in my monogamous (and in no way monotonous) sex life taught me to be creative in my sexual writing life. I wrote sex scenes that I had never experienced, coming up with ideas that I wanted (and did) try in my own life. And I wrote about some of my own experiences in some of my fiction, giving my characters the treat of engaging in activities that had given me pleasure.

Writing is a very sexy occupation. Writing turns me on. It stimulates my brain, which, as has been said, is the sexiest organ of them all. When I write I feel turned on. I feel passionate, creative, energetic, breathless, joyful, powerful, confident, present, fully alive, and hot. The most important element of a sexual experience for me is whom I am sharing it with. I have to be completely in love with the person I am sharing my body with. I can be in love with her for five minutes or a lifetime. It doesn't matter. What matters is, at that moment, I have to think she is the most fascinating woman in the world and there is no one else I'd rather be spending my time with. It is the same with writing (or reading) sexually explicit material. What matters are the characters. I have to be hypnotized by them. I have to be mesmerized by them. I have to be utterly captivated by them. I have to feel that there is no one I would rather be spending time with—not other characters in a book or other people in real life. I have to care about the characters so much that I feel their lust, their passion, their joy, their rage, their sorrow. And in the case of smut, I have to be able to see the blush spreading across a character's heaving chest. I have to be able to hear the exact pitch of her gasps and moans. I have to be able to smell the aroma of her damp underarm. I have to be able to feel the texture of a character's dimpled thigh. I have to be able to taste the luscious liquid between her legs. Otherwise, frankly, I'm bored.

To accomplish this, to "make me swoon"—as I implore writers who send me stories to consider for my series of anthologies, *Pillow Talk: Lesbian Stories Between the Covers* (Volumes I, II and III)—one does not have to come up with amazing sexual techniques or scenarios. One has to come up with amazing characters. Maybe it's a female thing, maybe it's a femme thing, maybe it's just a Lesléa thing, but what's most important to me in a sexual situation I am either experiencing, reading about, or writing about, is the emotional component. The intimacy. Often I write short stories (whether they are smut or not) in the first person, because I believe the most intimate portrayal of a character can be accomplished only from inside that character's head and from hearing her tell her story in her own, unique voice. Or perhaps I just enjoy fiction writing's biggest perk of all: being able to experience someone else's life from the inside out.

In my short story "Eggs McMenopause," which follows this essay, my narrator couldn't be more different from me. First of all, she's a butch. Second of all, she's a good 10 years older than I am. And lastly, she's single and hasn't had sex in "a long, long time," and as I've already mentioned, my sex life, though monogamous, is anything but monotonous.

Without giving too much of the plot away, the reason the story works (in my humble opinion) is that the reader gets inside the character's mind. The reader knows some of the character's history, knows she's in the throes of menopause, a time of great hormones and horniness. The reader also knows the character's yearnings (a good lay), her frustrations (her body's not what it used to be), her insecurities (will anyone ever love me?), her hopes (maybe tonight will be the night), and her dreams (to live happily ever after). And once the reader is privy to these thoughts, the character becomes human and thus very similar to the reader, whom we can assume is also human. Additionally, the character charms the reader (she's a butch, after all), so when the character finally does have sex, in a most interesting and unique way, the reader is right there with her, unbuttoning her lover's sweater, licking her nipples, fucking her with a… Oh, but I don't want to ruin the story.

When I sit down to write a story or a poem or a novel or an essay, I don't know if it's going to be a piece of smut or not. (In fact, I don't know if I'm going to be lucky enough for anything to happen on the page.) Writing is my master. I am my writing's slave. Writing controls me. I am at my writing's mercy. When I try to take control, to dominate, to make my writing do what I want it to do instead of the other way around, it is always a mistake and I am always more than sorry. When I behave myself, my writing is very, very kind and rewards me with words that fill page after page after page. When I am bold enough or, more accurately, stupid enough to disobey, my writing is very cruel. And though the punishment is always the same, and I always know what it is, it is still utter torture: My writing simply gets up and leaves. And worse than that, my writing doesn't tell me when it will be back. Or if it will be back. All I can do is show up, pray, plead, beg, promise to be good, pick up my pen, and wait to see if I am once more worthy of receiving words that add up to something. I must be patient. The tension is excruciating, yet I have to admit there's something I like about it too. The release—the flood of words—is exquisite, but it is hardly over before the whole process starts over again. I can be good—I can be very, very, very good—for a while, but then I can't help myself. I have to be bad again. I have to try to take control. To be the master of my master. To top my top. My writing just shakes its head and walks out on me again. So far, my writing has always returned, though the fear that it won't remains (and becomes greater each time). I never, ever, take my writing for granted. And that is the best way I can describe the thrilling, maddening, pleasurable, painful, sexy relationship I have with my writing. I guess—and this will come as a big surprise to my girlfriend—I'm really nonmonogamous after all.

Eggs McMenopause

By Lesléa Newman

Insomnia equals insanity. And believe me, I should know. I haven't slept in two years. *Two years*. Ever since September 10, 1996, when my period stopped on a dime. Damn. Who knew I was out of eggs? Not me. It's not like I got any kind of warning or anything. One month there I was, bleeding away like a stuck pig, and the next month, bam!—dry as a bone.

So the question is, Would I have done anything differently had I known? Thrown myself a party? Saved my last bit of menstrual blood in a jar like Paul Newman's spaghetti sauce? Found some guy to fuck at the Last Chance Motel so I could finally be a mother once and for all? Not that I ever wanted to be a mother, you understand. It's just that once I knew I couldn't be, all of a sudden that's exactly what I wanted to do. Grow big as a house. Give birth. Breast-feed. The whole nine yards. It was ridiculous. Sort of like pining away for a lover after you've broken up with her. You know how it is—you don't want to be with her anymore, *you're* the one who called it quits, you can't even stand the fucking sight of her—but as soon as she has her arm around somebody else's waist, you want her as much as you've ever wanted anybody in your whole life. More. And if you make the mistake of telling her that, and if she makes the mistake of running back to you, then—poof!—your desire disappears as finally and completely as my last egg. That's human nature for ya. Go figure. We all want what we don't have until we get it, and then we don't want it anymore.

Like my period. God, when I was a teenager, I was dying to get my period. I was the last kid in my class to get it. All the other girls wore their sanitary napkins like badges. "I can't have gym today, Miss

Allbright. I have *my friend,*" they'd say in a stage whisper loud enough for all the other girls to hear. They carried their bodies differently too. Like they had some holy wisdom between their legs that I was just dying to get my hands on. *Please,* I'd pray every night before bed. *Please, I'll do anything, just let me get my period. Please.* I'd rush to the bathroom every morning, shut my eyes and listen to the sweet music of my pee hitting the toilet water. Then I'd take a deep breath, wipe, and open my eyes. But every day that pink toilet paper came up with nada.

Then one morning I pulled down my pajamas, and before I even sat down on the pot, I saw they were stained with thick, brown blood. I was so surprised, I didn't even know what it was. I thought I was dying. I had no idea how I cut myself down there, as I didn't spend any time down there at all, much less with a sharp instrument. I told my mother, and she slapped me. Twice. Slap-slap, once on each cheek. It's a Jewish custom, though it's also a custom not to tell you it's a custom, so of course I thought I had just done one more thing to make my mother mad. After the slaps, she gave me a belt and a sanitary napkin and told me to be careful, I was a woman now, and I'd bleed once a month until I was at least 50, so I'd better watch myself, soon all the boys would be after me.

Well, she was partly right, my mother. I did bleed until I was 50, but the boys were never after me. The girls were after me, or, to be more precise, I was after the girls. Girls with their periods, girls without their periods, tall girls, short girls, fat girls, thin girls, I didn't care. I wasn't fussy. I just wasn't happy unless I had some sweet, warm, female thing in my arms. Which I haven't, in case you're wondering, for a long, long time.

It's not that I'm a dog or anything, you understand. It's just that menopause, in case you haven't gone through it yet, doesn't make you feel like the most attractive woman in the world. First of all, you bloat. I looked in the mirror one day and thought, damn, who the hell sneaked in here when I wasn't looking and injected helium under my skin? I looked like a balloon from the goddamn Macy's Thanksgiving Day Parade. Second of all, you sweat. Night sweats, day sweats, morning, afternoon, evening sweats. God, I grew hotter than hell and didn't wear a winter coat for two whole years, and New York City in fucking February isn't exactly Miami in July. I couldn't bear the thought of anyone coming near me; in fact, I could hardly stand to be near myself. And on top of all this, I got pimples—pimples!—at my age. I looked like a walking, talking case of Acne Anonymous. And then, of course, I was so sleep-deprived, I could have walked right past Miss America (who happens to be just my type), and I wouldn't have even noticed.

So one night when I couldn't sleep, I started doing the math. I got my period when I was 16, and it stopped when I was 50. That's 34 years, times 12 months a year, equals 408 periods. Four hundred and eight eggs. Could make the world's biggest omelet. Or something.

Call me crazy, but I got obsessed with the number. Four hundred and eight. They say your ovaries are the size of two tiny almonds, so how could they hold 204 eggs apiece? That's a lotta eggs. Being a visual gal, I wanted to see them. I wanted to feel them. So I bought them. Went down to the corner store and bought 34 dozen eggs. A few dozen at a time. I might be crazy all right, but I don't want the whole neighborhood knowing just how loony I am. Luckily I live in New York, where there's a corner store on every corner. I just worked the neighborhood and bought a few dozen here, a few dozen there…

At first I just stacked the cartons one on top of the other in the living room. Four stacks in the corner: two stacks of eight dozen, two stacks of nine. To tell you the truth, I was a little afraid of them. I had to live with them for a while, you know, get used to them. I mean, to my mind, they represented my unborn children, in a twisted sort of way. I even started naming them. Went right through the alphabet: Annie, Bonnie, Carol, Delilah, Ellen, Francis, Grace. You get the picture. Then I started in with boys' names: Adam, Barry, Carlos, David, Eddie, Frankie, Greg. I had to do it 15 fucking times. Abigail, Betty, Claire, Deborah…Allen, Burt, Craig, Daniel…Amy, Barbara…Angel, Bernie… Pretty sick, huh? That's nothing compared to what I did next.

Next I unpacked them and started placing them around the apartment. Now if you've never been up here, let me tell you, this place ain't exactly the Plaza. It's pretty tiny, just three small rooms, and I haven't redecorated in a while. Since the Ice Age, as a matter of fact. But I'm not complaining. My hovel is perfect for one person. One crazy person and her 408 eggs.

The first place I put them was on the couch. Eight dozen fit there, and another eight fit on the bed. Three dozen covered my kitchen table, and two dozen filled the shower. A dozen fit in the bathroom sink, and another dozen filled the sink in the kitchen. Twenty-three down and 11 to go. I had no choice then but to lay them out on the floor. It looked kind of like an inside-out Yellow Brick Road. The floor was covered with eggs except for a twisted, windy path that led from the bedroom through the living room, through the kitchen, and out the front door.

When I was finally finished—I have to say it—I felt pretty damn proud. Sure I had used up my eggs—nothing much to it, women do that all the time—but how many women have actually replaced them? I stood in the narrow path in my apartment, looked around and felt smug. For about two seconds. And then I started feeling incredibly horny. All those eggs! I mean, have you ever felt an egg, I mean really felt an egg? They're very sensual, you know. They've got a little weight to them; they're heavy and smooth, not unlike a woman's breast that fits just right in the palm of your hand. I took two eggs off the floor and held one in each paw for a minute, closing my eyes and just bouncing them up and down a little. God, I felt like a cat in heat. No, not a cat, a pussy. I wanted some, and I wanted it now.

So what could I do? *Go out, you old fool,* I said to myself. I hadn't been out for about a million years, and the thought of it was more than a little daunting. Had I lost my charm? (Had I ever had it?) There was only one way to find out. Go out. So I did. I got all dressed up in a jacket and tie, did something with my hair, put on my motorcycle boots, and hit the street. I didn't even know if the bar I used to haunt was still there—part of me prayed it wasn't, and part of me prayed it was. I heard the disco beat half a block away, and it pulled me inside like a magnet. God, it felt good to be out with the girls.

Now before you jump all over me and tell me I should be calling them women, let me tell you, these were girls. To my mind, anyway.

I wasn't quite old enough to be their mother, you understand. I was old enough to be their grandmother. Sure, you do the math. Eighteen and 18 is 36, plus 18 more is 54. Which is just a year and a half shy of how old I was. And how shy. I almost turned around and marched out the door the second after I marched in, but traffic was going against me, so I went with the flow and headed straight (so to speak) inside. I mean, what the hell, I had dragged myself out of the house and there was no one back there waiting for me but the ingredients for about 200 Egg McMuffins. I might as well pretend to enjoy myself.

I headed for the bar and parked it on an empty stool. Asked the bartender for whatever was on tap, leaned back on my elbows, and looked around. Luckily I didn't have to look far. There were two gals to my right, one more gorgeous than the other. Were they together? It was hard to tell. Both of them were dressed in black from head to toe: black sweaters, black stockings, black skirts, black shoes. So I doubted they were lovers, because, after all, what can two femmes do together? But then again, this is a new generation. Femmes go with femmes, butches go with butches, hell, I've even heard that the newest happening thing is for girls to go with boys. Though what's so new and radical about that is beyond my imagination.

I pretended I didn't notice the two babes, of course, but I kept my eye on them and tried to eavesdrop on their conversation. Easier said then done, as the music was really pumping, and though I hate to admit it, my hearing isn't what it used to be. I can't believe I'm turning into one of those old sows who walk into a bar and whine, "Why does the music have to be so loud? Can't they turn it do-ow-ow-own?" But like I've already told you, age does strange things to a person. So I couldn't really hear, but I could see all right, and let me tell you, both these broads were drop-dead gorgeous. One of them had that short, bleached-out blond, rhinestone glasses, dog-collar-around-the-neck look. Very East Village, not exactly my type. The other one, though, I'd lick her boots any day. She had black hair down to her waist, and she was at least six feet tall, even without the five-inch platform shoes. God, her legs went on forever, and I couldn't stand that they weren't wrapped around my waist that very minute. But before I could even ask the bartender what she was drinking so I could send one over with my compliments (a move that makes them swoon, or at least did in the old days), she turned from her gal pal, tossed all that glorious hair over her shoulder in a huff, and flounced into the crowd.

Now let me tell you, if there's one thing I love even more than dykes, it's dyke drama. I sidled up to Miss St. Mark's Place and asked, "Is she your girlfriend?"

"Why don't you ask her?" She pointed to the object of my affection, who had obviously changed her mind and returned to the scene of the crime.

Well, I always was one to follow orders. Pointing to the blond, I asked the goddess standing before me, "Is she your girlfriend?"

"What did she say when you asked *her*?" Mademoiselle thrust her fists onto her hips and looked at me with blazing eyes.

This was beginning to feel like therapy; every question I asked was being answered with another question. "She said to ask you." I looked the towering Glamazon in the eye and held her gaze as she snorted and shook her head. "C'mon." She held out her hand, to my delight and amazement. "Let's dance."

Well, she sure didn't have to ask me twice. I slid off that barstool like a greased pig and let her lead me to the dance floor, where I attempted to move these old bones to the music, if you could call it that. All I could hear was some kind of throbbing, pumping techno beat. Perfect for humping, I thought, and as if my girl had a Ph.D. in mind reading, she pulled me into her and started working away. I hate to admit it, but my knees actually buckled, and I had to hold on for dear life. Luckily there was a lot to hold on to. Like I told you, this girl was beyond tall. Her crotch came up to my hipbone, and her breasts were at eye level. I smelled her sweat and her juice and her perfume and just kept my hip jutted out so she could go to town. "Ooh, baby, you are something else," I murmured and somehow found her nipple in my mouth. Cashmere never tasted so good, let me tell you. A few times I tried to look up at my dancing damsel, but her eyes either were closed or focused in the direction of the bar. Was she using me to make her girlfriend jealous? Did I care? Hey, a revenge fuck was better than a mercy fuck, though to tell you the truth, from this babe and a half, I'd have taken either.

When the music changed, we headed back toward the bar, but much to my relief, the blond bombshell was gone. I couldn't tell if Mandy was pissed, relieved, or disappointed. (Once her come was all over my jeans, I figured I had the right to ask her name.) Without a word, she hopped up on that still-warm barstool, drained what was left of her gal-pal's drink, and drew me toward her by wrapping those mile-long legs around the base of my butt. I felt her muscles clench as she held me tightly, and I realized I couldn't get away even if I wanted to. Which I didn't, in case you're wondering. I may have gone bananas in other departments, but I wasn't so far gone that I'd look this gift horse in the mouth.

"You live around here, baby?" Mandy whispered, letting her tongue roam the highways and byways of my grateful left ear.

"Just a few blocks away," I panted, and let me tell you, it was a good thing she had me by the butt because my legs were beyond Jell-O.

"Let's go." She released me, and I commanded my skeletal system to get a grip as we made our way out the door. Once outside, I tried to lean her against a lamppost and kiss her a bit, but it was embarrassing for her to have to bend down an entire foot just to get her mouth anywhere near mine. Clearly I had to get this girl on her back as quickly as possible, so we hustled down the street and up the steps to my apartment. I thought of carrying her over the threshold, but when I opened the door, I couldn't believe my eyes. The eggs! I had forgotten all about them. Would she notice? I decided to play it cool, since after all, what other choice did I have?

"Walk this way," I said, bending over like Groucho Marx and waddling down the narrow path to my bed, which was of course completely covered with eggs. I thought of whipping away the bedspread, like a magician who can pull a tablecloth out from under plates, glasses, and silverware without disturbing them, but that would have been too dramatic. Besides, it wouldn't have worked.

But Mandy, bless her heart, was foolish with youth, liquid courage, or just a wacky sense of humor. "The yolk's on you," she said, reaching for an egg, which she cracked with one hand on the bed frame like a young, beautiful Julia Child. Then she deposited the contents of the shell expertly and neatly right on top of my head.

"Allow me," I said, and with cool yolk dripping down the side of my face and neck, I send all eight dozen of those babies flying with one grand, gallant sweep of my arm. As they rolled, cracked, and crashed to the ground, I prayed Mandy wouldn't forsake me and run screaming out the door. But not too worry. I sure know how to pick 'em, if I do say so myself. Mandy just flopped down on the now-clear bed and rolled onto her back, with her hands behind her head and a look that said loud and clear, *OK, I've done my job; now it's up to you.* God, I love those femmes.

"Over easy," I remarked as I bent down to unbutton her sweater. She wore no bra, and damn if her breasts didn't remind me of two eggs sunny side up. I cracked an egg onto her chest and licked her nipples through the yellow goo. She laughed and opened her legs, which had somehow worked their way out of her skirt. Crotchless pantyhose—what will they think of next? Clearly Mandy had been expecting to get some action that night, but being fucked with an organic egg by a butch three times her age probably wasn't exactly what she had in mind.

I moved the lucky egg slowly up one magnificent thigh until it was right up against the path to glory. I pressed it against her and rolled it around and around until the shell was slippery and slick. "You move, it breaks," I said, teasing her clit with the tip of it.

"It breaks, you eat it," she replied, squeezing her legs together and cracking that ova in two.

Well, suffice to say, my cholesterol level skyrocketed that night clear through the fucking roof. I had egg on my face, and I didn't mind one bit. We crunched our way through my entire apartment, and that Mandy wasn't squeamish in the least. I licked egg off her toes, off her nose… We fucked in every room, and by morning there wasn't an egg left to scramble. Four hundred and eight eggs smashed to smithereens. That's gotta be worthy of the *Guinness Book of World Records,* don't you think? I tell you, I was so spent by the time the sun came up, I didn't know if I was wide awake or dreaming. And I still don't know, because later that evening I woke up alone in my bed, fresh and clean as a newborn chick, the apartment clean as a whistle. Mandy and the eggs were gone, and so were the bags under my eyes. Was it all a deranged fantasy due to menopausal madness? Perhaps. Or perhaps there's a young girl out there who now knows menopause is nothing to fear. Youth is not wasted on the young. *Au contraire,* my dear: The best is yet to come.

GOING TOO FAR
By Felice Picano

I was sitting minding my own business, performing one of my more prosaic weekly chores, opening and reading the mail that came into the post office box of the Gay Presses of New York, one afternoon in the early spring of 1984, when out of an overseas envelope spilled a bunch of much-stamped official looking documents from the United Kingdom Customs and Overseas Commerce Ministry. With them was a short note scribbled by one of the partners of our company's British distributors explaining the purport of said papers.

It seems, Aubrey wrote, that GPNY's shipment of sea-voyaging books had been restrained at a docks in Liverpool and opened by the authorities. The official had gone through the sealed boxes of shipped books, scanned their contents, and chanced upon a title that he looked at a bit more closely. He then declared it to be "Obscene and Pornographic—Unfit for Sale in the U.K." While the other titles had been eventually released to Gay Men's Press, all 48 copies shipped of this particular GPNY title had been impounded, and after sundry authorizations were signed by one of Aubrey's partners allowing him to receive the other books in the shipment, the entire box of the offending title had been formally burned to ashes on the dock.

The volume in question was my collection of short stories titled *Slashed to Ribbons in Defense of Love*. By 1984 the book was in its third printing, with some 8,000 copies in print. When published the year before, the book had been featured on the cover of *Writers* magazine as well as reviewed inside, along with collections by such literary luminaries of the day as Donald Barthelme, Ann Beattie, Raymond Carver, and Alice Munro. "Short Story Renaissance!" the cover had proclaimed. Since then, the stories had been positively mentioned in the few extant gay media outlets of the day and had appeared for several months running, albeit in a lowly position, on the *Christopher Street* magazine best-seller list. So, obviously, I was surprised to see my work labeled as obscene and torched like someone accused of witchcraft. Or heresy.

Looking more closely at the official papers as I phoned my GPNY partners to tell them the news, I saw that the official had written, "with especial regard to material found on pages 131–144." I turned to those pages in my copy of the book, and there it was: my story "Expertise," the story I have chosen to reprint in this anthology.

While outwardly outraged during my discussions with my partners and my attorneys as well as in letters to my congressman and senator and to the British Counsel offices in New York and Washington D.C., I have to admit, secretly I was pleased.

Very, very, pleased.

How often has anyone written 13 pages that have been found so offensive by someone else that it they to be impounded, then destroyed by fire?

It meant that I was now officially bad.

I was thrilled.

Clearly, I was upset too. Since someone had failed to understand my intentions in writing the story, I had to now wonder how many other people had also misunderstood it.

According to our British distributors, it was they, not me—a barely known foreign author—who were the Customs Ministry's target, singled out and persecuted by the authorities during that Orwellian year. Their intent was clear: to harass Gay Men's Press and the Gay is the Word bookstore in London as much as possible. And, by putting various sorts of pressure on them, to keep them from getting and selling books from abroad. Or merely even to make it too expensive—by destroying incoming books—for overseas shippers to continue to service their account.

I realized all that. Intellectually, at least.

In my heart, I knew I'd at last gone too far and was reaping the ambiguous rewards of such an exercise.

For years, my parents, my schoolteachers, my college professors, not to mention various friends, had warned me that someday I would go too far. Now I had done so. I had proof.

So in a sense I had succeeded. I was fulfilled.

✍

From the first, whenever writing gay-themed material, I noticed that I seemed to do what today we call "pushing the envelope." I didn't actually do this consciously, say, like Voltaire or Evelyn Waugh, to *épater le bourgeoisie*. It was simply the way I saw life around me, the way I thought of it, how I evaluated it, and, as a result, the way I wrote about it. To me, my writing about gay life was more or less reportage, informed a little by my peculiar tastes and my weird sense of humor.

Of course, when I was first writing, to write anything at all about gay life and try to publish it was going too far. Did this stop me in any way? No. When I had completed my first (to myself) successful short story, titled "Slashed to Ribbons in Defense of Love," I immediately mailed it off to *The New Yorker.* Two weeks later, some secondary assistant associate fiction editor there actually hand-penned a rejection note and mailed it back to me. He did not ask to see anything else of mine. Didn't those philistines know art when they read it? It would be eight long years before that story was published by anyone. And when it came out in *Christopher Street* magazine and then in the magazine's fiction anthology *Aphrodisiacs,* the story's ending was edited. My story was still too much for even an openly gay periodical!

Meanwhile, I was writing poetry—and it seems that I was again going too far. Although I'd written and published three mainstream novels by 1977, my first gay book to ever be published was the poetry collection *The Deformity Lover.* Its title poem was about a homo who sought only handicapped and disfigured men to have sex with. A commentator on a New York public radio station not only read the poem, he also strongly objected to the poem and disparaged me as its author. Or so I heard secondhand.

Other poems in that tome, however, proved no better when it came to sensitivity or political correctness. One was about drugged-out dance fags, another about overly fastidious phone-sex callers, another about hypocrite leather queens, another about S/M stupidities, another about an exhibitionist jerking off while riding a bicycle in public. There happened to be a few magazines of the time that dared publish such poetry—*Mouth of the Dragon, Fag Rag, Gay Sunshine.*

And to me, these poems, most simply put, were my subject matter. What I saw around me. Also, they were what made my book new. As in Gertrude Stein's dictum: "Make it new." Needless to say, the book was reviewed by scarcely anyone outside the gay media. And inside the gay media, *The Deformity Lover* was met with what could charitably called a "mixed" response. I remember going around chanting what Edgar Allan Poe had written in a letter a century and half earlier about the reaction to his poem "Annabel Lee." "My poem is damned!" Poe wrote. "Damned in the quarterlies. Damned in the journals! Damned upon the pulpits and within the salons. Damned in the coffeehouses and taverns of all the seaboard cities! Damned, I tell you. Damned!" And yet someone must have read my book: It sold out three editions in five years, and was back-ordered for years.

Having learned little from my experiences with the short story and poetry, I stumbled on. My second gay book, a novel, *The Lure,* was and perhaps still is 22 years later one of the most sexually explicit gay books put out by a mainstream press and promoted by a mainstream book club. It has been translated into eight other languages. *The Lure* dealt with the nighttime scene of gay life in Manhattan during the late 1970s. And I do not mean black-tie parties at the Frick Collection or charity galas at the Metropolitan Opera. It was dark; it was dirty. But it was real. I'd lived it, dated men who closed bars at 4:30 A.M., then caroused at after-hours parties. I knew what I was writing about.

Having written the damned thing and having found people nuts enough to publish it, I compounded my act of chutzpah and dedicated this in-your-face fag book to whom? To my parents, naturally enough. Obviously, I had ceased to care whom I offended. With the expected results: The entire collective of the Body Politic and a few other active gay groups put me on the top of their hit lists. Someone actually shot at me. Bullets lodged in the outside wall of my apartment building near my study windows. I decided to leave town until things quieted down.

I foolishly thought that my third gay title, *An Asian Minor,* being distanced in time some 3,500 years, might calm these people down. It was, I admit, a bit cheeky. A retelling of the Greco-Roman Ganymede and Zeus love affair, it was not penned in elegant silver-age, Ovidian rhymed stanzas but instead in contemporary everyday prose, as told by Ganymede himself. That lovely lad I characterized as a tough, knowing, contemporary street hustler in search of the ultimate sugar daddy.

Again the reviews were "mixed." Many older homosexuals, academics and the type I used to call "classic-fags," found the novella deeply odious, profoundly repugnant. But it too sold well. And it eventually became a stage play, *Immortal!* that ran off-Broadway awhile.

When, a year later, unredeemed in any way by these experiences, I came to collecting and titling the 11 short stories I had written and had published in various periodicals over the previous nine years, I decided to purposefully go too far. The novella "And Baby Makes Three" was about a love affair begun when one participant was an adult, the other a toddler. The story "Hunter" was about a young gay man who ended up having a supernatural sex affair. Another was about a blow job I got from a (thinly disguised) movie star. Another, about an equally ill-disguised classical musician and his infamous affair with a young hustler. "Xmas in the Apple" is about three gay men's various but mostly depraved and depressed holidays. "Teddy the Hook" is about a handsome guy with a misshapen, if sizable, penis who finds sexual paradise in gay Vietnam. "Mr. World Buns" is about a national contest for the prettiest rear end and was specifically subtitled "A Story Without a Moral." I hoped there was something in the book to offend everyone. I even thought of titling the collection "Gay Tragic Romances," after various woman-oriented magazines of the 1950s. (Note: *An Asian Minor* and *Slashed to*

Ribbons have been reprinted in one volume by Alyson Books, titled *The New York Years*.)

And yet, strange to report, until that letter arrived in 1984, no one had ever hinted that I had succeeded in going too far with "Expertise." What was worse, since the stories had been published to less than the usual annoyed reviews (maybe they'd given up on me?), I'd felt a bit liberated. So much so that I had charged ahead and written the first of my memoirs—or perhaps anti-memoirs, as André Malraux had cleverly called his own such book—*Ambidextrous: The Secret Lives of Children*. That publication told what it had been like when I was a child, age 11 to 13, growing up in a middle-class, melting-pot New York city suburb. And it did so without pulling any punches whatsoever. In print ever since and now considered something of a gay classic, *Ambidextrous* itself, soon after the receipt of that fatal British letter, began to undergo its own attempts at censorship, as publisher after publisher turned it down. To a person, they found its mixture of material disturbing: I might have easily written about gay and straight sex among children who were sniffing airplane glue, looking at gay porn photos, and vending straight poetry porn, one wrote. Except that I had dared to write all that and then to place it—as in truth it had occurred in my life— alongside such acceptably fond childhood memories as kids' softball games, bike rides through cones of autumn leaves, classroom antics, arts-and-crafts valentine exchanges, and school museum trips. One editor took me to an expensive lunch at which he explained why he could not publish that book: I had yoked together preadolescent gay sex and military heroism from the Korean and Vietnam wars, in the end demeaning all war veterans: I, and my book, were patently offensive and egregiously unpatriotic.

When *Ambidextrous* was published by my GPNY partners in the United States, it was reviewed hardly anywhere. The *Publishers Weekly* reviewer evidently read only the first six pages. In the United Kingdom—saved from the torch there, I'm guessing, by its childlike cover art—*Ambidextrous* was reviewed by someone in *The Manchester Guardian*, who wrote, and I quote, "Mr. Picano. Children don't have sex. Period," to which I responded. "Mr. ____. Check your

OED. This book is not fiction. It is a memoir. Children did have sex. And this is how they had sex. Period."

Since then, however, two straight women have told me they wrote favorable reviews of *Ambidextrous* for (1) *The Village Voice* and (2) the *San Francisco Chronicle,* reviews that were turned down by the book editors who had assigned them and thus were never printed by those allegedly liberal organs. Again because I had gone too far.

Subsequently in my writing career, I have made it a point to go too far, no matter what I pen. When Dr. Charles Silverstein chose me over several other more obvious choices (including a very disgruntled John Preston) to coauthor *The New Joy of Gay Sex,* Silverstein said it was on the basis of reading *Ambidextrous* and the next memoir, *Men Who Loved Me* (a title found monstrously pushy and egotistical by many).

When we commissioned the artwork for the sex book, I instructed Deni Ponty, who did the beautiful color paintings found in the front of the original edition, that his initial sketches were OK, but the men weren't close enough to each other. Ponty wanted to know how close they should be. "You shouldn't be able to slip a piece of paper between their bodies," I instructed. When the equally talented Ron Fowler, who did the black-and-white illustrations, asked if he could he depict anything and anyone, Silverstein and I said sure. Thus we got pictures of men of all sizes, shapes, and colors, including skinheads, midgets, and a guy in a wheelchair—fucking, sucking, sixty-nining, masturbating, having circle jerks, pissing on each other, and, in one unpublished drawing, with barbed wire twisted around their scrotum. HarperCollins's art director and editor found that last art a bit too controversial. I couldn't see their point, but we took it out anyway. Because by then I understood how I'd no longer be able to take discretion as the better part of valor, or in fact as the better part of anything.

✍

Unlike "Mr. World Buns," "Expertise" is a story with a moral. Or sort of a moral. Or something that might be construed as a moral.

Which makes the story being taken as obscene especially jejune.

I wrote the first draft of "Expertise" in 1979 at my rented summer cottage in Fire Island Pines as all the brouhaha was getting started around the publication of *The Lure*. I revised it in May of 1980 in Manhattan.

"Expertise" was, naturally enough, based on my experiences in bathhouses, on boardwalks, and in sex clubs of the day but especially in the club specified in the story. That site was either the Glory Hole, located in Manhattan on 11th Avenue and 22nd Street, midway between two leather bars, the Eagle and the Spike, and operated by a pair of entrepreneur lovers from Texas; or the original Basic Plumbing in Los Angeles, located somewhere on Fairfax Avenue (does anyone know the exact address?) within a young man's orgasm distance of West Hollywood.

I was seriously dating someone, but we had one day a week "off" from each other. He liked bathhouses on these nights. So I went to the other kind of clubs. Actually, I liked these other clubs better. One needn't spend as much time in them or make as much of a personal commitment as was required in a bathhouse environment. You could sail in between beers, suck dick, get blown, then sail out. Often I'd be home hours earlier than my guy, able to read a book or listen to a few LPs before he arrived.

Little by little, I began to notice that some men always seemed to be in these clubs whenever I rushed in for a quickie. I began to notice, then to watch, and later on to spend time observing these regulars. They had their favorite booths. They'd wait around outside them while others were inside, then dash in as soon as they could and stay there for hours. They had little rituals, connected with hours-long stays in the booths. One arranged his bottle of butyl nitrate, cans of 7-Up, and joints of grass, in between regular cigarettes, along a wooden shelf. I began to notice well-known gay men in these clubs. A few authors. One of the Village People. A celebrated avant-garde playwright. Manhattan's top commercial illustrator. A mulatto physique model. A bearded Japanese classical musician. A well-known pianist–cabaret artist. Two guys from the first U.S. punk band I ever heard. The club in Los Angeles was even more dotted with recording stars, professional athletes, and actors. I had sex with all of them.

I never became obsessed, never myself became a "regular," but I found it all fascinating, especially the writing on the walls: "I sucked off a hunky, well-hung Catholic priest. He came twice in a row, moaning 'Jesus loves you!'" "Got butt-fucked six times. Number 7 felched it all out." I felt it was a unique site, a uniquely gay male experience, and it and its various denizens just had to be written about. The last visit I made to such a club was to Basic Plumbing in Los Angeles in midsummer of 1981. It was a cloudy afternoon. Quiet. I was about to leave when I noticed two handsome, big men come in. The white guy was my type, but I couldn't get his attention, Meanwhile, the black guy was after me. When we stopped to chat, I told him I wanted his friend. He suggested a three-way. We found a booth that could hold all three of us. We took turns doing everything to each other, ending up with me being "Lucky Pierre" between the two of them (like a slice of meat between two thick slabs of Italian and pumpernickel bread). Afterward it turned out they were football players—Los Angeles Rams. I felt I had experienced the most sexual gratification to be found in such a setting, and could never top this experience. So I never returned.

"Expertise" was first published in *Blueboy's* May 1981 issue and collected in *Slashed to Ribbons in Search of Love and Other Stories* two years later. More recently (1997) it appeared in the United States and the United Kingdom in *The Mammoth Book of Gay Erotica*, edited by Lawrence Schimel, who told me it was one of his key gay stories.

I'm not sure if I'd want my writing to be represented by "Expertise" alone. I doubt if I'd approve of gay life or even the gay"70s being solely represented by it. But it's a true story. And while sensual and erotic, it's not in any way obscene, I think, nor pornographic. What it is is reportage, with a sly little comment at the end.

Since "Expertise" and, in fact, since the story collection, I've not written that much gay erotica. Only one or two scenes in my big novels *Like People in History* and *The Book of Lies* could be considered erotic. With my novel *Onyx*, however, to be published in 2001, I have returned to describing a series of erotic experiences between two men. The relationship in *Onyx* between the gay Ray Henriques and the younger, "straight," married-with-children workman Mike Tedesco is based on a seven-year relationship I experienced, in which—at his request—I homoerotically educated another man. Like "Expertise" and my other stories and novellas and poetry, it's my attempt to accurately yet also artistically report on a life experience.

Expertise

By Felice Picano

When his third lover walked out the door, Alex decided he'd had just about enough of gay romance.

Bradley had been as beautiful as an old Arrow Shirt ad model, as delicious as Entenmanns's chocolate chip cookies, and alas! in the final evaluation, about as nourishing. How long could love go on with the perpetually wounded vanity of one partner and the adoring selflessness of the other? Yet it had happened to Alex before: with Tim, with Lenny, and now—most disastrously—with Brad. Enough times, Alex concluded, to qualify as a bona fide self-destructive syndrome.

What he needed was to look after himself for once in his life. Yes, to cultivate selfishness: an enlightened selfishness.

So, after the requisite day and a half of tears, the usual two weeks of increasingly bored sympathy from friends, and the necessary month of depression and self-recrimination, Alex decided to turn a new leaf.

He would transform himself into a sex object, and as this sex object, he would seek out none but other sex objects. They at least would have the realistic insecurities of their humble origins, the confidence of their developed narcissism, and a healthy respect for anyone who'd accomplished as much.

In a city like New York, Alex knew that taking this step would soon assure him of: (1) innumerable one-night stands; (2) invitations to all the hot parties in town and on Fire Island; (3) as a result of those parties, more one-night stands of even higher quality than before; (4) memberships in private discos, discriminating baths, and sex clubs; (5) as a result of those, invitations to even hotter parties in the city and even more distant—to Los Angeles and San Francisco; and (6) as a result of all that, extreme, intense, nonstop, mindless self-gratification.

Alex inspected himself in the full-length mirror hanging in his bedroom and thought, *Well, it's worked for people with far less raw material than I have to start with.*

His evaluation was born in that total objectivity that often follows despair. His face was attractive enough—although scarcely magazine-handsome. At least it had the character that accompanied ethnicity (Greek-American) without a hint of immigrant to it. Large, light-colored eyes that some had called hypnotic. Dark, straight hair that required little care. An obvious but rather nice nose. Cheekbones that could only become more prominent with age. Of course his body could use some work, he thought. But mostly detail work. Five foot ten, fairly lean and well proportioned, his limbs weren't apelike like some porno stars people jerked off to, not cutesy-doll short either. His back was straight, his posture and walk fine. Detail work: a few months swimming and playing on the rings at some gym; a touch of weights to build up his pecs, laterals, and deltoids. As for dress—that all important system of codes and invitations to the knowing—Alex already knew what he would need to buy, what he would have to discard, what he would have to pre-age and partially destroy to achieve that particularly casual look. Sure, Alex wasn't a natural knockout beauty. But then, how many current Living Legends around him had been before they went to work on themselves?

He began the next day so that he wouldn't have time to find excuses. He phoned Jim Maddox, who cut all the hottest and most highly paid models in town, and set up an appointment. He joined a local health club with a great pool, extensive athletic equipment, and few sisters to distract him. He went through his closets and cut his wardrobe in half, then shopped in the Village, blowing about $600 in plastic that he would be sorry about next month.

He could already picture himself, 11:30 on a Sunday morning, his lean, tanned body half wrapped around some drop-dead number he'd picked up at the Ice Palace and necked with at the after-hours party at a Bayside pool house, sweeping down the boardwalk at the Pines, past an astonished Bradley.

It would be heaven!

And, six months later, it was heaven. But for one tiny yet all-important fact he hadn't taken into consideration months before when he'd begun his transformation plans—a fact that provided Alex with a rather icy awakening.

Henrik turned over on the double bed and seemed to brood. Brooding, Henrik looked as breathtakingly handsome as Henrik seductive or Henrik comical or Henrik intensely following the progress of a spotted beetle across a beach blanket. His golden-blond hair shimmered in the champagne haze of the ocean afternoon. His skin glimmered in the venetian blinds' mottled light, now red, now pale blue, now the faintest hint of green against his deep tan and against the striking diamond white-on-white pattern of the designer sheets.

Henrik had gone limp once more, however, which was why he was brooding, and all of Alex's tactics to revive the flagging erection proved failures. Alex knew it was his fault without being able to say exactly why it was his fault. They'd started off so well on the beach, doing a *From Here to Eternity* number in the swirling surf, despite the passersby, despite the critical commentary from surrounding beach blanket occupants, even despite the two little tots who insisted on playing with beach pails only three or four feet away. Started off so well, so hot, so frantic, Alex and Henrik had finally stood up, rearranged their hard-ons in their tiny Speedo bathing suits, and trekked back to the house. Where they had continued hot—until they'd fizzled.

"I guess I turned you off?" Alex said, knowing it wasn't a question at all.

"Oh, no," the gloomy, polite, deep-voiced bed lie.

"What was it I did wrong?" Alex persisted. "What didn't you like?"

"Nothing. Nothing at all," Henrik insisted, looking at Alex with eyes of the bluest depths of a fjord in summertime. Then those eyes seemed to widen and narrow, as though Henrik were trying to gauge Alex's capacity for truth, vulnerability, and all the connecting links between. He must have decided Alex could stand more truth than flattery, because in the next minute he slowly said, "I suppose my problem is that I'm more used to—well—to experts."

"Experts?" Alex asked, then realized what exactly was being said; he became embarrassed.

"It's what American men are best at, you know," Henrik said, gently, firmly, decisively. "All over the world it's known. I have a Finnish friend, Ole, who comes to America two weeks a year on vacation just to get American blow jobs. He saves up all year for it. He hasn't missed a vacation here in 11 years."

Alex surveyed Henrik's pale, long, flaccid cock and thought, *Well, I did the best I know how; no one else ever complained. Not good enough,* the little voice within him replied. *Not good enough for beautiful Henrik. Not good enough for the other beautiful men you want. Not even good enough for your goddamn country! What kind of patriot are you, anyway?*

Because Alex was silent, listening to the little voice, Henrik took this as encouragement to go on. He described the five best blow jobs he'd received: their circumstances, setting, the other person, the techniques employed, and any other interesting little details. Then Henrik described Ole's travels across the country by train, plane, car, and Trailways bus in search of the perfect blow job. He mentioned the small, out-of-the-way towns where Ole had been astounded; the times he found himself suddenly surprised by luck on the backseats of buses, in the lavatories of jets, at truck stops, at public toilets—places he'd returned to again and again.

Every phrase reproached Alex; reproached and shamed him. They also excited him. He wondered if this was because it was Henrik, beautiful, sexy Henrik, telling it or if it was because such anonymous, mechanical sex must of necessity be more exciting.

"Here," Henrik said in conclusion, reaching for Alex, "let me show you how it should be done."

The neighbors two houses down the beach must have heard Alex when he arrived at that orgasm.

"Now that," Henrik said proudly, "was what Ole would have called a blow job."

Alex too. But he was afraid to try it himself, fearing his lack of expertise would cause yet another and even more embarrassing failure. Handling the Swedish Adonis' own now splendid erection, he asked in what he hoped was him most enticing tone of voice:

"How would you like to fuck?"

✍

It was a turning point. For the next few months, Alex continued to go to Fire Island, to parties, to the baths, to bars and orgies. He continued to meet handsome men anywhere and everywhere and to get them into bed with little or no trouble just about whenever he wanted to. And though it was all undoubtedly more satisfying than having to put up with Brad's moods or Tim's tantrums or Lenny's falling asleep on him whenever he wanted them to make love, something was missing. As though for all his new, rugged looks, his posed stances, his rehearsed words of seduction, he'd still not made that last final step in his planned transformation.

During these months, however, he began to realize that one group of men completely eluded him. Not a real group—more like an amorphous assemblage, but a distinct one. They weren't the best looking nor the best connected, not the most talented or talked-about—but they were the most desirable. Alex seldom saw them at bars or baths or orgies, and whenever he did see them they were always with each other, always being private, obviously together, without any attempt to hide it or, more to the point, to include anyone else in. They dressed no differently than Alex or thousands of others, yet they had an altogether distinctive aura. Their flanks looked longer and flatter, their asses more delectable in denims or bathing suits, although they wore the same button-fly Levi's and Speedos he wore. Their chests seemed more defined, less pumped, more natural. Their mouths looked more sensual, their hands more eager and experienced, their crotches more...everything! Alex didn't know what it was they had, but they knew they had it. And they knew he didn't. He never once received even a half-curious look from one of the group, never mind a cruise, never mind the hint of a pickup.

✍

"It's really only a matter of expertise," Jeff said. He and Alex were sitting at a Formica-topped table in a booth in a coffee shop of utterly no distinction across the street from a shoddy, abandoned gas-station bathroom where Alex had followed Jeff's offhand cruise a half hour before and where Alex had gotten the best blow job of his life. "You simply have to be committed," Jeff went on, "to want to be the best and then to practice until you are."

Jeff—no last name offered—was about 10 pounds overweight—around his waist, where it showed even in a loose T-shirt. He was balding at the back of his curly-haired head. He was prematurely gray in his beard, at his temples, and on what Alex could see of his chest. He didn't dress well, nor was he more than ordinarily good-looking (certainly not in Alex's class!), yet Jeff was one of that group Alex lusted after. He was always among those seen sleazily grinding their hips into each other at 8:30 in the morning at Flamingo and always amid those seen leaving the Ice Palace for a private morning party where who was excluded was more important than who was invited. So when Jeff cruised Alex on the street, Alex knew he would be late for the movie date he had with a woman friend: He couldn't pass this up. He followed Jeff into the bathroom and gave himself up to Jeff's expert hands.

Now, however, Alex had to know why he and so many others desired Jeff or his ilk so much, so hopelessly. That was why, after the blow job, he'd talked to Jeff, asked him to this hepatitis dispensary, why he made himself completely miss the film he was supposed to see, why he sat here with Jeff, why he could bring himself to ask the embarrassing question Jeff had answered so succinctly.

"Practice!" Alex said. "I practice all the time."

"Where?"

"The backroom bars, the clubs, the orgies, the parties, the bushes, the baths, at home, in bed. Everywhere!"

"Too many distractions," Jeff said, all-knowing. "What you have to do is find a place where distractions are at a minimum, where you can concentrate on what you're doing, where face, body, personality, character, past history, social connections, none of it can get in the way. You need a still, intense focus. It's an art, you know, and like all arts must be practiced purely!"

When Alex paid for the coffee and pastry, Jeff reached into his own wallet and pulled out a tattered, yellowing card.

"Go here. Use my card until they get to know your face. It's very private. Not anyone is allowed in."

Alex stared at the card, defaced by wear to a few lines and cracks. "What is it?"

"Blow job palace. Two-fifty and all you want."

Alex thanked him, wishing he could bring himself to say something about seeing Jeff again. After that lecture, it seemed entirely out of the question, unless Jeff brought it up.

"I hope this works," Alex said.

"It will. Oh, take my phone number. When you think you're really ready, give me a call."

✍

Alex waited a month before going to the place. He put off going week after week, telling himself he wanted to be certain he would go there in the right frame of mind—horny, experimental, perhaps slightly frustrated, perhaps somewhat detached.

Even so, when he did finally go to the club it was more by chance than by design. He'd had dinner with some old friends in the neighborhood, had drunk a bit more than usual, had smoked more grass than he usually did, and was feeling—if not all he wished to feel— at least horny and bored with the prospect of trying to pick up someone in one of his usual haunts this late on a weeknight.

The club was two floors of what had once been a storefront years ago. A small foyer led to a large, high-ceilinged room, surrounded on three sides by small, closet-size rooms, divided by wood planking. In the middle was another freestanding series of closets. Each one locked on the inside by a simple latch and was unfurnished except for a low, rough-hewn stool. All very ordinary, except for the obvious irregularity of large holes at lower torso level in each partition—more oval than round, not big enough to put your head through, but sufficient for most genitalia. Alex supposed they were made that way to accommodate men of differing heights.

Inspecting the almost empty club, he discovered that most of the closets had similar layouts except those located on corners, which only had two holes. Later, he would discover that the two middle rooms within the freestanding group were large enough to hold two or three people, with six, seven and even more holes hewn out of their partitions. Evidently these rooms were favored by couples, groups, teams, and insatiable singles.

Aside from the closets were only the most primitive amenities: a sort of waiting room with two benches and floor ashtrays, a cigarette and soda machine, a small bathroom. It was all moderately lit—not as dark as most of the discos and backroom places he frequented. Disco music of the funkier sort was played over six speakers on each floor, the records spun by the same guy (youngish, cutish) who took your money at the door and gave you a coat check.

As Alex wandered exploring, several men came in, making him feel more cautious. He went into a booth, locked the door, sat down on the stool, and lit a joint. He smoked, hearing the sound of doors opening and closing around him. None of the three booths that opened up to this were occupied. It must be too early in the evening. *Here I am,* Alex said to himself, *all ready to practice.* He didn't feel drunk or woozy or overstuffed from the meal nor even sodden from the grass but, as he always felt while cruising, oddly extra alert. He tapped his feet lightly on the wooden plank floor to the beat of the music, leaning back against the door.

Before the song was over or the joint in his hand half smoked, the door in the booth to his right opened, and Alex made out someone come in and saw the figure turn to lock the door. Now something Jeff had said before was clarified: Unless the other man bent down, Alex couldn't see who he was, could only see part of him, certainly not his face. Alex leaned forward to get a better look and a longish semierection was immediately pushed through the hole in his direction. Alex took a final toke of the grass, smashed its embers out on the floor and began to idly fondle the erection.

Practice time, Alex said to himself. *No fooling around tonight.*

The guy must have been really horny—he got stiff instantly and came in about three minutes flat. *Hardly enough time to be considered anything but a warm-up,* Alex thought, turning away to find that roach he'd dropped and relight it. He was somewhat pleased with himself, even though he knew this had been too simple to be any different from his past experiences—certainly not different enough to place him on Jeff's level of expertise. By the time Alex had located the small piece of joint and lighted it, he found two more erections facing him from the previously unoccupied booths. One was olive-skinned and thick with a fat head, the other smaller and red on top as though bruised. Choices, choices, he thought, playing with both of them for a minute. Then he decided to take turns, jerking off one while blowing the other and then switching it around. He got two more rather quick orgasms and was soon facing another erection from the other hole. Was this beginner's luck, or was it like this every night? he wondered.

When Alex emerged from the booth some two hours later for a soda and a rest, he'd given more blow jobs than he could keep count of. He'd also received the third and fourth (after Jeff and Henrik) most spectacular orgasms of his life, thanks to guys on the other side of the partitions.

He still had a long way to go before he could attain Jeff's seemingly effortless degree of expertise, he felt, a lot more practice before he could begin to be comfortable with Jeff and his group.

✍

Having found his first experience painless and fun, Alex began going to the club more often: first a night a week, then two nights a week, then three nights a week, clear weather or foul, from midnight to three in the morning, sometimes staying later.

He also began to experiment with moods and mood-altering agents to see if they helped or hindered him. Some nights he'd merely have a vodka or smoke some grass before going: That always made him horny and seemed to turn on the other men. Sometimes, if he were feeling a bit tired, he'd sniff a bit of coke before leaving his apartment. Other times he'd drop half a quaalude, which definitely made him feel looser, sleazier. But that could also prove counterproductive to practicing, as he would be swinging on a really nice large cock while high on a down and decide he'd really rather take it up the ass, which was cheating. He almost always supplemented whatever mood he had designed with poppers. So did everyone else. He tried heavier drugs once—mescaline—but it wasn't as good: He became too distracted by the music, lacked alertness, forgot what he was doing, got overly imaginative about the man attached to the cock.

In less than a month, Alex encountered more different cocks than he'd ever imagined existing, even though he'd had his share before. Maybe it was because they were so emphasized here. In one night at the club, he would bring off long ones, thin ones, thick ones, lily-white ones, flaring purple-headed ones, angry red ones, black ones, tan ones, fat ones, flattened ones, bent ones, squarish ones; some with tiny little pointed heads, others consisting of almost nothing but head: several had a network of bulging veins, some had no apparent veins on the shaft at all; some smelled of colognes and powders, others of wintergreen (athletes?), some of urine, others of perspiration—ranging from metallically acrid to sweeter-than-butterscotch; most smelled of nothing at all.

In those early months, Alex practiced on each one that came his way. Even if it was small and thin, even if it was so large he could scarcely encompass it with a hand, never mind get his lips around it. He made it a point with each to find the right angle of approach, much as one does when first meeting a person socially, as though the cock were the entire individual encapsulated, personified. Some were to be handled gently, others more roughly. For some, he had to drop onto his knees, squat, and angle up; others had to be gotten at from the left side or the top.

Alex naturally also observed others: the holes in the partition provided enough room to view. Between increased practice and observation, he learned how not to gag, how to use the top of his palate, how to tongue the sensitive, vein-rich shaft bottom, how to titillate the area beneath the head. He learned how to stroke, caress, lick, grasp, grip, and fondle each scrotum. He even learned how to hold both genitals—if they weren't too large—together in such a way that he could blow both cock and balls simultaneously.

These technical matters aside, Alex also discovered there was a right attitude and a wrong attitude to take in sucking a cock. Demanding orgasm was meaningless—even wrongheaded. If he was relaxed, in time with the music, and thoughtlessly sucking away, he became nothing but an internal muscle—the ideal state. Often he'd be without a thought in his mind, almost oblivious to where he was, what he was doing, or how much time had passed when the telltale sign of a sudden new thickening in the head told him he was about to get another little explosion.

One night he stood up from one of the larger, center booths and saw a handwritten scrawl that read, "Brought off 20 guys here tonight!"

Alex laughed. Only a tyro would bother to keep count—or to crow about it.

He'd become comfortable in the club. He got to be known to the two guys who alternated at the door and spinning records. He started to know almost instinctively the minute a man walked into the foyer whether he'd be good for one orgasm or more. He even began to size up cocks from how their owners walked, from how they played with themselves through their pants.

Soon men were flinging their bodies against the partitions, moaning and calling out in orgasm when Alex had hold of them. One night someone fell backward against the door of the booth. Another forgot to lock his booth and fell right out—into someone passing by.

Alex became sought after in the club. Booths on either side of his were seldom empty. He began to feel easy, casual, confident, effective.

After not too long, he felt ready for anyone—anyone.

When Jeff walked into the club, he must have been stoned: He walked right past where Alex was sitting on the waiting room bench without noticing him.

Jeff had lost weight, and his gray hair had spread to an even salt-and-pepper over his beard and curly head. He looked terrific.

Alex followed him around a bit, trying to get his attention, but Jeff still didn't recognize him and finally entered a booth flanked by two occupied ones. Alex stood against the wall, lit a joint and waited until one of them emptied or Jeff came out again.

Alex had progressed from being completely promiscuous to being utterly selective. He didn't need practice anymore. Now, whenever he stepped into a booth, it was to give someone he'd chosen a special treat. He usually stayed out in the waiting area until someone exceptional arrived—someone attractive, well-remembered, or simply new to him. He would then follow the man around, cruise him, watch until his intention was clear. Most guys he cruised, cruised back pretty fast, picking up on his supercharged sexuality. Most of them remained outside a booth until they could find one adjoining his. But there were times when the place was so crowded only one booth was available. Alex would open the door and invite the guy in. All of them entered, and all of them stayed.

Afterward, sitting on the front benches sharing a 7UP, a cigarette, and a desultory chat, most of the men offered Alex their phone numbers, and a few asked for his. It didn't take him long to make a good-sized collection. But the few times he called up guys he'd met at the club, there always seemed to be a lot of talk and endless grass smoking and interminably long foreplay before they got down to what interested him. After a few turnoffs like this, Alex still took phone numbers and said he would call, but he never did.

But he was known now. Whenever he went out to parties or bars or discos, all the most attractive, most desirable men knew him. Some fondled his nipples as he passed; others groped him or patted his ass. All at least nodded or said hello, including most of the men in that group he wanted to know so badly before. Especially them.

Finally a booth next to where Jeff had entered flew open and a tall, good-looking guy stepped out. Alex went in, sat down, and looked. Jeff was sitting down too. He needed a little motivation.

Alex had evolved a little ritual, which seldom failed to interest. He would walk into a booth, lock the door, play with himself through his denims until he was hard, slowly unbutton his fly, open up, draw it out hard, play with it a little, take out his balls, rub them a little, unloosen his belt, slowly push his pants down to his knees, all the while turning his cock to various angles for differing views, then he would unbutton his shirt, pull off his T-shirt, let them look at his lean, muscled abdomen, then kneel down and present his face. It was as certain as a spider web, and most guys stayed not only to reciprocate but often for a second blow job.

It worked with Jeff too. It took Jeff a while to extricate his cock from his shorts and then a bit longer to get the studded cock ring untangled, but finally it was free—still flaccid but large, with exactly the right size balls, exactly the right color, the head just thick enough, the cock shaft exactly the right degree of veininess. His lower torso was perfectly muscled. Even Jeff's pubic hair had a shape that excited Alex.

It took Alex a while to get the thing stiff, but when it was, it felt so right in his mouth and hand that he gave it the benefit of every trick he had learned: the palate rub, the hand slide, the ball tug, the sideways shaft lick—he pulled out all the stops. When Jeff finally came, he lunged against the divider so hard he banged his head. He emitted a low, guttural sound and spurted a long time. Then he staggered back, dropping onto the stool like a bag of beans.

Alex had caught the substantial load straight down his throat—no more messy moustaches for him—and it still tingled with heat and a slightly alkaline taste. He stared at Jeff, hoping he wasn't having a heart attack.

Jeff's stunned look met his, and there was a momentary smile and mumbled thanks. Jeff still didn't recall him. It must have been over a year ago they'd met. Then Alex was hard and pushing himself through the hole. After a few minutes of that, he asked Jeff to join him in his booth.

There, Alex stripped Jeff, necked with him, sucked him hard again, turned him around, and fucked him. All the while, hands from other booths were sticking out, caressing them. Mouths, faces, eyes were pushed up against them through the holes, wanting to share. When Alex came inside Jeff, it was a moment of total triumph. He'd never felt so good in his life. He'd outdone an expert.

On the bench in the waiting room, Jeff put him arm around Alex's shoulders.

"I was pretty downed out when I came in. I'd only come an hour before too. I sure didn't expect to find anyone like you here tonight."

Alex smiled. Then he reminded Jeff of their meeting in the gas station bathroom and their conversation in the coffee shop. He enjoyed Jeff's surprise, the gray eyes narrowing in sudden recognition, then widening in satisfaction.

"Well, I'll be damned," Jeff said, and pulled Alex closer.

People came and went around them. They could hear doors opening and closing in the large room.

"Tomorrow's Saturday," Jeff said. "You don't have to work, do you?"

"No, why?"

"Why not come home with me. We'll get some shut-eye, then take up where we left off tonight. All day tomorrow if you want."

Alex suddenly didn't want to. He felt cold, distant. A year before this would have been perfect. But now…well, things had changed in a year. He had changed.

Jeff went on to talk about the big disco party the next night. He and Alex would fuck and sleep, fuck and then go out to the party, dance sleazily, make out, get each other and others hot too, then go home and do it all again on Sunday. Jeff was amusing, offhand about it. All Alex could read was Jeff's eagerness: his uncool eagerness, his desire to possess Alex alone because he was just as good.

"Well, how about it?" Jeff asked.

"Maybe another time," Alex said, trying to soften it. "I have to see some friends tomorrow night."

"Well, how about tonight, then?"

Alex read even more eagerness in Jeff's eyes.

"Don't think so," Alex mumbled. "I'm sort of beat. Got a dog to walk when I get back. Dishes in the sink..."

He felt Jeff's arm slide off his shoulder. They sat next to each other for another awkward minute or two.

"I sort of like you," Jeff offered, all casualness gone.

"Me too," Alex said. It came out wrong, hard, wrong. Alex decided to let it pass. He didn't care.

After another few minutes during which he was afraid Jeff would do or say something even more tactless, Jeff stood up, straightened out his pants and said, "OK. Another time."

That was better. "See you," Alex said.

The minute Jeff left the club, Alex realized he hadn't even offered Alex his phone number.

What a phony, Alex thought. *All he wanted was a one-night stand. All he wanted was me fucking his tired old ass.*

He angrily lighted a cigarette and smoked it, thinking what a phony shit Jeff was. It was 3:30 now. He ought to go home. Why stick around. Nothing but pigs here.

He was just getting up to go to the coat check when someone walked in: a lanky blond with full, darker beard and denims molded so that every inch of his heavy-headed cock could be made out.

Alex exchanged a cruise with him, then a heavier one, and watched his sultry, slightly bowlegged walk to the booths. His jeans were so rubbed around his ass, they looked white. They looked as though they needed spreading.

Alex could probably get him off by eating through the denims.

He got up, went into the room, cruised him again, then found a booth next to another empty one. Inside he went through his ritual body showing. His cock never looked as ready, his rippled stomach more touchable. He knelt and faced the open hole and saw the erection push its head at him. He began to fondle it till it was really stiff.

He suddenly remembered Jeff walking out of the place after the best fuck of his life without even offering his goddamned phone number. Fucking phony!

Then a fat, warm cock head was brushing against his lips. Alex opened his mouth. And was pacified.

What Do Women Want?
We Want to Be Big Slutty Fags, Among Other Things
By Carol Queen

Some years ago I was invited to make a presentation to a women artists' conference. On a panel with several other creative women who use sex centrally in their work, I got to talk about my creative process and concerns when I write fiction as a woman. Since I've never been a man (except, perhaps, on paper), these issues did not seem difficult to pinpoint: As a matter of fact, I think my gender is fundamentally central in my fiction and erotic memoir, so that teasing out what I would write if I weren't a woman seems like an impossible exercise. It might be useful, don't get me wrong; I just don't think I could do it.

Back when "gender studies" just meant "women's studies," not "How many genders are there?" I experienced my femaleness as self-evident, immutable, and yet problematic. It wasn't problematic because my sense of my own gender was in question, but in that women's studies kind of way: Mars, Venus, 72 cents on the dollar, Take Back the Night, etc. I read feminist theory, criticized sexist social construction, and lionized androgyny (ironic, though, that so many women's studies types were so deeply suspicious of *true* androgyny, especially if it came packaged in a transsexual person). I read Freud and feminist critiques of Freud, and I got extremely cranky when he asked the $64,000 question: What Do Women Want?

What the fuck do you mean, Sigmund? Women want *equality,* you pig! We want you to stop analyzing our goddamned dreams like a cocaine-snorting voyeur! That's what we want, you bastard, and we don't fantasize about our fathers either, you dirty-minded old fuck.

That was my response, and except for those crazy French feminists who were in the process of rehabilitating Freud by dressing him up in post-structuralist drag, it seemed like everyone else's response too. (Anyway, we hadn't quite discovered *New French Feminisms*. It was still OK to talk and write as though you were trying to communicate with an ordinary person; that would soon change.)

Along with this theoretical immersion in feminism, I immersed myself in women's sexuality: my own, my lovers', and that of the entire lesbian community. I shouldn't, perhaps, have to spell out, but I will, that in those days I actually thought I could know and understand the entire lesbian community—even though my experience was severely limited and in fact I was talking out my ass. But I was hardly alone in this. We wanted so deeply to create an alternate reality for lesbians that we pretended a single, comprehensible, and comprehensive lesbian community existed. Anyway, I explored hidden desires and new erotic adventures with my girlfriends, learned as best I could how to pleasure them, and was very certain my erotic world differed greatly from that of men. Like almost all of us, I believed that women's sexuality was knowable and that we were mostly alike, except for the obvious differences rooted in our sexual orientation.

Parallel to this immersion in womanity, though, I still got turned on to men; for a decade that part of my sexuality mostly popped wheelies in a cul-de-sac, all fired up but no place to go as I lived my life in Lesbian Nation. As I've written elsewhere ("Beyond the Valley of the Fag Hags" in *PoMoSexuals*), the way I accommodated these desires was to direct them toward gay men. I was a politically correct dyke (more or less) with a dirty secret: fag fantasies—but even those were more PC than the other alternative, my response to which I studiously repressed, bikers who looked like a cross between Jesus Christ and Satan. (I've always had such a soft spot for those guys.)

This should have shaken my firmly held notions about female sexuality, but for a long time I resisted any insight about my own erotic complexity: it would have been too threatening in 1979 to think that I would never be a *real* lesbian (whatever that was). Bisexuality was pretty much off the map.

But my own complexity remained, and not only that, my lovers were complex too—*differently!* I never did figure out how to make one of them come; of course I never simply asked her what she wanted, how she did it herself, *if* she did it herself, what she fantasized about. And that wasn't even all. Lesbian Nation was "engaged in a great civil war, testing whether that nation, or any nation so conceived and so dedicated, c[ould] long endure." Yeah, that's Abraham Lincoln talking, not Gayle Rubin, but the feminist sex wars pitted sister against sister as surely and often as viciously as the rhetoric of North and South. We screamed at each other about S/M, porn, sex work, and pretty much everything "male-oriented," whatever that was. For a while I uncritically accepted that appellation, until I noticed that *I* actually wanted to do some of those "male" things, or had been doing them all along. Uh-oh. And it seemed many other women wanted to do them too, hence the fuss.

Sigmund, I apologize. What the fuck *do* women want?

I think the answer would confound old Siggy at least as much as the question. Women want to love; explore; seek pleasure; throw off the chains of gender oppression, and that means the ones on our clits as well as the ones on our paychecks and psyches; then some of us want to attach real chains to our clits for fun. Women want to make love while bungee jumping, sneak into a bathhouse and fuck all the men up the butt, recapitulate the *Story of O* playing all the roles, masturbate while we shoot up the New York Stock Exchange with a really handsome semiautomatic weapon. Oh, the list goes on. And some women, it seems, want to spend lots of time scrutinizing what other people want and then get very, very worked up condemning it, which is to say that some women are shameless voyeurs and bluenoses to boot. Roll over, Sigmund: It's way too complicated for a 19th-century guy like you. *I* can barely keep track, and I'm a trained professional.

✍

So when I sit down to write, the creative world I access includes not just my experience and fantasies—from which I draw very liberally—but also the entire social discussion about female sexuality. (I also draw from my male friends' experience, my experience of them, and much social theory about male sexuality, especially in the queer world, since I still tend to like my men queer. I think I draw very believable men, but I do not grapple with and invest in those characters in the same way I do writing women.)

Since I have felt personally shamed by (lesbian and) feminist ideas about correct female sexuality, which is the late-20th-century version of "proper" behavior, I explore an erotic realm in which women mostly do not have the constraints of correctness and propriety, in which the "you own your own body" ideal of feminism is a done deal, and women mostly are free to do things that nice girls don't do. For one thing, this is a crucial cultural function of erotic literature: It always serves as a kind of protest literature exploring (and exploding) taboos, gender roles, and socially imposed notions of appropriate sexuality. So says the erotologist, the academic analyst of erotica, in me, but more than that, it is crucial to me personally as I try to carve a space for myself in the world that acknowledges the true possibility of an alternative female sexuality that is exploratory, voracious, curious, pansexual, open to multiple sources of pleasure.

I suppose I could be setting these explorations on another planet, but to me the erotic stories I write work best as literature when they exist in and even grapple with existing taboos. That way the tension lives within the story and I don't have to make my characters get into arguments, commit adultery, and feel guilty about it, or shoot up the stock exchange. I think the overarching tension shaping my work is the notion that women aren't supposed to want or be able to experience these things, whether or not we dress as boys to prowl our back alleys. Clearly, "nice girls don't" is one taboo I have no use for; I'm not much happier with "feminist women don't," so I am always engaged in a dialogue with feminism, even when the rhetoric usually associated with that kind of discussion is absent. (It *does* appear, often, in my essays.)

But that's only part of the way my work grapples with issues of femaleness. It's all very interesting to change gender on another planet (although those characters really lose my interest when they do it just to reproduce), but I am interested in gender play, masquerade, and change on *this* planet. Characters in *The Leather Daddy and the Femme* (from which "After the Light Changed" is excerpted) almost all have some problematic and interesting relationship to gender, sometimes in the context of their own transsexuality (Ariel and Jacy), other times in relation to "correctly gendered" desire in the queer community. This is where my many years loving fags and sneaking off to read fag porn transmogrify into my characters' real lives: Randy/Miranda cross-dresses to lure leather daddies, and Jack decides to transgress the bounds of fagdom and play with her anyway, even though she's "no ordinary boy"; later in the novel we meet Peaches, who was born to cross-dress, the John who only likes women with big cocks, and Demetrius, who comes into his erotic attraction for men through being fucked by a bigendered, biracial domme.

Girls will be boys and boys will be girls, partly because we have different erotic energies and personae with which we can play when we step outside our own gendered reality and also because there is a great and largely unexplored/unarticulated space *between* boy and girl—this is where many queer folk, in fact, live, and it radiates possibility. That I might be growing up into a world where gender would, for the first time on a substantial scale, be contested territory, its spies and double agents exposed, was not clear to me as a pained, trying-to-be-politically-correct baby dyke, but now I find it the most extraordinary and compelling aspect of the queer world we have made. I can't express how glad I am to have grown up to live in (and try to sketch) it.

Still, I do not think this brave new world takes me out of my own femaleness; it just casts my gender (sometimes) in a new light. I still can't go to the baths and dive into the orgy room (usually), and I am still fascinated by the visible but still separate sexual culture of gay men. So in "After the Light Changed" (and the stories that follow, especially "Ganged") I let my protagonist Miranda inhabit a seemingly gay male identity long enough to enter a world of sexual adventure that's mostly closed to me because I'm a woman (and, well, because I'm a woman). I know enough about this world to appropriate some of its signals, certainly to be suffused with (and convey on paper) its eroticism. It is a deeply significant part of my own sexual orientation—not the alley crawling, but the erotic appreciation of fags and fag space. Yeah, I know the fags went to play in the tree-house together and pulled the ladder up; I don't care. If only because my (subconscious) strategy for nurturing my own bisexuality in a strict lesbian world was eroticizing fags, it's always part of my sexual point of view. Yet, also like Randy, I don't want playing a boy to remove me from my femaleness. Really what I desire is a pansexual world in queer community clothing, a world in which "male" and "female" are more shape-shifting sources of possibility than Great Walls of gender role and restriction. I write to make it so or at least to give myself (and those with similar issues and desires) a place to retreat for a while: a San Francisco very like our own but with fewer dot-coms, lots more time to fuck, and where nobody throws anybody else out of bed, not even for eating crackers.

✍

I write to explore the issues and eroticism that most compels me, and in a real sense I write to create more role models for myself. (The person who showed me this was worth doing is Pat Califia, whose *Macho Sluts* blew a hole in the dam of female erotic silence that washed me right out of my backwater of shame.) It turns out that other women often respond strongly to my work, especially women who, like me, have felt limited around not only propriety but also the constraints of a community we hoped would free us from those of the larger society. Who knew we would be exchanging one set of rules for another? When I write erotic memoir I am specifi-cally speaking to an audience (even more than when I write fiction, when I often speak primarily to myself—then I share it with readers, whom I hope will be as aroused, amused, or provoked as I was when writing it). Since I still do not believe the cultural space for women's erotic expression and exploration is large enough, when I breach its walls I want to advise that it can be done. I also want to leave a doc-ument that describes a journey I was not supposed to be able to take.

In stories like "Sweating Profusely in Merida," "The Best Whore in Hillsboro," "Social Skills," "Like a Virgin," and "Knife," for instance, I wrote about scenes I lived that surprised even me: Something about those experiences was supposed to be impossible, and yet there I was. It's one thing to do the erotically taboo or improbable in fiction—and I think it's useful—but there's something about true or mostly-true stories that serves a different function. Memoir maps a *real* country, not an erotic Middle-earth that, no matter how compellingly it's drawn, may not be accessible from here.

Still, I like my fiction best when it feels plausible, even as it crosses boundaries strong enough to render it improbable—when the characters don't step entirely out of reality even when the scenario in which they live is rather far from my own day-to-day reality. I think this is because I *do* have an activist motivation when I write: I want to uncircumscribe sex and see what happens to us and to it when we slip the bonds, are free of certain constraints. The more improbable the scenario, I think, the less we are invited to learn from the characters' journeys.

For all this talk of taboo-breaking, I've occasionally been criticized for being a sort of Pollyanna of sex writing, Rebecca of Sunnyfuck Farm—so sex-positive that there's not enough for critics who like that cutting-edge style that wallows in taboo and shame, nouveau de Sade. All I can say is, I don't find that stuff especially compelling or relevant to my life. I want my characters to get up and fuck another day, and any critic who thinks it's *normal* for real-life sex stories to have happy endings hasn't gone outside in the last 20 years. They can write those stories, and I'll write mine. In fact, that gives me an idea: Little Rebecca goes out to the bunkhouse on Sunnyfuck Farm, sees Hank the farmhand masturbating the horse while Big Jim the overseer fucks his hungry ass, and Rebecca creeps up the ladder to the loft so she can watch. But the farm dog has followed her in…

What do women want? A really good view from that loft. A ladder sturdy enough to scramble down and join the action.

After the Light Changed
By Carol Queen

I was looking pretty boyish that evening. Maybe that's why he looked twice at the stoplight when my car pulled up next to his motorcycle. Usually guys like that are moving, you just see a gleaming blur of black and silver. But here at the light was a real done-up daddy, sitting stock-still, except for his head, which turned in response to my eyes fixed on him and found what he saw noticeable enough to make him turn again. When boy-energy gets into me I look like an effete young Cambridge faggot looking to go bad; round spectacles framing inquisitive eyes and a shock of hair falling down over one. Not classically Daddy's boy, something a little different. Maybe tonight this daddy was looking for a new kind of ride.

A real done-up daddy, yeah. His leathers were immaculate, carried that dull gleam that well-kept black leather picks up under streetlights. Black leather cap, high boots, everything on him black and silver except the well-worn blue denim at his crotch, bulging invitingly out of a pair of chaps. I eyed that denimed expanse quite deliberately; he noticed. He had steely-blue daddy eyes and a well-trimmed beard. I couldn't see his hands under the riding gloves, but they looked big, and from the looks of him I bet they were manicured. I love these impeccable daddies. They appeal to the femme in me.

And his bike! A huge shiny animal, a Harley, of course, nothing but classic for this daddy. The chrome gleamed like he did the fine polish with his tongue—or rather, used the tongue of some lucky boy. I'm more for polishing leather myself, but if this stone-hot daddy told me to do his bike, of course I'd get right to it.

Ooh, he was looking right into my eyes, taking in my angelic Vienna-choirboy face and my leather jacket, much rattier than his with all its ACT UP and Queer Nation stickers. Does he think I'm cute enough for a walk on the wild side? I could hear it as he dished me to all the other daddies: "Yeah, this hot little schoolboy, looked real innocent but he cruised me like he knew what I had and wanted it, so I let him follow me home."

On the cross street the light turned yellow. I did want what he had. This was it. I leaned out the window and said, just loud enough to be heard, careful to keep my voice low-pitched, "Daddy, can I come too?"

The daddy grinned. When the light turned green he gunned the Harley, took the space in front of my car, and signaled for me to follow.

An apartment South of Market—oh, this was perfect. At 3 A.M. on any given night he could probably open his bedroom window and find a willing mouth down here to piss in—I've heard about this alley. The entryway was dark. Good. I parked my car and caught up with him there. I fell to my knees as he pulled his keys from his belt. By the time he had his door unlocked I was chewing on his balls through the denim. He let me go on that way for a minute, and then he collared me and hauled me into the dark foyer. I barely had time to grab my rucksack, which I'd let fall beside me so I could get both hands on his hard, leather-clad thighs.

Inside, I pulled off my glasses and tucked them away safely in my jacket. Daddy pushed me back onto my knees, and I scrambled to open the buttons of his Levi's. I wanted his cock, wanted it big, wanted it down my throat with his hands fisting the hair at the nape of my neck, giving it to me hard and rhythmic. I wanted to suck both of his balls into my mouth while he slapped his dick against my cheeks. Cock worship in the dark—use me, Daddy, no, don't come yet—I have a surprise for you.

I don't know how long I went on. I get lost in cock sucking sometimes, it's like a ritual, it disconnects me from my head, and when it's anonymous all the more so. I hadn't even seen this cock I was sucking, and that made me feel I could be anyone, even an adventurous gay boy in a South of Market alley, sucking Daddy's big hard dick. Any second now he could realize that I was no ordinary boy, and that gave me a great rush of adrenaline, a lust to have it down my throat. Until he discovered me I could believe this illusion myself, and with most men this was all I could expect, a cocksucker until they turned the lights on.

Daddy was moaning; guess as a cocksucker I got a passing grade. I felt the seam of my Levi's, wet where they pressed into my cunt. Jesus, I wanted it, I wanted it from him, I wanted him not to care. The scents of leather and sweat filled my head. Finally I pulled my mouth away from his dick, no problem speaking in a low voice now, shit, I was hoarse from his pounding. "Daddy, please, I want you to fuck me."

He pulled me up at once, kissed me, hard. That was a surprise. I was swooning, not feeling like a boy now, whatever a boy feels like, but all womanly, my brain in my cunt. And I was about to be discovered. His hand was sliding into my jacket; any second now it would fall upon the swell of my breast. This was where most guys freaked out and sent me home to beat off. That was OK usually, but God, it would kill me to break this kiss.

But the kiss went on even when his fingers grazed first one breast, then the other...when his other hand followed the first under my jacket, then under my shirt, as if for corroboration, and he felt my nipples go hard under his touch. He squeezed them, eliciting a very unboyish moan, thrusting his tongue deep down where his cock had been, so that even when he twisted the nipples into the shape of morning glories, furled around themselves, I couldn't cry out.

The kiss went on even when one hand slid down my belly and started undoing the buttons of my jeans until there was room for him to slip a finger down between my pussy lips, root its way, almost roughly, all the way into my cunt, pull the slick finger out again and thrust it into my mouth, where our tongues sucked it clean. The kiss lasted until he'd slid his fingers back in and fucked me all slow and juicy and excruciating and I finally broke away to beg, "Oh, Jesus, please, make me come!" He stroked in faster, then; I came like a fountain into his hand. He rubbed the juice all over my face, licked some of it off kissing me again, then pulled me down the hall into a lit room. I felt weak-kneed and wildly disheveled; he was immaculate yet, but his cock was out and it was still hard. For me.

Those steel-blue eyes were lit with more than amusement, and when he spoke, in a soft, low, almost-drawl, I realized it was the first time I'd heard his voice.

"Well, little boy, I must say you had me tricked." He laughed; I guess I looked a little proud. "Do you make a habit of fooling guys like me?"

"Not very often," I managed. "And most men don't want what they get."

"No, I would imagine not. A little too much pussy under that boy-drag. A man wouldn't want to get himself...confused. Hey, where'd you learn to suck cock? A bathhouse?"

"My brother taught me. He's gay."

"Shit, bring him with you the next time you visit," said the daddy. "I'll die and go to heaven." He pushed me back on the bed then and knelt above me. His big cock dangled above my face, and at first he held me down, teasing me with it, but I begged and he lowered it to my lips, letting me have just enough to suck on like a baby dreams over a tit. "Good girl," he said, smiling a little, running his fingertips over my skin in a most enticing way. The boy-energy was gone, but I didn't want to stay a little girl with a man this hot. Anyway, he wasn't acting like a leather daddy anymore.

I don't know what gets into me. When I cruise gay men as a boy, I know full well that I have to stay a boy the whole time. Unless they send me out at the first touch of curves, the first smell of pussy, they only want to play with me if I can keep up the fantasy. I lick Daddy's boots and suck his cock and get on my face for him, raise my ass up at the first brush of his cock on my cheeks. I beg Daddy to fuck my ass and promise I'll be his good boy, always. But deep inside, even as he's slam-fucking my ass and I'm screaming from the deep pounding pleasure of it, even though I love being a faggot for him, I secretly wish he'd slip and bury his meat all the way deep in my cunt. I love being the boy, but I don't like having to be two separate people to get what I want. I really want the men I fuck to turn me over and see the whole me: the woman in the boy, the boy in the woman. This daddy, this leatherman whose name I didn't even know, was the first one with whom that seemed possible—and I wanted to make sure. I wanted to know if he would really play with me.

So again I let his cock slip from my lips. "Daddy, will you let me up for a minute? I want to play a new game, and I really want you to like it." He released me, looking at me quizzically as I reached for my bag and pulled the last of my clothes off. There. A femme hates having pants bagging around her ankles.

Feeling sleeker already, I took the bag into the bathroom, promising I'd be right back. Everything there, shoes, clothes, makeup. It was time to grow up.

The dress was red and tight and hugged my small breasts into cleavage. Its back plunged down almost to the swell of my ass. Black stockings and garters (the dress was too tight to wear a belt under, only a black G-string), and red leather pumps with high, high heels. The kind of shoes drag queens named so aptly call "come fuck me" pumps. You're not supposed to walk in them; you're supposed to offer the toe to a worshipful tongue or lock them around a neck while you get pounded. Which is what I hoped would be happening to me shortly.

With some gel and a brush my hair went from boyish to chic. Powder on my face, then blush. I darkened my eyebrows and lashes, lined and shaded my eyes with green and violet, and brushed deep crimson onto my lips. An amazingly changed face, all angles and shadows and eyes and cheekbones, looked back at me from the mirror. One last glance: I was sufficiently stunning. In fact, the sight, combined with the knowledge that I was about to emerge from the little room into the leather daddy's view, had me soaked, my heart pounding, my clit buzzing. I get so very narcissistic when I'm femmed out. I want to reach for my image in the mirror, take her apart and fuck her. No doubt I'd be riding this energy into the girl bars tomorrow night, looking for my image stepped through the looking glass, out looking for me.

One last flourish, a long sheer black scarf, sheer as my stockings, flung around my shoulders, hiding nothing. I stepped back into the leather daddy's room.

He'd taken his jeans off from beneath the chaps. His jacket was off too, hung carefully over a chair. His dick was in his hand; he'd been stroking it, staying hard. Bands of leather drew my gaze to the hard curves of his biceps. Silver rings gleamed in his nipples. I felt like a *Vogue* model who'd stumbled into a Tom of Finland painting. He was gorgeous. He was every bit the spectacle I was, body modified and presented to evoke heat, to attract sex.

He looked at me hard, taking in the transformation. I saw his cock jump; good.

"So, Daddy, do you still want to play?" I said "Daddy" in a different voice this time, let it be lush with irony, like a '40s burlesque queen. A well-educated faggot ought to pick up on that.

There was a touch of wonderment in his voice. "Goddamn. I don't believe I've ever picked up anything quite like you." Then suspicion. "So what's your trip? Trying to turn the heathens into hets? No wonder all those other guys threw you out."

I experienced a new rush of adrenaline. I thought to myself, *Go ahead, be uncomfortable, baby, but don't stop wanting it.* I took a couple of steps, nearing the bed enough that I could put one foot up on it. I moved into his territory, gave him a view of the tops of my stockings and the wet, pussy-redolent G-string. I narrowed my eyes. "Did I suck your cock like a het? You think I can't take it now that I have a dress on?"

He persisted. "Why waste this on gay men? Straight boys must fall over for you."

"Straight boys don't know how to give me what I want." I ran my eyes down his body. "Besides, your cock says I'm not wasting this on you."

He made no move to try to hide the hard-on. His voice was more curious than accusatory when he said, "You get a perverse charge out of this, don't you?"

"Yeah, I do. But I really want you to get a perverse charge out of it." I moved to him, knelt over him so that only the insides of my knees touched the smooth leather of the chaps. He was close enough to touch; I had to stop from reaching. This was it, the last obstacle. His hard cock almost touched me. "I'm no ordinary boy, Daddy, and I'm no ordinary woman. Do you want it? Just take it."

There is so much power in being open and accessible and ready. So much power in wanting it. That's what other women don't understand. You'll never get what you want if you make it too hard for someone to give it to you. He proved it: He lifted his hands to me, ran them once over my body, bringing the nipples up hard through the clinging dress, pinned my arms at my sides, and brought me down into a kiss that seared and melted, a kiss I felt like a tongue in my cunt. I felt myself sliding along his body till his cock head rested against the soaked silk of my panties, hard and hot, and he stroked against my clit over and over and over. He released my arms, one big hand held my ass, keeping me pushed against him, the other fisted in my hair. He held me fast, and once again my cries of orgasm were muffled on his tongue.

When his mouth left mine it went to my ear, talking low.

"Pretty girl, I want your cunt so hot you go crazy. You got all dressed up for me, didn't you. Pretty bitch, you want it rough, you like it like that?"

"Yes!" I gasped, still riding the last waves of come, wanting more.

"Then tell me. Ask for it. Beg me!"

He pulled the scarf from around my neck, threw me easily onto my back. He pinned my arms over my head, bound my wrists with the scarf, talking in his low daddy voice, playing my game:

"You want it, pretty bitch? You're going to get it, Miss Special. Think your cunt is good enough for my meat, do you? Can't get what you need from straight boys? You're gonna need it bad before you get an inch of it, baby... Spread 'em, that's right, spread for me, show it to me, let me have a good look. I haven't seen something like this in a long time... You know what I usually do with this cock, don't you? Is that what you want, is that what straight boys don't give you? Want it in your ass, make you be Daddy's boy again, hmm? No, you want it in your pussy, baby, I can feel it. Just shove it all inside you, you want to feel it open you up, can you take it?"

Now he was reddening my ass with slaps, the dress pulled up to my waist, and from nowhere he clicked open a knife. I gasped and whimpered, but he just used it to cut the G-string off, and it disappeared again. He slapped my pussy with his cock, scattering drops of my wetness, stopping short before I came, whispering, "Want it, pretty bitch? Want it all?" And I writhed against him and begged him, "Jesus, please, give it to me, Daddy! Please...please!"

He was a consummate tease, this daddy; I wondered dimly if his boys tried to wiggle their assholes onto his just-out-of-reach cock the way I was trying to capture it with my hungry cunt. Not so much difference between one hunger and another, after all.

He reached for a rubber, worked it over his cock head and rolled it down the shaft. The encasement made his big cock strain harder. As he knelt between my spread-wide legs, I murmured,

"Give it to me, give it to me, give..." And in a long plunge, he did.

It felt so good to be filled so full, with the smell of hot leather and cock and pussy and the feel of the chaps against my legs. The second thrust came harder than the first, and a look of sexy concentration played across my leather daddy's face as he settled in for a long, hard, pounding ride.

It was my turn to talk to him. As I met his strokes with thrusts of my own, letting my pinned-down body fill with the delicious tensions that would build up to even more intense peaks.

"Oh, yeah, just like that, give me your cock, baby, fill up my pussy, yeah... Give it to me, give it to me, you know I can take it, hard, yeah, come on... Fuck my cunt like you fuck your boys' asses, make me take it from you, yeah, don't stop, don't ever stop, just try to outlast me, Daddy—you can fuck me all night, fill that rubber with a big hot load and I'll come just thinking about you, just give it to me... Just give it to me, make me, make me... come..."

And it was all lost in cries and sobs and breath taking over. Somehow he'd untied my hands and I held him and came and came and came, and the wild ride was over with half a dozen bucking thrusts. I heard his yells mingle with mine, and I reached down to pull cock and rubber free of my cunt and feel the heft of jism in my hand as we lay together in a tangle of sweaty limbs, not man and woman, just animals, two sated animals.

I drifted off to sleep and woke again as he was working the tight, sweaty dress over my head and off. My red leather shoes glowed against the white sheets.

"Hellion," he said as my eyes opened, "faggot in a woman's body, bitch goddess, do you intend to sleep in your exquisite red shoes?"

I held them up for him to take off, one and then the other, and he placed respectful kisses on each toe before he set them on the bed.

"No," I said, "that's pretty femmey, even for me."

"And what does a man need to do with you around," he continued, pulling off my stockings, "to get fucked? Call your brother?"

He hadn't seen all the contents of my trick bag. I reached for it and spilled it onto the floor; three dildos, a harness and a pair of long rubber gloves fell out. I promised that in the morning he could take his pick. I was dying to show Daddy what else a femme can do.

By Scott Brassart (a.k.a. Jesse Grant)

You could not have grown up in a more sexually repressed household than mine. I never saw my parents kiss. Never saw anyone walking around the house in a state of undress, half dress, anything but full dress. When my grade school friend Jeff came for a sleepover, my first ever, I was shocked when he prepared for bed by stripping to his underwear...and then stopping. No robe. No pajamas. No fuzzy animal slippers. Just little white Jockey shorts with a blue stripe adorning the elastic. "What if my mother comes in?" I asked, stupefied. I couldn't imagine being seen by my mother while wearing nothing but underwear. And here little scampering Jeff was, risking being seen by *someone else's* mother. I was very relieved when we crawled under the covers before she came in to turn out the light.

A few years later, in fifth grade, my all-white, middle-American public school taught Sex Education. Sex Education: written with capital first letters, uttered in a deep, principal-like tone. Our parents, who hadn't learned about sex in school, were collectively mortified— *first Darwin, now this!*—but oh, so pleased to be relieved of this otherwise familial duty. My classmates, unlike our parents and very unlike our teachers, were, of course, rabid with anticipatory glee.

I did not share in their enthusiasm. They were titillated; I was lost. I suppose some of them were ready for it, far enough along physically and mentally—*sexually*—to process the information and apply it to their own bodies, selves. The adventurous kids, kissing under the Ping-Pong table at recess; my friend Angie, with budding breasts; my classmate Billy, taller than my 13-year-old sister. But the hormones of discontent had not even *begun* to foment in *me*. The most pressing questions in *my* life had nothing to do with intercourse or masturbation; they were more along the line of "Excuse me, Miss Librarian, are there any new Encyclopedia Brown mysteries?"

Taller-than-my-sister Billy lived in one of two duplexes standing sentinel at the entrance to our ranch-style tract home neighborhood. My mother *hated* the tacky orange brick duplexes. She never said as much; far too refined for that. But she never looked at them or spoke of them. She *ignored* them. A dead giveaway. When my mother truly despises something, she deletes it from her world. Simple. For instance, she has never said the word *gay*. The point of this digression, in case you're wondering, is that Billy, on top of living in an ugly house, used to set fires in trash cans. So I suppose that although he very likely benefited from Sex Education, he probably had other, more pressing needs. As did the young man I met last Saturday.

I had an agenda of errands and was running late. I was also hungry. I debated rearranging my day—moving clothes shopping to *after* my haircut—to squeeze in a late breakfast. Fast food loomed on the horizon, and the deal was sealed.

The Saturday late-morning crowd was surprisingly sparse—a few old people milking their refillable coffee over the morning paper, and a fat, loud couple with a couple of loud, fat kids, collectively engulfing a table by the rest rooms.

Maître de, please, a table by the can.

I took my piping-hot sausage and egg biscuit, hash browns, and medium Coke instead of coffee, please, and sat at the raised counter for single diners—a setup I'm noticing more and more fast-food joints incorporating into their decor. I don't know that I like this. But I oblige the corporate minds that devise such schemes by sitting in the designated area when dining alone. They're getting paid a lot of money to make these decisions. They probably did research. They probably care. I don't want to show them up.

As I unwrapped my food, I began to feel vaguely uneasy, as if I were being watched.

As it turns out, I was.

A kid, probably 18 or 19. Unkempt, adorned in oil- and dirt-stained blue work pants and an oversize white jersey turned inside out. The shirt and pants and even his shoes were tattered. But he was cute. A teenage Lenny Kravitz. As he waited for his food, he looked at me out of the corner of his eye with…what?

Is he cruising me?

He sat to my left in the single-people section, leaving a seat between us. Empty tables abounded. He smiled, said "Hi," and then looked away, embarrassed.

Is he flirting?

He opened the syrup for his French Toast Sticks, dipped a stick, held it in front of his face, examined it with adoration. His tongue escaped his lips and reached out and lovingly gathered a growing, soon to drip dollop of sticky-sweet syrup.

Does he have a clue? Any clue at all?

He opened his mouth and tilted his head back and slid in the French Toast Stick, biting halfway. On his first chew, he looked my way.

"Good?" I asked. I'd never tasted this particular establishment's version of one of my favorite foods, so I was a little curious. But I was more curious about what was going on behind that gangsta facade.

He dipped the remaining half-stick and popped it in his mouth, nodding vigorously in the affirmative. Then he suddenly laughed.

"What?" I asked.

"My sister pretends she's giving blow jobs when she eats these."

"Oh?"

He nodded, smiling.

"Is that a turn-on?"

"Naw," he said emphatically. "She's my sister."

"Oh. Yeah." Then I dropped a bomb he wasn't expecting: "Is that what *you* were doing? Just now?"

He got suddenly bashful—caught—and changed the subject. "You know, one other time I was in here and talked to somebody, some guy. But I think he was retarded."

I raised an eyebrow, indicating healthy curiosity.

He looked at me and said, "He thought I was a chick."

"What?"

"Well," he said, "when I slick my hair back, you can't tell. I could be walking down the street and you wouldn't know if I was a girl or a guy."

How do you respond to that? He seemed almost proud of it. "Well," I said, "you look like a guy to me."

"A hundred percent." Then, after an awkward moment, he said, "What time is it?"

I don't wear a watch, but my 10-year-old car has a clock that actually works. So I had a decent idea of the time. "I think it's a little after 11."

"I'm supposed to be at counseling at 11," he said, biting into another toast stick.

Counseling? "You're late," I said. "It's at least a quarter after."

He shrugged, nonchalant, showing off. Letting me know he never had any intention of going to what I strongly suspected was a court-ordered, mandatory session. Then he said, "She does it with tasty links too." This made him laugh, look away.

I realized he meant his sister and pretend blow jobs. When I regained my equilibrium, I said, "Tasty links? What are those?" I knew, of course, but wanted him to tell me.

"You know, sausages. Except big." He demonstrated their size, utilizing a familiar-looking two-fisted gesture. Then he stuck out his tongue and took a quick few pretend sucks at the imaginary tasty link. Imitating his sister, I supposed.

He seemed suddenly surprised at the brashness—the freedom—of his actions, and he popped the last French Toast Stick into his mouth.

And then, as abruptly as it began, the encounter ended. He stood, said, "Well, gotta roll," and ambled away.

Outside, the bright, hot, nearly noon sun beat down from the sky and backlit the uneven edges of his shaggy Afro, creating a smoggy halo. In minutes, I knew, the blistering oppression of summer would raise a light sweat on his dry Hershey's Cocoa and melted butter skin.

I thought, *Chase him!*

And then I thought, *I'm not done eating.*

And then I thought, *Too late now.* Because it was. He was gone like smoke. A quick breeze and…poof, no more. Probably for the good.

Like I said, he had more pressing needs than sex education.

Later, I deconstructed this odd, oddly erotic encounter. I decided that yes, he did know what he was doing. Sort of. I decided that no, he did not want me to pursue him. Very much. I decided he would go home and lie naked on his bed and jack off thinking about me. And I would write a story about our encounter—my own form of jacking off—with a different ending, of course.

So how did a little boy shocked by the sight of another boy's underwear grow into a man who writes, edits, and publishes erotica? How did a child who cringed all through Sex Education become lead editor of an annual collection of gay erotica (*Friction: Best Gay Erotica*)? How did sexually repressed Scott Brassart become sexually explicit Jesse Grant? How did I get from there to here?

To answer, I must first pose a slightly altered version of that question: *Why* did I get from there to here?

I did it because I had to. When I came of age, Ronald Reagan was president, and a young gay man in an extremely conservative, extremely rural area had two choices. He could become a flaming queen and have the crap kicked out of him, or he could keep his mouth shut and fantasize. I chose the latter option—the easy way out. I kept my hands and my thoughts to myself. And whenever I was in a big city, far from home, I would sneak off to a dirty bookstore and buy a gay magazine.

In those few and far-between magazines my fantasies were brought to life. I found pictures of naked men, sometimes with other naked men, often with hard-ons. And, even better, I found written fantasies brought to life: gay pornography—a phrase I uttered only to myself and always with the same reverence my fifth-grade classmates reserved for *Sex Education*.

Please notice that I said gay *pornography* and not gay *erotica*.

There is a difference.

A big difference.

That difference: Story.

Pornography is sex for the sake of sex, grainy film with bad music and multiple come shots. Wham, bam, thank you, ma'am. I mean, thank you, *sir*. Erotica, however, is sex for the sake of *story*. Pornography is written or filmed to get you off. Erotica is written (rarely filmed) to set the mood, to prime the pump, to get you ready to get off. Pornography works on your dick (or clit or whatever the hell sex organ you have). Erotica works on your brain. Pornography is what I found in gay magazines in the '80s. Erotica is what you'll find in this book.

As you may have guessed, I have grown to prefer erotica. After all, the largest erogenous zone in the human body is the brain.

So, with that said, I will answer my original question: *How* did I get from there to here?

The answer is simple: I read a story by Pat Califia. And suddenly the pornography I'd been reading lost its appeal. Califia's tale— about *lesbians,* no less—was the hottest thing I'd ever read. I am at the very far, very queer end of the Kinsey Scale, and I jerked off to *lesbian* sex. I was dumbstruck. And Califia's work stuck with me long past ejaculation. I'd remember the *story,* and then I'd be hot all over again. Suddenly my brain was bigger than my dick.

Califia, perhaps, said it as well as anyone when he (yes, he: see "Califia Ch-Ch-Changes," *Lambda Book Report,* June 2000 issue) wrote in the introduction to M. Christian's short story collection *Dirty Words,* "The best writing about sex is also about something else." In other words, the best writing about sex is written for the sake of story.

It doesn't have to be much of a story, but it does have to be compelling. For instance, in the tale I chose to accompany this essay, "Onions and Green Pepper," which first appeared in my book (published under my pen name, Jesse Grant) *Men for All Seasons,* the plot is extremely simple. Boy meets boy, boy makes pass at boy, boy gets punched. Conflict: the first element of story. Followed by the second element: resolution. In this case, the boy who threw the punch shows up with pizza, beer, and an apology, then drops his trousers and takes it like a man. It's all very romantic. Honest. Which is what makes the story—two young athletes coming to terms with their sexuality—compelling and one of my favorites. (I decided against submitting the extended, embellished version of my fast-food encounter, another of my favorites, because it repeats much of what appears at the beginning of this essay. And repetition bores me.)

When I took over the task of editing the *Friction* series, I remembered my reaction to Califia, to story, to *erotica*. And when I select the pieces to be included in the *Friction* books I keep that in mind, choosing work on the basis of story first, sex second. Because if the story works, so does the sex. What I have learned from editing the *Friction* series and other erotic story collections is that *any* sex can be hot as long as the reader is enthralled by the story in which the sex takes place. You don't have to like leather sex to enjoy a story that unfolds in the back room of a leather bar. Or, closer to home, you needn't dig women to get off on a lesbian encounter.

Over time I have come to know, both personally and professionally, most of today's best sex writers: gay, lesbian, bisexual, and even straight. And what I have found is that they all have the same philosophy: story first, sex second. I call these story-first writers "The San Francisco School" because so many of them—Califia, Christian, and too many others to name—live in the Bay Area. But, of course, just as many live elsewhere. R.J. March resides in rural Pennsylvania. Felice Picano is my neighbor in Los Angeles. So perhaps Califia's term for this crew of scribes is better than mine. He calls this cadre "Glamorous Nerd Pornographers." Although I could easily make an argument that none of us are glamorous, nerds, or (by my definition) pornographers. Actually, I take that back: Shar Rednour is glamorous.

The point of all this, of course, is to bring to light the possibility that you too are journeying from there to here. Your starting point—your *there*—obviously differs from mine, just as your ending point—your *here*—will differ. But your life, your back story, is what makes your sex life special. For instance, the unexpected thrill of my breakfast encounter was not that it led to sex (because it didn't). The thrill arose because of who I once was and who I have become. I could empathize with a young man's sexual confusion and at the same time rejoice in the baby steps I saw him take toward a happy, fulfilled life. My personal story turned a short conversation into an erotic moment that means more to me than at least 90% of the actual sex I've had. In much the same way, your story, your own "from there to here" both can and should turn raw sexual experience into real-life erotica you'll treasure forever. So as you read on, I hope you'll examine your own life and find in it as much titillation and arousal as the contributors to this book, who have perfected the art of "sex for the sake of story," find in theirs.

ONIONS AND GREEN PEPPER

By Scott Brassart (a.k.a. Jesse Grant)

Neil is shorter and stockier and plays safety. A run-stopper who hits the gaps between the linemen and linebackers and big blocking fullbacks and takes the legs out from under the quick little scat-backs so prevalent now in the Big 10.

The conference used to be known for huge, hulking backs. Guys from Michigan or Ohio State or Purdue who could run through a brick wall. But now, the wide-open West Coast offense has made its way to Middle America, 10 years behind schedule, like fade haircuts and Hugo Boss suits.

The West Coast style is why Neil is so valuable. We need a speed guy that hits like a jackhammer, and he's that guy. Hardheaded. Mean. Not interested in thinking, just doing. Just hitting. Tackling.

Defending the west coast offense also requires a prototype NFL cornerback—tall, fast, and smart. That's me. 6 feet, 3 inches, and 210 pounds, the same weight as Neil but four inches taller. Big enough to bang large receivers, fast enough to stick with the little guys. And smart enough to know what the other team is doing even before they do.

If our knees hold up, we could both make it in the pros.

After all, making it is what we do best.

✍

Neil has the greatest ass. It's the first thing I noticed about him. I showed up at a preseason meeting my freshman year and there it was, this Levi's-encased bubble of muscle. I wanted to drop to my knees and start licking it right through the denim, right in front of the team and the coaches and everyone. But I didn't. Football players don't do that shit. So I sat next to him and smiled and stuck out my hand. "Jesse," I said. "Defensive back."

"Safety?" he asked.

"No. Cornerback." He seemed relieved; we played different positions, so there would be no competition between us for a roster spot. We could be friends, supporters. And maybe, I thought, if I played my cards right, I'd get a taste of those buns.

But for long weeks nothing happened. We went to practice, eyed each other furtively in the shower, told lies about fucking cheerleaders we'd never even met, and did our schoolwork—me struggling to finish a double major in four years, Neil struggling to stay eligible.

Meanwhile, the team got better and better. Our new quarterback, a redshirt freshman, was eye-poppingly quick with a cannon for an arm. He wasn't the most accurate guy I'd ever seen, but what an athlete! (And hung for days!) If we could keep him from throwing interceptions, we'd score a lot of points.

Stopping the opposition, however, was going to be a problem. Our linemen and linebackers were quick but small, and the returning defensive backs lacked talent. The previous year, Big 10 foes had scored on the team at will, resulting in a last-place finish for our school. Which is probably why, three days before the season opener, Coach Tanner called Neil and me into his office and told us we were starters.

True freshmen. Starters!

"Neil," said Coach, "you're the guy that has to stop the run. If you can shoot the gaps and make plays, we can slow teams down. Jesse," he said, turning to me, "you've gotta take out the number 1 receiver. Every play. You've gotta take him outta the game. Make him a nobody."

✍

Neil and I hung out the next three nights—Wednesday, Thursday, Friday—in the film room. We studied game films of our opening opponent, Kentucky, a nonconference rival we hadn't beaten in four years. The first two nights, Wednesday and Thursday, Coach Tanner sat with us, talking us through game films, pointing out the tendencies of UK's all-American quarterback—how he bobs his head just before he lets fly with a pass, how on running plays he alters his cadence to throw off opposing linemen. We spent more time learning Kentucky's offense than on we did on our schoolwork, and by Thursday night, we were ready. I knew it. Neil knew it. Even the coach knew it.

Coach told us to take Friday night off, to relax and get loose for Saturday's game. But Neil and I had been enjoying the film sessions—the dark room, the air conditioning, the silence (except for the whir of the VCR and occasional instruction from Coach).

Coach would sit near the VCR, starting and stopping it, pointing to the screen. Neil and I sat next to each other in chairs across the room, at first not touching, then with our thighs touching, then our shoulders, and by the end of the night we'd be leaning into each other pretty good, squishing around, finding the comfortable position. But not so much that Coach would think something was up.

"Coach," I said. "I know we're ready, but I'd still like to see more film. Can't we come in tomorrow night?"

"Yeah, can't we?" said Neil.

"Sure," Coach said. "But you can do it without me. Cuz I'm gonna get me some poo-oo-oontang." He tossed us the keys and said, "Make sure you turn off the VCR when you leave. Otherwise it'll be on all weekend."

✍️

So Friday night it was just the two of us in the film room. Alone with film and a six-pack Neil had brought. "I know we're not supposed to drink the night before a game," he said, "but it *is* Friday night. And we *are* in college."

"You don't need to convince me," I said. I popped a couple of cans, keeping one for myself and handing the other to him. We toasted our first-string status and settled in for a football junkie's Friday Night Movie.

Two hours later we were both a little buzzed and—I thought—horny. Neil, who'd been nestled on my right side with his head on my shoulder and his arm across my lap, stood to change tapes in the VCR, which rested on a table about waist high. He could have squatted to get to eye level with the machine, but instead he bent at the waist.

That ass!

So I did what I thought he wanted. I sauntered over and ran my hand up the crack of his ass.

And he punched me. Hard. Right in the face.

I wasn't expecting it and went down in a heap.

He glared at me, then left without saying a word.

✍

The next morning I showed up for the game with a tremendous black eye.

"Where'd ya get the shiner?" asked Coach.

"I tripped and hit a rock."

"Yeah?" He said it like he didn't believe me. "Well, don't do any tripping out on the field today. We need you sharp."

Neil stood at his locker, a few spots down from mine, and said nothing.

✍

As soon as I stepped onto the field, the incident with Neil was forgotten. How could it not be? College football is the greatest spectacle in sports. The stadium was packed with 50,000 screaming fans decked out in red and white and silver, and even a few blue-clad Kentucky fans who'd made the journey north. I could smell hot dogs and barbecue and beer from tailgate parties. I could see little kids lined up along the fence surrounding the field, seeking autographs, jaws dropping at the sheer size of the behemoths who rule the gridiron.

And I could see Kentucky—the team, the cheerleaders. The frustration of the night before turned into hatred. I wanted to shred them. I wanted to hurt them. I wanted to leave them black and blue and wistful.

And I did.

All game long I stuck like glue to Kentucky's top receiver, which frustrated their all-American quarterback. His first option was covered, so he had to look for other receivers. Meanwhile, our defensive line, undersized but quick, was finding holes in their elephantine offensive line, pressuring the quarterback into quick decisions. Bad decisions. Just before halftime, needing a score, he decided to go to his top receiver—my man. He threw a dangerous pass over the middle of the field. The receiver and I ran full tilt into a crowd of bigger players. We leaped into the air simultaneously, raising our arms for the high pass. My superior height won out. I made the catch. Unfortunately, my ribs, exposed when I reached up, took a pounding on the way down. A crushing blow knocked the wind out of me, but after a few moments I was up and ready to battle some more.

Neil also played like a man possessed, making game-breaking tackles all over the field, including a drive stopper late in the fourth quarter that turned the tide permanently in our favor.

At the end of the game, a shocking 14–13 upset win, it was clear that Neil and I were the stars. Our teammates jumped on us and hugged us and gave us whopping head-butts. (A few of the guys didn't even have their helmets on.) It was only later, in the locker room, that I saw the huge bruise covering the entire right side of my rib cage. I'd gotten it on the play where I'd made the interception, when I'd reached up to make the catch and exposed my ribs. Now that the adrenaline from the game was fading, I was starting to hurt—a lot—my ribs even more than the shiner Neil had given me.

But neither injury hurt the way Neil's rejection hurt. We'd been having so much fun. It had felt so right. Why did he hit me?

✍

Most of the players were going to a big fraternity party to celebrate our victory. Several guys, including Randall, our quarterback, who'd also had a big game, scrambling for both of our team's touchdowns, asked me to tag along. I declined as politely as I could, saying I planned to go home and ice my bruises.

Neil stood nearby, smiling at the same invites, saying, "Yeah, I'll see you there," and, "Will there be chicks? I need to get laid." He was assured of chicks aplenty and that after the making the game-saving tackle, he'd have his pick. Blond and busty, red and raucous, brunet and brainy, whatever he wanted would be there for the taking. All he'd need to do was take.

When the assurances of scoring some pussy were made to Neil, the guys would turn their heads to me and say, "You too, man. Superstars get laid. Superstars *always* get laid."

"Who knows," I said. "Maybe some hot number will come to my dorm room and lick my wounds." Hot number. No gender. It left a bad taste in my mouth.

The conversation soon degenerated into a group comparison of "sloppy pussy" encounters, and I quietly slipped out.

✍

Two hours later…agony! I felt as if I'd been hit by a car. My black-and-blue ribs throbbed, my eye throbbed, and amazingly, my dick also throbbed—though in a much different way. Whereas my ribs and eye felt like mush, my cock felt like tempered steel—an oversize railroad spike. I wished for some beer to dull the pain, but of course I had none. And I wasn't about to limp to the liquor store only to have my fake ID refused by some stringy-haired, pimply-faced ass-hole of a clerk. I decided to jerk off instead.

I used my unbruised left arm to slip off my sweatpants and Jockeys and checked myself out in the mirror across the room. Not bad, I thought. Penetrating green eyes, square jaw, the beginnings of a beastly goatee, big shoulders with arms and pecs to match, a little fuzz around my nipples and down from the middle of my chest to my navel and cock—eight inches straight up and thick, balls pulled tight like always—heavy muscles visible all down my thighs and calves, size 13 feet. Yeah, I thought, not bad at all. The only blemishes were the bruises on my eye and right side, and even those were pretty hot in a fucked-up way.

I leaned against the pillows, trying to find a semicomfortable position where I could still see myself in the mirror, finally settling on a seated position with my legs raised, one resting on the edge of my desk, the other on the back of a chair. In the mirror I saw my favorite porno pose: legs up, tight little acorn of an asshole with just the right amount of fuzz, nuts, and hard cock. I'm pretty much a top, so I don't usually get off on my own ass, but I was horny, and ass was all that was on my mind since I'd met Neil. I practically came just looking at myself.

I started to stroke, licking my hand for lube, wishing my bruised ribs didn't preclude using my right arm. I wanted one hand for my dick, another for my ass. Wanting another active hand, of course, made me wish for Neil.

I got a pretty good rhythm going, working my dick with my spitty hand, humping my ass against air, watching my bud contract in the mirror like it was squeezing a dick, like I was getting fucked by the invisible man. Like Neil hadn't slugged me. Like Neil was in the room with me. Like—

✍

A knock at the door.
I froze.
A louder knock.
"Who's there?" I asked.
"It's me. I brought pizza." I recognized Neil's voice.
I couldn't find my underwear, so I pulled on just my sweats. My hard-on stuck out like a branch on a tree.
"Hurry," he said. "This pizza's hot."
I let him in, hard-on and all. I was happy to see him, and there was nothing to do about my dick except hope he wouldn't notice. Fat chance.
He noticed but didn't comment, instead saying, sheepishly, "It's extra cheese. I wasn't sure what to get. I figured extra cheese is safe."

"I like extra cheese. Everybody likes extra cheese. Safe is good."

"Yeah. But what do you *really* like?"

I took my time answering. "Onions and green pepper."

"I like that too. Sometimes."

"Oh?" I asked.

"When I'm expecting it." His gaze had fallen to his feet, but he raised his eyes to mine to say, "I'm sorry I hit you."

"That's OK," I said. "I just thought—"

"I promise not to hit you tonight," he said, still looking me in the eyes—serious—and then he smiled and shyly looked away.

I wasn't sure why he was smiling. I thought it was odd.

"I figured you might want somebody to take care of you. You know, get more ice for the ice pack. Keep you company." He held the pizza in one hand, a six-pack in the other. He lifted the beer and held it by his face. A peace offering.

"I *could* use a beer," I said.

We sat on my bed and launched ourselves into the pizza and beer, devouring all but the last slice, each of us eyeing it but not wanting to be rude. Finally Neil shoved away the box and stretched out on the bed, stomach down, ass popping three-dimensional right at me. He looked at me over his shoulder with the same odd smile I'd wondered about earlier. "I feel bad about last night," he said. "I think maybe I should be punished." And then, after a pause, "I should be spanked."

"Spanked?"

He wriggled his ass.

I slapped it.

He said, "O-o-oh." He lifted his ass and slid over so he was draped across my lap.

My ribs exploded with pain, but after a moment, as I had during the game, I forgot about them.

"Spank me."

I slapped his ass, harder this time, and he ground a hard-on into my thigh.

"Pull down your pants," I said.

He buried his face in my sheets that hadn't been washed in at least three weeks and that I'd been sleeping on and jacking off on in the late-summer humidity. He wriggled his jeans down to just below his ass, but no farther.

I smacked him good this time.

He moaned, "O-o-oh."

"Take them down."

"All the way?" he asked.

I nodded.

He stood and stripped, then braced himself against the desk, naked except for gray gym socks and his black and red high-tops. His feet were spread. His hands were on the desk. His ass jutted out atop his gladiator legs, leading to the valley of his back.

Through that very sexy valley runs a stream. And in that stream swim the most beautiful trout. I decided to retire there and fly-fish forever.

I ran my fingers from the nape of his neck, down the valley, to the top of his hard little ass. I ran my finger down his crack and he didn't hit me. I suddenly slapped his ass.

"Yesss," he said.

And then I did what I'd been wanting to do since I first laid eyes on him. I dropped to my knees and pulled apart his ass cheeks and soul-kissed him.

He threw himself back at my face and yelped like a wolf cub and shot his come onto my desk between his goalpost arms like a field goal, his hole clenching on my tongue. Then he threw himself forward so his stomach and chest and face were all in the warm come he'd just shot. "Fuck me," he said. "Slap my ass and then fuck me."

I slapped. "Spread your cheeks." I slapped again. And again very hard, contacting his pucker, still wet with my spit. I could see his dick bobbing below him, half-hard and dripping. I reached into my desk drawer for a condom and my half-empty, family-size bottle of lube, which so far I'd used only for jacking off.

I slipped my middle finger up his ass. Tight, but willing. Ready for more. I left it there for a second while Neil rocked back and forth, whispering and whimpering. It "popped" when I pulled it out.

"Nice," I said.

"Fuck me. Take me."

I shoved my cock to his hole and pushed into him until he screamed and said stop. I let him catch his breath, then leaned forward. Half a dozen starts and screams and stops later I was grinding my pubic hair against his ass crack. After a few seconds, he began to rock back and forth on my cock, just as he'd done with my finger, again whispering and whimpering.

I reached with my good arm and grabbed him by the hair and pulled him into a standing position. I licked the back of his neck and he arched back and I kissed his ear the way I'd kissed his ass. I dropped my hand to his dick, slick with his come, and stroked him in time with the movement of my cock inside him. Slowly. Kissing and whispering for only him to hear.

When he was fully hard again, I spit on my hand for extra lube and jacked him in earnest. And I pounded into his tunnel like he'd pounded into the Kentucky running backs. Bam! Bam! Bam! Bam! So hard I thought I'd go numb. But I didn't. I felt everything. And Neil screamed and his ass clamped like a python snake and I pushed through his muscle and came. I came into a condom slick with the juice of his ass. And then I collapsed, and he carried me to bed and kissed my wounds and tended to them with ice and aspirin and more beer until Monday, when we both had class.

✍

A year and a half later, Neil and I are in an "on" stage of our on-again, off-again relationship. He is coming to my off-campus apartment tonight. (I couldn't stand living in the dorm.) He'll bring a six-pack and we'll order pizza and I'll read him this story. We'll laugh at the onions and green pepper part, and then I'll fuck him.

ALL IN MY HEAD
By Cecilia Tan

So there's this word, *fantasy*. Walk up to the average Jane on the street and ask for a definition, and you're likely to get one of two answers, either it's a genre of storytelling, like science fiction, that has magic and stuff in it. Or you must mean *sexual fantasy*. As in what you have when you *fantasize*.

Two separate meanings, for most people.

But not for me.

I started writing smutty science fiction when I was too young to know what sex was. I don't mean I didn't know about reproduction and intercourse—my liberal mother and medical doctor father explained that when I was about 6 years old and a potential baby brother or sister was on the way. When it came to sex, I didn't really know what *lovemaking* was all about. I didn't sneak peeks at porn books or magazines when I was a kid, didn't see a porn movie until I was almost 20. And at age 10, 11, 12…I still hadn't had any of my own. So exactly what went on *in bed* was a mystery to me.

As such, trying to imagine what sex would actually be like was an interesting exercise, as intriguing and exotic as imagining, oh, what life would be like on the planet Xurg, where women ruled and gravity was only half what it is on Earth. Trust me, when I was 10, this was intensely interesting. And more often than not, well, it turned out to be the clothing-optional planet Xurg, where women ruled but were required to do one day a week of sacred whore service. Just to give an example of the kind of fantasy I would have. When I fantasized, it was fantasy of the other kind too.

Let's not forget the erotic "let's pretend" games I played with my friends, as well. When I was 5 years old I had a friend who would come over to play Batman and Robin. Yes, even at that young age, the erotic undercurrent in that TV show was detectable to me. As such, what we actually played, usually, was Batman and Catwoman, taking turns being tied up and threatened with various tortures, including "the urine trap." Sorry, I don't recall the exact details of that particular trap now…I do recall I used to masturbate myself to orgasm after my friend would leave. Yeah, 5 years old. Explains a lot, doesn't it?

Then there were the fantasies about Captain Kirk, specifically that time he was sent to the slave planet and forced to kiss that alien woman. Or how about the time the crew were being controlled by these godlike characters and Spock and Uhura were forced to kiss? I'm sure if I try really hard, I can dig up some more examples from my subconscious, but you get the drift. Sci-fi equaled sex in my mind from the very earliest. Fantasy equaled fantasizing—it only seemed natural.

And notice how the word *forced* keeps coming up. Who can say whether these early influences steered me toward S/M or whether my already natural inclination and interest in power games attracted me to those scenarios? I certainly can't decide which came first, the chicken or the egg. But certainly one thing pushing me toward fantasy and sci-fi settings for my sexual fantasies was the fact that, even at that age, my sexuality was far from mainstream, and there was more room for me to fit myself into far-out scenarios than into "real life."

I was always interested in bondage, multiple partners, bisexuality, and gender play. Looking around the "real world," I didn't see much evidence of that—Catwoman was my one S/M role model, David Bowie my one bisexual role model—and let's face it, Bowie was pure science fiction himself back then. It took changing the setting to faraway planets or strange societies unlike our own for me to come up with fantasies I could inhabit for myself.

Of course, hindsight is 20/20, and now I can see how significant all that was to my writing career. When I started trying to write actual stories in my teens, I even produced some erotic science fiction. I still have one manuscript, in my spidery, impatient handwriting, which details a woman being raped by a woody, plant-like alien that grows protuberances with which to penetrate her. This was *way* before the anime squidgy tentacles fad, and way before I'd ever been penetrated with anything other than my own finger. OK, there was that disappointing experiment with the Ballpark Frank (they plump when you cook 'em, you know), but that was just that once…

And I wrote smut for my friends, casting them and the celebrities they drooled over in the starring roles. One of my old high school friends got back in touch with me recently and sent me a manuscript I'd written about myself and a famous person. The really funny thing is, I later actually slept with that person. But you'll have to wait for a different essay to hear those sordid details. This essay is about *writing*. As I was saying, it's now so obvious how significant these early fantasies were to the direction my career has taken. Because combining fantasy and *fantasy* is what I'm known for, what I've built a career on.

When I was 23 years old, I moved to Boston and was single for the first time in many years. This, I thought, was the time to both start my writing career and forge the adult identity that I'd been held back from previously. And for the first time in my life, writing came easily. I sat down and wrote a story from start to finish, and I don't think it is a coincidence that this story summed up everything I desired at that point. It was also the first story I had ever written where I knew it was ready to be shared with the world, where I knew when I reached the end that it was complete.

I had just discovered that bondage and S/M existed in the "real world," but I hadn't yet gone out and experienced any of it. I knew I wanted to surround myself with a pansexual community, gay, straight, bisexual, trans, all mixed together, but I didn't know if that community existed. I knew I wanted to explore the relationship between masochism and submission and the contrast between being owned and being subdued, not to mention the stark difference between rape and consent. All this stuff came to a boil in my mind, my libido, and my imagination, and out came a story called "Telepaths Don't Need Safewords."

The story was like a magic spell—or a prayer, perhaps. The power in a spell or a wish or a prayer is in *defining* what it is you want—

you make it all that much more likely that fate or circumstance will deliver your desire to you if you can articulate what it is. Fate, as it would happen, would deliver to my door shortly thereafter a living embodiment of Arshan, the main character in the story. A few years later he broke my heart, but that only goes to prove that real life and fantasy do diverge.

Or do they? Another story I wrote shortly thereafter, exploring another desire, featured my current partner of almost 10 years. I saw him at an S/M party, playing with someone else. It was love at first sight, and I practically fainted. I had to leave the room while he was tied up and being beaten. I went home and wrote the story "Heart's Desire," placing myself as the narrator, a woman who gains a princely slave. The story again worked like magic, and a few weeks later, there was my own princely slave in my bed, and he's still there, nine years later.

I suppose this means my writing is my sexuality, to some extent. I was writing erotica before I knew any other kind of fulfillment, and I'm still doing it. In fact, during the years when I wasn't writing erotica, I was neither creatively nor erotically fulfilled. It wasn't until I wrote (and self-published) "Telepaths Don't Need Safewords" that I felt I had arrived as a whole person and as a whole writer.

This was before I found my old, old teen manuscripts, and so I thought I was discovering something totally new about myself. But of course the themes had been there all along, the slavery, bondage, forced sex, as well as the writing itself. I guess what I'd had to do was rediscover it as an adult, bring it into my conscious rather than unconscious mind.

And that's pretty much what I think every story is. I write some stuff that has neither sex nor science fiction in it too. But any story reveals the subconscious. Sometimes like a hypnotic confession, sometimes like a cryptic tarot reading. Ultimately, that is what some of the best sex does too, allowing us to lose our self-consciousness and reveal another plane of emotion, understanding, or self. So once again, sex is like writing, writing is like sex. Writing *is* sex. Writing is identity and loss of identity at the same time, just as good sex reaffirms who we are even as we lose ourselves in each other.

Telepaths Don't Need Safewords

By Cecilia Tan

Arshan tugged on the leash and gave me a bare-toothed smile, insistent and yet as catty as if he had winked. I replied with a sullen look, half a sneer, really, saying with the look what I thought—*You know how much I hate this leash and you know how much I love this scene.* He dangled the leash over his shoulder, leading me across an open plaza toward the Hall. I kept my eyes down, not out of submission but to watch his feet. Arshan stands about 6 feet 4 inches. With the leash over his shoulder, I didn't have much room to avoid his long legs. I may have been playing the slave, but the last thing I wanted was to look like a klutz. I could feel him smiling.

At the door we exchanged looks again, and he thought, *It's been a while.*

I know. But I'm up for it if you are, I assured him, making a last mental check on our costumes. He carried no weapon, no instrument, no tool, save pieces of his costume that had more than one use. We'd worked hard perfecting it, the belts, the waist length cape, the boots. His colors, as always, were black and dark green. My own costume had fewer elements, just a basic black halter stretched over my breasts and black mid-calf dance tights, bare feet. Oh, and the leash. I draped myself against him as he presented our pass to the doorman. We donned simple eye masks and proceeded down the carpeted hallway. *Think people will remember us?*

✍

The Hall has a ceiling is at least 50 feet high, perhaps higher, and one long wall made entirely of glass, overlooking the Galdarin River.

Echoes of laughter came down from balconies on the opposite wall, and crystals and lights and chandeliers flickered everywhere. Arshan made his way straight for Cleopatra, one of our old friends.

She dripped with black beads, completely covered, yet not covered at all by a complex network of beaded strands, hanging in long wings from her arms, and cascading down her back from her black hair. She turned from the conversation when she saw us, throwing up her hands and kissing Arshan on the cheek. "Arshan! You've arrived! We've missed you, you know. And you, Mriah," she added, turning to me. "It got very dull here for a while." She sighed, fluttering her eyelids. I love Cleo's act. And she loves ours.

Arshan smiled. "It's good to be back."

"Easy for you to say," I said, tossing my head.

He turned on me, shortening up the leash and speaking harshly. "I am trying to converse with the Lady Cleopatra. Now, will you be quiet or will I have to cut your tongue out?"

I gave no answer at all except to nod my head toward Cleo.

She smiled. "As I said, it was getting very dull around here."

✍

We were lounging by the pool later, with some people we knew and some we didn't, when Arshan slapped me at last. Maidi and Bivonhad been taking turns whipping Danielle, and when they were done, she thanked them for it on her knees. Gallen, a blond-haired fop Cleo favored, started in with "She's a proper pretty one. All slaves should behave so well, don't you think, Arshan?"

"She's very beautiful," Arshan said to Cleopatra.

Cleo swallowed a bit of plum. "I believe she's for sale."

"Oh?" Gallen sat up a bit in his lounge chair. "Maidi, how much?"

Maidi and Bivon sat on the grass, coddling Danni between them. "No, she's not for sale," Maidi said.

"I'd say she's worth 40,000," Gallen continued. "Whereas I wouldn't pay more than 5,000 for one like yours, Arshan."

"Not that I would go with you, anyway." I replied from where I sat at Arshan's feet. Arshan jerked on the leash.

"You haven't broken her yet?"

Cleo laughed. "Arshan likes them with their teeth intact."

Gallen was unfazed. "Imagine that. I think she needs a lesson."

I sneered. "From you? I'd rather put out my own eyes."

Arshan jerked the chain so hard I pitched forward onto my hands. "That will be quite enough, slave." He sat up in the lounge chair a little, then settled back, shortening the chain so I remained on all fours. "I can handle her myself, thank you." He smiled obsequiously at Gallen.

"Oh, it's no fault of yours, I'm sure." Gallen picked up a plum from the bowl between Cleopatra and him. "Still, I can see why she's talking back. You don't even have a bat for her."

"I've never needed one."

Cleo applauded the point by tapping her own crop in her gloved palm. "Arshan has many methods."

"Still, I wonder how she would respond to some of mine." Gallen stood, placed himself in front of me, snapped his fingers. "Look at me, slave."

I drew my eyes up his leg, stopped at his crotch. I let half a smile onto my face.

"I said, look at me."

"I am."

He lifted my chin with his boot. I held his gaze for a moment, then dropped back down to admire his groin again. There wasn't much to see really, at first. But as he grew more angry, he grew. I watched the bulge thicken as he made a fist. "You have to put fear into her, Arshan. Like this." He drew back his foot to kick me.

Arshan was up in an instant, between us. "Think again."

Cleo laughed, tugging on Gallen's velvet sleeve. "No one strikes her but Arshan, dear, and she obeys no one but him."

"Well, what good is she, then?" Gallen said sullenly, sinking back down into the chair at Cleo's side. I was already holding on to Arshan's leg. I let my hands run up and down his thigh. I closed my eyes and rubbed against him with my cheek. *That was close.*

He's obviously an asshole. I'd let you bait him more, except I think he's dangerous.

I don't know... I drew my hand between his legs to caress his crotch, letting the heat from his stiffening penis flow into my fingers. *Shall I show him what good am I?*

Arshan made some meaningless small talk with Cleo as I came around his leg to kneel in front of him. The loose-fitting pants he wore didn't end in seams on the inside. And Arshan never wore underwear. I had his cock in my mouth then. "You see," he was explaining, "she is extremely loyal. And always grateful." I would have added something of my own, but my mouth was full. Using my lips, I squeezed some precome into my mouth and swallowed. I let my tongue work the underside, the tender cleft just at the base of the head until he was having trouble keeping up the conversation. I felt him start to go, his hips began to buck, and then I ducked.

Semen shot out over the grass; a fair bit spattered the golden edge of Gallen's green waistcoat. Arshan recovered immediately. He grabbed me by the chin and scolded me harshly. He gripped the halter at the center and pulled it over my head, with two knots he tied my hands behind my back using it instead of rope. Then he knelt in front of me, holding my head still by the hair at the base of my neck, and slapped me with his right hand across my cheek.

Do it again, I thought.

He raised his hand high this time, and I tried to flinch, but his other hand held me still. "Don't you move, now," he said, almost growling, as he brought the slapping hand down to fondle my bare breasts instead. He squeezed the nipples between the knuckles of his first and middle fingers, then forced my head down to the grass. The blades prickled against my chest, cool and rough. "Are you ready to apologize?"

"I'm sorry, Master."

"You needn't apologize to me. Apologize to this gentleman, whose finery you've ruined."

I kept my mouth shut. Gallen was on his feet now, towering above us. Arshan stood, picking up the end of the leash again. "Slave." He gave it a jerk, and I sat up. But I kept my head down. "Slave," he repeated.

"Screw you," I said.

You're pushing it. "Maybe I haven't made myself clear," he said, wrapping the leash around his hand until he held me fast by the neck. "I think you owe this man something, and I intend to see he gets it." He lay me on my back in the grass, leading me by the neck. "Gallen, may I borrow your knife?"

"Certainly."

He handed down his pearl-handled dagger. Arshan slipped it deftly under the waistband of my tights and with one stroke ripped them open from my belly button downward. Uncoiling the leash, he wrapped the other end around my right ankle, binding my foot near my head. The left leg he bound with one of the belts from around his own waist, by wrapping my knee to my shoulder. I felt my wetness drip down the crack of my ass, as my pussy was now open to the wind. "Gallen, I believe this slave owes you something. So long as you do not strike her, you may do as you will."

What? I started to object. But Arshan didn't answer me. Gallen opened a cock slit in his own tights and brandished his penis. "With pleasure," he said as he motioned for two male slaves to lift me up onto the table. He pressed the head of his cock against my ass. "I will gladly spill some seed in return," he said, and with that he rammed into me. He got about an inch in, holding me by my thighs. His cock was so dry, it burned as he thrust deeper in. I saw his face twist and wondered if it was unpleasant for him too. But then I felt his balls against my ass, and he started pumping. I clenched my teeth tightly, staring him in the eye as he worked. I don't think he liked that, but it didn't matter because soon his eyes were shut. The motion became smoother as precome leaked out of him, but I kept my teeth bared and didn't relax. As he began panting, I growled, and he came inside me, shooting hot white blood up into my insides. I looked away while waiting for him to recover. He opened his eyes, and nodded to Arshan. "Well," he said, his dick still inside me. "She is good for one thing." I opened my mouth to speak, but he clamped a hand over it. He pulled his leather gauntlet off the other with his teeth and began stroking my pussy. His index finger probed down between our stomachs. He brought it out from my vagina, moistening my labia with the juices there, then stroked my clit upward a few times, smiling as I shivered involuntarily.

He worked his large, rough thumb back and forth. I tried to fight him, but struggling only increased the contact. My hips began moving with him as I hungrily sought my release. I bucked forward, trying to increase the pressure, when I felt his shrunken penis slip from my ass. "O-o-oh, looks like I'm done," he said, stepping back from me. "I hate you," I whispered between clenched teeth. With my hands behind my back, there was no way I could finish the job he started. He was laughing. "The poor little thing, look at her struggling. Ha!"

Arshan released my legs and made me stand up. I trembled, tried to rub up against his leg, but he slapped me again. "Down. You're a mess. I think you need a walk through the pool." As he led me to the edge of the water, he asked me *How are you doing?*

Loving every minute. I still don't like Gallen, though.

He winked. *Yeah, but at least I got the knife away from him.*

✍

We mingled near the buffet for a while. Arshan picked at bits of bread and fruit. Occasionally he would drop something into my mouth as he made his point or changed the tide of a conversation—when he wanted me shut up. My thighs hummed with the energy Gallen had built up. It made me quieter than usual; all I could think about was Arshan's penis, which I had held in my mouth not so long ago. From time to time, as we circulated though the crowd, I met the eyes of guests, willing them to touch me. *Look at me, how can you resist me? My breasts bared for you, my hands tied, the gaping rent exposing my mound, how can you not bring your hands to me?* But they touched only with their eyes, some with curiosity ("Wish I'd seen that scene") or disdain. Very few were masked like us, I realized. Perhaps we were outdated. Finally, bored, I began nuzzling Arshan's shoulder. I rubbed my breasts against the woven fabric of the short cape, feeling the nipples contract to become rock-hard.

"I think the civil unrest will resolve itself," he was saying to a man I didn't know, who also had a slave on a leash. The slave, a male, was wearing nothing at all, and he posed and pranced after his master like a show horse. Arshan held me still with his gaze. "Haven't you had enough? No favors for you until I'm finished eating."

The other man chuckled. "Poor thing, she looks like a hungry one."

I tried to rub my head on Arshan's chest, but he backed up a bit. I lowered my head then, and went for the man, pressing my chest against his side and begging silently with my eyes. "Oho! Arshan, I do believe you have been depriving the girl."

"Ah, she gets like this sometimes, uncontrollable. But she hasn't deserved me yet. What shall I do?"

The man stroked his mustache. "Slave," he said to his own slave, "Kneel." The slave obeyed. To Arshan, as his eyes examined me still pressing against him. "I believe we might have some amusement?"

"By all means."

Arshan handed the leash to the man, who held me from behind by my shoulders. He untied my hands as he moved me forward, until I was less than an inch from his kneeling slave's face. The slave licked my stomach. "Lie down," he said, pushing me down as he said it. He held my wrists fast above my head and called for two other men to hold my ankles. Two other guests gladly did, spreading my legs in front of the slave. "Now, slave," he said, speaking to his own, "follow my instructions very carefully."

"First, run the back of your fingers up the inside of her legs, but stop about halfway up the thigh. Good. Again. Keep that up. Now move forward on your knees, run your hands up her stomach, cup her breasts. Take each nipple into your teeth, the right one first."

I twisted as he bit, not hard enough to draw blood but enough to send goose bumps down my whole right side. I moaned when he took the left.

"Now pinch them both with your fingers, keep your thumbs over the tips of the nipples, rub as you would a lucky coin. Ah, she's moving now. Fetch ice from the table. Good. Now take one cube in either hand, and hold it against her breasts. Rub. Good. Now with the ice, down the center of her sternum, down to the belly button, slowly now, slowly down the center of her abdomen, stop. Leave the ice there."

I felt the cold water melting down over my pubic hair.

"Now take some ice cubes in your mouth. With a cube in your right hand, slowly draw a line from the floor, up past her anus (I shivered again) up to her vagina, stop. Can you push it in? It has melted already? Get another, now up, up, press it to her clitoris, slave. Do not rub, simply press."

I gasped. The rubbing Gallen had given me seemed to flood back into me; I felt my labia swelling and my clit begin to throb under the ice.

"Now, keeping the ice in your mouth, extend your tongue, touch her clitoris."

The rough surface of the tongue, as cold as ice, made me jump. The slave began a circular motion with the tongue, then switched to a straightforward lapping. I couldn't stop moving my hips. I tried to pull my legs free—I wanted to wrap them around his head and keep his icy tongue there forever, but the men held me fast. I began moaning.

"Now, slave, please immerse your penis in the ice. After this, he pulled a cock ring from the pocket of his brocaded jacket. The slave had trouble at first but finally succeeded in putting it in place. Good. I wanted him long and hard and inside me. Even if it will be ice-cold.

The long, frozen shaft penetrated my throbbing cunt one millimeter at a time. I moaned, trying to move up farther on his pole, but he kept the distance where he, or rather his master, wanted it. When he was all the way in, they held more ice to my nipples, and then he pulled just as slowly out and iced his cock some more. Then he came back in, slowly, and out. More ice. Then slowly in…I thought I would go insane. He tickled my clit with the icy tip then, and a spasm ran up my spine. So close! Then he plunged into me and began grinding in a wide circle. I moaned loudly but kept my eyes on the man holding my wrists. After all, it was really him fucking me, through his slave. I imagined it was Arshan inside me then and I gasped; the slave began pumping in and out of me so fast I was just beginning to wonder how long he could keep that up when I came and came and came. One leg came free as I spasmed and they all let go and I clung to the slave with all my limbs, holding him deep inside me. I rolled him over onto his back and sat up, riding him. I threw my head back and began rocking, pushing immediately for that second explosive orgasm I knew I could have. It blossomed quickly, the energy traveling out my limbs and up through the top of my head as I cried out.

I slumped forward and Arshan lifted me off the slave's still-stiff penis. There were people applauding politely, I think. He bound my hands in front of me then, and let me lean, eyes closed against him, covering my shoulder with the corner of his cape. "There now, much more docile, you see."

"So I do see," the man was saying. Then to his slave, "Well done. "He removed the cock ring. "He has been instructed not to have an orgasm or ejaculate until I say he may," he explained. "I am pleased."

We moved off into the crowd then. *Thank you,* I thought dreamily. *You're welcome. But you're not done yet, are you?*

I sent him the image in my mind of his penis probing the very dark corners of my soul, of the fire spreading up my limbs and back through him with a kiss, building and spreading through every pore in both our bodies. *In time,* he replied. *But. I think I am going to let one more scene pass.*

He rarely gave me hints about what he was planning, unless that was a part of it all.

Yes, I think I'll trade you for someone else for a while.

What?

Trade you.

Arshan, I don't like the sound of that.

You can tell me to stop anytime. We'll go home.

I bit my lip. *Not yet. Not yet.* Even through his thoughts I was unsure if he was serious. Aftershocks from orgasm were making things jump in and out of focus. He held me tight as he led me to a place to sit, a chaise lounge along one wall.

When I looked up he was smiling. *It's just I have a few interests,* he thought.

Oh? I haven't seen much worth fishing for.

He shared with me the image of Cleo, black beads covering them both. *Hah. How do you think you're going to maneuver that? Cleo doesn't do public displays anymore.*

Who said it would be public? But not just now, I'm thinking of more ready game. You remember Mor?

How could I forget him? Mor was an old partygoer who had played with us a few times. He had luscious dark brown skin and long black straight hair. *But he's—*

He's here tonight, as a slave. I don't think I'll have to trade you for him, but I do want him.

I returned the smile. *Let's go for it.*

✍

I had to admit Mor was stunning. I had always seen him heavily adorned in black leather. But tonight he wore only body paint in elaborate and colorful designs. His hair drawn back in a long top-knot, he seemed a bird out of a jungle paradise, alien and irresistible. His master we also knew, Martin, who had once been a student of Mor's. I suspected this was a sort of graduation gift. Mor's and my eyes met while our masters talked. If I hadn't known better I would have thought he had me hypnotized. I admitted to myself I wanted him, but he was Arshan's choice. The thought of his body and Arshan's together warmed me all over. A crowd was gathering.

Suddenly Arshan dropped the leash. Martin picked it up, and I was pulled outside of the circle that was forming. I resisted the urge to call out to Arsh. I couldn't see him, and a knot of panic started growing in my stomach. I looked at Martin. He smiled, remembering me, and it calmed me. Arshan could take care of himself. But I still wished I could watch. Martin shrugged and let go the leash then and pushed his way back into the crowd. Free, lost, I circled the knot of onlookers aimlessly.

I'm not sure when it happened. At one point I could sense, even though I could not see, Arshan approaching orgasm. Perhaps it was at that moment, when the leather-gloved hands covered my mouth and nose, a strange smell invaded my brain, and try as I could to think, to send a message, I could only slip down into the darkness.

I awoke what couldn't have been more than a few minutes later. Gallen leered as he closed the last binding on my ankle. I was spread-eagled on a cross in one of the small playrooms. I sensed other people behind me—three? four? From their breathing they sounded like men. Gallen straightened his gauntlets and crossed his arms.

Arsh? Arshan! There was no response. I could sense him fuzzily— no telling if it was the drug that made me weak or if he was just too busy to hear it or both. Like me, he was always weakest after an orgasm. I looked Gallen in the face. "What do you think you're doing?"

He didn't answer, except to pick up a short whip and to come to lean against my side. I was at about a 45-degree angle to the floor. He caressed my breasts with his leather-covered hands, and my nipples stood up defiantly. I didn't have a shred of costume left now, even the collar was gone.

Arshan, did you plan this? Arshan! But there was still nothing. I cursed at Gallen in Ardric, now only half-acting.

"Screw you," he replied, but mildly, as he tickled my nipples with the tip of the whip. He ran the leather under my chin, bringing up goose bumps, tickling the inside of my ear, making me shudder. "There, now." He used the tip like a feather, searching me all over for ticklish spots until he ended by tweaking my clit upward with it, not quite hard enough… I moaned. I was becoming wet. I hoped Arshan had set this up earlier.

Gallen lifted the end of the X and it locked into place with me parallel to the floor. Twisting my head, I could see the others, three men I didn't know. I was going to hiss at them, when I felt the handle of the whip enter my cunt.

I looked up at Gallen. The handle was rough, and though I was wet, it did not go in and out smoothly. He smiled as he fucked me with it. It was the smile that frightened me. I tried to read him more closely, but his mind was sealed tighter than shrink-wrap.

"You like that, don't you?" He twisted it back and forth, never pushing it far enough in to touch my cervix. Just enough to make me moan again. "You like the whip," he said more to himself than to me. He pulled it out then and tasted the wet end of it. Then his tone changed and his smile disappeared. "I promised you a lesson, didn't I?"

"You've had your fun," I spat. "Let me out of here."

"Such a feisty act you two have. Let's see how long you can keep it up." He cracked the whip, and I and the spectators jumped.

"If you lay that whip on me, I'll kill you," I said matter-of-factly. "Believe me, Gallen, if I don't, then Arshan will."

He raised his eyebrows at the use of his name, and cracked the whip again.

"Gallen," I repeated, "stop it, now."

He circled me, rotated the X again so that I was upright. The blood was rushing from my head as I tried again. *Arsh, get your ass in here!* I struggled against the bindings, but they were as real as they looked. "I am going to kill you!"

And he struck me. The whip lashed me on the chest, just above my left breast. Pain and adrenaline flooded me. *Arshan!*

Yes?

I tried to tell him what was happening, but all that came through to him was a white-hot burst of pain as I was struck for only the second time in 10 years by anyone other than he. Perhaps that got the message through more clearly than anything. I was panting. "You will die," I said. Gallen lashed out again and again. Sweat broke out all over my body as I fought to contain the pain. I tried to breathe deeply, but I shook too hard, he gave me no respite between strokes. He tricked me, cracking the whip into the air sometimes, or raising his arm and then stopping. I did not scream.

And then Arshan's voice in my head. *The door's bolted. Hang on!*

"Please, stop," I was saying. I looked at the three spectators. "Someone, make him stop!" One of them started forward, but Gallen cracked the whip in front of them. He struck me again, on the cheek. I think tears ran down my cheeks with the blood. "Gallen! Stop!"

He was laughing. He let a few more strokes fall, each one seemed harder than the last, and then he threw the whip down and unsheathed his penis. He pushed the table back flat and stood between my legs, rubbing his penis against the inside of my thighs with his hand. I mustered up the strength to spit at him and he thrust into me. "Still warm, I see," he said as he fucked me vigorously. Trembling, I tried to pretend he wasn't there. I closed my eyes this time, *Arshan…?*

We're almost through, he answered. I could almost feel the clenching of his teeth.

Gallen must have heard the door beginning to give, for he redoubled his efforts and was exploding into me just about the time Arshan came exploding through the door. Arshan leapt straight over the table and knocked Gallen flat on his back. One of the spectators pressed the release and tipped the table forward. I stumbled to my knees, shaking life back into my arms. The two of them struggled. I saw Arshan thrown backwards and Gallen stand up.

I tackled him in the midsection, forcing him back against the wall, and swept his feet out from under him. Once on top of him, I smashed my fist into his face. And again. "I could just drive your nose up into your brain and kill you instantly, " I heard myself say, "But I'd rather beat you like this." I held onto his collar, lifting him up with my left hand and then beating him down with the right. His face felt fleshy, crunchy, knobby all at once. I pulled him up to a sitting position and switched to back-fisting him, then roundhousing him, then back-fisting him…the resounding smack of meat was all I could hear.

Mriah! Mriah! Stop it! Arshan finally grabbed my wrist and I wondered how long he had been trying to get my attention. He pulled me off of Gallen, and I collapsed, sobbing. Gallen just lay there.

He picked me up gently, wrapping me in his cape. I couldn't think at all; I just cried for a while, and he rocked me in his lap, humming a song softly in his throat. He kissed my bruised cheek, smoothing my hair with his hand and holding me. At some point I realized we were in the car, the smallness of the space comforting me. I kept my eyes closed as he caressed my face. I kissed him, drawing his energy deep into my chest as I inhaled. *I love you* was the first thing I could think. I drew him down on top of me then, kissing him and kissing him, not opening my eyes even once. He seemed to touch every part of my body then, the whole and the sore, warm and soft. I felt his skin, the long smooth plane of his back under his shirt, and the bony curve of his hip against mine. *Come inside me, heal me,* I thought. He held me tightly, arms circling my rib cage completely. He came into me gently, probing as I opened for him. I tucked my legs behind his back, bonding us together, one animal. *You make me whole.* I felt the energy building in my womb. Our minds open, I shared it, felt the waves of blood-warm pleasure feeding back to me. Up and up we went until shuddering and shaking as one, we passed the peak and slipped back down into oblivion. As I was drifting into sleep I heard him say, *Now I remember why we stopped partygoing.*

In his arms I smiled. I answered, *But now I remember why we started...*

Porno, Ergo Sum:
The Incredible Lightness Of Being Male
By www.JackFritscher.com

Ask me no questions and I'll tell you no lies. The British critic Edward Lucie-Smith told me that if my once-upon-a-time lover Robert Mapplethorpe had written a monograph on how and why he shot his photographs, the world would have had an invaluable insight into his work. Because Robert wrote nothing, his beautiful work stands on its own. Answering why and how I write my literary erotica is like skating a figure 8 on an ice cube, naked. Anne Rice and I started out on Castro Street at the same time; both of us have double careers writing fiction and literary erotic fiction. Behind the mask of eros, I write literature. Erotica is literature with velocity. My writing is like thinking while coming. I'm Gatsby's Daisy: "I write because men are so...so...beautiful" and because of the incredible lightness of being male. I enjoy being a guy.

Readers and critics feel my writing is autobiographical when it's only vérité. In truth, from 1965 to the present, I've been downloading my personality into books, magazines, video features, and telephone tapes. Jeez, I have lived it up to write it down; but my work is no more autobiographical than the movie *Platoon,* which director Oliver Stone said, "is not about me, but if I had not been in Vietnam, I could not have written and directed such a film." So it is with my signature novel, *Some Dance to Remember,* which is a gay history novel of the golden age of liberation, 1970–1982, in San Francisco. *Some Dance,* full of real tales of the city, weaves its emotional and historical and erotic ropes around a specific group of people in a specific place at a specific time. My "quantum style" folds time, squeezes a dozen years into 562 pages so structured with Aristotelian unities and limned with stream-of-consciousness that readers willingly suspend their disbelief, which is the aim of fiction. "Daddies" who were at the '70's gay renaissance party write me that they make their "boys" who missed the party read *Some Dance* to experience the high-water mark to which gay culture once rose before plague and politics destroyed the most erotic decade in American history.

Born the year after Thomas Wolfe (*Look Homeward, Angel*) died, I grew up as the other Tom Wolfe (*The Kandy-Kolored Tangerine-Flake Streamline Baby*) popularized gonzo journalism, in which the writer must participate in the story. I came of age on the rhythms of James Joyce, Scott Fitzgerald, Hemingway, and cried when at 15 I first read Walt Whitman, forbidden at my high school as filthy erotic literature. I wondered why the parts the teacher thought dirty seemed so achingly beautiful. I've been balancing Whitman with Rimbaud ever since. Some of my writing is erotic, porno vérité, because Oscar Wilde was right as usual: "Nothing can cure the soul but the senses."

"In the end, he could not deny his human heart."
—*Some Dance to Remember,* 1990, opening sentence

I confess. I breathe in experience. I exhale fiction. Feeling, emotion, is the oxygen of my fictive voice. Stories for me begin as raw emotion felt, or a disembodied "voice" heard. As a humanist, who is neither a feminist nor a masculinist, I welcome all emotions as well as women's voices and men's voices that I channel. As literary critic Michael Bronski points out, "In *Some Dance,* there are nine plotlines and 15 major characters sweeping through the epic story of the rise and fall of everyone who was ever anyone." Those plotlines and characters are intricate to the way I write: avoiding stereotype (Freud), going for archetype (Jung). Slice-of-life stories rule, because that angle best matches our human lives lived in slices of time, emotion, and awareness.

Fiction should render the writer invisible behind strong story arcs and layered characterizations and strong dialogue. Fiction actually "works" when the suspension of disbelief tips the reader into saying,

"Aha! This is real. This happened. This is autobiography." Perhaps what is recognizable is my intention to try to reflect something universally human about "the autobiography of the reader's inner self." Readers of my erotic adventure fiction want to know how I read their private sex journals, how I read their dirty minds, how I know what they did last summer. The storyteller is a trickster, a conjure man. Sex is only three degrees of separation.

At the baths one time, a man whose tits were in my steely fingers slipped down past my face, my cock, looking up at me, saying, "Do to me what you did to that guy in that story." I sent him on his way. My sex life is not a tour of my Greatest Hits of Fritscher Friction Fiction, but erotic reputation is a pisser after more than 30 years in adult entertainment—literature and photography and video. With more than 8,000 pages in print and around a thousand photographs in magazines from *Drummer* to *Bear* to *Unzipped* to *Honcho,* and more than 140 feature videos, I've been a busy boy living a wonderful life. My mantra is, "He who dies with the most column inches wins." That's a joke. Personally, I *am* leather; I *am* Wicca; I *am* bear fetish. But in my poker hand, my wild card as culture critic trumps leather culture's full house to top me; trumps satanic culture's four aces of spades to claim me; trumps bear fetish culture's hearts and diamonds to seduce me. I create erotic videos but, maverick, neither join nor validate any adult directors' guild or video archive. I am a unique hybrid: I am personally leather and a pioneer action figure in leather culture as well as a scholar-historian of gay male leather culture but not part of the establishment Leather Reich of "Mother-May-I S/M". In my *Porno Manifesto,* art for art's sake may go beyond the pale of consent.

✍

Actually, critic John F. Karr wrote in the June 27, 1985, *Bay Area Reporter* that from 1972, with the first publication of my novella *Leather Blues,* through my creating *Drummer* culture's heart, image, and style as *Drummer*'s founding San Francisco editor in chief: "Jack Fritscher is the man who invented the South-of-Market prose style (as well as its magazines, which would never be the same without him)." In the '70s hardly anyone was writing, photographing, drawing erotica. In the right place at the right time, I had 20 years of magazine and journalism experience in writing and photography as well as 10 years in leather and S/M when I became editor of *Drummer*. Supply and demand. A nasty job, but somebody had to do it. It was the dawn of gay culture. The times cast me as the hot boy editor…and luckily, as in "A Whiter Shade of Pale," the crowd called out for more. To put content, ethos, and style in those pages with everyone else out fucking and dancing, I had to fill that magazine cover to cover out of my own dick and brain, inventing the first articles on cigars, tits, daddies, all the hot tickets that have become the usual "themes."

In truth, I wrote two years' worth of *Drummer*, 11 issues—the thickest, juiciest, most original issues *Drummer* ever had—mostly at the baths, with pencil on yellow legal pads in small rooms painted black under a naked red light bulb. Arriving at 8 P.M., hard with anticipation of how the Barracks/the Slot/the Everhard/the St. Mark's/wherever, would pick up by midnight, I mainlined (metaphor only) the anticipation of the action into the veins of my stories, feature articles, and interviews. I channeled the high energy of the sexual revolution at the baths into my erotic art (which is the other side of my "legit" literary writing). My porno I write with my dick in one hand. Like the reader later falling into the story, I, the writer, must fall into the story while creating it. I must believe the fiction or the feature article ("Prison Blues," "Pumping Roger") to the degree that my dick stays hard driving the words, just as the words ultimately must drive the dick of the reader into hardening—and coming—in what I feel is the most interactive art in the world. The ultimate porno review is a reader shooting his load.

Others may deny that, because they're gay puritan fundamentalists who swing "politically correct." I'm as fucking nice a bobo (bourgeois bohemian) as you can get, but no one fucks with me—who successfully escaped the censorship of the Roman Catholic Church and Vatican politics—when it comes to writing, photography, and videography. What you read is what you get: no agenda, all entertainment. It's sexual truth, personal and raw, the kind you can't write if you suck off publishers, editors, workshops, museums, archives, or, worse, write for the failed Marxists in "politically correct focus groups." Fuck 'em all. As Sondheim writes and Streisand sings in "Putting It Together," it's all about the work.

Porno is an act of aggression that tops the reader, making him go nucking futz (like now), making a party in his pants. Erotic writing is so Fritscher-Rechy "outlaw," so much like shooting an "indie film" outside the studio system, that the "proper" academic gay rags have yet to acknowledge the literary merits of the only real gay writing there is—erotica—in reviews or awards. But God spare us from gay erotica becoming academically institutionalized. Teaching novels as assignments for class ruined the reading of fiction. College film courses assigning movies for term-paper critique destroyed the enjoyment of film. The irony is that 20 years after erotic "outlaw writing" is written, the mainstream begins to suck it up into respectability. It's hard to be edgy; it's harder to remain edgy. For a good time, give me a heaven with wild fucking saints who aren't canonized.

Too bad the future of an art form lies in the prejudices of its audience. The straight press thinks I'm "gay." The gay press thinks I'm "erotic." (The San Francisco International Lesbian and Gay Film Festival thinks my videos are "not gay enough." Go figure.) I'm professionally trained in literature. I know writing. Most gay writers who want to be on the straight best-seller list are perpetually angry because the straight mainstream literary world judges "Gay" and "Lesbian" writing as just another genre, like "Westerns," "Mysteries," and "Romances." I witnessed the 1998 Key West writers conference at which the president of the Writers Association abruptly and indignantly ended the conference sending all of us—including the other excellent writers in attendance, Tony Kushner, Edmund White, David Leavitt, Michael Bronski, agent Michael Denneny, and that sweet writer whose pseudonym is Andrew Holleran—out into the street. We were given the bum's rush not so much because Larry Kramer as usual went ballistic onstage but because the readings and panel discussions had started to turn in the tropical heat from "lit'rature" to "erotica." Key West wanted us to talk about AIDS as a

Literary Genre. Instead, steamy, sweaty, promiscuous gay writing and culture got too icky to deal with. We'll always be driven into the streets like hated queers until the exclusionary gay literary establishment owns up to the reality that gay writing is quintessentially erotic and therefore legitimate because eros drives human nature—particularly gay human nature—the same way that erotica drives new technology: VCRs, DVDs, the Internet.

So much goes on behind the scenes of porno I could write a backstage musical. Back in the '70s, I advertised my tutorial services in the pages of *Drummer* with a display ad called "Writer's Aid." Having been an associate professor teaching university journalism and literature for 10 years, and needing other writers' work to fill *Drummer,* I took on, during those first years of gay lib, aspiring writers to tutor them in both creative writing and journalism of the erotic kind. Two of those students were "Jack Prescott" and Anthony F. DeBlase. I counseled Prescott to take back his real name, John Preston, and then I did the final rewrite on his raw manuscript, *Mr. Benson,* and published it; from this draft Preston finally polished up the "unedited version." Tony DeBlase, years later, actually paid money to buy the ailing *Drummer* and became its publisher. Other '70s graduates of Writer's Aid include some wonderful current erotic writers who can reveal their own names *ad libitum.* So actually, John Karr in the *BAR* was right about my conscious nurturing of the South of Market leather fetish porn style. Lesbigay conferences, hosted by historical-revisionist groupies, are full of certain gay authors of a certain age claiming they and their exclusive circles invented gay writing. Fucking weird, man. No one invented gay literature anymore than someone invented Irish literature or African-American literature.

✍

Erotic content for me spins out of specific characters in a specific place at a specific time, so that the convergence of the quite "specific" nails a certain "universality" of human truth. Some people think Robert Mapplethorpe was a photographer when he was actually first an artist who was second a photographer. Never take this writer-editor-photographer-videographer, who was a founding member of the American Popular Culture Association in 1968, for anything less. That pop-culture sensitivity and my education, which I earned in my—as writer Dorothy Allison loves to repeat like a mantra—"working-class family," trained me with a Ph.D. in American literature and criticism so that I was prepared, with my homework done, to take on gay culture's ignition at Stonewall and blast off into the Titanic '70s for the cruise altitude of *Drummer*.

When the love that dare not speak its name began to scream, the golden age writers' duty and necessity was to name those unspoken acts, facts, and people. Erotic writers are endlessly inventive creating infinite synonyms for sex organs and sex acts. Actually, I had to determine for the '70s "Gay Culture Style Guide" that *cum* would be spelled "c-u-m" to match the Anglo-Saxon "f-u-c-k." and that *hardon* had no hyphen. My name being "Jack" tuned my familiarity with the word *manjack,* as in "every manjack for himself." So I wrote a *portmanteau* word by planting the word *man* as a prefix as in "mancock." Oy and vey! Every imitator on the block has prefixed everything but the "mankitchen sink" into what is now a total cliché of "manporn." (Nothing's worse than jerking off to some writer's story and realizing he's imitating your style. Bummer.) Pioneer writers had to create new vocabulary to spin-spin-spin queers from hated stereotype to heroic archetype. Stereotypes can be down-and-dirty shorthand to create a quick villain, but heroes need to be archetypes. I admit I write as a Platonist; out there somewhere exists the perfect lover. Quentin Crisp, who was not a Platonist, told me there was no such thing as the perfect tall, dark, and handsome Platonic ideal. I told him, "Of course there isn't. He's blond."

That first night when I first saw Kick, I recognized one of life's long shots at the Perfect Affirmation. He was a man. He had a man's strength and fragility, a man's grace and intensity, a man's joy, and a man's passion. He seemed my chance to celebrate the changes in me as growth. He was so fully a man, he was an Angel of Light. To him I could say nothing but *Yes*. One thing, you see, I know for sure: Nature very rarely puts it all together:

looks, bearing, voice, appeal, smile, intelligence, artfulness, accomplishment, strength, kindness. That's what I looked for all my life: the chance to say *Yes* to a man like that. I look in men for nothing more than that affirmative something that grabs me and won't let me look away. Maintaining my full self, to have some plenty to offer back in balance, I've looked for some man who fills in the appropriate existential blanks, for some man to be the way a man is supposed to be, for some man to keep on keeping on with, in all the evolving variations of friendship and fraternity, beyond the first night's encounter. I've looked for that to happen: to be able to say *Yes* inside myself when a good, clean glow of absolute trust settles over the world. Honest manliness is never half-revealed. When it's there, it's all right there in front of you. The hardest thing to be in the world today is a man. When Ryan first saw Kick, I dare say, his fantasy spanned a million years.

—Aria, "Archetype," from the novel *Some Dance to Remember*, published 1990, to be republished 2002 by Alyson Publications

✍

Erotica is storytelling. Erotica is pillow talk. Erotica is what you whisper into an ear to seduce. Erotica is what you say in bed to bend your partner into three more inches. Erotica is what you promise afterward to make sure you get sex again. If I may make a comment as one of the first and longest-living gay writers-editors, lesbigay authors in the 21st century need to get their storytelling shit together. Lesbigay writing should be as good as straight writing or better if the fantasy is true that lesbigays have better taste than straights. Look at the lesbigay magazines. Most of the illustrations look like the drawings of mental patients. Most of the models, pro or amateur, have dead faces. Much lesbigay writing reads the same: mental and dead. Humorless. Lesbigay narrative is largely unimaginative: "I went to a bar, met a god who took me off on his bike, fucked me, and left me, but I'll never forget him, because he was my first time." Lesbigay writers need to develop titles, story arcs, character back stories, dialogue, points of view other than the first-person narrator, and certainly not one more sensitive soul coming-of-age story that deserves the "No More Wire Hangers Award"!

Just because writers' laptops print out instant-gratification columns—formatted to look like writing on a book page or a magazine page—doesn't mean that the writers need not go back over the first draft to polish it 20 times. I started writing *Some Dance to Remember* in 1968 and finished it in 1982, with final edits in 1984 and publication in 1990. Be patient, but always keep focused. I could only write the novel as fast as history happened. I knew this *Some Dance* diary of gay culture was a three-way love story told against the epic rise of gay lib, but I had no idea in 1978 that HIV would enter the novel the way the burning of Atlanta entered *Gone With The Wind,* to which *Some Dance* has been compared by, among others, *The Advocate.* On the other hand, I wrote my nonfiction memoir of my bicoastal lover, *Mapplethorpe: Assault with a Deadly Camera,* in 90 days while over and over as loud as possible I played the soundtrack from *The Crying Game.* Suggested reading: *The Writer's Journey: Mythic Structure for Storytellers and Screenwriters* by Christopher Vogler.

A trained cultural analyst, I mention this huge problem in gay storytelling because such process analysis reveals the construct of what my erotica attempts. I'm tempestuously Irish (romantically independent) and Austrian (romantically aggressive), a Gemini born during the noon hour on the summer solstice. My first nonfiction book was about sex and the occult, *Popular Witchcraft: Straight from the Witch's Mouth;* my second was *Mapplethorpe: Assault with a Deadly Camera.* Patricia Morrison, the writer who attempted the horrible biography *Mapplethorpe,* named me, based on my journalism in *Drummer,* "The King of Sleaze," showing how shocking she—as a straight interloper—found gay-culture vérité to be. Was Patsy pissed that my frankly honest *Mapplethorpe* memoir beat her puritanical Catholic schoolgirl biography into stores and was the first book on Mapplethorpe ever published? Anyway, this King of Sleaze thanks Ms. P.M. for her rant, which in the inverted gay world is wonderful, actually, for quoting on covers of books.

Educated in Catholic schools, I can't seem not to write "sexy." I try, but even my earliest stories, published in—believe it or not, Roman Catholic magazines—are erotic subliminally, written as they are about virgin-saints fighting impurity, martyrs suffering joyously under the sadistic hands in the Colosseum, and revolutionaries in Latin America nailed to the roofs of cars by the *policia* in my 1961 story, "The Untimely Death of J. Cristobal." (Get the coded name?) My stories were "out" erotically before I was, in fact, before I knew that sex or homosexuality even existed. For a fictional memoir "take" on this, check out the year 2000 prequel to 1990's *Some Dance to Remember*, titled *What They Did to the Kid: A Post-Confessional Comedy*. *Kid* is totally overheated eros told from *inside* the closet, so it is a new kind of gay erotica that takes place before there is any coming-out story.

When straight people ask me what I write, I say, "Men's adventure stories." All my stories are relationship stories disguised as adventure stories ("Wild Blue Yonder"), comedy stories ("By Blonds Obsessed"), revenge stories ("The Lords of Leather," very Edgar Allan Poe), fetish stories ("Cigar Sarge," "K-9 Dog Dik," "Foreskin Blues"), war stories ("The Shadow Soldiers"), leather stories ("S&M Ranch"), bear stories (the one-sentence, 3,500-word "Three Bears in a Tub"), gym stories ("Father and Son Tag Team"), muscle stories ("Buzz Spaulding's Training Academy"), sci-fi stories ("Roughnight@sodom.cum" which won the Richard LaBonte Different Light award for best title), twinkie stories ("A Beach Boy Named Desire"). I write stories of the future ("Earthorse") and the past ("Titanic," the gay version) as well as ethnic stories (the Irish "Chasing Danny Boy," the Native-American and German "Buckskin Foreskin," and the Latin "From Nada to Mañana"). Hell, I even write lesbian stories and novels (*The Geography of Women: A Romantic Comedy*) that win awards, despite being told by one prestigious reviewer: "I know how to review your gay male porno, but I don't know how to review a man writing about women." Duh. Such antihumanist bigotry! Could he review *A Streetcar Named Desire*?

I'm known for helping editors out at the last minute when other writers don't meet the deadline. Editors beginning new magazines often invite me in to their first issue for good luck on the kickoff (*Skin, Just Men, Bear, Fetish Noir*, etc.). To sustain a porno career, and a writing career, one must stretch, grow with the times, as in changing my byline name to www.JackFritscher.com. I'm famous for pastness, memoirs, but also hot on the latest. I'm always trying to refresh the gray column inches of gay publishing, books and mags, with alternative erotic genres: plays ("Corporal in Charge of Taking Care of Captain O'Malley," which was the only gay play published in the canonical collection *Gay Roots*), screenplays ("Buck's Bunkhouse"), and features written in Internet E-style ("The Genome of Bear" for *Bear Classic 2000*, "The Genome of Leather" for "The Leather Magazine of Record," *Checkmate Magazine*). I've written a ton of lesbian erotica for major straight publishers (Larry Flynt), because I'm a humanist and not a slave to the failed Marxism of political correctness and will defend to the death my pal Pat Califia's right to advise gay men about their penises. Camille Paglia and I not long ago appeared together on a British TV program titled *Priapus Unveiled* defending the penis as erotica for both women and men. These female-male gender liaisons occur because writers are thinkers, analysts, and maybe cultural weather vanes as well as storytellers. I write literary erotica, as bipolar as Anne Rice, who is A. Roquelaire (all forms of sex), because it plays to a double audience: those interested in literature, and those interested in intelligent sex. "My porno starts in your head and works its way down."

I like to be in America. OK by me in America, where box office maps pop culture. *Some Dance* has sold nearly 23,000 copies; *Mapplethorpe* in hard cover, 42,000; the other 10 of my soft- to hard-core books, 70,000. That's approximately 130,000 book copies, coupled with more than 250,000 units of my 130 erotic videos. That's major sales, and a rubdown with a velvet glove on the balls of a culture, especially when there are from one to a dozen places to jerk off in those 380,000 pieces of entertainment. (That's the sexual pun in "Palm Drive.") That's say, conservatively, 4 million masturbatory loads out there in the dark, which is something to a Catholic boy who was raised to believe that masturbation is a mortal sin that condemns the masturbator to hell for all eternity. Is that why I write? Christ meets Dionysius? Or do I just get off knowing every night that out there someone is whacking himself into a moment of sublime pleasure, his only joy after a day of a shitty job or of taking care of his elderly parents?

Sometimes tiny Stanislavsky quirks sneak into the writing method: Sometimes I get naked; sometimes I dress up in leather or sex gear; once upon a time I sometimes smoked a cigar or sniffed poppers, because nothing clarifies erotica like amyl nitrite, which in its purple haze turns Godzilla into God and the brain comes down with some little mantra, three or four words of essence, as valid as Gertie Stein's experimental writing. Art is a delicate balancing act: living in one's brain waves at alpha (14 cycles per second) in a beta-driven world (18 cycles per second). No one sane ever does it; sane people make money. No one without the discipline of a monk and a marine can do it. The secret of art, of the art of writing, of porno, of literature, or of the art of literary erotica, is putting your butt in the chair, with all the notes on pieces of paper to cue the next paragraph, the dialogue, the feeling. I write three pages every day, five if it feels good, but no more. The spirit is willing, but the flesh is aged beef. At five pages I begin to foreshorten. I stay hungry, eager, at three pages, so the next day the drive continues into the next three pages. Until a book is actually bound, until an article or story is actually in the publisher's hands, the writing is never over: visions, polishing, revisions. A person has to be very brave to write porno and very secure to publish under his own name, because sooner or later "everything you say can and will be used."

✍

For better or for worse, critics always mention my style. "Fritscher is a stylist." Style for me is strong word choice, rhythmic phrases, colorful metaphor, filmic editing of space and time and memory, distinct objective dialogue as well as the streaming-consciousness, the convoluted monologue of thought and conscience that reveals characters seen by themselves in contrast to how other characters see them.

In this filmic age, I attempt stories vivid enough to jump directly from page to performance. *The Geography of Women* and "Rainbow County" are virtual plays/screenplays. Like it or not, in our culture, literary pages are validated by the screen, which is why I enjoy the high concept of turning my written fiction into porno videos and vice versa, as in "Buck's Bunkhouse Discipline." The final test of writing is reading the text out loud. If as a writer I stumble, stutter, when reading the lines, something is wrong with the lines. Rewrite. Find the rhythm of the words, of the sex, of the scene, and write that rhythm. Faced with the huge difficulty of writing such a "confession" as this, I am tempted to retract the veracity of all these factual words and turn fact into fiction, presented in a way that shows how reality is reshaped by fiction, how autobiography turns to drama, how experience turns into entertainment:

Not arrested, but picked up, questioned about what he did and how he did it, he told everything revealing nothing. On the table before him, the tips of his fingers, sensitive from years of typing, drummed the wood, impatient with the interrogation. From an ashtray, blue smoke from a half-twisted butt rose like incense at a seance toward the naked light bulb. *He breathed in experience.* He could feel the heat on his forehead. *He exhaled fiction.* Under the metal shade, the bulb hung like a burning pear, a scrotum, on a cord. He sat in the intense circle of light. He studied the detectives' movement in the darkness beyond the shade. His cock hardened untouched. He looked for the faces out there in the dark.

Other hands, other intentions, shuffled the evidence spread across the table, turning pages, trying to sort fiction from non-fiction, examining photographs, advancing videos frame by frame. He smirked. Excitement tweaked his nipples. Someone had tampered with the evidence: cum had spurted across his thousand photographs of naked men; more cum glued together the pages of his 69 stories in four volumes; cum, mixed with sweat and tears, curled the pages of his 562-page ransom note he couldn't even dance to remember. *Everything you say can be held…against…hard against…fill in the blank,* he figured.

At 14 he had bet he could get away with murder. At first, all he needed to pull off the job were yellow legal pads, then a manual typewriter, then a Selectric, and finally a laptop. He moved on to cameras, black-and-white print film, 35-millimeter transparencies (mmm, that first willing lifeguard on the beach in Chicago!), 8-millimeter, Super 8, 16-millimeter, video. He was an analyst. He lived it up to write it down. He was a part of all he met and vice versa vérité, baby. He nailed a warning above his bed: "Enter here to become a story told at night around the world." He could have sold space in his books and stories, so eager were the accomplices wanting to be mentioned in code or in reality, desperate for him to write, "When the hero came into the bar, he walked by X who stood by the pinball machine."

He could have admitted to none, some, much, most, or all of the fiction that was truth that was fiction, but he didn't. His pen was the mighty. He was a rich man with a big dick driving a fast car. As they had when he played football, everyone patted his ass. He always knew exactly what he was doing, who he was doing, when, where, and how he was doing it. His brain was his ultimate hard-on. He had the last laugh.

By www.JackFritscher.com

William Blake's "Thel":
On My Back to the Future
through the Tunnel of Love...

Inch for inch, pound for pound, Big Boyd Grymkowski was the best buddy a flyjockey could want back in those bombs-away days when our lives depended on each other in the United States Air Corps. Boyd was the aviator, the pilot, the captain, the jock, the stud. He even had a girl back stateside. Sweet Lorraine.

I was his ball-turret gunner, squished like a human booger into the all-glass nose of his airplane. He called me that. His "Booger." Wrapping his big arm around my neck. Giving my crewcut head a, wow, ow, dutch rub with his big knuckles, asking me, "What's an air cock?" Shoving me down between his thighs, dropping his big stud dick into my willing mouth. High in the skies over Europe, we were higher than any high-wire act without a net those last days of WWII whistling "Booger Wooger Bugle Boy," because that was the nickname we strong-armed our flight crew into painting real bold behind the nose of our plane, them not knowing the real "Booger" joke or how it was between Big Boyd and me.

I remember one of our last times together, me and Boyd, heading out before dawn across the wet tarmac, outside in the last deepest dark before the French dawn, ahead of the other flyboys, who were still combing their wet hair, acting in the mirrors like they were God's fucking gift, which most of them were, since you measure a flyer by his groomed looks, his attitude, his build, and the size of his cock, which every Joe knows, always side-glancing in the showers, sneaking peeks for the biggest cock of the walk, always hoping you won't be the peewee. Not that anybody ever said anything. Except about Big Boyd, who was hung so big everybody talked, like once a cock gets to be a certain size nobody's embarrassed to talk about it. There wasn't any flying ace who wasn't sort of in awe of the size of his 13-inch gun.

"If I had me a dick like that, I'd screw me Rita and get my roll in the hay-worth, I'd gobble Betty Grable, and I'd show Lana Turner a few new turns. And they'd all die with smiles on their pussies where my dick went in and grins on their mouths where my dick came out." We were nuts. We were young, with scores of our last high school games still stuck in our heads. We were American warriors. We were on a charted dead-set bombing mission. Berlin or Bust!

Anyway, that hour before dawn, those other dickheads were still tucking their pricks away in their skivvies while Boyd and me, strutting down the runway, all suited up in our sheepskin-lined brown-leather flight suits, coveralls they were, both of us laughing because of our wild fuck the night before, crawling this morning out of the secret rack we'd hidden in the back of the hanger, skipping our showers to make the sweet smell of our sex last longer, sucking the taste of come from our tongues and of sweet ass from our moustaches. He was so blond and hairy, I felt I ought to comb my teeth.

Boyd pulled me up short. Not hard to do, me being 5 foot 7 with an eight-inch propeller. We stood alone under the dark shadow of a B-52 wing. He grabbed me by both shoulders and looked down at me from his full 6 foot 3 and 220 hard pounds. The squadron had nicknamed us "Mutt and Jeff." I confess we were both easy on the eyes. Everyone said so. I was fair and ruddy with red-brown hair. Big Boyd, well, Big Boyd was the blondest Polack I ever did see.

He squeezed me in tight with his big arms, real romantic, and kissed me, tubing his big tongue like a second cock through my lips, dribbling his sweet saliva that tasted like my come he had sucked off, one last time, only minutes before, in the maintenance room behind the latrine. God! Was I in love with him! Me, 21, a cracker lieutenant from Little Rock, A-R-K. Him, 26, a crackerjack captain from Pittsburgh P-A's Little Poland. Without a war we'd have never met.

He sucked hard on my tongue. My dick hardened. His was always hard. Polish sausage. Kielbasa, he said. It rode hard. He carried it hard. It showed hard even through his thick leather coveralls.

"Hey!" He held me out at arm's length. His voice was deep and smooth like blond honey poured over warm gravel. "Don't sit under the apple tree with anyone else but me!"

"Till I come marching home," I said.

That song was our secret code those days when no one talked about how easy and how natural sex, and sometimes real and abiding love, could come to lonely soldiers who, faced daily with sudden death, dared to sleep with other young soldiers. Thank God, I knew passion. Thank God, Big Boyd was my one great passion.

In my life, I never regretted what I'd done, only what I didn't do.

If it hadn't been for that war, we'd have never met.

If it hadn't been for that war, I'd never have been killed.

Without that war, I'd have had to live my whole life managing the Woolworth's in Little Rock, serving my three never-to-be-born kids free Cokes at the soda fountain, not knowing what I missed, never having fucked around with the XYY-likes of Boyd Grymkowski.

Don't be cynical. TV networks make series out of being dead. Only I'm not dead. Not anymore. I'm as alive as you are. This day. This year. But whoa! I get ahead of myself. Heaven can wait. Ask Warren. Ask Shirley. When a man like Boyd Grymkowski tells you to sit under the apple tree, you sit, obedient as Adam in Eden. And you wait. Anyway, we're all old souls in a new life who turn and turn again, and if you don't believe that, they won't let you drink vegetable smoothies in Southern California, Venice, precisely, where Boyd went after the war…

The weekend after that morning, when I nearly got my balls blown off in the ball turret, which is maybe why the bastards call it that, our squadron barracks was empty. Unbelievable. Luck. Chance. Destiny.

The military's more perverse than fags, because war is first of all having to live with too many guys in too close a space for too long a time. So far so good. Not a shabby concept for shitting, shaving, and showering with every Tom, Dick, and Harry. Voyeur's heaven!

A hundred guys times, what, 6-inch to 8-inch, shit, say 7-inch, dicks, equals 700 inches of cock, or 58 feet of meat! Fuck privacy! Give me any day hundreds of young soldiers' buck privates, cocked, blue-veined, hung, dangling right or left so you knew how the guy jerked off when he was a growing kid. Pricks tenting under sheets at night. Skivvied meat hardening at the mere mention of blow jobs. Buns, hard bubble buns. Athletic pecs. Lean, hard chests. Nipples rosy, flat as quarters, erect as Hershey's Kisses. Shoulders broad as gun racks. Armpits dripping drill-sweat through red and blond and brunet hair. Hard arms. Proud biceps. Some tattooed with "Mom" or "Betty" who'd long since sent her "Dear John." The bitch.

Corded forearms of handsome mechanics. Sculpted hands. Long fingers. Grease-crescent nails. Lucky Strike Green hanging from lips surrounded by Barbasol shaving cream. New cookie-duster moustaches. Old Spice aftershave. Corn-fed farmboy thighs, ah, yes, high school football thighs, wrestling thighs, varsity letter thighs. Flat sit-up-till-you-throw-up bellies. Torsos lightly uphol-stered tit to tit. Hairy butts. Farts lit in the night. Screams of jackass laughter. Hairy legs. The sinewy curve of instep on a hard foot spied under a john partition. Beautiful, suckabilly toes. Anonymous hard cocks porting through wooden glory holes into anonymous warm mouths. Every manjack among them in full bloom. Too young, too fresh with semen, to give even a hint of going to seed, to pot, to rack and ruin, and every one so ravenous for sex that given the right time, the right place, and the right liquor...

Boyd loved my lust for life.

I loved his.

It nearly killed him when I died.

At dusk that Saturday evening, he returned to the barracks cov-ered with grease from working on "Booger Boy" and soaked with sweat from a hard workout in the squadron gym. I don't know who he had been wrestling, but I could tell the other guy hadn't won. No one beat "The Grymko." Ever. Victory turned Big Boyd Grymkowski on. (Pit him and Hitler in a ring...Fuck!) Boyd's 10-inch shaft, plus its three-inch bulb head, was hammocked hard in his tight red wool wrestling singlet.

What a combo! The grease of a mechanic and the sweat of a competitive grappler. He stripped slowly, teasing, wiping the back of his hairy blond hand across his mouth. He dropped the thin straps of his singlet down. He reached his big arms behind his neck and pulled his T-shirt up from the hairy-ape nape of his neck. First his navel appeared on his belly like a button on a washboard. Then the line of thick blond hair that ran up to his twin-pack pecs peeled out of the T-shirt he pulled over his unshaven, greasy face. Finally he husked the T-shirt off his head of short blond hair.

He grinned, and his blond moustache spread golden as dawn's first light flat along the horizon. Shit! He knew what he did to me. His blue eyes. His rosy nipples like twin islands in the sea of his blond-haired pecs. He laughed. He hawked up a luger—we were all sport-spitters—and spit it end over end toward me. A perfect shot. The flume, white as come, landed on my hard cock and hung like a juicy rubber band.

"Bull's-eye!" he said.

I lubed my tool with his spit.

"What you got there, kid?" he said.

"My cock," I said.

"I mean what you got in inches?"

"I got," he wasn't trying to humiliate me, only tease me, but I was a sass-mouthed match for him, "maybe 16 inches."

"Sixteen! Why that don't look like more'n about eight to me."

"It is eight. I was just planning on fucking you twice."

"Right after Helen Keller crowns Eleanor Roosevelt Miss America."

I savored each hard-on fetish word: "You ever going to strip off that…sweaty…red…wool…wrestling…singlet?" He knew I liked kneeling on the floor in front of him any time, every time, he stripped. He always peeled real slow, the way big-muscled guys do who, sometime before, in boot camp locker rooms figured out that normal-size men couldn't take their admiring eyes off them while they stripped off their uniforms, showered, and dressed, never in much hurry. Boyd was born cock of the walk.

He spread his broad shoulders, ran his hands up and down his hairy arms, palmed across both his furry pecs, and slowly slam-dunked both hands down his hairy belly, sliding his fingers into the red singlet. I beat my cock watching him, with his tongue between his teeth and his eyes fixed on his crotch, as he started the slow roll of the red wool singlet down from his steel-belted waist, down his hips, toward the revelation of his huge blond cock. His fingers out-lined the full shape and length and circumference of his 13-inch piece of work. The muscles in his linebacker thighs corded into groups like soldiers in V formation. I wanted his cock. He wanted his cock. I adored his dick. I loved it. But no one loved it better than Boyd himself. It was big, handsomely shaped, heavy-veined, Polack stud cock.

I knew what was coming.

"Lay back on the floor," he said.

I looked up at him, 6 foot 3 and 220 pounds of him, as he walked up the length of my body. His huge hairy legs dripped with sweat. His bare feet smelled rich from wet leather boots and damp wool socks. Standing, he straddled my chest. His pecs were beautiful. His shoulders…his face…I loved him.

"You ready?" he said.

I rubbed my hands up his hairy legs to wet them with his sweat and, wet-palmed, started salt-stroking my cock.

He leaned over me and tongue-funneled a long stream of spit from his mouth that ran Niagara to mine.

He smiled. I swallowed. Finally! Finally! Finally! He rolled the red wool wrestling singlet down to mid thigh. His porcelain-white cock, studded with blue veins, rose from the matted sweat of the blond hair in his crotch. His big bull nuts dropped loose and free, rolling in the play of his big palm like two billiard balls cupped by a hard-stick pool stud. His dick turned like a gun turret, heavy firepower, stand-ing straight up and straight out.

He looked down at his big rod over the mounds of his pecs. This night I knew he was putting on a special show to pleasure me. He laughed. His blond face broke open, the way sun at 3,000 feet breaks through fog over Europe. Nothing lasts. Not in war. Even the best is bittersweet. I was determined to beat the odds. I wanted to remember forever so I could find him again, his sparkling blue eyes, massive chin, big grin, and the kind of white teeth peculiar to born jocks, big white perfect teeth with spaces between them like pickets in a fence around a yard where you'd like to live. Alone. With him. Worshiping forever his big cock.

"This one's on me," Boyd said.

He was a born exhibitionist. He dropped to his knees over my chest, his drayman thighs triangled across me, below my nipple line, leaving me space to reach one hand through his crotch to beat my meat. My other hand roamed across his pecs, down his belly, juggled his balls, and wrapped around the base of his 13 inches. I squeezed. The veins purpled up under the blond skin. A big drop of clear bubble pearled in his piss slit. My tongue darted for it. My lips stayed put on the mushroom head of his meat.

He toyed with me. Slowly face-fucking me, rimming my lips with his cock head, planting the knob end of his three-inch cob in my mouth and slow-stroking his 10-inch shaft, taking pleasure in himself, giving pleasure to me, who was received like a guest into the personal pleasure he found in his own masculinity. He was like that, I knew. He liked having sex with anyone who liked to be part of him having sex with himself. Like me. Like Lorraine.

That thought, after I was dead, saved my life.

With his dick in my mouth, I was never more alive. His cock was so big jutting out in front of him, he was like the rider of one huge stallion, which he took from trot to canter to gallop, flogging hard flesh deep into me, ramming inch after inch deeper into my mouth, sliding over my tongue, breaking through the glottis, burrowing down my throat, hard, proud, yet so graceful that his insistent force seemed gentle for all my choking, salivating, and gasping for air around his sweet blond stud cock. He face-fucked me deep and hard, falling forward over me, 220 pounds of hairy Polish beef, counting cadence push-ups, his dick divoting down my throat, my nose buried in his redolent crotch hair, then on the upstroke, the wild suction of his dick pulling up and out of my tight throat like a plunger pumping a john. He push-up fucked me to 50, then 70.

"Ten more," he said. "Hard ones."

Eighty.

"Give you something to remember me by."

Ninety.

"The last 10," he said. "Animal fuck!"

He gave me what I wanted as he headed to a hundred. How much is 13 inches times 100? My lips were splitting. My tongue was tangled. My throat was bruised. Blood came from my nose. Yet he did not come. On the hundredth stroke, he pulled his slick dick from my face and leaned over and kissed me.

"Love me, Mutt? Ya love me, Booger?"

He took his cock in one big meat hook. He was a southpaw. He held his 13 inches like a boy's ball bat. He rubbed his right hand across his big pecs, flicking his nipples, while his left began the beguine on his enormous cock. He knelt directly over my face, over my open mouth, bringing his fully hard rod to full bore, cocking the trigger, pulling the piece, shooting his sperm-luger load all over my face, into my open mouth, up my nose, down my chin, on my nipples, on my chest. He scooped up a dripping load of his come on his big fingers and fed me. I sniffed the smell of his seed, tasted the sweetness of his sperm.

"You swallow up all my little babies." He was talking like a daddy, sticking his big hairy fingers down my throat. He dropped down full weight on top me and kissed me. "Jeff loves Mutt," he said.

My heart took off for the wild blue yonder.

Which brings us back to that kiss before dawn on the tarmac. That mission was my last. This ball-turret gunner bought the farm without ever seeing Paree. Big Boyd nearly died, my death grieved him so.

Later that spring, VE Day changed everything. Boyd, his uniform dripping with medals, stopped off in Pittsburgh to see his family and to marry Lorraine, crossed swords and all, which seemed the right thing to do, just as right as him taking her and a couple Samsonite suitcases and moving to Southern California, where a lot of other vets were toodling around like wild ones on motorcycles, still restless from the war, not ready to settle down. But Boyd, already settled with Lorraine, always wanted everything, thank God, both ways. So

Lorraine, who was no fool when it came time to worshiping 13 inches, didn't mind too much when Boyd rebuilt an old Harley better than new, didn't mind it as much as the tattoos he got on both his hairy arms. Plus she had to admit she had been bored shitless with Pennsylvania, so anything "California" that Boyd wanted to do was OK with her, except have a kid, not too soon anyway.

I watched all this. My lover, Boyd, pumping up on some iron, becoming a blond-bearded 235-pound biker, pretty sexually straight those days, with always a little playing on the side, mostly with guys who liked to worship and adore his muscle. Some things never change. (Can you imagine being dead and jealous?) I still loved him. I still wanted to be around him. One thing I know, some folks don't. They think we all just come back as somebody anonymous. No way. I know smart old souls can put in an order and wait. So I did. And any fool can guess what it was.

The fucking Santa Ana winds were blowing, the winds that make all L.A. crazy, making Lorraine crazy for Big Boyd's big dick, but this time I knew he wasn't planning on coming in her face. He fucked her hard and deep till she was screaming and climbing the wall and the more she bellowed the more of a big rutting, fucking, blond biker beast he became. They were wrecking the bedroom, and all of Venice Beach could have heard them. It was what I wanted. It was what I'd been waiting for. It was passion. I wanted to be a son born of his lust. When he grunted deep and low in his throat, "I'm coming!" And she screamed, "Come in me!" And he threw back his head of long blond hair, raising his face up, I zoomed faster than the speed of light like a bullet through his forehead.

I lodged in his pituitary, where I took first car in the roller coaster of his come that exploded in a starburst of energy, partly me coming in, that shot down under the blond bristles on the back of his thick neck, down his well-muscled spine, straight through his prostate, picking up other seed all along the way, me picking the best one to attach myself to, then rocketing around the double-8's inside his big bull nuts, and finally, launch time, I hit the first micrometer of his 13-inch cock, poised, perched, ready like a shot in a sling, when his toes curled under, his big butt tightened, his thighs hardened, his pecs and belly bulged, his powerful arms flexed, and the column of his neck stood corded like a huge cock.

His orgasm tore me at about a million G's as I shot down the inside cannon of the 13 inches of his cock. Not only did I have to beat out a couple million other anonymous sperm, I had to hit the target with Lorraine bouncing like a bitch in heat. But what's a ball-turret gunner good for, if he's not a hot shot?

So, for one brief moment, I was sailing along inside the 13-inch cock of my lover who, I knew, still grieved for me, but bingo!, not for long, not when nine months later he held me in his big daddy arms and said to Lorraine, "We'll call him Mutt."

"His name is Michael."

"So we'll call him Mutt."

"No."

"Then we'll call him Booger."

"I'll call him Michael."

"I'll call him Mutt."

The way he said the names I knew he recognized me. He kind of crooned under his breath and noodled my chin singing, "Don't sit under the apple tree."

And that's how my lover became my dad and we were the first ones on motor scoots and surfboards and everything was very California because, I was no fool. I made sure that his sperm I connected up with was genetically XYY-coded to be built big and muscular, blond, hairy, and hung like my old man with a 13-inch dick.

He always got off on himself so much, he liked me even better when I grew up looking every day more and more like him.

"You're Boyd all over," Lorraine always said.

There's nothing better than when the lover becomes his beloved. Or close to it. His beloved's son. I had quite a boyhood, a better adolescence, and when my old man hugged me on my 18th birthday like he'd never hugged me before, well, what goes round comes round, like father, like son.

Would a man with a 13-inch penis lie?

My Writing Life, or, Everything Old Is New Again
By Laura Antoniou

I'm a pornographer, by choice, by trade, by political affiliation. I'm somewhat prolific, with porn of every variety having issued from my word processor at one time or another. You might have read my Marketplace series of novels, about a modern-day real-life slave market, or perhaps seen an anthology or two—or six—of mine. You've possibly read me having no idea it was me, in little digest-sized magazines full of "true" letters and stories or on the shelves in the gay men's erotica section or even in a publication intended for straight men.

I was going through some of my work to prepare for writing this essay and found a few memorable moments in fiction. See if any of them sound familiar.

A young person brimming with promise becomes an apprentice to an older, wiser, sardonic, and mysterious teacher whose demands often seem cruel and whose history contains elements of suffering for the sake of a higher goal.

Two women meet at a bar, take a liking to one another, and for their first night together, the more dominant one teaches the other to polish her boots the right way. Mention is made of lashes earned for boots polished the wrong way...

Two strong, hotheaded youths are matched against each other in battle for the idle entertainment of their master, who wagers on them and murmurs, "I will have the winner," much to the amusement of his guests.

A low-ranking trainee is set upon by her higher-status roommates, who taunt her for failing to show proper respect and then leave her hog-tied on her bed while they go laughing off to dinner.

A lengthy session with a nine-foot single tail, three pages to get through 10 lashes, each of which draws blood, until the recipient staggers against the chains and slumps, only to hear, "Ten more..."

Recognize any yet? How about this excerpt?

"Garret put the finishing touches on his Lord's right boot, and his hands were shaking. When Renton had noticed the flaw in Garret's usually brilliant shine, the lad had received a vicious kick in the ribs. Although Renton had retired in a good mood, it seemed that his slave would bear a constant stream of abuse nonetheless. If Garret thought ill of such treatment, neither his face nor his eyes gave him away...."

Something from one of the Marketplace books, right? Or perhaps from one of my gay male S/M novels or short stories?

Actually, all of these situations and the excerpt are from a novel I started a little bit earlier than my more recent works. It's unpublished, actually, and will never be published. But then, how many works do you think survive rewrites starting at age 13?

Now, did I think this was porn when I was writing it? No, I thought of it as high fantasy, that sort of standard sword-and-sorcery, going on a quest to get the ancient relic kind of thing. In fact, its original title was "The Sword of Truth," which I changed to "Where's the Magic?" during a sudden fit of adolescent despair that lasted about 100 years.

John Preston, in his essay "How Dare You Even Think of These Things," mentions a similar experience as a teenager, writing a fantasy about a handsome, manly lord type riding through the fields of his estate and gazing at the muscular bodies of the men who worked for him and deciding which will be chosen for his pleasure that night. I wrote that sort of stuff too, but probably at age 15 or later, and all of those stories are gone now, consigned to flames in a panic-stricken night when I thought that when I ran away, someone would find them and…I don't know what. Know I was a pervert, I guess.

But my fantasy novel was different. It had a plot. (Albeit a convoluted, monstrously derivative and not very well-thought-out one.) It had character development. It had magical stuff! Somehow, all of these things added up to making something of greater merit than the sum of all the parts that would make my heart pound when I wrote them.

It's difficult to piece together exactly what I thought when I was writing this stuff. The first draft, underneath the clumsy construction and awful dialogue, still shows signs of a measured buildup of mystery and attraction to danger and power. Through two alter-ego characters, I made a case for both the "How can you live this way?" view of the outsider who sees black uniforms, strict discipline, and a fetish for obedience as alien, and for the military leader who sees the world as a series of superiors who must be obeyed and inferiors who must be controlled.

And it's pretty clear whose point of view I favored too.

But in the rewrite, I see that I had started to strip away some of the more blatant, sexualized pieces of fetish behavior for a more subtle approach. I had always struggled with my erotic impulses. I couldn't deny them and didn't really want to. But neither could I reveal them, and I knew that very early. I can see that I had started to embed them deeper into the story, to not make a big deal out of— oh, for example, a scene where one character backhands another. I think I had begun to realize that if I set the rules of my fantasy world to include such things without comment, then no one would know how much it thrilled me to think about them.

In later years, I took the world of this aborted novel—all 300 pages or so of it (even back then, I had a problem with length)—and I turned it into my world for an Advanced Dungeons and Dragons role-playing game. As I read through these pages, I wondered, was this world of mine always so shallow? Wasn't there more?

Yes, indeed, there was…created for small groups of friends to help me in my erotic imaginings, whether they understood what they were doing or not. Through my college years, my simple world built up around a simple story became much richer and more personally fulfilling. With the help of other sexually maturing friends, my world began to fill with things I had dared not write about. Consensual adult incest, intergenerational sex. Group sex and polyamorous relationships—long before I had ever heard that word. Pain play. Sex with professionals because they did it better, not because they were available at a tavern. And all of it packed into pretty standard action-adventure stories with a little bit of the "Kill the monster/Take the treasure" thrown in to appease the traditionalists.

It was during that time that I found a lover who also had as rich a fantasy world as I had made, and finally, I revealed the truth behind all this plotting and magic. It was an excuse to tell a story of an attraction to power and the loneliness and hunger that comes when you get that power, the drive to serve one greater than yourself, and—of course—every ritualized beating and boot polishing and whack across the face that brought us through the tale. We spoke porn to each other and acted it out, and I discovered that the real thing is ever so much more fun than just writing about it.

Now, years later, I find myself 300 pages into the fifth book in a series about attraction to power, the need to serve, etc., etc. And in an ironic twist, now I am overburdened with plot, which I must sometimes suspend in order to include the very scenes that were my excuse for plots when I first started writing!

What has happened here?

What was I always really writing about?

At first, it was easy to point at the obvious fetish pieces, ranging from my adolescent daring in suggesting that same-gender attractions might actually be preferred in a military setting, especially one in a world without reliable birth control, to the multipartner, bondage- and S/M-inclusive, possibly incestuous groupings that popped up from time to time.

But the real story that hooked these scenes together—or gave me an excuse to imagine them and write them—is also familiar.

I see a main character, bitter because of a lost opportunity, who nonetheless excels in her field and dedicates herself to making someone to replace her.

I see the confusion of someone who has been both drawn to and frightened of power, who both struggles with new concepts of right and wrong and embraces them with all the desperation of one of those "gifted children" who will do just about anything to impress a distant parent.

Power struggles abound in every rewrite, getting more and more subtle. Blatant threats in the early version become veiled, silky, dangerous in that understated way of someone who doesn't have to bluster to threaten. There are people sworn to service who hate the ones they are sworn to serve nonetheless. There are slaves taken in battle and as war prizes who grow to have affection, respect, and even love for their owners—much to the discomfort of those owners. (Was I unable to completely imagine such a thing? Or was I so sure that any moral person would not want to be loved by someone who could not freely choose to be with them?)

Everyone who had power found that it came with a cost attached to it. The warrior-king who could not be slain by any weapon except one in the hand of his second in command was forbidden to love. The woman raised to believe she would be a champion found out there would be another after her who would actually take on the task she was trained to do—and that she would have to make this person ready to do it.

It was all a romance—a soap opera with elves and swords. Melodrama in the classic sense of the word, because what is a teenager if not melodramatic? Questions of good and evil came up, as they will when you are writing fantasy, and I delighted in making my evil characters honorable, my fun-loving ones amoral—if not apathetic. Even back then, I didn't want things to be too easy. Honor and loyalty, pain and betrayal, deep love and hate that can't be mentioned out loud, quests and adventures, looking for the magical thing that will solve it all—romance.

And what am I writing now? A soap opera with whips and chains. About a character who misses a chance at becoming something he has always dreamed of and instead finds himself training others to be that which he desires for himself. A lengthy quest adventure through the modern S/M fetish world as a woman searches for the magical solution to her identity and desires, looking for that perfect happy ending and finding it's not that simple. Master Trainers who look at the pain they cause and mutter things like "omelettes and eggs..." and then get back to the work they have to do. Honor and loyalty, pain and betrayal...etc.

And still I am caught between wanting the sex and power and S/M all spelled out because that's what turns me on (and, presumably, the other readers), and wanting it to be such a given, built into the structure of the world, that readers can understand that it will happen—but there is no need to read through 20 pages of it when three will do. Not unless it advances the plot and shows some of those wonderful character conflicts and resolutions.

OK, so I am writing the same story. (The lead character even has the same name, although the spelling and gender have changed.)

But believe me, it's much better without the elves.

The First Time
By Laura Antoniou

The first time I was bound, she wound strips of a mutilated white cotton nightdress around each wrist, chiding me for my rude behavior. How dare I make fun of her exquisite gowns, delicately edged in lace, gathered slightly below the bodice and sweeping to cover my feet while floating above her own delicate ankles. I'd laughed at them, these gently worn, sensual garments of such feminine intensity that I could not even imagine them near my skin unless they were clinging to her body, her body then pressed next to mine. But wear such a thing? No, not I.

When she picked up the scissors, I laughed aloud and shivered in mock fear. When she made the first cut, just below the neckline, I started to reach for her, to stop her from destroying such a pretty thing. But her arms tightened and all the concentration in her eyes pinned me to the bed. I had to watch her tear through the thin cotton, making ragged, long tears that rapidly became the neat strips of anonymous white material, ethereal yet stronger than I might have guessed.

I pulled one hand away, testing her fortitude, and she slapped me with an imperious look. It was delicious. I let her pull my hands together, wrapping them around with one strip and then across with another, and then relaxed back onto her rich linen sheets and hand-embroidered pillowcases.

I let her touch me, smiling and sighing between the giggles, and reached for her as if to fight, aching for the strips to be tighter, to keep my hands above my head so there was no way I could impede her progress as she continued to make her points with maddeningly light slaps to my body. I reared up once to kiss her, and she pushed me back as easily as I could push her slight body around, and yes, I let her.

I wanted to see what she was going to do.

Because no one had bound me before.

But we were young and shy, and the boldness we showed onstage and in the dark corners behind the scenery vanished into the awkwardness of authentic intimacy. She reared back herself, and during the silence we both made our decisions. We were apart before long, and she remained a sharp reminder of the dangers of straight women, the perfidy of femmes. And she made me hunger for shadows of her for years, until at last I laid myself down for a woman in a gown and sighed in perfect release and abandon.

Or, maybe it didn't happen that way at all; maybe I imagined it.

Because the first time I was bound, it was to my own bed, by a man younger than I, an aching, beautiful boy, expertly instructed and coached by the one who knew exactly what she wanted. He danced and ran and shook his body in delight, never still, never at repose, even when he snuggled up to me in the coldest moments of the night. He grinned when I sought his eyes and told him it was time, and he eagerly handled my toys and used them in a careful progression, making me crazy with need and then falling on me with a passion so pure it had to be exactly as he claimed—virginal. We gave each other a sacrifice that year, cutting into ourselves and handing over the warm, moist parts that were our secret passions.

I bared myself for him, and he bared himself to me. He struck me with all his youthful strength and crammed folded towels in my mouth to muffle the cries, and held on to me later on, when his body twitched in a sleep without rest. He didn't tease, couldn't know how to tease, and so he satisfied me fully and made me feel that I might actually have a way to fulfill this desperate need in me.

I knew precisely what he was going to do; I was his instructor.

I needed to be in charge; no one had ever bound me before.

And so he knew where the tools were and knew exactly the kinds of stimulation I wanted, where, how often, for how long. No one could know me better than he, because I had told him everything he needed to know. I was in absolute control of my tender young faggot, my sweet lonely lover, and was able to surrender to my passions, if not to him.

Or maybe it didn't happen that way at all.

Because, really, the first time I was bound, it was by a stranger. A tall, powerful woman who could have lived my life twice with time to spare. She buckled worn leather cuffs onto my wrists and locked them in place and slapped me hard. I could not look at her while she completed the rituals that transformed her from the rough-voiced seducer of a crowded and smoky bar and into the sleek, silken seductress who could charm the most frightened young woman into a very dangerous game. I knew the proper words to say and the proper games to play, but still I went with her to a place I did not know, leaving no one behind to call for me or know whose hands I had given myself into.

She stripped my body and tied me up tight, and for the first time, I truly felt the pull against restraints placed on me by another, the weight of my own body, the limits of my own strength. And she stroked my face tenderly before striking me again and again, and kissed the blood from my teeth and lips so I could see it on her when she drew away. In a too-late moment of indecision, I tested the bonds and found them locked onto me, impossible to slip or lift off. And I knew what it meant to be truly helpless, at another's mercy. Alone, with a person who was known for being merciless.

I had no idea what she was going to do.

I was terrified, because no one had ever bound me before.

She brought weapons before me, silky, dangerous weapons like herself, and let me be romanced by them before they launched into brutality. Opening my bruised mouth, she commanded words from me and got only sounds, and her fury was so magnificent that I knew she was beyond human. She demanded worship. And in the end she got it. At a price so great, I was never to see her again.

No, it didn't happen that way at all.

The first time I was bound, it was by words alone. "Stay there" and "stand still" and "don't move," uttered with a playful, casual simplicity, punctuated by stinging cuts that threw ripples of distraction all along nerve endings. A light voice and soft hands and a test that was designed for me to fail. I ground my teeth and set my body and keened out lengthy screams that echoed in my skull but actually came out in hisses and gasps. And the more I obeyed, the harsher it was, until the agony exploded and waves of nausea swept through me. Drunkenly stubborn, I locked my limbs in place—I would stay there, stand still, and not move until rivers of blood covered my body, until my lungs couldn't draw another breath, until the starbursts of pain behind my eyelids became one bright red light and I fell to the floor and didn't know any more.

And I did fall, but not to the ground. Instead, I spiraled inward, and my obedience to these commands left my body no choice but to ignore those petty, spiteful stings. They faded into distant jabs that distracted me from myself, and when they rose in a flurry of angry impotence, I ceased to mind them at all.

I didn't know what was happening.

I had never been bound before.

Not much later, hands beat against my locked arms and fingers and bent me forward and at last I moved, and the sizzling, crackling awakenings of my body finally made me cry out. I could barely hear him, cradling me, his once-cynical voice trembling with shame and horror and fear as he asked over and over again why I had not moved. I knew then that he could hold me no longer, and so I let him soothe me and did not remind him whose bonds had held me so fast. I knew that he hated me then, and I allowed that hate to fill me with the much-belated pain and freed myself minutes after he left me for the last time.

No, it couldn't have happened that way.

No, really, the first time I was bound it was after years and years of bondage, when I was handed two pairs of cuffs and told to put them on. When I passed the rope I cut the night before under the bed legs and lay down in a genuine state of fear. Not fear of her, but fear that because I had never been bound I shouldn't have been there, hadn't earned my way to that strange bed and those accurate hands.

And with the two items I had brought and the one she had, she taught me what it was like to be tied, to be spread so wide that there were no safe places on my body. She taught me that the place I had gone before was not accessible through her, and when at last the tears came, I gave myself to them wholeheartedly, never losing myself, never turning away.

The cuffs were snug and light, and when I pulled against them, I did nothing but press my body wider for her. And in time, when I was turned and moved, it was her voice that held me, and the bondage seemed almost superfluous. I struggled against the ties and sighed in agony as they refused to give, and in one blissful moment reared against them, fingers curled and my entire body tensed to tear them from their anchor points. They held. What a luxury to be so tightly bound.

"Luxurious, ain't it?" she breathed into my ear.

And I cried again, clean tears that poured through me, soaking my face, my hair, the sheets beneath me, because I was so grateful for that moment.

You see, I'd never been bound before.

And when the bonds were gone, I found that they stayed with me anyway, and I slept in them and wore them for quite some time. The marks were not to fade from my body for months, years maybe, but the cuffs are still there, waiting for the rope under the bed.

But maybe that wasn't the way it happened at all.

Maybe it's still to come.

Screaming Underwater
By Lucy Taylor

Sometimes I think God made me a writer so I wouldn't have to turn into a serial killer—and a writer of *erotica* so I wouldn't have to become a hooker. Writing gives me a legitimate way to relish and delight in the forbidden. It allows me to imagine down to the last gritty detail any number of things—from the lewd and lascivious to the outright homicidal—that I might otherwise be tempted to act out in real life. Hopefully, of course, moral scruples and fear of prison would prevail, but on a *really* bad day, who the hell knows?

Although much of my work includes an erotic element, more often than not the sex takes a back seat to horror for the simple reason that I prefer passion with a dash of derangement, lust with an undercurrent of malice and madness. Without the tang of terror, the threat of slice-and-dice in the midst of fucking and sucking, my interest tends to flag—in fiction, anyway. Real life's another story. For a few years, I tried the date-a-psycho route and learned what I suppose most people already know, that nutcases are a lot more fun when they lurk in my imagination than they are when they lurk in the bushes outside my house.

As far as writing erotica, though, I got my start in the mid '80s, working for men's magazines like *Cavalier* and *Magna*. At first I got a huge kick out of being paid what at the time seemed like a large amount of money to write what basically amounted to porn. For a while I even had a monthly column called "Women in Lust: The Cutting Edge of Sex" in *Penthouse Forum*. Although I cringe to think of some of those articles now, they *were* fun. I specifically remember the one about penises, when I polled my girlfriends and gay male friends about the most unusual dicks they'd ever encountered and got descriptions of all manner of penile oddities—strange colors, bizarre bumps, shafts with more kinks than a fetish orgy.

I soon discovered, though, that no matter how kinky the activity or how numerous the participants, the human body is limited to a finite number of limbs and orifices and even the most elaborate orgy allows for only so many possible combinations and permutations. I got bored with writing erotica and moved on to erotic horror, a genre that allowed me to combine the gore of splatterpunk with the kink of porn.

Since then, most of my work has been in the horror genre, though on occasion I still write erotica. "In Heat," for example, the story in this volume, was written a few years ago, shortly after I'd spent a Fourth of July with a friend on Solana Beach near San Diego. I don't recall any fires raging, except the libidinous kind, nor were there any lost loves, deceased or otherwise, in the picture, but the physical appearance of the "runner" in the story is based loosely on a person I encountered there.

Having said that, I need to add that, in general, I tend to avoid writing about experiences and people taken from my own life. Whether writing erotica or any other kind of fiction, I've always thought that sticking too closely to the truth was a bad idea—just because I find something I've experienced to be fascinating doesn't mean the reader's going to share that enthusiasm. What I try to capture, though, is the tone of a situation, what I like to call the emotional landscape of something I've experienced. And then I transfer that atmosphere to an imaginary plot.

I particularly like writing from a gay or lesbian viewpoint, since either offers a vicarious break from my normally hetero lifestyle, and I've done enough gay and lesbian pieces that I feel comfortable crossing the fictional border. Given the choice, I probably prefer writing gay male fiction to lesbian fiction simply because as a (more or less) straight female, the objects of my sexual interest are generally male. And though nature has unfortunately denied me the opportunity to command some hot male slave to "Get down and suck my dick!" nobody can prevent me from enjoying the fantasy.

Overall, the greatest challenge that I find in writing erotica is balancing the sex scenes with plot and characterization. I hate it when a writer skimps on story line and character and simply throws big chunks of fuck 'n' suck into the story just for the sake of sex. In real life, fucking just for the joy of it is an excellent thing—it should be an Olympic event, as far as I'm concerned—but in fiction, "just sex" often bores me to the point where I find myself desperately hoping one of the participants will whip out a machete or chain saw just to get the whole thing over with.

Why do I have such a penchant for mixing the erotic and the macabre? Well, you might say it's an inherited trait—bizarre perhaps, but one I've gotten so much fun out of over the years that I can't really complain too much.

Actually, I owe it all to my mother and grandmother, who regarded sex as only slightly more revolting than public puking or a hands-on tour of a leper colony.

In my family of origin, sex and violence were inextricably linked. Now, I can hear my grandmother writhing in her grave right now (because God knows sex was never discussed outright, *ever*) but the aura of sex and fear was a subterranean text permeating the icehouse of repression in which I grew up. Men weren't just vilified as boorish louts who (like my father) abandoned their wives and children or (like my grandfather) drank beer and sometimes couldn't hold down a job, they were vicious sexual predators, human-looking and acting (sort of) but really a form of subhuman beasts. Should a woman make an off-color remark or wear something slightly slutty, these brutish thugs would perpetrate all sorts of unspeakable horrors upon her. Since these abuses were never actually described, it was left to my imagination—with a little help from *Webster's Dictionary*—to try to figure out what the hell they were talking about and how I was going to get some of these dastardly male despoilers to practice their perversions on me.

"Oh, yech!"—I can hear my grandmother exclaim at the sight of a bare-chested man on TV. Her disgust and revulsion made an impression, all right, but not in the way that she wanted—those half-naked men, especially if they happened to be endowed with an abundance of body hair, came to seem not only hopelessly unattainable but more desirable than my next breath of air.

So what does this have to do with writing erotica? Or writing anything for that matter?

Well, like many people whose childhoods were something less than sane, I started escaping into my imagination early in life and have kept the world of fantasy as a sort of second residence ever since. I like to think of it as an endless attic, full of strange, bizarre, and fascinating things, always offering up new nooks and crannies to be explored. It's scary too, but as is also often the case with sex partners, a dash of danger only adds to their allure. And since it's *my* attic, the place where my psyche stores its darker, more disturbing treasures, it's full of all manner of decadent and erotic inclinations.

My family of origin did not intend me to embark on sexual adventures as an adult, much less make money writing about them, (under my real name, no less!), but by treating sex like the proverbial rhinoceros in the living room that you are never supposed to think about or notice, they pretty much ensured that I would think about it all the time and, for many years, indulge in sexual excess with the addictive zeal of one who naively believes that in sex lies a form of salvation: I fuck, therefore I am.

But before I took up writing,(or fucking, for that matter), I was trying other forms of self-expression. Back in the '50s and '60s my mother and grandmother and I spent countless stultifying summer days by the pool of a pseudo-elite establishment known as the Westwood Club. The isolation was as unrelenting as the heat, and the embarrassment of being dragged around by these two embittered and eccentric Southern "belles" was ghastly, but I'll spare you the details. What I discovered, though, was that I could take a deep breath and dive down beneath the cool, chlorinated water and scream at the top of my lungs, scream my fury and frustration and adolescent rage, and no one could hear me or punish me for my feelings. Underwater was my place for self-expression when no other place was safe or possible, the place where I discovered primal scream therapy before it was ever in vogue.

Far better than screaming underwater, though, I later found that writing opens the door, not just to the release of angst but to a cornucopia of vicarious pleasures, unimpeded by age, gender, lack of opportunity, absence of a penis, or deficiency of moral scruples. If I'd like to kill the people up the street, I can do so on paper. If I'd like to fuck them first (or after) that's OK too. And there's an exhibitionistic quality to writing erotica, a legitimization of the relentlessly carnal mind, that I enjoy immensely. Everyone thinks about sex—that's a given. But the people who think about sex and then write it down are not only *admitting* it, they're inviting the reader to wallow in the same, lush, primal bogs that most other people keep private.

The reader may never know if the author is writing from imagination or memory or some combination of the two, but you now know, irrevocably, that those thoughts percolated in the writer's mind, that *this* story, novel, or whatever was among the items in his or her psychic attic.

And, although it may seem incongruous to some, the fictional avenue that I find most compelling at this stage of my life is the exploration of the erotic and the spiritual. I've touched on this in some of my work, "Thief of Names" from *The Mammoth Book of Short Erotic Novels* being one example. It seems to me that a great misconception in our society lies in the polarization of these two—sex is relegated to the tawdriest of sideshows or mechanical exercises— insert member A into slot B, shake well and thrust—but too often bereft of real sensuality or passion, while spirituality is conceived of in the driest and dreariest of terms—the image of the castigating and castrating Puritan God or the asexual holy person, narrow-minded and carnally stunted.

Spirituality or sexuality, the right arm or the left, is what the choice seems to come down to, but no God I can imagine would ever demand such a soul-withering sacrifice. Rather, I think the erotic and the spiritual are not mutually exclusive but as intimately linked as Shakti and Shiva, as the yoni and lingam. Only because of the Puritanism inherent in the Judeo-Christian tradition have the two been so often and regrettably polarized.

Whether I will ever completely achieve the merger of the erotic and the spiritual, either on paper or in the bedroom, I don't know.

What I do know is I will continue to write about sex and horror, because both fascinate and intrigue me.

In a sense then, every time I sit down at the computer, every time I write something that another person might find to be shockingly decadent or a forbidden turn-on, I'm still screaming.

But I'm not underwater anymore.

In Heat

By Lucy Taylor

Dennis left me the night the fires started in Malibu.

It was just before the Fourth of July in Southern California, and the summer had been especially dry and hot. The grass on the hillsides overlooking the sea was tinder ready to explode. The people who live in those hills know the risks, but even when their houses burn, more often than not they come back and rebuild on the very spot where the first home burned.

The first few nights, bored and desolate, I drank too much and sat in my darkened living room, listening to the sound of the waves slapping the beach, flicking the remote.

Pictures flying past: a rooftop turreted in flame, the cars of those evacuating the hillsides, a woman distraught because the cops were blocking the road and she had two dogs in her home on the hills.

The wind kept whipping the fires into new and terrible configurations. Firefighters fought the blaze while I battled the urge to call Dennis and try to make things right.

By the end of the week, five firefighters had died and many hundreds of acres had burned, and I still hadn't called Dennis.

Fuck him, I thought, *I don't need him.*

Instead of continuing to play the part of channel-surfing zombie in front of the tube, I began to imagine new opportunities. I spent a lot of time walking on the beach, enjoying the fantasies of all the new options now available to me. All the textures of bodies and timbres of voices. The delectable curve of an unfamiliar jaw, the sheen of oiled pecs on a bodybuilder, the whole vast and beckoning territory of unfamiliar flesh. Scoping out the fuckable surfer dudes in their skin-hugging rubber suits, lugging their long, phallic boards, and the lean, shirtless Rollerbladers on the sidewalk outside the condo, even the beefy middle-aged security cop with the inviting bulge in his pants. Basking in the heat of carnal possibility. Anticipating. Working up my hunger.

Teasing myself with fantasies of who I might have, what I might do.

Or so I thought. In truth, it was like going off a diet and then discovering you have no appetite. I still missed Dennis, damn it. I missed his scent on the sheets, the curve of his full lower lip when he pouted over some slight, real or imagined, the sweet sound of his balls slapping my butt when he angled his hips and plunged into me.

The fantasies of what might be paled against the memories of what no longer was.

So it was a relief when I finally spotted a guy who made my sappy memories of Dennis collapse like a kid's sand castle going splat under a wave. The object of my sudden, unequivocal lust was running toward me on the beach. Not traveling at the speed of your basic recreational jogger but at an out-and-out run, as if something dreadful was in desperate pursuit.

It was around dusk on the kind of cool, cloudy day that's not unusual for L.A. even in early July, and there were few other people on the beach. I like to think I'm too cool to stare, but this guy was running through the surf, splashing water, running directly—or so it seemed at the time—at me. He had a broad, athlete's chest covered in black hair, muscular legs and arms that pumped as he ran, black curly hair. I couldn't tell his age, he could have been 30 or a very much in shape 45.

I risked a glance at his face and saw that there was no expression there, that although he seemed to look right at me, in reality his dark eyes were miles away. Only at the last moment did he become aware of me and veer away from a direct collision, not slowing down, not faltering in the slightest.

I turned and watched him go, waiting for him to slow his pace as the beach sloped uphill. He didn't. He ran harder. He kept on running until he was out of sight.

Back in the condo, I'd left the TV on as I always do whether I'm watching it or not (one of the things Dennis and I often fought about).

The local news was on, and they were showing shots of the terrible fires up in Malibu that had already destroyed over 100 houses and taken several lives. An exhausted-looking fireman was being interviewed. I switched the TV to another channel, stepped out of my wet bathing trunks, made myself a vodka tonic and carried it out onto the balcony.

That was when I saw the runner standing down below. He must have run up the wooden staircase leading down to the beach—a good eight flights—because he was panting. I could see his chest heave and broaden above his concave belly and solid-looking rib cage. He was dripping wet, and the thick mat of hair on his torso was plastered flat against deeply tanned skin.

In the dusk, I didn't think he could see me. I stared down at him and felt my dick stir. Idly, I started to caress myself, imagining myself parting and plunging between those muscular buns.

I was standing there, slowly stroking my hard cock, when the runner looked up and saw me. He couldn't have seen my dick—the balcony wall was in the way. What he did see, though, was my expression, one part longing to two parts lust. I got a jolt of adrenaline— Did he guess that I was jerking off? Did he want me too?—but he looked away. I thought I saw him shiver. Then he walked on past, toward the row of hotels farther along the beach.

✍

That night I dreamed the runner ran toward me up the beach.

He was naked, and his cock, magnificently erect, was bright with flame. Flames capered in the springy thatch of his pubic hair. They climbed the dark tree on his stomach and spread across his chest like avid fingers. I woke up with a hurting hard-on. I reached over in the bed for Dennis, wondered for a second why he wasn't in the bed…then woke up fully.

No Dennis. Why wasn't I used to it by now?

Oh, well, I could do better anyway, couldn't I? Hadn't I secretly always thought so? Dennis wasn't even my type, not when I really thought about it. He was too pale, too short, he never managed to work off that extra 10 pounds of flab around his middle. Yet it was Dennis who'd had the nerve to walk out on me. I was still smarting from that. I was the good-looking one, with my ash-blond hair, smooth chest, and good looks that an admirer once compared to Hugh Grant's. I'd always figured Dennis knew he was lucky to get me.

"I can't take you flirting with every guy you see," Dennis had yelled at me that last night. "I go out of town, you're at the bars all night. I can't trust you. It's driving me crazy."

"Leave if you don't like it."

"I fucking well will."

And he'd done it, damn him. Gone to stay with a friend of ours in San Diego, a lesbian sculptor who did performance art with her lover in La Jolla.

&d

Fourth of July on Solana Beach is always a big deal. Everyone treks up to the Point to drink beer and watch the fireworks. A lot of people build campfires, so the beach is lit with the eerie flicker of flame and shadow against black sand. The evening on the beach was a tradition with Dennis and me ever since we'd gotten together four years ago, and I was stubbornly determined not to let his absence spoil it for me. I'd watch the fireworks, then go home and shower, hit the bars. There was a little place in downtown L.A. that I'd read about—baths and naked "slaves" on call, an orgy room and a dungeon complete enough to satisfy De Sade.

I spent the late afternoon lounging on the sand, then ate dinner, stuck a six-pack in a cooler and went back to the beach. I found a spot that was secluded enough so I wouldn't have to be distracted by the kids and the straight lovers and built a fire for myself using wood I picked up off the sand.

As the shadows lengthened, however, I found myself thinking about Dennis, and the flames shooting skyward in front of me seemed to burn cold.

"You alone?"

The voice was so soft and husky I almost didn't hear it above the crackle of the fire, but I recognized the silhouette immediately. The runner from the beach the night before stepped past the fire and sat beside me.

I moved over on the blanket to make room for him. His body smelled like it had been doused in some musky, pheromonal perfume. The hair on his body glistened with what must have been sweat or salt spray.

"It's no good spending the Fourth of July alone," he said.

I shrugged. "My lover Dennis and I broke up a few days ago."

"Yeah," he said, "I know the feeling."

"You too?"

"Something like that."

I forced a smile. "Hey, no sense grieving. Their loss, right?"

He nodded. "Xavier was a good guy, but I never loved him."

Then neither of us wanted to talk anymore. Hunger and heat crackled between us like an inferno gathering force. I saw the tiny bead of sweat glistening in the cup of his navel, and I was suddenly parched. I wanted to drink from his body: his saliva, his sweat, and his come, to become drunk on him and never sober up.

His hand slid inside the waistband of my trunks and stroked my thickening erection. In seconds, I was so hard I ached. His other hand trailed lightly from the small of my back up to my shoulders, leaving a wake of gooseflesh before his fingers buried themselves in my hair. The fire made strange patterns on our flesh, eerie arabesques of ocher light and shadow.

His tongue found my nipple, then traveled up to the hollow at the base of my neck. He whispered, "I want to fuck your brains out."

Which was an understatement about how I was feeling about him. I wanted him to fuck me until I felt like someone else, until all the pain and restlessness inside me fired out the end of my dick and left me empty and sated.

I felt safe where we were, curtained by the darkness, the cliff side at our back, the fire in front. The few people who were passing now were hurrying toward the Point, anxious to get there before the fireworks began.

I grabbed him by his furry chest and pulled his face toward mine.

The kiss blistered its way to my belly and into the tip of my dick.

I flattened out on the blanket, pulled his trunks down, and took out his cock, which was the stuff wet dreams are made of—eight inches of thick, hard flesh.

He leaned back on his elbows. I tongued from the veined shaft up to the head, which was as pink and silky as a rose, swished my tongue across the tiny hole, then took all of him into my mouth.

At first he lay still while I slid my mouth back and forth over his dick, then he began to thrust. The length of his shaft was slick with my saliva. His hands were in my hair, clutching, pushing. My face was pressed against the hard, hairy plane of his belly. I slid my hands underneath him, gripped his cheeks, and lifted him toward me.

The fire crackled, spewed hot ash across our skins. He arched and gripped my hair so hard it hurt. I could feel the need in him, the power gathering behind his coming orgasm. Then suddenly he thrust me away and sat up abruptly. "I don't like doing this so close to the fire. Where I saw you on the balcony the other day—was that your place?"

"Just up the beach."

"Let's go."

Inside my condo, the lights were off. Only the pale glow from the TV screen illuminated the bedroom. We embraced and kissed in the shower, rinsing the sand off our bodies, teasing and licking and suck-ing. We lathered each other with soap and ground our wet, slippery bodies together.

He turned me around, dropped to his knees, and licked from the base of my balls up the crack to my asshole. I could feel the hard, probing tip of his tongue penetrating me while he worked my erection.

"I want to fuck you."

I considered the need for a condom, but long ago I'd discovered that a fuck spiced with danger and risk is a fuck to die for, and who cares if that could literally be true.

Fuck safe sex, I thought.

I leaned forward and braced myself against the wall while his cock hovered at the entrance to my anus. His hands gripped and spread my cheeks as he opened me and eased inside. I felt the dick-stiffening satisfaction of being parted and filled. He started slowly, and every now and then he stopped moving altogether and just *filled* me until the suspense was almost unendurable and I pleaded with him to go on.

"You like that?" he teased.

I was ravenous. It was as if over the years with Dennis I had forgotten how to fuck with my whole being, how to desire. Now that my body was remembering, my hunger had returned in all its force.

While he reached around to pump my cock, I fondled my own nipples, arching my face into the spray from the showerhead. His hand buried itself in my hair again and he yanked my head back, riding me like a horse on a very tight rein. His tongue was in my ear now, his teeth sinking into the fleshy part of the lobe.

My come jetted. I lifted his hand to my mouth and sucked my jism from his fingers, licked his palm, and kissed the sinewy wrist. He was inside me to the hilt now, pounding into me while the water sheeted off my back, over my head. When he came, his cock pulsed like a muscle spasming. He reached past me and cut off the shower. We toweled each other dry.

I found myself already wondering if he would stay the night. Wanting him to.

Naked, we lay sprawled on the white shag rug in the living room, listening to the distant explosions of the fireworks. The light from the TV set flicked on our skins. CNN showed more scenes from the Malibu fires. Smoke pluming from the roof of a Spanish hacienda-style split-level. Firefighters chopping their way through heavy brush.

They started listing the names and showing pictures of the five firefighters who'd died—three men and two women. I reached for the remote but for some reason didn't click it. The runner looked riveted to the screen.

The TV showed a close-up of a Hispanic man with small, penetrating eyes and high cheekbones. Xavier Ramon, age 33, the announcer said.

"That name?" I said. "That isn't...?"

The runner grabbed the remote away from me, clicked off the set. We sat in silence.

"You knew already?" I asked.

He nodded. "I found out he'd been killed two days ago. He was on a slope when the wind changed. He tried to run, but the fire moved too fast." His voice was tight and strained as if someone had looped piano wire around his throat. He said, "He was a fuck buddy and a nice guy, but I didn't love him."

I must have opened my mouth to say something, but no words came.

"I'm...sorry," I finally said. Words that were monumentally inadequate as well as imprecise. Was I sorry about his lover's death or sorry he hadn't loved him? Or just sorry he was denying it now?

"I don't want to think about that now," he said. "It can't be changed. I want to think about being alive."

He reached for me again. We went out onto the balcony. The sky above us was coffin-dark and the fireworks were over, but people were still camped out on the beach. I could see the lights of their fires. I went down on my knees and sucked the thick, heavy length of the runner's dick, and he moaned and closed his big fists in my hair.

We stayed that way for several minutes, until I felt his thighs begin to tremble and a roar like something wounded came from his throat.

He arched and I felt the come pumping out of him into my mouth. I swallowed most of it, but some of it dribbled down onto my chin and dripped onto my chest. It was like being anointed with some thick, musky-scented oil.

"Stay the night?"

He shook his head.

I wasn't surprised and I wasn't really sorry. His dead lover was there with us now. The condo felt too crowded.

He didn't offer his phone number. I didn't ask.

After he left, I went back to the balcony and watched the flickering of the campfires out on the beach and the dark orange glow of the fires raging to the south.

I thought about Dennis, and I stared at the phone. Along about dawn, I called him.

AN INSISTENT AND INDELICATE MUSE
By Patrick Califia-Rice

"The truth is often rude."
—Mikal Shively, queer sage and Daddy Bear archetype

Asking why someone would write about sex is rather like asking why anyone would eat at a five-star French restaurant. The inherent pleasure of the activity in question seems rather obvious to me. As a pornographer, I am in the same position as the restaurant critic. I get to do something I love while being paid for it. Why would I ever *stop* writing about sex?

Of course, this is a simplistic description of my vocation. It omits the deadbeat publishers who try to bowdlerize writing that scares them; checks that never quite stretch to cover all the bills; the disapproval of family, fellow pagans who are stuck in the cultural feminism of the '70s, and other nonfriends; the lack of serious critical attention (because everyone "knows" pornography requires no serious literary talent); the angst of putting something so personal out for public perusal; watching my dot-com friends buy new cars and houses while I agonize about when I can afford to change the oil in my 10-year-old Honda Civic and dodge calls from the landlord; and the mind-numbing challenge of finishing a collection of sexually explicit fiction despite chronic pain, yet another hacking chest cold, or a dry spell in which I haven't had a new trick to inspire me for the last six months, thank you very much, Aphrodite.

Some of these obstacles exist for any writer, no matter how staid. Creative work is badly paid and underrated. The rodeo announcer's cautionary opening statement, "Mama, don't let your babies grow up to be cowboys," might more aptly be rephrased as, "Mama, don't let your babies grow up to be artists." Anybody who can look at the hump on a Brahma bull's back, not to mention those very pointy horns, and still persist in the delusion that the creature is meant to be ridden gets no sympathy from me. But then, I have never felt the rope burn of desire to sport one of those silver-and-turquoise trophy belt buckles as big as a dinner plate. (My Western genes do, however, predispose me to own a lot of multicolored, pointy-toed boots, and I prefer a big saddle when I go for a ride. Alas, I digress.)

I *have* experienced the jones to write while stuck at a desk in Chevron Oil's word-processing pool, watching precious irreplaceable hours of my life tick away like the sand in the Wicked Witch of the West's hourglass, while I sent out form letters about credit cards. It hurt. A lot. I write because I must. I am motivated by a strong desire to avoid the pain caused by not writing. Any parallels between being an artist and a junkie are too obvious to be mentioned here.

If it weren't for pornography, I wonder if I'd ever have become a writer. In my early 20s, I was unable to keep (or publish) anything I'd written. The minute a poem or short story came out of the typewriter ,I loathed it so much that I destroyed it. The only way I got myself past this self-destruction was to make myself write something that was so forbidden and exciting that I wouldn't be able to stop myself. I also told myself I never had to show it to anybody else. (This trick still works.) I'd never tied anybody up or spanked anyone, but my sexual fantasies were all about bondage and discipline. I found them scary and shameful but could not relinquish the pleasure they gave me. So I had to find a way to own or integrate this part of myself. The result was "Jessie," which later wound up being excerpted in *Coming to Power* and published in toto in *Macho Sluts*. At the time, it was the only piece of lesbian S/M porn—or lesbian porn of any sort, for that matter—that most of us had seen, so it circulated in photocopies of photocopies. For all I know it still travels in this samizdat format, encouraging more budding perverts to wear black velvet suits and put candles up their booties.

Because there was no tradition of sex writing by and for lesbians, I had to use my imagination a lot. There were no clichés for me to fall back on. I did not know anyone who actually engaged in the acts

I described, so I had to devote more time than porn writers usually do to filling out my characters. The challenge was to make the sex believable, to use the female characters in such a convincing way that the reader would be led step by step into a world where women actually said such things and got what they were begging for. Of course, I was also leading myself into that world. It was a case of life imitating art.

I kept writing leatherdyke smut because I had to create the audience that would appreciate my work (and let me live out some of my fantasies in the real world). That is one thing that I believe makes my fiction unique, the fact that it built the very community that it celebrates. The message of *Macho Sluts* was "You don't have to just think about these things. There are other women who want them too. Come and find us."

It will be interesting to see what happens to my fiction as a result of this gender transition I am making from female to male. I'm well aware that I've gotten away with breaking a lot of the rules because I was perceived as a woman and a dyke. Defending free speech and public sex and writing hard-core tales were unheard-of occupations for a lesbian in 1977. I worry that some of the things I have to say will be dismissed or seen as not particularly interesting if they come from a person who is living in a male identity. Right now I am struggling to figure out my relationship to the body of work I created before I started taking testosterone and using male pronouns. It's very hard for me to do readings because my voice has changed. (Literally.) I understand how important it is for many lesbians to be in women-only space. I don't want to ruin this safe place for women who need it. Yet I feel that I'll probably continue to write lesbian porn, if only because there's something rebellious and dangerous about two women looking for their hot zones together. But will lesbians still be willing to buy my work?

Transgendered people are already turning up more often in my fiction. I keep asking myself, "Who will read this stuff? For that matter, who will publish it?" These worries slow me down. I'm 46, and I have a painful autoimmune disease. I don't know if I have it in me to once more build a community by writing about it as if it already existed.

At least I don't have to start from scratch this time. Many leatherdykes have gone before me and come out as FTMs. There's a strong international FTM movement, but a lot of transmen are freaked out by S/M and homophobic to boot. Do the rest of you care enough about gender issues to be interested in the sexual adventures of trannies? Does that turn you on?

Even though I sometimes feel as if I am building a bridge out over the thin air of the Grand Canyon, I can't imagine being able to stop writing about romance and all the other packages that sex comes in. The work itself is reinforcing, because as I write, I too am entertained, aroused, and educated. The things that hurt me lose their sharp edges and become more like a finished jigsaw puzzle than a Colt .45 with one bullet in the chamber. The act of creation is almost always an act of faith. It's impossible to know, while you are making something new, exactly what it will be when it is finished or what will happen to it when it leaves your hands. The future is none of my business, partly because if I focus on the consequences, I will never have the tunnel vision and warped concentration of energy it takes to spin words into sentences. Although I don't see anything wrong with writers and other artists being good businesspeople when it comes to attracting an audience for their work and the material means to continue it, I also think that the postcreation marketing stuff is the least important part of the entire process. It's sad when a great painter, for example, is not appreciated until after his or her death. The probability that there are other great painters whose work will never be seen at all is even more tragic. *But the work was still valuable,* no matter how obscure. Each image was still a vocation and an obligation that the painters had to fulfill, just as the lion must fulfill its mandate to hunt and the tides must follow the moon, rumpled like the bedcovers of a restless sleeper.

Here are some of the other things I've learned in my career as a pornographer.

By the time I put the manuscript of *Macho Sluts* together, I had discovered and read quite a bit of heterosexual and gay male S/M porn, and I found that a lot of it was unrealistic. When I read about sex acts that I knew were life-threatening or just physically impossible to perform, it bumped me out of the narrative-induced trance and made me feel uneasy and icky instead of aroused. Much of my fiction is written as much to entertain me as it is to grab a reader by their short hairs. I wanted images of S/M play that was edgy but doable. This seemed to me to be much more subversive than the mass-marketed pulp paperback stuff that was far-fetched or all about people being maimed or killed. Bad, mass-market fetish porn implies that its subject matter could never be translated into the reader's daily life or relationship. I wanted to depict people who got off on extreme things who still had jobs, apartments, bills to pay, and lovers to argue with and fuck.

Even though I write about male-female sex whenever the urge strikes me, on the whole my work is about the perfection and grace of queer sex. When Dr. David Reuben said in the first edition of *Everything You Always Wanted to Know About Sex (but Were Afraid to Ask)* that one vagina plus another vagina equaled zero, he was just saying what most heterosexuals believed in 1969, albeit in a crude and piggy way. Straight people didn't just hate dykes and fags then; they thought we were ridiculous, a dirty joke, struggling to make two identical bodies fit together in a way that would never work. Our determination (or compulsion) to succeed at this impossible task simply confirmed our mentally ill status. Queer sex (especially lesbian sex) wasn't just seen as being wrong, illegal, or sinful; it was seen as being on some level *impossible*. (Unless, of course, two hot chicks were making out while a straight guy watched, in which case it was just very effective foreplay for a heterosexual ménage à trois.)

My earliest ideas about sexuality came from a crazy fundamentalist Christian religion that sanctions only about 5% of the many possibilities people have for experiencing pleasure with one another. I was terrified to be gay. But when I actually experienced putting my body up against the body of a woman, all I felt was flesh on flesh. I was troubled by my ambivalence about having a female body, but I could not feel any wrong being done. Skin to skin, mouth to mouth, with our hands and our lips we crafted a sensuality that exceeded anything I'd known in my few shabby heterosexual trysts. Even though there is a large body of same-sex porn available now, it is still important for us to keep writing about this, the fact that when two men or two women desire one another, something morally good, spiritually rewarding, and physically gratifying transpires. We are not zeroes. We are like pi. We could go on to infinity without repeating ourselves.

While I may tell myself that the trash I'm typing is for my eyes only to get the rough draft out, an appreciative reader is just about the only anodyne for the painful and repetitive revision process that makes fiction inkworthy. This is a roundabout way of saying that I've often written about sex to seduce somebody. In fact, the dedications of most of my books are to people who no longer share my bed or my good graces. I once had a lover ask me to promise to never dedicate a book to her, as she feared this would jinx our relationship. If we define sex as stimulation that leads to orgasm, I could claim to have had sex with thousands of people via the pages of my books. (And all of it safe sex at that!) When I create some especially fiendish scene, one that might make readers inhale suddenly and sharply or get goose bumps, there's a certain kind of pleasure to be had from topping all those strangers.

My sexually explicit fiction documents the vagaries of my personal life, but it's about everybody else's love life too. Porn is one way to write sexual history—the slang, fashion, community institutions, music, controversies, mores, the signifiers and significance of sexual expression at various points in time and in several different sexual minority communities. Some authors would find that a horrifying prospect. They strive to create an archetypal erotic story that will be timeless. So they avoid, as much as possible, descriptors that would nail down a story's location and time. Sometimes they also strive to eliminate descriptive details of their characters' appearance or personalities. Their goal is to create an erotic Everyman or Anywoman, Piers Plowman at the Last Chance Lap Dance Saloon. *The Story of the Eye; Harriet Marwood, Governess;* and *Spanking the Maid* are amazing achievements in this genre. When writers with less skill attempt this feat, it blows up in their faces, because it's pretty easy to blunder and wind up with a story that is colorless and boring and looks like a lazy, halfhearted effort at realizing a fantasy.

But it's almost impossible to separate action from context. In time, these works too will provide readers with historical data as well as arousal, though they won't be as rich as *Fanny Hill* or *My Secret Life*. These two books are good examples of the strategy I prefer, because I believe it makes the work more potent—diving into a wealth of detail, creating a complete picture of where the sex is taking place. I think this plunges the reader more deeply into a vicarious experience. But every technique has its weakness. The writer who wants to convey an accurate sense of the times they live in risks seeming quaint or unintentionally humorous to the next generation. (I know who among you have laughed at the author's photo in *Macho Sluts*.)

Clothes, language, religions, governments, and table manners come and go. But a new generation of readers can overlook a few anachronisms if they find something in a narrative that reflects their inner life. That's why I believe it is so important in fiction, whether it's erotic or not, to focus on the emotions, beliefs, and needs of the characters. Human nature has not changed all that much in 7,000 years of recorded history. The epic tale of Gilgamesh and Enkiddu is still comprehensible to the modern reader, even if we miss some of the religious references. Beowulf and the myths of Egypt still fascinate us because we want to know what is going to happen to all those people next, even if we think their clothes are weird. If a writer is able to accurately portray how a character feels, the work stands a better chance of holding up under Father Time's big pink eraser.

If anything renders a piece of fiction quickly obsolete, it is an absence of desire, whether the author's point is to convey a sense of its frustration or fulfillment. I write porn in part to balance out all the Western fiction that makes it invisible. I've never understood why so many writers willingly extirpated sex from their narratives. How can we understand any character in a play, short story, or novel without knowing something about their pleasure-seeking behavior? Jane Austen should always be read alongside contemporary explicit depictions of sex. The understanding of one can only enrich our understanding of the other.

One of the things I love most about describing passion is the chance to imagine or empathize with how it affects people who are very different from myself. There was such a need for sexy lesbian entertainment that I put most of my energy into this kind of work. But I live in the whole world, not a gay ghetto, and I wanted to get inside the heads of straight men, straight women, gay men, people who were violent, people who were victimized, people who lived in different worlds. It really pleases me when I hear from heterosexual readers or genetic gay men who have responded to stories that were about people like them. I also like what happens when sexual minorities begin to read one another's scripts for reaching orgasm. We all have enough in common to motivate us, hopefully, to be kind to one another, and enough differences to keep us seeming exotic and attractive.

Most subcultures rely on staying underground to survive. We often want to keep our secrets because we are afraid that other people will distort or misuse the very personal experiences that make our lives meaningful and happy. Any work that celebrates a stigmatized way of being in the world cuts two ways. It is both celebratory and revealing, sometimes dangerously so. I've often been asked how I feel about straight men reading my lesbian porn, and that would be hard to answer without taking it case by case. I've only gotten one letter from a straight guy who was so utterly clueless that he interpreted my work to mean women like abuse. I'm pretty sure he held that opinion before he ever ran into my byline. Gay culture is no longer the secret property of the friends of Dorothy. It's out there for anyone to scrutinize. Many straight men don't like lesbian porn written by and for lesbians. Why should they? There's no role for them in those scenarios. On the other hand, just as there are dykes who love boys-only videos, there are some heterosexuals who like to go someplace else when they are fantasizing. *We have straight allies.* There are people who are not gay who like us and enjoy participating in certain aspects of our lives. Heterosexual men also read lesbian-identified porn to educate themselves about female sexuality. If just one straight girl got a decent bit of head because her boyfriend read one of my books, I'm happy. I think that if we keep quiet about our fetishes and rituals, we make ourselves seem less substantial or real, even to each other. Whatever safety we might be able to buy by eschewing representation of our excitement or orgasms isn't worth the damage it does to render ourselves mute and blind.

Oddly enough, a lot of the smut I write isn't necessarily intended to stimulate a mad bout of jilling or jacking off. I like to use the cover of eroticism to entice the reader and make them emotionally and psychologically vulnerable to new ideas or discomfiting information. I hold out the reward of dirty talking in exchange for the reader stretching their political muscles. People are reluctant to think about many of the issues surrounding sex and gender. Or there's a knee-jerk reaction that reflects what "everybody knows" to be true. Some of the topics I've chosen to tackle this way are barebacking, relapse from safer-sex precautions, AIDS and lesbians, rape, drug laws, queer youth, police brutality, domestic violence, censorship, addiction, racism, and class differences. The bittersweet presence of sex in these narratives hopefully motivates the reader to hold on to the ambiguity or conflict that is often more accurate or truthful than coming down on one side of an issue or the other. The lesson to think, question, and humanize rather than blame, judge, or jump to conclusions lingers far longer than it would have after a lecture.

Most of the political or ethical criticism in my work is aimed at the larger society, because that is the locus of the hatred and discrimination we live with every day. As sexual minority communities become larger and stronger, I think it's important to also question the mores or policies they develop to socialize new members, regulate the conduct of insiders, and handle relationships with outsiders. This is pretty hard to do, since oppressed minorities already take a lot of grief. But very few people become saints just because they are persecuted. I'm uncomfortable with anything that's written on stone and handed down from the mountaintop by a superior being. I want to live in a world where women are taken seriously, pleasure is not stigmatized, there's good sex education and equal access to health care, and my people are valued instead of persecuted. A lot of that is beyond my control, not in the power of anyone who owns a leather jacket to give or take away. But we can also be pretty nasty to one another in our marginalized subcultures, and I like to remind fellow outlaws that we are accountable for this bad behavior. I would like to live in a world in which everyone who's a minority would not be looking for somebody who is farther down in the hierarchy so they can stomp on their head.

My work is founded on respect for the reader. I assume that most people can tell the difference between a book of fantasy and a how-to manual, and I believe we should all seek out diverse points of view, to keep our brains from fossilizing. This presupposes a certain level of intelligence and maturity that censors can't credit the average person with. (Protection is not the same thing as respect.) Even though I write about pain and suffering (which are two different things), I hope my work is infused with a sense of compassion as well. Sadomasochists are able to express love for aspects of their partners' being that are usually objects of repulsion or scorn. We represent the capacity to seize hope, love, and dignity under adverse circumstances. By celebrating what is beautiful and righteous about forbidden forms of intimacy, I try to provide comfort and a sense of connection to others, both mortal and divine. There's so much loneliness, depression, fear, and loss in the world. This is the spiritual dimension of sex writing for me: to create fellowship and community so that we can take care of one another, to praise the material or physical manifestations of our creator, and delineate the value of tragedy as well as ecstasy.

I have lost so many of the people with whom I began this journey of sexual exploration—lost them to AIDS, drugs, car crashes, murder, suicide, old age, cancer. I continue to write about topics they would find amusing because I have been left behind to bear witness. Every controversy I foment, every pair of knickers I tie in a knot, are my memorial to the beloved dead. The project of ending sexual repression and hatred of people who are bisexual, homosexual, or transgendered is still necessary. If I cannot heal the grief I feel, I can at least make it a little lighter by making myself useful.

The Code, Chapter 1: "You're a Goddamn Masochist"
By Patrick Califia-Rice

It was so cold. She had been outside for hours, watching his house. Her breath looked like smoke, expelled into the frigid air of this winter night. She had to keep moving constantly—stamping her feet, chafing her hands, hugging herself, rubbing her face—to feel the cold, rather than a dull and empty numbness. It was ironic that so much effort went into keeping herself sensitive enough to feel the pain of being slowly frozen alive. It was so much like her entire inter-action with the Master. The whole courtship had been conducted this way—haunting his footsteps, keeping a respectful distance, but always being available, always ready with a polite offer to open his door, fetch him a drink, watch his bike; and him ignoring her, walk-ing right past the greeting and the proffered service, pretending that he (who missed nothing) could not see something that distressed all the men around him. But each snub, each rejection, only intensified her suit. She did nothing now but follow him everywhere, and if she could not go where he went, she waited outside until he emerged and could be tracked again. She had lost hope long ago, and grimly decided she could go on without it.

It had not been easy, waiting in the peculiar toxic darkness, a black rendered gray by cigarette and cigar smoke, of that unwashed bar, whose every surface seemed to be slick or sticky with old, spilled semen, Crisco, and beer; the only woman there, knowing the patrons heartily wished her in hell, seeing the bartender smirk, getting jos-tled or stepped on by burly men in leather, keeping her eyes focused only on him, the Master she had decided to serve, whether he would or no. It is not easy to be that available. You must stay hungry, eager, taut as a retriever waiting for the shot and the falling bird. There is nothing passive or lazy about it. It is exhausting. It hurts as much as a beating but lacks the consolation of the sadist's gratitude.

Despite the cold, she wore the uniform she had worn during the entire quest: her boots and jeans, a white T-shirt, a motorcycle jacket, and thin leather gloves. Her belt was plain leather (studs were an ostentation she did not deserve), and her keys hung on the right. She felt instinctively that he would disapprove of a bandana, even a black one, and anyway, if it was appropriate for anyone in the scene to fly a colored flag, it was not her, whose ambition was merely to be noticed. She tried by this simplicity to speak to his own formality, his old-fashioned strictness. Often, in despair, she wondered if by doing so she had not doomed herself to obscurity, made herself even more invisible than women normally were in his masculine world. Or if she had not made herself ridiculous, as if she were imitating an ideal her physiology would never allow her to achieve rather than making a statement about her deepest and truest self.

If that was true, if she could have attracted him by displaying cleavage, wearing gaudy new-wave leather, offering him a handful of cocaine, or tearing one of his epaulets off, then her shrine was empty, the god was not present, and this ritual was pointless. She knew, the way a violin string knows if it is properly tuned or not, that he was Code. He went by the book. And much as her fantasies revolved around whips, chains, shouted orders, shining boots that kicked or crushed their victims, to possess or wield this paraphernalia was not enough. The words had to be spoken by one who was properly anointed and ordained. Each black leather item of apparel had to be a badge of honor or a medal of valor. The ceremony of humiliation and bondage had to have a secret meaning, and that could be revealed only by an initiate. She hungered for the mysteries. And she knew that on some level, by even asking him to lay his hands on her, she had violated the Code. Even if he wanted to, it might not be possible for him to induct her into this discipline.

But times change, and even the gods change with them. Leather was no longer a persecuted cult. It was a fad. Victims no longer hunted for masters in sailors' bars and truck stops. Instead, elaborately dressed voyeurs and exhibitionists confronted one another in leather bars, and if they went home together, it was with the understanding that most of the expensive and uncomfortable gear would come off before "the action" got started.

Well, she was not a poseur. Pain called to her. If no one would administer it, she would give herself a hard task and grind it out alone, with as much purity as possible, and hope the endurance, the stamina she was building, would someday flatter and encourage another, who could be crueler than she was to herself.

Jamison must be nearly 60 by now, but his temperament was such that he would have been of the old school even if he had been 21. If the Code meant what she thought it did, he would not be deceived by appearances. He would sense her obsession, her devotion to duty, even if her sex distracted him.

She walked up and down, shuffling her feet, hands tucked into her armpits to get them warm enough to put up to her ears, to bring the blood back into them. It was getting even colder, and a sharp-edged wind was blowing up the alley. It was a very clear night, every star a tiny, mute explosion. Too cold to snow, damn it. She wished for an empty oil drum. She would have made a fire and huddled over it like a tramp and kept her vigil in a little more comfort. She could not feel her toes on either foot, and the tip of her nose was similarly numb. That was frightening. For the first time, she wondered about frostbite and even freezing to death. She supposed it could happen, even in this day and age, with only the wall of his building separating her from warmth and light.

She should go home. There was still a half-bottle of good Scotch, left over from Christmas. She could kill that, pile every blanket she owned on her bed, and climb underneath them, suffocating and drunk but warm. She probably wouldn't even need to masturbate before she fell dead asleep.

But some mulish streak in her would not turn her around for the main street, a taxicab, and home. The vigil had to be kept. She knew instinctively that only extreme methods would persuade him to appear and beckon to her. Never mind that the windows were dark. Never mind that she had kept this up for six long months—every day or two. She fixed in her mind a portrait of his face—the iron-gray hair beneath his visored cap; the intolerant hazel eyes; the thin, unforgiving mouth; the tyrannical jaw and chin. His hands were things of beauty, like instruments of torture on public display, and his entire appearance was immaculate, shining with a black light, his back straighter than mere bone and muscle could achieve. He was a gentleman, but he was also an outlaw, and woe to the fool who forced him to remind them who he really was.

She would stay. Tonight she realized that she was not going home until he had either accepted her or driven her away. She would not rest or eat until he either cursed her or took her in for questioning. She could not bear one more night alone, without a purpose, ignorant, untutored, useless. She would not return from this wilderness without her vision.

Her pacing had brought her underneath a streetlight. She stood under its cone of yellow light and stared up at his mocking, empty windows. She stared at them so hard that tears came to her eyes, and she never saw the light at the foot of the steps come on or heard his door open and close. When she heard "Get over here!" pitched to carry, in a Midwestern twang, she jumped out of her skin.

The light was behind him, so she could not see his face. As cold and stiff as she was, she tried to stand at attention for this crucial examination. If that pleased him, she was not told. Instead, she was ordered to put her hands against the wall and lean into it, with her feet far apart. Then he searched her. The flat surfaces of his palms were as impersonal as a doctor's, as thorough as an X ray, squeezing her sides, sliding down each thigh, patting her butt. He confiscated the folded knife in her back pocket. Having then judged her defenseless, he bid her, "Get in there," and she went up the stairs and inside the front door, but not quite far enough inside, because he had to shove her to make room for himself and to close the door.

The warm air was making agony bloom in her hands, feet, and ears. "How long were you out there?" he asked.

"Since 7 o'clock, Sir."

"Fool."

Whether that referred to her keeping watch or to her use of his honorific, she could not guess. But he gave her time to adjust to the heat, watching without impatience or disapproval as she jogged and flexed her limbs. She knew he knew she was in pain. She could not help showing it. But she did not show it off, and so at least she did not irritate him.

"What did you think you were doing?"

"Waiting for you, Sir."

"Why?"

"To serve you, Sir."

"Have I asked you to serve me?"

"No, Sir."

"Then what gives you the right to tag along wherever I go and hang around me?"

"I have no right, Sir. All I have is need."

"Need?"

"I need a Master, Sir. And you are the only Master I have ever met."

He considered this. Was he enraged, amused, disgusted, indifferent? She could not tell. Like an animal, he had no facial expression; a human being could only imagine he must be showing this or that emotion. She honestly did not know if he was about to kill her or embrace her, and neither one would have surprised her.

His house smelled like wood smoke, dogs, leather, old books, and cooking oil. He did not smoke, and she had been close enough to him to discover that he did not wear aftershave or cologne. He drank moderately—hard liquor, never beer or wine. He would eat if he was in the company of others who wished to dine, but he never gorged. His passions did not tempt him to indulge his own flesh. He was addicted to the sensations he could provoke in other men, not to some craving of his own body's making. He looked so refined, but profane, an ascetic libertine, a horseman who rode other men, the confessor and the vice confessed and the expiation. Who was she, next to this man whose life was a treasury of love crimes and hateful caresses? Just a pale, naïve, determined girl—nobody special to look at; you wouldn't notice her at all unless you made her scream.

"Take your jacket off and hang it there," he said, indicating a coat-rack. He went farther into the room and sat in his favorite chair, pulled close to the fire. She did what he had ordered, then stood where he pointed, once more at attention, not quite believing he had allowed her to stay.

"Have you had any dinner?"

"No, Sir."

"Drink this." He handed her a bowl half full of soup. It was lukewarm, but she drank it gratefully. Glancing at him, she saw him staring meditatively at the fire. The bowl had come from a TV tray by his armchair, and there were some crackers and slices of cheese on a plate, with an empty glass that had held milk. It reminded her that he was an aging man, alone in a big house. She remembered hearing that his lover and slave of three decades had died last summer. Jamison had not replaced him. In fact, he had been almost a recluse, emerging from solitude just about the same time that she began to stalk him. Her stomach growled at the soup, and she blushed, not knowing what to do with the bowl. When he continued to ignore her, she stepped to the side and leaned forward to put it back on the tray. This meant coming between him and the firelight, and he gave her a sharp look.

"You presume a great deal," he said frostily.

But she had noticed that he was wearing full leather—hardly typical dress for a lonely dinner of canned soup. He had put on his leathers before he went to greet her. Nothing had ever made her this glad.

"Yes, Sir."

"Don't you think you should apologize?"

"If I have offended you or intruded, I am very sorry, Sir."

"But not sorry enough to offer to take your jacket and go home, isn't that right?"

"Yes, Sir."

His nostrils looked pinched. He had the appearance of a hanging judge.

"But if you wish me to leave you, Sir, I will go back outside."

"Oh, of course you will. And the next time I walk into the Brig, you'll be two steps behind me, trying to buy my drinks and brush off my bar stool."

She laughed. "Yes, Sir," she admitted cheerfully. Those eyes had not been dead, had not been glass. He had seen her. She was real, took up space, existed in his world—even if it was only as a confounded nuisance.

"I am not amused," he barked. She snapped to, and regretted her lapse. He came at her anyway, rising from his chair with more grace than a boy athlete, and cuffed her until she fell against the mantlepiece. It was a brief beating, but it was savage, and she had to fight to control her protests. The only thing she would allow herself to do was protect her neck. That left him the rest of her, and he abused it heartily. Then, his feelings apparently somewhat relieved, he sat down again and pointed once more to the place where she was to stand and answer.

She panted, but he did not. "So you presume to think I might have need of your services," he sneered. "You are certainly original in your folly. What do you think you can do for me?" All the scorn for women implied by men loving one another was contained in that question. It would be so easy to answer him with fury, like a rejected representative of her gender. But she knew if she could not swallow and answer that scorn, there was no apprenticeship or indenture to him. She had endured misogyny her whole life. She could not endure futility.

"Sir, I would be your student."

"Am I a teacher now, holding a roomful of brats hostage to reading, writing, and arithmetic?"

"No, Sir, no. You are the Master of a craft, a code I want to learn. I think I have wanted this my whole life. I would give anything to learn it. And that is what I have to give you. I do not think you want to die without having passed your knowledge on."

"A long speech for a beggar."

Chastened, she made no reply.

"Your cheek is bruised."

She touched it tentatively. "Thank you, Sir."

"At least you have fairly decent manners." He chewed his lower lip and thought about his bed and his own right hand. "Who taught you your manners?"

"No one taught me, Sir. It just seemed appropriate. According to the little I know about the code."

"Then you've never played S/M games with pups your own age?"

"Yes, Sir, I have."

"Then why don't you go back to them and keep on playing games?"

"This is not a game to me, Sir. I can't get what I need from other beginners. I need this the way I need food or air to breathe. If I want sex, I know where to get it, Sir, but this is more than sex, it's...life."

"So it is, so it is," he mused, and then snapped, "Throw your shoulders back and suck that gut in." This threw her breasts out, but that no longer bothered him. She had a good body—young, solid, resilient. It was a body with staying power, he sensed. He wondered if it was true that women had a greater capacity to tolerate pain than men. God knows the serious masochist is as rare a commodity as the true sadist. Most bottoms just want some entertainment, like spoiled children who must always be the center of attention, who throw a tantrum if they can't have their favorite food or watch their favorite show. They would promise you anything to get you home, then chicken out before you even got warmed up and try to manipulate you into something demeaning that was closer to their real notion of sex. He called it being "whip-teased," and it made him as bitter as being cock-teased ever made a high school boy. If one of these phonies succeeded in talking you out of working them over, the next day they would call their friends and tell them you were really a pansy. If they failed (and got what they had consented to and were starving for), they would tell the same friends you were a maniac. Goddamn it, it would upset all the penguins and patent leather queens at the Brig if he showed up with this one in tow. What a monumental piece of blasphemy that would be! It would almost be worth it just to get the collective blood pressure to go up that high.

She saw a series of disillusioned, then mirthful, expressions cross his face, and waited, wondering what it was all about.

He had been a Master so long that he didn't even hesitate when he finally recognized what he was feeling. He was one of that handful of people who forge ahead without hesitation when they come to a fork in the road, so they always look as if they know where they are going. A proper approach had been made, and he was intrigued. This affair was at the cusp, and there was only one way to resolve it. He would begin by doing what she claimed to want and get more information. If it was a horror show, he could kick her out with a clean conscience, and no one would believe any tales she told out of school.

But she knew none of this. "Unbuckle that and put it on," he told her suddenly, pointing to his boot. She knelt at his feet and felt for his ankle. The sharp edges of the metal buckle bit into her hand as she drew the soft strip of leather out of it. Her head bowed as low as it could go without touching the floor, she fastened the collar around her own neck and waited, afraid that there was still some mistake, some misunderstanding, and he would put her out, excommunicate.

Then he stood and brought her head up against his hip, her face brushing the buttery softness of his leather, one side of her body ablaze, and his fingers showed her tongue where to run up and down the zipper, down the thigh; to be eager, but not to use her teeth, not to leave a mark on the smooth perfection of his armor. He slapped her away from his hip to see if she would come back, and she did, being careful to keep her mouth gentle. He rewarded her with another slap, and another from a different direction. There was no way to reach him through this barrage, but she kept trying, and his swift, punishing hands held her up with blows to the face. The side of her cheek that had been bruised was swelling, she could see the fat curve of it at the bottom of her field of vision. The edge of his hand clipped the lobe of her ear once, and she was glad she had taken out all of her earrings. That, too, would be swelling.

As it is below, so it is above. He showed her what making these small injuries had done to him, let her come close while he rolled a rubber cap-and-nipple down over his distended flesh. She was a little surprised; she didn't know any gay men who used condoms. But then it seemed appropriately old-fashioned, fastidious. Of course he would want to keep a barrier between them, even now. For a little while, he let her taste his sex, but it was not lapping that he wanted. He wanted her to accept the surging length of it, a spear in her throat, and when he was housed, he was urgent for the friction of her tongue and the suction of her cheeks and mouth. She understood that if he was to use his tools on her, the whips and clamps and ropes, the straight razor and the enema nozzle and the stock prod, he must also be able to use this tool, and she must learn to respect it and take it with the same dignity and skill that she would take torture or deprivation. If she could not please him with her squirming now, he would not care to see her squirm for whip or spur. So she swallowed him whole, completely penetrated, and showed him he could make use of her, that she was useful for this, not unwilling. Finally he drew away, but they both knew he could easily have obtained as much bliss as he liked from her mouth, and it was only his whim (not her failure) that made him seek consummation elsewhere.

"Strip."

This was not easy to do. For a moment, she was jolted out of this new and wonderful rapport between the two of them, back into the outside world, imagining the condemnation of others, imagining him critical of her body simply because it was female. But disobedience would cost her all her self-esteem, so she removed and folded and stacked her clothing. He approved, then showed her that he knew how to hold and constrain her, letting her enjoy the feel of his leather against her naked skin but permitting her no freedom. His still-hard cock glided, wet and suggestive, against her thighs, between her legs, and he turned her, bent her, the arm of the chair rough but solid underneath her belly and breasts. Her nipples were as hard as his cock, and anything that touched them only aroused her more.

The term "spanking" is far too cute to describe what happened next. This was not something that should happen to a child, although it made her feel like one, an abandoned and hated child. She realized he was causing her more pain with his hands than any whip she had put herself under. It was a more intimate kind of pain, there was no way to have a relationship with the pain apart from its source. She could not go away in her head and pretend this was self-inflicted or came from a machine. For one thing, she could not seem to predict what he would do. Or get used to any of it. His hands soothed, then smacked and stung; squeezed, then landed like a plane crash. He aroused her skin, sensitized it, then outraged it. She tried to guard against making herself vulnerable, but his touch would be so delicious, her hips would rise involuntarily, and then his stony hands would collide with her passion. She was so upset by her inability to deal with what was happening that it never occurred to her to take credit for not saying "uncle," for not begging him to stop.

His long fingers flattened and separated her ass cheeks, and she knew then that he would not spare her from any trial simply because she was a woman. If she was to belong to him, to come under his tutelage and wear his tokens, then she would do for him what any boy lucky enough to come home in his cuffs would do. Which included the round, slippery, thrusting head—the lubricant it pushed into her—the initial catch, then the smooth opening of her hole, no pain but complete possession, which was more difficult to tolerate, his pleasure building inside her discomfort, his pleasure turning her discomfort into heat, lust, need, pleasure. She could not move fast enough, hard enough, on him. There was not enough of him to take, even though there was too much, emptiness vying with demand until they met, fit, and worked at each other as if only one of them could survive it. Then he had her, his hands about her waist, and she was open to him, for him, telling him she was taking cock up the ass and loving it, had waited too long for it, could not wait any more—and came, and wailed as he fucked her during her pleasure, past it and after it, and came himself, alone, her body spread under him like a ruined city.

Without being told, she brought a napkin to clean him. But he was removing the condom, and apparently this was a private matter, because he kicked her in the ribs, then ignored her. She stayed where she had landed until he concealed his sex and fetched her back to his thighs and groin. Her face buried in his crotch, she could smell her own juices mingled with his cum and sweat.

"Was that what you came here for? Have you had enough?"

She shuddered. Was this shame or shamelessness? "No, Sir."

He took her by the collar and showed her where the dungeon was.

She would have been happy to be strung up in a doorway equipped with screw eyes or strapped down to a bed. She was used to ignoring beige carpets, drapes with floral patterns, harsh overhead lighting, and the fumbling of an overeager, would-be top who was even more of a novice than herself. For this Master, she would have been proud to simply bend over, put her palms on the floor, and hold that position through any ordeal that pleased him.

But Jamison had been a Master for a long time, blessed with a stable relationship with a man 10 years older than himself who put all their savings into real estate. Mike, Jamison's partner, had outlived all the members of his family who might have challenged his will and thus left Jamison the sole owner of everything they had worked to accumulate together. He had lived in this house for 10 years and had the time and the money to make sure it provided for all of his needs.

There was a hallway that ran from the living room to the other end of the house. He stopped (stiffening his arm so she did not bump into him) and kicked aside a throw rug. One of the dogs, a male weimaraner with oversize puppy feet, came out of the kitchen and happily dragged it away. Jamison pointed to the floor.

"Open it," he said.

It was a trap door, and looked massive. But she put both hands through the big ring and pulled. It was hung with a counterweight, like a garage door. She went down the stairs, and he swung it shut over their heads. The door locked from the inside, but she was too caught up in the contents of the dungeon to notice how the hidden mechanism operated.

The walls were painted in glossy black enamel. The ceiling was covered with Mylar. It was a big room, containing at least four separate massive pieces of abusive furniture, but each area could be cordoned off by lightweight Mylar screens.

Music was coming from the far side of the dungeon, and she did not even realize the sound was drawing her to walk through the room. Lights also came up—indirect, subdued. The heat had been on for a while, since he changed into his leathers, so the temperature was quite comfortable. There were other lights he did not choose to turn on now—floodlights, focused to beat on the prisoner at any of the available interrogation stations. He did not want to dazzle or terrorize her now, just lure her, let her be a tourist for a bit.

She passed a set of shelves full of leather straps ornamented with buckles and D-rings. He called to her then and told her to find her size. She realized there were many, many sets of wrist and ankle cuffs, arranged from largest to smallest. She tried the smallest set of wrist cuffs first, kneeling to put them on. They were too snug, but the smallest ankle cuffs fit. When she had buckled herself in, he came to her, checked the fit with an index finger, and nodded approval.

From a pegboard on the wall he took down a weight lifter's belt and cinched it up around her waist. He fastened the wrist cuffs behind her back to rings on the belt. Then he used a handful of leather strips to make a body harness. After one fruitless attempt to bind her small breasts, he gave it up and just ran the leather crisscrossed about her torso.

Next to the shelves was a long row of boots, most of them black, most of them knee-high. Here he hesitated. It was his custom to keep the M in boots, because he liked the look of it and because boots were essential if he wanted to hang someone upside down. But he knew that none of these were going to fit her, and the idea of having her tromp and flop around in ill-fitting boots was ludicrous. She had been wearing boots upstairs, hadn't she? He couldn't remember, and anyway, it would ruin the whole thing for him to go upstairs or send her back to fetch them. Tomorrow they would take care of that detail. He put his hand on the back of her neck instead, shook her a little, and said, "Don't drool. You'll get to spend plenty of time with those. Later."

He took her to the most stressful (and simplest) areas of the dungeon, released her hands, and fastened them together again, this time in front of her body. A winch lifted them into the air. He knelt to fasten a spreader bar to the ankle cuffs. He explained that he enjoyed this act, kneeling to prepare the victim. It was the recognition due to the scapegoat, the perfect one singled out for sacrifice.

She did not need to fear being imperfect. Mistakes would not be allowed. Men, he remarked, felt incredibly vulnerable when you forced their thighs apart. He expected it felt a bit different when your genitals weren't dangling in midair, though she was (he determined by slapping it with his open palm) quite sensitive there. And her thighs seemed to spread farther, more easily, than a man's. Well, that was convenient, and he told her so.

Then he left her alone to begin that struggle with the position that makes standing bondage a little bit of hell. Having your arms fully extended above your head is more stressful than it looks. You have to learn to obtain relief by changing the nature of your discomfort. You can lean on the restraints, try to hang from the chains. Then you can take your own weight, insist that reluctant, strained muscles come into play. You twist your wrists in the cuffs, which have crept up around the tender bones at the base of the hands. You try to thrust your hands still higher into the air to ease this compression. You turn your head, hold it to one side, to make one shoulder stop aching and the other shoulder ache more. You center your head over your spine to distribute the pain evenly. With feet apart, you have fewer options. Fewer ways to twist in the wind. Still, you work at it. You have no choice. You can't release yourself. And you are constantly being reminded, by twinges and cramps, that being restrained does not give you permission to be passive. Good bondage gives the bottom a job to do.

Jamison was sorting through some of his whips. At first he picked eight or nine of them, ranging from sensual to severe. But the sight of them all, bundled up in his arms, made him lose patience. He hung them all back up and kept only the braided cat. If she could appreciate that sonnet, by God, he would let her heel him anywhere, and make any dumbass who questioned her right to be there eat his slurs.

Still, he began gently. He moved screens around them, to close in the space and create a feeling of security and to let her watch. For the longest time, he spun the whip and watched the tails barely touch her. She had very little latitude for motion, but it seemed to him that she was bowing under the whip, pushing as much of her body as she could back at him. Like an honest soul, she admitted as much as soon as he asked. And so he brought the whip closer, so she could feel the speed of the circles he was making, but he kept the contact light enough to glance across the skin. He was stroking her. Still, this hurt enough to make some men stamp and whinny. Although she clearly felt it, she was not acting like a restless pony. The skin between her neck and the kidney belt, the belt and her knees, was scarlet, and still she had not made a sound louder than heavy breathing. So he struck her once quite hard, and she screamed. The sound startled him. Then he remembered that of course her voice was higher. He made her scream a few more times to accustom himself to the pitch and timbre and filed it away for future reference. This was not the sound of panic, this was not rejection—this was the breaking-in noise, the kind of sound he would get out of her before the turning point. The turning point was that moment when panic and stage fright disappeared and the pain became a different kind of pleasure, something you could crave and ask for even if you still hated it.

All this he told her, wanting both of them to understand what they were about. He could have sworn her ears pricked back like a cat's, to catch everything he said. Every precious word. This was very nearly a tabula rasa he wrote upon. But the back was the surface he wanted to make his mark upon, the shoulders, where the bone and the nerves had no protection except muscle. So he labored there until the sounds she made came down an octave and began to resemble a bellow more than a scream.

"Can't take it?" he asked, polite, sardonic.

"Sir, I feel it, but I can take it. It's not a problem."

She was laughing at him! He got serious; covered her body with a series of deep, quick, stunning blows. He told her how to make it stop. She said, "Please, Sir, don't stop. By your leave, Sir."

Perhaps he did his worst then. It's hard to say. After a whipping was over, he always felt he could have wrung another increment of pain from his subject if he had achieved just a bit more rapport with the whip and the laws of physics. There was blood, though, and that was reassuring. Blood meant you had done your best—and more than that, the bottom man had done his best. This, at the end of the chain he was paying out, was not a man. If he had forgotten, kneeling to undo the leg-spreader would have reminded him. But he had himself a live one. Not a whip-tease, no, Sir, by your leave, Sir.

"You're a goddamn masochist," he said fondly, but she had passed out with her head on his boots. What wasn't purple on her back and butt was black or red. The lilac stalks of blooming bruises were crisscrossed with thin stripes of blood. It was gorgeous. He rolled her over, took off his glove so he could feel her breath on his palm, and stroked her face.

What Comes of Wanting, or,
Why I Write What I Write
By R.J. March

I'm not sure what it was that prompted me to write erotica. I wouldn't exactly call it a calling per se, although I've always felt the need to write, have always found a certain sense of solace through writing, not to mention grace and liberation and bitter frustration and, though not very often, a small sense of achievement.

I was born and raised near Syracuse, N.Y., and grew up living down the street from Oneida Lake, which figures in many of my stories, the lake being something of a hotbed of desire and a locus of sexuality for me—I don't know how it figured for the rest of my boyhood friends. By the time I was 12, I had a pretty good feel for my sexual identity. It came to me in a dream in which I had all the neighborhood fathers tied naked to birch trees. It came to me with the strange attraction I felt for my father (but one could trace back my male attraction even earlier, to the fascination I had with a favorite uncle's bare feet). It was hard at that age, knowing but not telling. Because it made everything I did feel furtive and dirty and therefore all the more exciting. I knew that I was different the sum-mer before sixth grade started, when my sexual experimentation with the boys of my youth became less experimental and turned into something more like a search for something—no, a search for some*one*—to make sense of the goofy morass I found myself stuck in, someone who was sharing the same odd libidinous sensations that come with puberty and are, at least in my case, intensified by the wrongness one feels seeing his father in a towel-wrap or his uncle stepping into white briefs or his cousin, already covered with hair like a man, T-shirt lifted, showing his new furry belly. Dirty snapshots, like that of my father in a bra, a picture I used to masturbate with, small moments of intimacy that bother me to this day and work their way into the fiction I find myself writing.

Not a calling, no. But maybe a need. Maybe I *need* to do this. Like maybe the way some people *need* to shoplift.

✍

I had not loved a married man when I wrote "Tension." Unless you're counting my father. I had not had an intimate relationship with a married man at the time, unless you're counting the chance encounters I had with some at video arcades. I hadn't *loved* a married man until it came time to choose a story for this anthology. At that point, I was having an affair with one.

I hadn't known at first that he was married at all. In fact, he'd given me a phony name from the start. I'd said sure, because it's always bullshit, what they'll tell you once they've come and are zipping up and looking for something to wipe their hands on. I learned his real name maybe a month later, after that first—actually, second—time together and that he was married about a month after that. But, even double-tricked like that, I could not stop it. And so I found myself, like the protagonist of my story, enthralled and helpless, waiting for calls from roadside phone booths and the twice-a-month stays in town that seemed to quickly dwindle once we decided, once and for all, that we were in love with one another.

This story doesn't end much better than "Tension." I ended up the way I started out, which was alone, so maybe I lost less than the narrator of my story, whose wife left him. But then, my Kevin—actually, *not* my Kevin—was always kind and decent and, I always thought, confounded by what he felt for me and surprised when I ended the relationship and also relieved, I think, to be rid of someone who wanted so much from someone with so little to give and so much to give up, whereas the character Ford is calculating and dismissive and bordering on evil—a nasty but excellent fuck.

But what sad stories, I'm thinking now, "Tension" *and* my own—the "nothing there" at the end. And I ask myself, like the nameless character in my story, What *does* happen to tension?

✍

I can't look at married men the same way anymore. I still find myself attracted to them, to the ring and their blandness. They seem so settled and agitated, preoccupied with the stuff that husbands and fathers are concerned about—but what is that? I can only guess. Mortgages. Boats. The lawn. Orthodontics. Eighteen-year-old girls. The man stepping up beside him at the urinals. College football. Receding hairlines. The quickest way from here to there. His mid-section. The stock market.

I was at the mall yesterday to buy a watch battery, and I saw some-one's husband sitting by himself at one of those sitting places, eating something iced, and I saw his ring and the hair of him rising up out from under the collar of his oatmeal-striped shirt, and I could not *not* think about Kevin. And I couldn't not think of him without a flash of anger, which was transferred to this poor guy sitting there spooning an iced cappuccino into his mouth. *Fuck you and your stupid wife,* I thought, irrationally, pathetically. One of the things I have become painfully aware of is that there are an inordinate amount of married couples. You can't swing a dead cat around and not hit two or three Mr. and Mrs's. They're everywhere, I swear to God.

✍

I'm not always thinking about sex when I write erotica. I think first about a situation: Boy Meets Boy. Better put: Boy *needs* to Meet Boy. And then I think, Well, who is this boy? What does he look like? What is he wearing? Does he have long sideburns? What kind of music does he listen to? When did the Abercrombie & Fitch ads start bothering him? And then maybe I'll wonder about what turns him on. (Usually what turns on my protagonists will turn me on too, which is limiting, sure, but makes, I think, for a more intense read. I'll never forget how daunted and disinterested I was when an editor asked me to write a "leather story," the end result only remotely having anything to do with the fetish.) Eventually I have no choice but to think about sex, but I've often found myself on page 6 or 7 without a single ejaculation, and, as my favorite editor, Fred Goss, once said, "That's not exactly what we're shooting for here, Bobby."

Everything's a story for me, or fodder for a story—everything gets pulled in and recycled. For instance: Kevin's oddly—badly—circumcised penis is attached not uncoincidentally to a character named Kevin in a story called "Killian or Welch"; my father's bare back is featured in more than one story; and in "Tension," the skunks of Saratoga Springs, N.Y., where I spent two weeks at a writers workshop, the sparkled ceiling of a New Hampshire motel I once stayed in, and the lilac bushes of my childhood neighbor's backyard. I find inspiration in Martha Stewart, Abercrombie & Fitch, David Hockney, razor blade commercials, and Howie Long. I was driving to work once and saw three boys packed tightly in the cab of a scabrous pickup, one of them asleep. Who were they? Contractors? Landscapers? Ruffians? Who knows? It was intimate and masculine and highly charged and stuck like a thorn in my imagination. I've used that image again and again—three boys tightly packed. I cannot help but wonder about the smell inside that cab, the pressure the one in the middle received from either side, what the sleeping one dreamed, if anything at all, what song was playing on the radio, and who, if not all them, worried about the early-morning erections he suffered, trapped like that with the two loves of his life.

✍

I write erotica because it's all there for me, waiting. Because I am haunted by boys at the gym with their shirtsleeves shorn off, their slim sides bared; because I am haunted by an image of my father, helpless once, his collarbone broken, asking me in his bath to please wash his back; because I cannot stop myself from thinking about the hair on the backs of Kevin's hands.

Sometimes it's like playing with ghosts. Sometimes it's just like that.

By R.J. March

Ford touched me, put his hand on my shoulder. "You're all right now," he said, his fingers coming to rest on my clavicle. We're at the door still, the screen door, looking out at the black nothing, his dark front yard. Ford's wife laughs at something Connie said. We can hear them both laughing in the kitchen.

His hand comes off me and he pushes the screen door open. It was his idea to go for a walk. "Oh, no," Diane said, "nothing doing. Skunks everywhere," she said, turning to Connie, "and Lloyd got sprayed last week." Lloyd's tail beat on the floor, his eyes on his leash hanging on a nail by the stove. "We're staying put, aren't we, baby?" Diane said, putting her bare feet on the blond lab's side, making his ears dance, his head rolling on the kitchen floor.

I step out of the house. The air is heavy, doesn't move. There's a porch that runs the front of the house with rockers and ferns, a swing. Ford steps around me, his arm brushing my side. He's whistling. I follow him down the short stairs, my eyes adjusting to the night, making out the darker edges of bushes, of trees, the sudden light of blooming borders.

Once we're down the road, out of sight of the house, Ford stops us. He finds my hand and puts it on his chest so that I can feel his heart's panicked gallop. I can see his smile, how it comes and goes and comes back again. He doesn't let go of my hand but lowers it to his crotch, to the hard jut his penis makes and its wetness. I get my hand back and pocket it, my fingers curling around my own cock, its swelling just beginning.

"It's been like that half the night," he says, as though I hadn't noticed. I don't say anything now. There is the noise crickets make, loud and mechanical, and the odd feeling I have that someone is watching us, and I start walking, turning my back to him recklessly, a man with a gun. I can hear him laughing. He lets me get away, gives me a good head start. I'm walking as though I live here or have been here before, as if I have a destination in mind. I stop on the dirt road and wait for him to catch up. A close section of crickets go silent. I can see him in the distance, in the night light that makes everything blue. He doesn't look so tall to me now, not the way he did in the kitchen, standing over me, and not the way he did at the door, his hand on my shoulder, reminding me of my father.

Long-armed, he embraces me. "You're all right," he says, his mouth next to my ear. He leans onto me, hanging from my shoulders, his face suddenly closer to mine than I'm comfortable with, but there's no pulling away now.

"Why do you keep saying that?" I ask him, turning my head. To my right there's a wall of trees, tall firs, rowed like corn. Connie and I grew corn this year in our backyard—stalks grew tall, yielding nothing. "It's a metaphor," Connie said. "It's a simile," I countered. We were drinking beers; she tasted hers. "It's a semaphore," she said finally.

"Because you are all right," Ford says, his arms roping mine to my sides, pinning me.

"Connie," I say.

"And my wife," he adds, conjuring something. His fingers under my shirt tail. The smell he has. I squirm away anyway, and he lets me. "Come back," he says.

✍

He calls me at my studio. "It's Ford," he says. I pin the receiver to my shoulder and wipe my hands on a towel, ruining it.

Connie has invited them to dinner. She loves Diane, finds Ford "amusing." Ford has wild eyebrows; he's cocky. "And you can see his dick in his pants," Connie said. "Why is that?"

I shrugged, sipping some wine, feeling caught in some bad act.

"Because he wants you to, that's why," she said, pointing at me with a spatula.

Ford, on the phone, breathes so I know he's there. "I'm at the Fremont," he says. "You know where that is?"

It's around the corner. It's the kind of motel dead bodies are discovered in. "Yeah," I tell him. I am folding up the towel and hiding it in the vanity. He tells me his room number, tells me to pick up some beer.

"I can't," I say.

"The beer or come?" he asks.

"Both," I say.

"Sure you can," he says. He wants to watch me undress, wants to see me walk across the room, naked. "I won't touch you," he says. "I just want to see you."

"I'm not like that," I tell him.

"I don't have time for this," he says.

Silence settles between us.

"You're making this more difficult than it has to be," he says. He says, "Your hand is on your dick now, thinking about it." He's wrong, but I say, "Yes, yes, it is."

I say to him, "You could come here," looking at my painting the way I look at my own reflection, trying not to hate it. "No, not here," I say, changing my mind.

"I'm waiting," he says.

&

I like it, being watched. He sits in a chair, long legs crossed, his chin in his hand. He wears khakis, a heavy silver bracelet, another denim shirt, this one newer, darker, indigo. I take off my shirt first because I went to the gym today and my chest is heavy, feels massive. My nipples are soft and brown, their areolae very wide, spreading drops of milky chocolate. He watches me like a play—it's theater to me, his observation. I fold my shirt carefully and put it on the bed. "Not there," he says, shaking his head: bad luck. I put it on the bureau behind me, wondering if anyone ever stays here long enough to unpack any clothes, wondering if anyone comes here with a suitcase to unpack at all. I touch my belt buckle but decide to take off my shoes instead. I touch the wall to steady myself on one foot. The wallpaper is flocked, rococo, avocado-ish. It moves under my greasy palm; I feel it even after I take my hand away to pull off my socks.

"That's fine for now," Ford says. He scratches his head. "Do you have the opportunity to do this sort of thing often?"

I feel my face redden.

"You work out," he says, his face blank, unappreciative.

I feel like an applicant, and I feel as though the interview's not going very well.

His eyes wander; they leave my face and come back to it. I see there's paint on my wrist that I missed. He combs his hair with his fingers, squinting.

I don't ask myself what am I doing here. I don't ask myself why I am doing this. I ask myself: Should I take off my pants now?

"This is my favorite thing in porno movies, and it's so often skipped or cut out or whatever," he says, animated, sitting up in his chair. I'm undoing my belt. "It's the unveiling and the softness, the beginning of arousal. The type and brand of underwear, the first sight of pubic hair, the damp package."

White briefs, major-labeled. All my hair is below my waist, a shocking mat of black hairs. I look as though I am wearing uncommonly white (and completely brand-new) underpants over furry tights.

He tells me where to stand. He wants a three-quarter shot, some of the ass, most of the crotch. He frowns, and I tell him I can't get undressed without it happening.

"Every time?" he asks.

I nod.

"When you're alone?"

"It goes away fast," I tell him, but it doesn't.

The light coming through the turquoise curtains is hip, and I feel good. When I go down a bit, I start the slow push of the waistband, the unveiling. My dick wobbles and swells; my balls drop in their sac; the hairs on my legs stand up. I bend over, thick-thighed, to retrieve my briefs, tossing them to Ford, who catches them deftly. My cock is upwardly arching, stiff and quivering. It creates its own tension.

I am not what he imagined. Better? Worse? He doesn't say, just not what he'd imagined. "In clothes you almost seem slight," he says. "It's the way you move, I think. Walk around my chair now, please."

Halfway around he stops me, has me bend over to touch my toes. Blood rushes to my head and stays there. He comes up behind me on his knees. He sniffs out my asshole, and I feel the hard, wet glide of his tongue. He sucks the wrinkled lips, my tight purse. He gets in, his tongue erect, he gets it in me and moves it around, and I squat for him, wanting more. It's what I'd always wanted. I reach around and clasp his head, locking him in, his nose bent against my coccyx. It's a black forest he's in down there. His fingers dig into my muscled cheeks, drag down my thighs. He goes between them and grabs my dick.

His tongue inside me, his hand stroking my cock, I moan a little and surprise him with my sudden spill of semen. He shakes it off his hand and I apologize. I am not sorry, though—I am relieved.

I straighten and feel dizzy. He has his dick out, still on his knees. It is fat and fills his hand. He holds half of it, jerks it, sliding the thick cowl of skin, baring and concealing the shining red-colored head. I reach inside his shirt, fumbling for his nipples, thinking he might like that. I find them encircled with long and wiry hairs, hard dots of flesh that roll in my pinch. He opens his mouth, looking up at me. He says my name. It's like a movie. He squirts my shins with his warm spray. "There," he says, out of breath.

✍

The phone rings, and Connie answers it. "Hello," I hear her say, "hello?" She makes a face hanging up. "Again?" I ask, and she nods.

✍

The next time I see Ford, he picks me up at the studio. I ask him in, but he's not interested in my paintings. "Not right now, anyway," he says. He takes me to a restaurant. We drive around behind it, parking there. It's a cool day, temperate and sunny, but we roll up the windows to keep out the stench of the Dumpsters.

"Blow me," he says. It's almost a request. He sits there, waiting for it. I look around us. Black birds fly in and out of the Dumpsters, and even with the windows closed, I can still smell the mixed stench of cooked and rotting foods. Where's the romance, I'm wondering, but my dick is set concrete in my jeans, and his is high and hard too. I've been seeing it, what I remember of it, in my dreams. I unzip his fly carefully, glancing again and again at the windshield, through it to the restaurant's back door. There are two black handprints on it, wide-spaced and high. He's wearing blue boxers, a beautiful blue, darkened in spots from leaking. I maneuver the hardened pole through the two flies. His cock is huge, huger than in my dreams, and is a muddy red, reminding me of a movie I'd seen of Brazilian men. His cock is Brazilian, with a curling, pouting foreskin. I grip the hot shaft and push my fist down to his pubes, exposing the slicked head, squeezing out another gush of precome. I look at the door again.

"Just do it," he says. I drop to my elbow, my face inches from his fat prong. It pulses in my hand. I lick the rubbery head, its sticky emissions. He plays with the hairs on the back of my neck, tells me to get a hair cut. He fills my mouth with cock. I swallow it back and make my lips firm against the smooth shaft. He's going into me sideways, at an angle, and his dick has no give to it, it butts the roof of my mouth, knocking the soft nasally tissue in back, and every once in a while he lets loose a sweet little flow that tastes better than anything I know.

He talks to me, calling me names. I can't believe what he says to me. He makes me moan on the pole, my spit puddling in the little concavity just above the base of his prick. I push hard on the front of my jeans and moan some more. I twist my head and get him down my throat, wanting to impress him. My jaw aches. He pumps his hips, holding my head against the steering wheel. He rises up off the seat a few inches and he fucks my mouth and comes heavily and deep, coating my throat. "Don't move," he says, and I hear the restaurant door open and Spanish. Ford's dick softens in stages on my tongue. He starts the engine and puts the truck in gear. "You can get up now," he says.

He looks at me, stopped at a light, a smile on his lips. His fly is still open and his dick lies in a soft curl on the shining teeth. "Wipe your mouth," he says gently.

At home, I slip into Connie, who is finger-readied, not surprised. She fakes an orgasm to goad me into coming more quickly: There's a capon in the oven. My lips smear against her tightened throat, and I squeeze my eyes shut. I feel the give of her body, its giving up, and I say his name in my head, thrusting fast, thrusting hard, coming inside her, inside a condom.

"You didn't have to do that," she said afterward, staring at the ceiling. "It's bad enough. Don't think about him too."

✍

He doesn't like my studio. "It's the smell," he says, but I think it's my paintings he doesn't like. We meet at the Fremont. He says he wants my ass.

I have to draw the line somewhere—I've drawn it there. I tell him no, and he's quiet for a while, but his hand stays sandwiched in my ass crack.

He calls me at home. He used to hang up when Connie answered— now he just stays silent, and Connie, her voice sounding impossibly bored, calls me to the phone. He usually hasn't anything to say: "I was just thinking about you"; "I wanted to tell you good night"; or, breathless: "I'm coming now."

What happens to tension? How long can it last? I think of guitar strings and how they fall out of tune, losing their fine adjustments. I think of a canvas tightly stretched going to slackness. Inevitable. Slack or snap, there's no maintaining it.

✍

"I want to fuck you."

I shake my head. I've fucked him. I fuck him all the time. "Do this for me," he says. He caresses my behind. "Fair is fair," he says.

"Fair is not fair." The room is damp, smells off. He's coaxed me into hardness with his mouth. His fingers play in the fuzz of my butt crack. He moves my balls to get at my hole.

The last time I fucked him was in the men's room of a diner on our way to Watertown to meet up with Diane and Connie. We locked ourselves in and Ford dropped his pants. He put his hands on the wall over the urinal and spread his legs as far as his pants would allow. I lifted his shirttail, his ass grown over with hair. I licked a finger and got it in him, his hot insides. He passed back a rubber. He shook his head at two fingers, tightening up on them, whispering, "Screw me." I unzipped my fly. I petted his ass cheeks with my cock. I pinched its head and smeared the wetness across his puckered cunt. I put the condom in my pocket.

He says, going between my legs, that he has to have me. His cock knocks my balls, wetting them. His mouth on my mouth, slides to my ear, and he whispers. I don't want to give in, but I've given in already. I wrap my legs around his waist, and he gives me a look. It's the last thing, last step, the final line, and I'm afraid. I stare at the ceiling and notice its glittered stucco for the first time.

"Nobody's ever?" he asks, trying not to smile.

He has me roll over, and I feel his nose and then his hot tongue flicking the hair patch around my hole. "We'll shave this sometime," he says. "Spread your legs."

He lies over me, his cock rutted between my glutes. He licks my back, maneuvering his hips, taking aim and missing. He does this again and again, slipping and sliding in all the spit he left down there for himself until he hits his mark, and I curse his hugeness. "Poor baby," he whispers.

He eases himself in to the balls, me gasping all the way. Filled to bursting, my innards rearranging themselves in accommodation. He breathes in my hair, licks, then bites, my left ear. He gets his hands underneath me to pull hard on my nipples, hurting me, but I like it and he knows it, and I think he thinks he owns me now.

"Harder," I tell him, my teeth unclenching. I push my face into the pillow where it's easier to breathe, the air filtered and warm and musty. He pulls his cock out and it feels miles long—he stabs it back in. He fucks me fast, filling me up. I lift my head and his fingers circle my throat. My dick rasps against the stiff sheets. He turns us on our sides, slamming deep. I get a hand on my cock and pull on it roughly because he's riding a spot that has me panting and barking. He stops us, laughing and telling me to quiet down. He gets back inside, barely moving, playing with my balls, petting the inside of my thighs.

"You're my wife now," he says. "You know that, don't you; you're my Mrs." He thrusts to make his point.

"Fuck you," I say. I roll my head back. He fingers my tits. I move my ass against him, penetrated; I do the work myself. He holds my hands up over my head. I fuck myself on him, slowly, deliberately. I hear my pulse and nothing else. He sticks three fingers in my mouth, going for the back of my throat, pulling me on top of him. I pump him, my heels dug into the mattress. He stops breathing and I know he's about to come, and I reach for my cock to join him. He grunts and shakes under me, says, "Oh," grabbing handfuls of sheet, lifting his hips to slam my ass, reaming me until I finally come.

✍

Connie leaves. "I thought it was going to be harder," she says at the door. She looks at me, into me. Whatever she sees makes her blink. She picks up a potted plant, holds it like a child on her hip. I can't think of anything to say to her. I feel like a broken bowstring, useless. She slips past me, and I can smell her smell.

✍

Ford stops calling, so I call him. He doesn't want me anymore, but I can't make myself not want him. I feel as though I've stepped into his shadow. I call and Diane always answers. "At the mall," she says, or "Gone to the movies." Or: "Out for a walk."

The last time I see Ford, he looks through me. "What is it?" I ask. "What's going on?"

"Going on?" he says, looking amused.

I touch his shirt. "Diane," he says, looking up at the house.

"You know she's not home," I say. I was just there. I reach into the truck and undo a button, another button. I touch the dip between his pecs. I go down farther.

He wishes I wouldn't, he says, but I lean through the window and open his pants. I pull out his prick. He sighs, seeing me, it seems, for the first time. He says my name and I don't like it, the way he says it. He shakes his head slowly.

"Fuck me," I tell him, his cock twitching in my hand. I pinch the end, the slack skin. He shakes his head again, smiling, opening the door slowly, waiting for me to step back. He walks up to the house but doesn't go up the steps. Instead, he walks around to the side. He looks back at me. "Come on," he says, holding his pants closed.

Behind a trio of lilac bushes, beside an old water pump, he takes off his shirt, lets his pants fall to his ankles. His cock is engorged, engaged, jutting heavily from his groin. I take it in my hand and go to my knees, getting him in my mouth. I slip my tongue into the taut skin sleeve and tickle the sensitive head.

The sun catches us. His pubic hair shines like gloss. I heft his balls, squeezing them hard. "Tell me you love me," I say, my lips on his cock tip, blackmailing.

"Don't be ridiculous," he replies, touching the side of my face, pushing his cock into my mouth again.

I suck him hard, lips riding his shaft, tongue concentrating on the rosy split head, swirling and teasing.

He pushes me off: "Enough." He spits onto his palm to grease his prick, and I take down my pants. He positions himself behind me and stabs into me.

"Christ," I say sharply, and he humps himself into my burning hole, holding my hips, daggering me.

"You're mine," I hear him say, "and I don't even want you."

He fucks me so hard I lose my stance. My arms buckle, my face hits the ground, the dirt smells reminding me of the ease of being a boy. He slaps my ass, jockeying me, pulling all the way out to my relief, only to slam back in. I push my prick backward to meet his swinging balls.

"This is the last time," he says, breaking. "Last time." His thrusts slow, become deliberate, less wild. He's there, he's there, and I'm with him and it's crazy, we're so like animals, like lions. He pulls out and hobbles up to my face, pulling it up, and I smell my ass on him and I taste it and then there's this flood of come.

"You were always mine," he says, and I swallow it all.

The house is big, too big. I wander from room to room. The phone doesn't ring. Upstairs, you can hear the clock tick in the kitchen downstairs.

I stand at the front door, looking out. I thought I heard a car. There's nothing there.

By Shar Rednour

"They saw her"—I paused for effect, leaving my mouth open, holding my next word hostage, turning my gaze on each member of our illicit club, until I saw in the eyes of each one that I held them completely captive—"titties bulging against her open-necked shirt. They got so excited they ripped it right off of her!"

"What happened next?" Eldon shrieked. We sat sandwiched between shrubs and a fence, separated from the rest, the regular ones.

I turned to face the slight boy mascot we girls had adopted as the other boys played only feet away, and I dramatically stared into his eyes, telepathically trying to control even his emotions. "I will tell you tomorrow. You must keep the story secret. If I find out that anyone tells, I will never, ever tell you even one more word of it."

Marisa said, "You can tell more now. Recess isn't over."

Tanya, my best friend, was leaning back against the fence all nonchalant. She was kind of my right arm. A supercute femme tomboy with blond hair and a tan. "She's not telling any more, so get out of here before the teacher notices." You could almost see the cigarette nine years before it would be attached to her fingers.

"You're not her boss."

"Marisa…" Was all I had to say and the 6-year-olds scampered.

Tanya and I coolly climbed out and joined the rest on the playground after we waited long enough to create a dramatic tension as they wondered if would we make it out before the whistle blew.

✍

I definitely did not register on a conscious level those days on the playground how much I loved the power I felt delivering others' desires to them on my silver-tongued platter. But I do know how I felt, and now that I'm older I can better understand those feelings. I'll admit I luxuriated in the power itself. I couldn't run fast, I wasn't the pretty girl, I wasn't the smartest, but I knew how to capture people with humor and drama. I've always been able to tell a tale and pull out a hearty laugh, a shocked gasp, or a painful tear— depending on my mood or my audience's. I also liked that I was good at something. I liked that my listeners were captivated and enjoying themselves. How could I not feel proud of the skills that transformed others' worlds?

My first stories to a gathered audience were "dirty" tales to those kids on the playground in first grade. Soon I branched out to include scary stories and, mostly, funny stories. I'm instructed by the esteemed master of this collection, though, to tell why I write erotic content—dirty tales.

I could elaborate on different angles that I know will titillate you the reader, but a large part of writing for me is no different than the funny stories I would act out to girl-jocks in high school gym class. We had an arrangement: They caught the ball in exchange for me making them laugh. Which, to a wimp like me, translates directly into they saved me from the brain explosion that would have resulted from the impact of a speeding softball. In exchange for saving my life, I stood beside them working out my material, only ever momentarily interrupted at the times I screamed, covered my head, and hit the ground.

And, like those who've seen me perform have heard me say, if I had my druthers, if I could make a living and reach enough people, I wouldn't write a word of it down. I would simply sit or stand next to willing listeners and tell a tale. It's really what I'm best at. Some writers stumble through readings required by their publishers. I'm the opposite; my material comes to life when I read it aloud. I like the audience. I work best with the interchange. I can feel when their interest perks and when it's waning, when I have to turn a curve and draw them in again. Sex is the best for that. Nothing like saying "Cunt pussy dyke dick" into a microphone to capture attention.

I have also been motivated by telling the truth, the *whole* truth, of what I know of my own fantasies and those of others close to me. When I tell a tale and I get to the sexual nitty-gritty, I don't back off. I go into it thinking, *You know what's in your head, Shar, don't back off. Don't be afraid to tell it like it is.* Sure, it would be easy to gloss over the details that would explode a reader's sensual synapses if she (or he) were really doing whatever it is I'm describing in a given story. That's what Hollywood does, right? But I tell it how I see it, wholly hoping you see it too.

Have you ever watched a movie where the lead characters have sex, fall in love way too fast (maybe reverse that order), and then go off to live extreme adventures like killing people or robbing banks, but you can't enjoy it because you're stuck on the opening act thinking, *Would I fall in love with a stranger in one day and then take incredible, life-threatening risks with this person I barely know?* OK, so that's what I get stuck on whether you do or not. But actually, when people have great sex they do fall in love way too fast. And then do extreme things because of that concentrated connection we call *sex*. Little else can connect humans so intensely, quickly, and intimately.

So many more movies would be believable if the screenwriters and the actors could convince us of that moment, that exchange, that electricity. I'm not saying I always succeed in doing this when I tell a story, but I try. I try to deliver that intense moment, the moment of no return when a character's soul is signed, sealed, and delivered via fist, cunt, and kissing that rips off her face and leaves her insides bare.

It was by that grade school playground fence that I learned the power of a juicy story. It works like this:

(1) People are afraid to do and say what they desire. (I don't use "what they desire" as a euphemism for who they want to fuck; I mean desire regarding anything: whatever a person wants to wear, the music he or she wants to listen to, the way an individual wants to pass time.)

(2) People who actually do what they desire are viewed as either eccentric, crazy, perverted, or courageous. Sometimes all of the above.

(3) If you do something perceived as eccentric, crazy, perverted, or courageous, especially if you put a little magical spin on it, then…

(4) You are viewed as powerful.

(5) People thinking of you as powerful makes you feel powerful. And then you *are* powerful.

As a storyteller, you see the desire you create in people's eyes and you want to somehow make them feel like they are living it. In *American Movie,* the documentary about aspiring filmmaker Mark Borchardt, Borchardt speaks about friends outside his door who want to help with his movie but need instruction: "Those people out there, I wanna give them destinies." Such a powerful statement. Borchardt meant that he wanted to put them on a path to great things, to open their doors to a fate that's historic and marks their future. I understood him well as a fellow person who got out of a small town and brought as many people as I could along with me. I helped get them out too so they could dust off their knees and get on the road to their destinies.

I think of a twist on Borchardt's words: "Those people out there, I want to give them *desires.*" Actually, I want to open the door that keeps them from their desires; I want to let their desires grow and expand into a brilliant sexual, spiritual extravaganza. Sure, many people who read my stories and books are sexually savvy folks simply looking for entertainment—and that's good enough for me. But there's nothing more exciting to me as a storyteller than the person who's just a babe in the garden waiting for spring, not knowing the extent of the explosion that will happen around her. And who, upon hearing or reading my words, is transformed for the rest of her life.

By Shar Rednour

Why I was there wasn't so important as just trying to keep my stomach down over the fact that I was. I couldn't help where my parents raised me, after all. I would get out. I would definitely get out. Patience is a virtue, and good things come to those who wait. I chanted these sayings any moment my head would empty and I'd start to freak.

So most anyone from the outside was at the least intoxicating to me.

Maybe it was the sprouting dreads with the close-shaven sides above her ears. Back then I'd never seen anything like it. (My hair was the opposite—long, silky-straight, and blond.) It wasn't that she wore a leather jacket but that it was a *worn* leather jacket from a *secondhand store* in *London*. I have to say, that alone could have made me come.

How did her family end up in Idaville? I wouldn't hazard a guess, but Idaville was like that, ya know. There was my sophomore year when Leda Hudson was my friend; she was from California, and she'd had blue hair there. She'd been sent to live with her grandparents in Idaville to clean up, but instead she got pregnant and I had to drive her to a neighboring state to get an abortion. That same year Brad Paganelli came to town from Flushing, N.Y. He was 23 and going to the community college—same sort of story as Leda's, but he'd done it on his accord. He knew how to fence and had a real sparring practice sword and went back to New York to go to acting school after he dried out. The next year Claudia Aguilar Garcia was an exchange student from Puerto Nuevo. She gave me a square finger ring with rhinestones across the top and told me, "How much I love you, you know. You are my special friend." I cried for weeks over her leaving and she did too. So even though you might ask what she, Gin, was doing in Idaville, all I can say is that kind of stuff happened. Besides, remember, we felt Mafia influence even though we were seven hours from Chicago.

Gin was half black and half white. Her mom was white and her real dad had just been plain African-American, but her stepdad, JB, was Jamaican. Jamaican, can you imagine that? JB cooked jerk this and jerk that. And he'd talk Jamaican for us, which sounded so foreign that he'd laugh and repeat what he'd just said but slower and without as thick of an accent, and most of what he said, I came to find out, was English. Gin didn't seem too impressed by him; she wasn't impressed by her real dad either. JB had taken Gin and her mom to Jamaica three times. Gin hadn't just seen the ocean; she'd slept on it, put her toes in it, probably made love to the sound of it. I had never even seen the ocean.

Gin wore painter's pants, like a lot of us did, but hers were old and that didn't seem to bother her at all. She wore T-shirts with them and that old cracking leather jacket, she said from 1967. Didn't matter the weather, she wore it. She smelled nice too, like vanilla and opium mixed together. She smoked every now and then but not "only when she drank," which I have never thought was cool. If anything, she smoked when she watched me.

She wore gold hoops in each ear. My left ear was triple-pierced, which meant back then that people called me "punk." I told them they wouldn't know punk if Exene came up and safety-pinned their noses (my own little joke).

Physically, Gin and I were opposites. I was golden-pale like a buttermilk biscuit. Thankfully, my pale skin didn't sizzle in the sun; I just got a few freckles on my nose and the rest of me even more golden like honey. I was skinny then, way skinny, hipbones stickin' out, wearing little T-shirts and sandals. I'd stopped wearing a bra. I only wore one my first couple years of high school, a size B, 'cause to not wear one meant you was advertising you were a slut. My tits are small, just a handful, with nipples that are constantly hard, sticking out like mini marshmallows. My family said thank God I had an ass and a smile or I'd be shit outta luck.

Gin didn't seem to want folks to notice, but she was actually quite curvy. She had tits that my mama had prayed I'd get. I learned quick that Gin didn't consider comments on those areas, no matter how flattering the words were, compliments. Her hair, jacket, and boots were OK to comment on. But her tits, no. Whatever. I loved her chest. I imagined her without a shirt and wondered if her nipples were hard and tight like mine.

One time I asked her if there was a word for half black and half white and she told me "mulatto." (I had to look up the spelling.) I used it for years after until somebody told me mulatto was "a pejorative," which I also had to look up. In any case, I think "mulatto" is a beautiful-*sounding* word, and I was sorry to learn that it was used to keep people down.

I could go on about Gin just the way I could go on about Leda, Claudia, or Brad—the way they taught me things, opened my eyes, that they could see that I belonged somewhere else, thus feeding my faith that I could get out, get to somewhere else, that I was meant for bigger places.

Gin was city, worldly; she could stand tall because she wasn't beaten down. She'd seen beauty; she'd seen the ocean. She didn't have to go by faith; she'd seen it with her own two eyes.

"Gin" was short for Ginger, but she couldn't have been a Ginger in a million years.

Some folks wanted to get to know her just 'cause of the stuff I told you. That's one thing I have to point out: I wanted to meet the outsiders, but I didn't throw myself at them. Give me a break—I was bored, not desperate. We had to click.

So others did throw themselves at her, and I let them.

"And you're going to barber school?" Gin politely asked Jane, one of my friends.

Jane giggled and said, "Beauty school, silly! But yes. We have shows and all. I'd be so honored if you would ever consider…"

Like that it was. Around the table at Pizza Den. Each of them.

I smiled when they were showing off, and she caught my eye. She didn't talk much, and that seemed to make *them* talk more, make them nervous, but not me. I seem to always be friends with the shy people. My friends stopped noticing her at some point, caught up in their own dull chatter, and she leaned over to me and said, "What do you do around here for kicks?"

My heart caught just a little from the attention but I smiled cool and answered, "Smoke pot and stare at the stars. Or get drunk and beat up your family."

She laughed then asked, "You got a ride?"

"Yeah, my car. How 'bout you?"

"A ride *is* a car, and no, I don't have one." She smiled again, and I could see she had charm in those dark hazel eyes. You know, you have to if you move around as much as she did; otherwise you turn out a loner. And that voice of hers. Her voice was low but not husky like mine. It sounded like some kind of nighttime river that could carry me.

We headed for the door, leaving my friends mouths' gaping as they tried to latch on and saw it wasn't going to happen.

When we got into Stella, my '75 Dodge Charger, Gin asked, "You mean, you got ganja in this forgotten armpit of Americana?"

I smiled, "Oh, shit, yeah. I don't believe there's a town made too small to toke, ya know? Plus, we are straight on the Mafiosos' run between Chi and Memphis. It's one of our few claims to fame." I opened the ashtray and let her light up first, then drove us to the lake.

That's where it started. I became her guide into strict, boring po-dunk, and she began to guide me in another direction.

I would drive her around in Stella for hours, tell her the dirt on everyone, get her pot, and try to find stuff for us to do. She would tell me stories about the places she'd been—Jamaica; London; Rhode Island; El Paso, Tex.; and St. Augustine, Fla. In a way, I earned every one of those stories by entertaining her in one fashion or another.

"In Jamaica you can drink all the rum you want and eat fresh juicy oranges. The sunset is purple, pink, and blue-violet. There is reggae music floating through the air anywhere you go." She stretched her arms to the sky as she told the story. We were lying beside the river, with a train track behind us, sharing a bottle of wine. "The sunset seems to take hours, but then the sun actually touches the horizon and it slips so easily into the ocean, no argument, acquiescing completely, swallowed whole."

She'd taken off her jacket. The sun was still high, beating down on us. I had on a halter top so I could feel the cool, slick blades of grass underneath my back. I slipped off my jean shorts, and I wasn't wearing panties.

"Make yourself comfortable," she said. Even then I heard the tension in her joke but wasn't experienced enough to label it desire.

"Oh, no one can see us," I replied. "Don't you ever go skinny-dippin'?" I could see even through her sunglasses the answer was no.

"Well, in case you're thinkin' about it, I wouldn't go in the Mississippi. There's shit, piss, and chemicals all in there. You'll only get ringworm if you're lucky." I spread my legs wide. "I love the sun when I'm spread open. I can almost feel the rays going inside me."

She rolled over onto her side and propped her head up on one elbow. "Touch yourself," she said slow and firm.

My clit jerked. I laughed and asked, "Do you dare me?" thinking she was teasing.

"Dares are child's play. I'm telling you." She pulled the keys out of her pocket and dangled them over my stomach, "I'll leave you. Touch your pussy."

"You fucker, you wouldn't leave me." I looked for clues but she had a poker face.

"You have no idea what I'd do." Her voice became low and thick, making my breath catch in my chest. "But it doesn't matter because I know you want to. Tell me you want to."

I called her a fucker a few more times and tried to ignore her until she raised her voice and pushed a key into my stomach, "Don't test me, Tina. Say it, or I'll leave you. Believe me, I can find someone else to pass the time with in this butt-fuck little town."

I flinched. That one hurt. Part of me still didn't believe her, yet she was right that I didn't care, because I wanted to do it. I just needed to know if she was fakin,' gonna make fun of me for doin' as I was told.

I licked my lips and said, "I wanna to do it for you, Gin. I want to touch myself. My pussy." My clit surged and stretched to the sun with my words. I pushed my purple-painted nails into my golden curls.

"Do your clit," she said.

I pressed the tips of my fingers into my clit and began smearing it in circles like I did when I was alone.

"You slut. I knew it. You want everyone to see, don't you? What if men are working on the river and looking over here? Hey, Tina-girl, a train is probably coming."

That was it; I cried out and clenched my cunt as I started coming in jerks into my own hand. I was grateful for the shades that hid my eyes as I stared up at her.

She laughed and reached out to briefly stroke my hair. "I bet you won't walk around like that. Why don't you flag down a train… bottomless?" she said and smiled.

"Oh, big deal. I love being naked. You city girls worry too much." I took off up the incline.

"I wonder, Tina, who needs to worry," her words came out slow and sure—not hitting me until I'd reached the tracks. My sandals slipped beneath my feet as I stumbled on the sharp black rocks between the creosote-covered railroad ties. I knew from experience that the creosote didn't wash off and was trying to avoid it.

"Straddle the rail," she said. Then her eyebrows raised behind her sunglasses. "This should be easy for a country girl like you. Or are you afraid?" My cunt was throbbing just from the exposure. The thought of people watching me felt so wrong, so nasty. "Stop slipping! Stand on the wood."

"It's called a railroad tie."

"Stand on it," she commanded louder.

I stood on it and realized that there was a train coming. I could feel its vibration beneath my feet. I looked past her but couldn't see anything in the glare of the lowering sun.

"You want to be tough like me? Let's see what you're made of. Squat."

"What?"

"Squat down and sit on the rail."

I squatted till my pussy hairs touched the rail. I could feel the heat rising from the steel. I let my knees fall to the oily tie and balanced my hands on the rocks.

She put her boot on the rail between my trembling knees. "Put your pussy on it."

"Do you feel the vibration?" I asked. "That's a train."

She looked over her shoulder. "I don't see it. But I could believe you. Maybe this vibration is what you need." Then she raised her voice again. "Put your ass down on it. Now! There's no room for arguing this time."

I did as I was told. My clit burned against the hot steel. My cunt juice instantly singed dry, only to be instantly replenished. The vibration excited me, and my breath quickened. My pussy swelled and my lips spread wider and wider, engulfing the rail. I pressed harder into it. I looked up at her then spit down between my leg; then I slid my cunt into my spit and began sliding back and forth on the steel.

As I was grinding my pussy faster and faster against it, Gin stepped back off the rail to reveal an engine taking the bend up ahead. As the vibrations rose my furious steel humping rose too.

"Come, you little bitch. You're not going anywhere until you scream, coming like you want to." As the engine roared closer her frenzy seemed to rise. "Show me how you come, Tina! Pinch those big nips, then throw back your head and come."

I pinched my nipples hard through the fabric and humped until my hips were out of my control. Gin said, "They're watching you fuck the rail so they can see you come. Now come, you little cunt!"

With that I screamed and started coming and coming against the rail. I let go of my tits, fell forward and grabbed the rail with the orgasm pounding my cunt into the steel over and over in waves. Gin grabbed my arms and dragged my jerking body from the track just as the train screeched by. I lost a sandal, and my shades went flying. She threw me down and landed on top of me. I could feel her chest heaving into mine, her leg pressing in between my thighs. And her smell filled me. "Are you all right?" she asked, our lips just inches apart. I wanted her to hold my wrists over my head, slap me, and then kiss me like some angry man in an old-fashioned movie.

"I'm fine. How are you?" I expected her charming smile but she just rolled off of me.

"C'mon, get your shit and let's go." She said and waited while I dressed. After the train had completely passed, she pulled my sandal from the rocks and then walked ahead of me to the car.

I headed us back to Idaville. The sun was purpling the sky before I broke our silence. "Do you like to watch me touch myself?" I swallowed and hoped my voice didn't reflect my nerves, hoped it was husky like normal, how she liked it.

"Tina girl, You know I'm bored. There's no beach, no bars, no fucking coconuts even."

"There's no coconuts in Rhode Island," I retorted.

"You don't want to know? OK, fine."

"I'm sorry, I'm sorry," I sighed. I tried again, "Anyway, you liked it, watching me?"

She shrugged. "I'm bored." She blew smoke out the window, then after a few minutes said, "You keep me awake, and I tell you things. Doesn't that make you happy?"

I drummed my fingers on the steering wheel. I liked it better when she was charming me, but what did I expect? At least she was honest. Fuck, who knew bored better than me? I reached into the ashtray and lit up a joint. "Are you going to tell me to do more things?"

"Maybe." She looked at me. It wasn't a question, but I suspected she was feeling me out. Probably not 'cause she cared but just 'cause she wanted to see what she could get away with.

"There's a lot you got to learn about the country, ya know. You say you're not gonna be here long but hey, you are here. The cities might be tough, but you gotta be tough here too. You'd be surprised what I can do, what I'm not scared to do. We won't get too bored. Besides," I looked over at her, "it'll give you another story to tell."

At the last remark, she shot me a glance that I couldn't read. I didn't like it like this. I wanted us talking, laughing, and her showing off telling stories and all. I ran my hand down her arm. "Oh, feel your muscles," I teased. The pot hit us and the tension eased as she curled her arm for me to take another feel.

After a few minutes she leaned back, put her elbow up on the window and said, "Yeah, Tina girl, we won't get too bored."

She did tell me more things to do. She watched me as she smoked or ate an orange, peeling a little, then eating a little, and on like that. She never touched me. And although we seemed to get closer as friends, I could see that she could leave at any moment. I, on the other hand, daydreamed about things besides me leaving, and that was a first.

Reality, though, always managed to rear its ugly head.

We always got a lot of stares as we rode around in Stella and a few names thrown at us. The first time it happened we'd finished paying for gas, buying snacks, and were getting back into Stella when a truck of guys drove by and yelled, "White trash nigger lover!" at me. Even though they sped away, I was totally reading them at the top of my lungs when Gin got me to "shut up and get in the car, they're gone." I was so embarrassed that that had happened in front of her, in my hometown, where I was trying to show her a good time. I was getting ready to apologize when she turned to me in the front seat, looked me over, touching my shoulder, my cheek, and asked with sincere concern, "Are you all right?"

Her worrying about me. She never showed herself. I faltered in answering right away 'cause I was shocked at her concern. I really looked at her and saw, only for a second, so much…anger, mixed with concern and protectiveness. "You're shaking," she said and rubbed my arms.

"I'm fine, Gin. Skinny girls like me shake when we get all riled up. Those fuckin' wimps, yell names then speed away." I touched her hand and asked, "Are you OK?"

She pulled away from me and was tough, cool-headed Gin. "Scoot over, I'm coming around. I'm driving," she said as she got out and slammed her door.

Funny that she seemed to be the one giving orders but more often than not I lead us into our little game situations, mostly *not* on purpose. Mostly.

We were trampling through rows of corn to an oil well in a neighboring field when she almost touched an electric fence, not knowing what it was.

"To keep the cows and horses in or out—it doesn't kill them. It hurts like a mother but only for a few seconds," I explained.

"This little wire?" she asked.

"Yes. C'mon, I'll show you the oil well."

"And," her voice was getting that tone, "what about humans?"

"No, Gin. C'mon," I practically whined, running my fingers through my hair.

"Oh, if you just would have answered. It doesn't hurt you permanently, does it? Don't lie to me."

Oh, fuck, here we go. But this time I wasn't instantly getting turned on. "Gin, ya know, I just don't know what to tell you," I said, exasperated. "Boys piss on it, but considering it's too tall for me to straddle, I think that's out of the question. So what are you going to do, huh?"

The slap came out of nowhere, hard and fast from the back of her hand. I went flying, but she clamped my wrist in her fist and pulled me to her chest. "Drop your pants." She pushed me off of her. My clit was literally throbbing from blood coursing through it. I wiped away snot and tears with the back of my hand.

I dropped my jeans, and for the first time I let myself wonder if she liked looking at me because just wondering it made me feel good, added to the burning. Gin walked up to me and cupped my face in her hands. "Spread your legs, Tina. That's a good girl." She put her boot between my feet but did not press up against me. She kept me almost at arm's distance. "I want you to piss on my boot. Right here, right now."

My face was firmly in her hands. I started to argue or to cry, but I stopped myself. I just looked deep into those hazel walls, smiled small, then closed my eyes. I focused on the burning, I pretended her fingers were holding my pussy lips instead of my face, then I took a deep breath and let go. Piss streamed straight down, hit her boot and splattered all over my ankles and the bottom of her jeans. I opened my eyes.

"Tina girl," she said and brought her face closer to mine. "Taste it. My boot, your piss. In New York they have bars where all people do is drink piss. C'mon now."

"When will you stop?" I asked, although my head was still reeling from the New York City comment.

"When you stop wanting it."

"Oh, fuck you."

"You know you want to put your ass in the air, kneel down, and taste it." Instead of playing hardball, she winked at me and whispered, "Just do it." And I did. With my ass high, I kissed her boot and licked the piss from my lips. I licked more and more, pushing the flat of my tongue against the salt of me and the hardness of her.

"Get over to the fence and take off your shirt," she ordered.

Later, when I thought about it, I realized I had stopped arguing with her and forcing her to threaten me so much.

I dramatically pulled off my crop top and flung it over my head. My hair draped over my arched back. My clit was hugely swollen simply because I was naked. I liked it, the whole thing—my pussy, my nudity, her bossiness, feeling her *desire*. I was getting that she wanted me. And it made me feel powerful yet bad—a good girl wouldn't be getting swollen from this; she'd be offended, hurt, she'd slap Gin and run. The slapping that the ladies who wanted to be taken did in the movies.

My pussy became so full and burning that I didn't think I could do anything, but I walked to the fence.

"I want you to stick those hard nips onto the fence."

"It might throw me" was all I could say.

"I'll catch you."

I wanted to tell her that it wouldn't do anything to my nipples, that my whole body is what would get the shock. But that wasn't the point. I could feel she really wanted to see my titties stretching out to the fence. I wanted to make her happy. More than anything in the world, I wanted her to get what she wanted. I pinched my titties, although they were already bullets. I leaned forward and pushed just one into the wire fence. I cried out and was thrown just a little. I danced around, shook out my hands then vigorously rubbed my boobs. Juice crept out of my cunt. I breathed deeply and smiled at Gin. She was frozen, just staring at me. Then, "Do the other one."

I did ,and this time I danced naked into her arms.

She moaned, threw me down onto my back and knelt between my legs. She pulled an ear of corn from a stalk and ripped at the husk, then threw it on my belly saying, "Deal with this." She pulled off her jacket, dug in her pockets, and pulled out a roach clip.

Take a deep breath.

She clamped it onto my pink bullet nipple. It bit into me at first, then warmness flushed over my breast. She pulled the shucked corn from my hand.

Just keep your mouth shut, don't say a word.

She spread my pussy lips open with her fingers; I gasped and almost cried. Her fingers were hot against me; I'd ached for them for so long. She shoved the corn into me and we both moaned. I flung my head back and grabbed at the stalks of corn. She plowed this corn-dick into me. Kernels burst against the hardness of my cunt and our fucking. She pulled me up by my thigh, and I hooked my feet on her shoulders. She slammed into me deeper and deeper until I could feel her knuckles banging against my cunt.

Bruise me, bruise me, give me something to remember!

"Pull on your tit. Make it bite." She pulled the corn-dick out and threw it to the side.

"More," I cried.

"I'm doing this. Shut up," she growled, then grabbed my free nipple and twisted it until I screamed. She licked the back of her hand and started working my pussy. Cunt juice and corn juice poured down into my ass as I kept taking in her fingers.

"Breathe," she snapped. Then to me, to my cunt, I don't know, she was almost spitting, "Take me, take me, damn it, Tina." Then, she groaned and I cried out as my cunt took her fist.

Gin reached up to my clamped nipple and slapped my whole tit hard. I screamed, and the burning seared a path through me, through my chest, my soul. "Take a fucking deep breath, girl." The clip came off, and immediately sensations hit. "Touch yourself," Gin commanded, and pulled at my nipple till I rose with it.

I clawed at her arm, crying, pushing down on her hand and rubbing furiously at my clit. Somewhere everything became white-hot. My fury burned, blurred into stillness. Screaming floated to my ears, my lungs ripped. All of me convulsed. *Gin is a little scared* floated inside of me but her voice melted in saying, "I've got you, I've got you, go away." White-hot became purple became green, white stars lacing all. Lips numb. My shaking hand finds my face soaked with tears and snot. Gin, like vapors engulfing me, warm, softness, breasts, I landed, her shoulder, neck, opium, vanilla. Rest. I flew, faintly aware that she watched, held my rope from the horizon. Somewhere far away another her left me, my pussy, cooling-blue on red, but it didn't matter 'cause I was still gone.

I woke to her stroking my dampened hair, waves of leftover orgasm still shuddering through my legs and sobs still jerking at my lips and chest.

She dressed me and drove with me curled into her arm.

Gin didn't call the next day or return my calls. We went out again soon after that but she acted as if she'd never touched me, and she wouldn't look me in the eye. I could hardly be around her but couldn't be away from her either. My throat tightened at the base like I was choking on a rock or like someone was strangling me.

Also, the games stopped.

We'd been getting stoned at Miller's pond when I caught a garden snake and tried to make Gin touch it. She jumped back, almost falling, and totally lost her cool. I laughed till I cried. Seen-it-all Gin losing it! Suddenly—me with snake still in hand—she grabbed my hair and jerked back my head, seriously pissed off, then she pushed me off with such force that I fell on my ass. "Do something, bitch, do something with the fucking snake, you think it's so fuckin' funny." She kicked dirt at my legs and paced back and forth, then turned to me again, "Yeah? Well?" She spit to the side, put her hand on her hip and stared at me.

With anybody else I would have been on my feet already, in their face, telling 'em to cool the fuck off, but Gin always confused me, and that confusion more often than not left me still. I raised my eyebrow and smiled, "I'll do something with the snake... Wanna see?" It was only about a foot and a half long. I held it behind its head in one hand. It dangled around while I reached down and unzipped my shorts, then let them drop. Gin barely gasped but she did. I knew she could see my swollen clit through my sparse blond hair. If anyone could have seen it, it would have turned me on, but it was Gin.

"Watch, Gin, don't miss this." I laid the snake against my chest, between my little titties. I soothed it with my voice and ran my hand down the length of it. The snake tried to crawl up me but I kept a firm hold on it. I curved it like a big smile under one breast, then the next. I grabbed its tail and let it wiggle into my belly button, tickling me. Her mouth hung open for a moment; when she saw that I noticed she clamped it shut. This became the game to me: In my head I was saying *I can see you, Gin, I can see you!* Then it was her jaw clenching or a fist tensing. She was moving somewhere. Was it anger? Was it desire? Part of me was screaming *You don't want me, fucker, so let me go.* Part of me wondered if she was just pissed at the snake. Those thoughts I knew I was having; what I didn't realize was that I was pushing, that I would break her. And I would find her.

"Do you like it? Or are you scared?" I asked, then laughed again as I let myself be tickled by the snake. I smiled but my eyes glared *Who's still now? Confused, Gin? Can't move, Gin? Caught in the headlights, Gin?* " I raised an eyebrow. I played how I knew to play. I played hard. "Here's where you like it, isn't it Gin? Down here?" I lowered the snake, its tail dangling close to my pussy. To the snake I cooed, "Oh, Mr. Snake, caught up in Tina and Gin's game, aren't you? You like Tina's body? Do you want to touch it? Gin never touched it much. I wonder," I looked up at her. "I wonder if she wishes she were you, snake." I laid the head against me again and slowly ran my hand down the length of it until just a couple of inches ran into my pubic hair. I let my hand smooth past it into my lips. "Not long enough, are—"

"Stop it." She said loudly, yet it fell flat.

"Oh but I like it, and snake likes it too, don't you?" I lowered the snake some more, then trailed my hand down its back. This time I pushed it against my clit and in between my pussy lips. "Oh, fuck Gin," I moaned, "it's so hard. Oh, it's wiggling." It did feel good. (See, I am a pervert.) I stroked those last inches of the snake, pressing it against me.

"Stop it," she said again and took a step closer.

Show me, I screamed in my head. *Show me you, Gin, you!* Out loud I said, "How come? How come, Gin? Why stop? Because you like it? Because I disgust you? Why?"

"Wanna play, Tina?" She said snapped out of her spell, "Yeah, let's play. Lie down and fuck yourself Tina. Do it." She folded her arms over her chest. Suddenly she yelled, "Do it!"

I completely lost it and threw the snake into the weeds. "Fuck you!" My brain was spinning, screaming with all the shit I wanted from her. "How come I couldn't win this time, Gin? Huh. You can't show it. You can't fucking show yourself. Well, then fuck you!" Tears were streaming down my face. "What do you want? Huh? Nobody knows." I threw my hands into the air and looked around to my invisible witnesses, "Do we know? No! Fuck us, huh, yeah, dumb white trash butt-fucks. Why?" I screamed at the top of my lungs. "Why can't *I* know what's inside? Is it really boredom? Huh? Was that all a lie? Is it lust? Desire? Fear? Are you fucking scared, Gin?"

She was trembling all over. I thought, *Kill me with you bare hands, I don't care.*

"Fuck you, Tina," she said, then turned and started towards the road.

"Brilliant, Gin. That tells me a lot!" I started after her. "I don't deserve to know what Miss High-and-Mighty-City thinks, do I? Leave me. Fine, just leave. Take my car. But I'll tell you what, you fuckin' son of a bitch, I tell you what, just keep on drivin', you motherfucker." My fear was rising and my screams became shrill with terror and nothing left to lose. Spit flew from my mouth and tears poured. "Leave me here to rot, rot in this hellhole, goddamn you…" I stopped following her and put my head in my hands, "Fuck us, fuck me, we're nothing to you. Is that what you wanted, to fuck me, Gin? No, never. You never wanted a piece of me." I fell to my knees and sobbed into my hands, mumbling this dialogue to myself.

"You," she stood a few feet away, I pulled my face out of my hands to glare at her. I could see tears in her eyes. "You don't need me to get out, Tina." Her voice wavered, "You might not know that now, but I know it. You are going to get out of this place, and you'll see me with different eyes when you do."

"Just go."

"I'm trying to tell you," she yelled and pointed at me. "You asked for it, so I'm giving it to you."

She took a deep breath then said quietly, "You'll see with eyes that have seen the ocean and with a mind that keeps going, never stops. And once you get out you won't stop, and you'll see me and see that I'm just some fucked-up chick on a bloody free ride. I'm not exotic, Tina girl." She sighed and looked away. "I had to take you while you could be taken."

I licked my lips, and wiped a tear away, "So," I tried to sound matter-of-fact, "that means you didn't want me?"

She started crying then. Simply crying. "Tina," she put her hands to the sky then toward me, "Tina, I'm in love with you."

I started crying uncontrollably again into my hands. "Don't leave me, Gin," I sobbed, "Don't leave me."

She knelt beside me and put her arm around my shoulders, "Tina girl," she whispered, "I'm just a game. You don't need me."

"Oh Gin," I sighed, "you know that's not right." I reached up and touched her face, "I'm in love with you too, don't you know? They weren't just games to me."

She grabbed me hard, pulled my head back by my hair and kissed me with all of our violence—no holding back.

We stood in that field kissing until my lips literally bled. She put me on the ground, our lips still not parting, and fucked me until I came into her mouth. We wiped each other's tears and I said, "So are we going to finally blow this pop stand or what?"

She zipped up my shorts and patted my ass. "I hear tomorrow's sunset is going to be amazing, all pink, purple, and blue." She smiled, grabbed my hand, and started for the car.

"What about today's?" I asked. "We could get some oranges and chocolate."

"Tomorrow's," she turned to me and smiled, "is going to be over the ocean."

I screamed and threw my arms around her, "No way! We can get to the ocean by then?"

Mondo Pomo Porno

By Simon Sheppard

"Welcome to the humiliating world of professional writing."
—Homer J. Simpson

OK, let's say you're at the video store and you're thinking, for some odd reason, I wanna rent something about the mysteries of identity and the mutability of human personality. Two films spring to mind. On one shelf there's Ingmar Bergman's *Persona,* a chilly, astringent work featuring an agonized Liv Ullman in tight close-up. And on another there's Hitchcock's *Vertigo,* a massively fun mystery that features luscious Kim Novak in fabulous gowns. Be honest, gentle reader, which one do you think you'll take home?

Well, that's how I think about smut. Yeah, it's "just" genre fiction, and sure, there's a whole lot of crappy porn around. But it is, I keep telling myself, surely possible to address deeply felt issues in stories more likely to produce a hard-on than a yawn. Or so I'd like to believe.

Sometimes, though, it's an uphill battle to believe it. There are the well-meaning folks who ask me, "Have you tried writing anything besides porn?" Meaning, of course, "How about trying *real* literature?" And there's disdain from the literary world as well. Each and every new mystery novel gets reviewed in your Sunday paper. But with the exception, maybe, of Susie Bright's *Best American Erotica* series, when was the last time first-rate porn got the critical attention given to some third-rate John Grisham wanna-be? The Lambda Literary Awards, the major awards for queer writing, do not have a category for Erotica, despite the skillions of dollars gay men spend on the stuff. Lambda lumps us porn writers in with authors of

General Fiction, where we're condemned to lose out, once and always, to Respected Gay Authors Doing Serious Work. There are award categories for Mysteries, Science Fiction, Humor, everything but a separate category for Lesbian Cat Stories. But Erotica? Uh-uh. It's not *real* writing, apparently.

I don't know, maybe things will change. When *Vertigo* came out, anyone who thought it worthy of serious critical attention would have been laughed out of the room. Likewise, there's only been a market for what I'll pretentiously call "quality porn" for maybe a decade, decade and a half. Thanks to trailblazers like Bright and John Preston, there's now a space to write explicitly about sex without pretending we're doing anything else (such as churning out redeeming social value). And, after all, who knew that Raymond Chandler's pulp work for *Black Mask* would someday be taught in college?

I do have a great appreciation for well-crafted genre work that doesn't aspire to be much of anything else. (*Vertigo* too deep for you? Well, how about John Woo's *Face/Off?*) And sometimes I just want to write a plain old stroke story, maybe funny, maybe sad, but one with no more relevance to real life than an Agatha Christie. (English cosy porn…now *that's* a concept!)

And then there's the ol' economic imperative—a girl's gotta eat, after all, and standard stroke stories can bring home the arugula. The problem, for me at least, is that a steady regime of writing formula stuff is so damn unchallenging and therefore unrewarding. At some level, I'd like to touch the reader's heart and/or mind as well as his dick. (It's the same for me, I'm afraid, when I have sex, even with a one-off trick. I'm so-o-o old-fashioned.) So on the one hand, there's the opportunity to spin out simple-but-bill-paying tales of lust for *Big Meat Magazine*. And on the other, there's that call for submissions for one of those high-concept anthologies, a collection of erotic stories about, oh, cross-dressing, differently-abled CEOs. Of color.

Of course, me being me, I'll choose to write for that damn antho. And I'll sweat over that story for weeks, potentially making less per hour than a Mickey D fry chef—if and when the story sells—only to have the manuscript rejected because they already had *another* story about a quadriplegic Thai peanut oil magnate. In a ball gown. Like I could sell that fucking story anywhere else. It's a hard world.

But yes, I keep writing porn. Because I believe, as Pat Califia said and as I never tire of quoting, "Pornography changes the world." *Well, now,* the rhetorical reader asks, *how does it do that?*

For starters, it should do what any enjoyable fiction does: entertain. Porn lets us pass a pleasant hour on an airplane, in the bathroom, in the park while we're surreptitiously cruising that guy over there. (Yeah that one lying on the grass, nice nipples, a slight paunch. Yeah, that one. He's *hot.*)

But erotic writing can do more, much more. Not that it *should* do more, but it can. It's one genre we all can relate to, firsthand. Not every mystery reader will solve a murder. Very few science fiction fans will actually journey to Uranus. But every one of us has had erotic desires, and most of us have actually had sex, of one sort or another. Even the pope has jacked off, I bet. At least once or twice.

The reader of erotica has a particular relationship with the text. Just as a persuasive piece of political fiction can lead a reader to join a cause, write a letter, or attend a demonstration, so porn can lead to action. It may only be jerking off. And that's fine. Masturbation is a perfectly respectable, long-standing tradition that deserves to be honored, and if I found out that someone somewhere had an orgasm directly traceable to my work, it would make me smile. Confession: I myself don't directly use text as jack-off fodder. That is, I'm not a one-handed reader. But there have been times I've read a story, put the book down, and found myself so horny that I just had to let the jism fly.

There's more that porn can do, though. Let's be clear here: I'm not saying you should read erotica because it's *good* for you. Yuck. I once heard a well-known erotic writer say that one of the best things about porn is that while the reader is all sexed-up and receptive, an author can sneak in constructive messages about race, gender, and class. I think that's exactly wrong. I'd hate to see a porn universe populated entirely by well-to-do buff white boys, true, but for the most part, unless it's directly about a political situation, porn should teach by example, if it must instruct at all. By all means, make that character African-American, but don't have him stop mid fuck to lecture his trick on the evils of racism. Because if porn is going to do explicit political work, it might as well as do political work around sexuality itself.

I'm not the first (or hundredth) writer to point out that human culture, Western culture, American culture, is awfully fucked up about sex. Sure, the signifiers of sex are everywhere we turn. But as the inevitable Michel Foucault pointed out, just because everybody's talking about something doesn't mean they're truly tolerant of it. Just because we're all *discussing* sex doesn't mean we've conquered shame.

So one of the things porn can do, especially well-crafted, thoughtful erotica, is help convince us that sex is worth not just talking about but thinking about. In depth. And not just thinking about in a Dr. Ruth "everything is groovy and sunny and, gee, sex can just be so much fun" way. Yeah, sure. But sex can also be dark and dysfunctional and even destructive and *still* be worthwhile. The difference between "erotica" and "porn" is groaningly, endlessly debatable. But maybe one useful distinction is that porn presumes that no one can be harmed by sex while erotica is given the freedom to speak of consequences, to admit that, yes, desire can be frightening and awful and truly destructive *but is worth pursuing all the same.*

And we can and should tell those darker stories too. Maybe in an Ingmar Bergman way. Or maybe in an Alfred Hitchcock or John Woo or David Cronenberg way; to my way of thinking, the first great film about AIDS was Cronenberg's remake of *The Fly.*

Erotic text is special. Badly-acted videos can only go so far. Photos of Calvin Klein–pretty hairless lads with hard-ons can only tell us certain things. But well-written erotica can communicate, in one way or another, so much more. Not didactically; nobody wants to be lectured to when his dick is hard. (Unless he and his trick are doing a schoolroom scene.) But it can communicate, nonetheless.

When porn goes beyond mere entertainment, when it takes its world-changing possibilities *seriously* (ick, there's that word again), it can open whole new worlds for the reader, even if it's just a matter of whom he'll consider fucking. (Did you notice how when I talked back there about cruising a hot guy in the park I gave him a little paunch? See, I was trying to subvert mass-market stereotypes of sexual attractiveness. Hope you didn't mind.)

A lot of the best erotic writing, even the stuff that seems like just plain old smut, can help us explore who we really are. Maybe feel better about it. Maybe even, on occasion, feel not so good about it, make us rethink long-held desires. But pierce us to the quick, in any case.

What we don't grasp, necessarily, is that nothing we can desire is truly new. Nothing. Somewhere, someone else got there first. So let's stop burying those squirmy little things in the back of our mental closets, OK? (I can still recall reading, years ago, a piece by a man who got off on the sight of a guy with his foot in a cast. "Oh, my fucking God!" I thought. "And I thought *I* was the only one!") The wider the universe of erotica, the more surely we know we're not alone.

The Andrea Dworkin antismut gang wants us to believe that porn desensitizes, that it gives readers permission to do all sorts of terrible things. And maybe, just maybe, Sociopathic Sam will use his copy of *Anal Sluts in Bondage* to convince himself that, yeah, women really do want to be abused, treated like shit. Or to confirm preexisting beliefs to that effect, beliefs that may be implanted by culture or may even be hardwired into the ever-fallible human animal. But most of us know the difference between flesh and fantasy, between right and wrong—most of us who've read Dennis Cooper don't rush right out to eviscerate anemic, drugged-up young guys. At least, I sure don't.

Still, one strange thing about being a writer is that you're never sure who your eventual audience will be. If I write a hard-core S/M story with lots of pain and piercings, who's going to pick that up and read it? Maybe some 18-year-old, still half in the closet, even to himself? And what will that story mean to him? Will it be so scary that he'll be shamed deeper into self-denial? Or will he be so turned on by the infinite possibilities of desire that he'll embark on a lifelong journey of erotic self-discovery? The cliché answer is that it shouldn't matter, that the writer should go where his imagination leads him and let the chips fall where they may. But I think the pornographer who truly, thoroughly believes that, without a single twinge, is either an irresponsible knave or a psychopathic fool. And that's probably even truer for writers of queer male erotica, where AIDS and homophobia have made the terrain all the more treacherous.

So what's an erotic writer to do? Self-censor, which is to say lie? Each of us draws the lines in personal, idiosyncratic ways, I suppose. When I was coediting the anthology *Rough Stuff* with my good pal M. Christian, the question of unprotected sex came up. What would our policy on condom use be? If a barebacking story came in, how would we handle it? Well, the solution I felt comfortable with, as conditional and muzzy as it may be, was this: It was just fine if a story featured sexy unprotected fucking, but we wouldn't accept a piece that explicitly eroticized the *unprotected aspect* of the barebacking. Am I being an uptight prude? Maybe. Or giving readers license to do risky things? Hmm. Am I contradicting what I just said about the influence of porn on the reader's behavior? Perhaps. But then, consistency never was my strong suit.

Listen, we're only human, even the guys with 10-inch dicks. And when we're having sex, we're humans with a dense complexity of needs, regrets, limits, impulses. At some level, even the dumbest stroke story might suggest that very thing, that there's more to sex than the plumbing involved. Not *should* suggest, but *might*. I don't care whether it's a tale of 10 Rumanian midgets fucking on a tightrope, a story can have authenticity.

Example: I truly believe that virtually anyone participating in a raunch scene or a verbal abuse scene or any of a variety of other edgy S/M activities has a bit, and maybe it's only a teensy-tiny bit, of self-disgust. Only schizophrenics wouldn't. Does that ambivalence make those scenes "wrong?" Of course not. If you ask me, that just makes them hotter. So if I'm going to write about that stuff, I'm going to include that darker side, or at least not deny its existence. That sort of truth-telling is part of what makes a story authentic.

Sure, fiction is made up, and writers are liars. But that doesn't mean we should be *dishonest* liars. Each of us has a truth to tell. Whether dark erotica or fluffy porn, genre writing can become transcendent if it's written from the heart. When we're talking to people about their deepest desires, when we're influencing what young queers think about themselves, when we're describing what sex is and what it feels like and the consequences it may bear, authenticity matters. For erotic writing to reach its fullest potential, not only to make readers sigh or moan or get a hard-on but to connect in one way or another with their deepest desires, then it matters.

People sometimes ask if I write stories based on my personal experiences. Well, yeah, some of my work, a small portion, really, is pretty thinly veiled autobiography. Other pieces incorporate just bits and pieces of places I've been, men I've been with, feelings I've felt. But nothing I've written, I believe, is completely divorced from my life and heart, from real things I've done and desired and gotten off on. And writing has, circuitously, opened my eyes to new ways of experiencing my life, sexually and otherwise.

The story that I've chosen to accompany this essay, "My Possession," pretty much reflects what I've been talking about. It's a genre piece, a cross-genre piece, actually, using the gambits of both fantasy-based fiction and sex writing to explore some dark places. It deals with some of what I think of as "my themes": impossible need, betrayal, transcendence, the mutability of power positions. You know, all that stuff. It actually has less sex in it than many of my other works; this is, I hope, a story about the acute edge of desire. It may not be conventional pornography, but I think it's very erotic; what can I say—I think need is sexy.

The story's also got a bit of postmodern smart-assitude about it. I employed literary devices—e.g., faux translations of nonexistent theoretical text, letters written to the narrator—to suggest deceit, self-awareness, and the masks we all wear when it comes to sex. It's all a bit on the ambitious side, perhaps, but I'm fond of the story. Whether it works I leave for you to decide. I'm hoping the tale raises a chuckle as well as a frisson and maybe a hard-on too. And I'm hoping that, however dense things get, it has a plot that keeps chugging along.

"My Possession" is, I can now reveal, based on some real things that happened to me, and I wrote it while I was still trying to make sense of betrayal and duplicity and some pretty self-destructive behavior on my part. Writing the story was part of my attempt to claw my way back toward sanity, and now, looking back on what seems like foolhardy, drama-queen self-indulgence, I can comfort myself with the writer's ultimate consolation: Well, at least I got a story out of it.

MY POSSESSION

By Simon Sheppard

When we first met, we "met cute," as they say in Hollywood. You were tied down to the rack in my friend Allen's dungeon. I was late getting to the party; perhaps 20 men were already there. You were naked, on your back, restraints around your wrists and ankles, a few ropes around your arms and legs, gas mask over your face. My pal Berkowitz was standing over you, his shiny black rubber suit showing off his notoriously big cock. When I approached, he smiled. "Want to try some rope tricks on him? I'm bored."

I took over, never even looking at your eyes through the shiny face-plate of the mask. I think that's why I fell for you: the sheer impersonality of the play. At that point, you could have been anyone. Anyone with great legs and a fat, uncut dick.

Unlike Berkowitz, with his desultory style, I went to work on you for real, feeding soft, white rope through the rough cord webbing of the rack. Entrapping you in a web that even then you, faceless, theoretically submissive, were willing into being. When I tightened the ropes around your hairy upper thighs, cinched them down and knotted them, your dick sprang to its full hardness. Your long, tight foreskin never retracted. Glistening precome pooled at its tip.

Watching your trim, naked body strain against the ropes gave me the deepest pleasure. As is often the case in the best of scenes, "time" ceased to mean anything at all. An hour, perhaps two, had gone by when Berkowitz returned. "Gotta go," he said. "Work tomorrow." He smiled. "Gotta take my gas mask."

Your face, when I saw it at last, was perfect. Our first ferocious kisses tore through my soul. Though the party broke up, we remained in the dungeon, playing until the unseen break of day.

Words are slippery things at best, so it's damn near impossible to put into language what happened between us in the dungeon that night. I'd never known such mastery in a scene nor received such a gift of absolute surrender. You swore to me your trust was complete; I took you at your word. In one position, then another, coils of rope always tight against your tender flesh, you went further and still further into the welcoming dark. And you took me with you, to where we both hungered to be. And then sometime near dawn, with wrists and ankles securely bound, you curled up to sleep in my arms.

Your first letter read:

The few days I spent with you were among the greatest times of my life. You taught me what submission truly is. You touched a deep, deep part of me, and I'm forever in your debt. I am yours, entirely yours.

I can't believe that you're now thousands of miles away. Returning here to my home was so difficult. I feel so empty. But I'll be back with you when I return in the fall. And I know that, no matter what, I'll never forget the time we had. Dearest Master, in a very real sense, I'll always be with you.

Our short time together had been intense for me as well, the kind of scene I'm always searching for but so rarely find. Just reading and rereading your letter made my dick hard. I'd load the video into the VCR, watch you in close-up, in slow motion, hungrily licking my stiff cock. You in the bed of your hotel, enmeshed in a web of ropes, your wrists and ankles anchored firmly to the base of your swollen dick. Your moans when I tweaked your nipples. You gazing at the camera, at me, in what looked like absolute surrender.

But...something in the tone of your letter was excessive. Too much commitment, too much devotion. In the back of my mind, a caution light flashed. Even then I began to suspect that you were addressing not me but your own desire.

When I wrote back, I tried to be totally honest. I realize now that that was, in some respects, a mistake.

The months went by. From time to time, I played with bottom boys, boys who were maybe substitutes for you. Some were generous and honest in their submission. Others were self-absorbed little pricks who just wanted to be entertained. Always the shaky promise of your return was there waiting.

Your letters kept coming, each more slavishly devoted than the last. You longed to be my property. To sleep at the foot of my bed. You were telling me what you thought you wanted me to hear. I knew you were. I fell for it anyway.

On nights when I had trouble getting to sleep, I thought of us in the dungeon, after everyone else had gone. You were wearing my black leather collar, being my puppy. Walking on all fours. Licking my hand. Taking my commands. Wagging your beautiful, naked butt. "Roll over." Yelping happily, you got on your back. I scratched your hairy belly. Your doggy dick was hard. Your pink tongue lolled out. I hoisted your hind legs over my shoulders and drove my dick deep into you. "Good boy. Good dog," I'd said.

I went to work for Doppelgänger Press, specialists in transgressive postmodern literature. *Vertiginous Desires* was the latest book by a hot French author whose pen name was Choderlos de Laclos. Nobody seemed to know who he really was. I set to work translating the French into English:

Yeah, you've betrayed me. It's why I love you. You, who've given up so much for me. When it started, so simply and cleanly, you were tied up, restrained, me tying the knots. I seemed to possess you. I knew so little. You, in your ignorance, have since taught me so much. At first, by going behind my back, seeking out another master though all the while pledging submission to me, it seemed as though you were just another "pushy bottom." As though you were out for power, even the power of slaves. But now, only now, I see the genius of your selfless love. Now, as I stand here, rope in one hand, dick in the other, you nowhere to be seen. You're with someone else, someone you sought out,

as the murderer seeks out his executioner. You giving him your body,
your orgasms. He your "master," you his "slave."

But you, stupid genius of desire, have at last given me the oblitera-
tion of "you." It's the gift we both thought we were opening when I tied
white rope around your arms, your legs, your cock, your cock which is
too dark for your body, your cock which can't even crawl free of its fore-
skin, your ignorant, precious cock. The ritual was supposed to mean
you were giving up selfhood and will. To me. For me. But let's face it,
you in your pride couldn't ever give me the true gift, as I in my pride
couldn't accept it. Until now.

And so on. I was struck by the parallels between *Vertiginous Desires*
and the story of me and you. It even sounded like your dick. Still, the
narrator's affair had gone terribly wrong. Ours hadn't.Not yet.

For some reason, we never once spoke by phone. Transatlantic
calls don't cost that much. I suppose that I didn't want to be pressed
for an immediate response to your pledges of devotion. I suppose you
feared that your voice might give the game away. It's easier to lie
when you're doing it on paper. "I want you to know, to believe, that
there are truly no limits between us, that my trust in you is absolute."
I read it again and again, let it roll around in my brain. What was I
going to do with you? How could I live up to what you believed me
to be?

The last days of summer faded into fall. You were due to come
back soon. I sat before the VCR more and more, stroking my hard
dick while I played and replayed the tape, watching the interplay of
flesh and muscle, trying to decipher your face. My hand reached into
the frame and pulled off silvery titclamps, leaving dead-white inden-
tations in your pink nipples. Circulation returned to bruised flesh,
painfully. You moaned and writhed. Looked straight into the camera.
Aware of the effect. As though you were acting for the eye of an
observer. As though that observer were you. Not me. I leaned into
camera range and spat in your face. And again. The moment when
you closed your eyes, licked my spit from your lips and said "Thank
you, Sir" almost always made me come.

Two weeks before your plane was due, I received your final letter:

It's so hard to write this. I am sorry to have to tell you that I have signed a full-time slavery contract with a man I met through an ad on the Internet. I'm afraid I won't be able to let you play with me during the next year, until the term of the contract is up.

It seems unfair that you, who taught me what submission really is, should end up the loser. But I felt in need of something bigger. Though he and I haven't yet met face-to-face, I know that MASTER Jeff is the man I've been seeking.

Please don't take this as a rejection. I hope we can still be friends. And I'll be free again in a year. I know I'll be worth waiting for.

I've always had problems dealing with people who deal in bad faith. It makes me want to scream and throw things, but besides being undignified, throwing things never does any good. Which is why I sent you a note saying only "Goodbye and good luck." Anything more would have been self-indulgent.

I would have let it go at that, or at least would have tried. But when you got back to the States, you made that damned phone call to me. For the first time in months, I heard your voice. "I can't believe the brusque tone of your note. You're not the man I thought I knew. I thought I meant more to you than just sex."

I responded, "I would have settled for less than a pledge of total submission. I would have settled for honesty."

You said, "Why couldn't you have written what I needed to hear? You never once wrote that you wanted to own me."

I said, "Listen, at the same time as you were telling me there were no limits between us, you were auditioning Master Jeff and who knows who else. I can forgive your wanting to play with someone else. But you lied. You're like some little kid who doesn't know he's doing wrong because he can't distinguish fact from fantasy. And you still want to be friends? Drop dead."

And that was that. I wish I could say I didn't think of you again. I wish I could say I didn't jack off to your image any more. I wish that *Vertiginous Desires* didn't make so much sense to me:

What a stroke of brilliance! What ascetic glory! Through your betrayal, you've discarded all the pleasures I gave you. Robbed yourself of my adoration. My very presence. Through your treacheries, you've made yourself worthless, lower than low. Valueless as shit. You, miserable little traitor that you are, lying groaning sweating stinking in the bed of some brutal man too stupid to know what he's got, you've given me what I always knew I wanted.

You've made yourself the dirt beneath my boots. How then can I do anything but love you? You, who've made yourself repulsive to me while I watched, you've allowed me not to be merely a "top" in the shabby little bedroom-games sense. Oh, I worried I was weak, but you've shown me by your cowardice, your blinding insincerity, how strong I truly am. You've allowed me to tower high above you. You've abased yourself so thoroughly that nothing, nothing will ever obliterate your shame. How then can I do anything but burn for you? Burn for you with the terror of the dying sun? You've destroyed me utterly with your faithless dick. And I, who longed to know the dark of death yet still live, I'm gone but still here, you arrogant bastard. I can taste the juice of immortality, while you, you've vanished without a trace. No, wait, that sticky-sweet, slightly rancid taste...IT'S YOU. I've gulped you down, you're part of me, my nourishment, my poison. Drinking you to slake my thirst. Pissing you out again. My love. I burn for you. Even as I, in the very act of writing this, showing it to strangers, I betray you. Risking all, even my freedom, I lower myself to you. My love. My deepest, worthless love.

I turned off the computer. I went to bed. I slept fitfully, as I often had since your last letter. I woke up in the middle of the night. You. You were standing, naked, at the foot of my bed.

"Use me, Sir, I'm yours."

"How the fuck did you get in here?" I said.

"Whatever you want to do, Sir."

"How the *fuck* did you get in?"

You were peeling back the covers, kneeling between my legs. Your mouth closed around my dick. Slight surprise: Your mouth was wet but cool, as though you'd just finished drinking iced tea. Your chilly tongue played with the underside of my dick until I swelled to fill your mouth. I lay back and stared at the blank ceiling as you sucked me deep into your mouth. Cool, with the force of a vacuum. You brought me really close, really quick. I reached down, tried to pull your head off me, tried to get you to back off for a minute. You hung right in there, took my dick all the way down your throat. Your hands reached around, grabbed my butt. Your fingertips lightly brushed my hole. I couldn't help myself. I shot, yelling as I came. You gulped down my spunk like a starving man.

When you'd swallowed the last drop, you let me have my dick back. "I'll be right back," you said, leaving my bed.

I lay back and drifted off to sleep, the soundest sleep I'd had in weeks. When I awoke, it was midmorning. You were nowhere to be seen. The door to my apartment was locked. From the inside. As though none of it had happened. As though it had been a dream.

In the days that followed, I wrapped up the translation. Though I'd previously worked in fits and starts, agonizing over every line, I now ripped through the rest of the manuscript at fever pitch and sent it off to Doppelgänger. And all the while, I thought about you. At the oddest moments—waiting on line for a cappuccino, working out at the gym, watching *Jeopardy!*—your face appeared before me, and I wondered if and when you would return. Each day, I impatiently waited for the postman, hoping for a letter from you, and felt pathetic in my daily disappointment. I toyed with the ache of desire like a child whose tongue can't keep from worrying a loose tooth. Loving the discomfort. I was, beyond a doubt, being a fool.

And then, in the second week, I was awakened by your voice. In the dim light I saw your naked form kneeling beside the bed. You said, "After we talked that time, you never wrote to me."

"I…I couldn't."

"Pride?"

"More like needing to know that if you came back, it was because of your need, not my persuasion."

"Pride."

"Maybe so. But did you expect to rob me of everything?"

"Tie me up."

"What about Jeff?"

"Jeff is gone. There's only you. Tie me up. Please."

You were mine again. Mine. Your body belonged to me. I circled rope around your torso, brought it from the sternum back over your shoulders, gathered your hands behind your back and wrapped the cords around your wrists until you were firmly restrained.

"Face down on the bed."

You knelt on the mattress. I helped you lower yourself down. I wrapped rope around your ankles, cinched it tight. Tied the ends to the windings of rope around your wrists. Securely hog-tied, you started humping the mattress. I reached between your thighs and grabbed your dick. Your faithless dick. Even there, your flesh was cool to the touch.

I looped a cord to the base of your balls and wound it around soft flesh until your ball sac was taut and shiny. I flicked my forefinger against your balls. It made me happy to watch you jump. And then you looked back over your shoulder at me. The same look that the video had caught. The actor, supremely self-possessed, pretending to surrender for the sake of effect.

I roughly grabbed hold of your hard, dark shaft and tried to peel back the tight foreskin. As I worked to stretch it back over your swollen dick head, your discomfort was real. I hope. Finally the foreskin gave way. Your shiny purple dick head, slick with precome, burst forth from hiding. I had you. You were mine. My possession.

"That's enough for now. You'll sleep at the foot of my bed." I freed your hands, put locking restraints around your wrists. Tied the restraints firmly to the legs of the bed. You'd have a hell of a time if you tried to get loose. You'd have a hell of a time just trying to get to sleep.

You'd gotten off easy, though; Part of me wanted to rip you apart.

In the morning you were gone. The empty restraints lay on the floor, still tightly locked. There was a limp pile of ropes where you had been, And the front door, when I checked it, was locked. From the inside, of course.

For weeks, there was no more sign of you. I started on a new translation. I should have been writing a story about you, about us. It's the only way I had to try to master you. *I'm getting a little old for this sort of obsession,* I thought. It didn't matter. You ruled my thoughts. *Maybe all I want is to be able to say "I love you" to your face and mean it. Or maybe I want to pierce the hidden head of your dick, slip a silvery ring through the hole, feed a rope through the ring and tie it to a stake through my heart.*

My VCR went on the blink and ate the tape of you. I was robbed even of your image.

Finally, I gave up. I swallowed my pride and wrote you a letter. It said:

I know now that my desire for you is real, that it exists not despite what has happened, but because of what has happened. Your lies and your betrayal have brought us to a point beyond mere bedroom game playing. And your knowing that I am not the Master you've fantasized but only the man I am will make your submission, if it comes, riskier, more radical, and more filled with love.

I signed it "With much love" and dropped it in the mail. For weeks, it brought no answer. "Typical," I thought. And I knew that whatever my faults, you were unworthy of me, of what I had to give you. My friends, when I told them the story, all had the same response: "He's a fucked-up, confused little liar. Forget him."

But by now, with the force of a brick to the head, the words of *Vertiginous Desires* had become real to me. I could have written them myself. All that transgressive, postmodern stuff wasn't just pretentious bullshit. It was realer than real. The struggle between irony and lust was over. Lust had won.

My new translation was going nowhere. I couldn't get to sleep. You. You were possibility, promise, the threat of closing doors. The uncertainty tortured me. Fucked up, I was real fucked up. I needed resolution, any resolution. Then one day I received a letter in an unfamiliar hand. It was from Master Jeff:

There's no easy way of saying this. I'm sorry to have to tell you that your friend is dead. It happened just days after we first met. We had played most of the night. He turned out not to be the boy I'd hoped he'd be. Too controlling. I had to work hard to show him who was boss. Finally, finally, I broke him down. When I was done, I tied him to the bed. I was dissatisfied, restless. I went for a walk. I don't know what happened. When I got back, fire engines were there. The house was in flames. He died there, tied naked to my bed.

I'm torn up about this. I just can't tell you. I'll never forgive myself. I tell myself it was an accident. It doesn't matter. I failed in my responsibilities, and now he's lost. Lost to both of us. And he seemed like a real nice guy.

Failed you. We both failed you, I as much as Master Jeff. More. If I had only been what you needed… And then I realized how stupid it was to think that way. Still, if only…

I drank myself to sleep. And in the middle of the empty night, I felt you crawling into bed with me. "I'm here," you said, and I was terrified, though not of what you'd expect. Death I can deal with. I've lost plenty of friends; we all have. I was terrified of how much I needed you, of how glad I was to see you again.

"I know all about you now," I said.

"You don't know what I am. You never did. I'm a mystery. A fucking mystery." You pressed your body against mine. I grabbed your hard, uncut dick. "But whatever I am," you said, "I belong to you." You smiled. A smile for the camera.

"I love you," I said. "I need to possess you."

"Just lie back," you said. Commanded.

You started at my feet, running your cold tongue between my toes.

You worked your way up my calves, licking behind my knees, then up my inner thighs. "I exist only to serve you. There are no limits between us. No limits." Your voice was coming from everywhere and nowhere. I ached to have your mouth on my dick. Instead, you threw yourself on me, grabbing my wrists and pinning them to the bed. "No limits. Not ever again," you said, your eyes full of chill blue fire. Your body felt weightless, but I couldn't move. You kissed me, hard, shoving your tongue down my throat, filling my mouth with an odd taste, a not unpleasant taste of earth and decay.

You slithered back down my body. Grabbing my ankles, you pushed my knees to my chest. "I need you in order to be real," you said, and plunged your tongue into my ass. It had been a long time since I had been rimmed. I'd forgotten how great it felt. I started to worry that it was unsafe for you until I giddily realized it didn't matter anymore. Inside me, your probing tongue felt like cold fire. Though the tip of your tongue was buried deep, your voice was distinct. "I'll never leave you again. Never again. I'm yours forever. No limits." My body began to tremble, then shake uncontrollably. The room became filled with cold blue flames.

At first you used your fingers to open my ass wider so you could bury your tongue deeper inside. Your sharp, icy teeth pressed against my tender flesh. Then your mouth was replaced by fingertips, then fingers. I'd never been opened up so wide before. You moved your bloodless hands inside me, spreading me, opening me. Surprisingly, there was no discomfort, but there was no pleasure either. The blue flames grew brighter. I closed my eyes. "No limits," I heard you say. And then you entered me, head first, sliding up inside me. Shoulders. Torso. Butt and hard dick. Giving birth in reverse. But slithery, silky-smooth. Your legs gliding into me. Then your feet. Your toes. I felt myself close up again. Your shape shifted, stretched, filled me entirely. I looked down. Your body was gone. My skin had an eerie blue glow. You were mine. All of you, mine. And as you filled me, I experienced something so near to ultimate joy, yet so close to death…

I came in big, shuddering spurts. And when I looked down past my come-spattered belly I saw not my pink dick but your dark, uncircumcised cock.

And now you've taken over. You're with me everywhere. When I look into the mirror, I see your eyes staring from my face. When I flog a tied-up young bottom boy, I feel your hand guiding mine. When I come, it's your cock that shoots. And when I finally get to sleep, you wait implacably for me until morning comes.

There are no limits between us. No limits. You own me completely. For now. Maybe forever.

The Smile of the Fool
By Thomas S. Roche

I've been writing stories since I could hold a crayon; the first pictures I drew were narrative. These quickly blossomed into 32-panel comic books of increasing complexity. Soon I was turning out my trash-culture chapbooks regularly. I chronicled the bizarre adventures of Biff Nolton, interstellar fighter pilot, moral crusader with a cleft chin, grenade-chucking blaster-wielding badass motherfucker.

Biff was a sort of Buck Rogers rip-off, inspired by Saturday-morning serials, which makes me sound a hell of a lot older than I am. I took Biff's adventures seriously—saving the world, liberating the oppressed, flying interstellar fighter craft at breakneck speeds and generally kicking mondo alien ass.

But there were elements of humor in Biff's portrayal, elements of the smart-ass epic antipoet I was destined to become if a Mack truck didn't grind me under its tires as I crossed the street one day on my bike. My Biff was the Fool of the tarot, perhaps blissfully unaware of the doom which awaited him, keeping up his smart-ass comments even in the face of certain doom. But always leading a charmed life, because he would endure and evade all attempts to bring him down.

There were elements of parody in those early works, though to call them early works seems hopelessly pretentious and at age 6 I could hardly have uttered the word parody, let alone, say, have constructed a telling satiric morality play with elements of Shakespearean drama. I was a kid, a fucking kid. All that half-assed pseudointellectual stuff comes later in life, when we learn that in order to be allowed to dream our dreams, we have to convince people we're smarter than they are.

The task of the writer in today's economy: to convince people that they are supposed to read what the writer has to write. Ideally, you must convince a lot of people all over the world, including those who speak Estonian and Hindi, that they are supposed to read what you have to write, and thus one day cheerful publishing company accountants in three-piece suits will show up at your apartment rolling wheelbarrows full of money and carrying Nobel Prizes. That's how it works. Trust me, I've read *Writer's Digest*.

But when I was 6, I didn't understand these complicated geopolitical and economic factors that have since come together to form the late-20th-century global-village literary-intellectual zeitgeist. Man, I just wanted to kick some fuckin' ass, blow away some Satan-worshipping Nazi aliens, liberate the oppressed, save the world, get some pussy.

I didn't call it pussy, of course, but that's what it boiled down to. Biff, like Buck, like Kirk, like Flash Gordon, always rescued the girl as well, and even if I didn't yet *know* what Biff and that crudely rendered flat-chested stick figure with long hair and no ass were going to do in the backseat of the interstellar fighter plane, I had seen enough James Bond movies and soft-focus scenes in *Star Trek* to know that they sure as hell were going to do *something*. And it was something of which, even at that tender age, I wanted Biff to *get a little*. Of whatever it was he was supposed to be getting.

✍

It always astonishes me when adults think that children are not sexual. It's as if acknowledging the sexuality in children's actions would become a license for adults to manipulate and use them inappropriately—as if adults needed such a license. Or as if adults who manipulate and use children in nonsexual ways, which includes every set of parents I've ever encountered, are somehow protected by the moratorium on children's sexuality. Well, I'm not going to go into a debate on that shit, because there's too much blood to be shed over that issue, too many children suffering and dying in silence in a society that will neither acknowledge their sexuality nor protect it from abuse by adults or, just as important, other children. But what little I do know, I know about myself. My behavior was not sexual—not in that context. It hadn't been translated yet, by my body, into sexuality. But the alphabet of sadomasochism was there in my early years as much as it is now—the vowels and consonants of a society built on nonconsensual power exchange. Even as sheltered as I was from the realities of the world's struggles, I knew that the guy in tall black boots with the riding crop could kick your ass if he wanted. And there wasn't a goddamn thing you could do about it.

✍

But what's notable here is that while Biff was going through his complicated rituals of destruction and rescue, he always found time to fall into the space aliens' clutches. My aliens were not multitentacled psychopaths that gibbered and drooled slime. I came of age well after *Weird Tales* but well before the little gray guys in mirror shades showed up on key chains around the world. No, my aliens were human, and I swear I am not making this up, in some of the comics I drew these aliens were Nazis. My moral fiber having been bred not on Jesus and Moses but on *The Magnificent Seven* and *Hogan's Heroes, The Longest Day* and *The Guns of Navarone,* and tempered by my older sister's explanations of what happened at Auschwitz and Treblinka, I superimposed upon the alien threat the mark of the worst evil I could conjure—the very face of the devil, spewing totalitarian vitriol. Maybe it's just that in my primitive drawing style, a swastika was about the only recognizable symbol of evil that I could manage. But I thought up complicated explanations for why the aliens were Nazis—Hitler had escaped Berchtesgaden on a teleportation beam; the aliens had preserved his brain in a jar; Hitler was an invading alien in the first place, only *pretending* to be an Austrian, and Nazism was, after all, a virus from outer space.

But whoever it was wearing the tall black boots, the main factor is that these aliens, both female and male, would kick Biff Nolton's ass with the abandon of Emperor Hirohito with a 14-inch strap-on.

Biff would get his ass kicked, his jaw busted, his body swathed in contusions and broken flesh. He would almost be consumed in the conflagration of his crash-landing fighter plane; he would battle his way unarmed through enemy soldiers and finally be taken in chains to the fortress of the evil alien lord; he would fight through seemingly insurmountable odds; he would endure the agonies of the damned under the cruel implements of his captors and never, never, never give up the safeword, oops, I mean secret plans, of course.

Sound familiar? Sound like fun? Sound like last weekend?

✍

These games I played with myself, these binder-paper epics of protosexual illumination and obfuscation, were obviously never intended as erotica. They certainly weren't perceived as such by the adults I showed them to, most of whom chuckled and made comments about how creative I was, occasionally saying things like "I thought these were aliens. Why do they have swastikas on their foreheads?"

Nowadays, I don't show my stories to adults. And the aliens don't have swastikas. And I am well aware of the details of what James Bond was doing with his girlfriend in the backseat of the Aston-Martin (and maybe with Q when the cameras weren't rolling). I have no doubt about what Buck Rogers and Wilma did in the back of the spaceship. I even teach classes on it. And my characters, most of the time, get much more than a little.

But the structure of those power relationships hasn't changed in my fantasies, any more than it's changed in the real world. On the one hand that's depressing: No matter how much progress we seem to make as a culture and a species, there are still guys in big black boots with riding crops—and the sad, terrible thing is that they are not—ever—aliens. If they were, we could just deport the mother-fuckers to Venus and be done with it.

But the shape of those boots, the texture of that riding crop, still become to me exactly what all my fears became in those early days of suffering and confusion. They became my fantasies. Because the process of suffering and surviving, the experience of being dominated and standing my ground, the process of resisting evil, is what everything in my life, from paying the rent to buying immortality with Fiction Stamps, is about. There are those in the real world who will get their ass kicked by Satan-worshiping alien motherfuckers in tall boots (or cops or soldiers or priests) without the barest hint of their consent, and it goes without saying that they won't like it one bit. Meanwhile, the sufferings of real-life people can fuel my darkest fantasies—which should seem like bastardization, theft, irreverence—but it doesn't. Because for me sex is about resistance, it's about strength, it's about struggle, it's about perseverance—it's about victory. And only through defeat, through submission, through surrender, can I know the taste of that which I most fear. Know its taste, savor its texture, relish its agonies. So when the real live black-booted motherfuckers come to kick my ass, I can spit that surrender out of my mouth. And kick their asses instead. With the smile of the fool on my face.

Broken and Entered
By Thomas S. Roche

"You know I'm gonna fuck you, punk. You can't wait."

It was just a statement—something obvious. But of course he meant it as a threat. Hearing it made my muscles tense and my head spin. Across the street, the clock in the church's tower struck 11.

I heard him laughing as he stood over me. "That's right. I can see your little pussy ass clenching when you think about it. Well, think about it good and hard, punk. Think about getting fucked, 'cause you're gonna get fucked, all right."

He knelt over me and put his hand on my ass. He squeezed my ass cheeks tightly, bending close so I could feel his hot, wet breath on my ear as he growled: "And this is where I'm gonna fuck you. Right here."

He squeezed my ass tighter and jammed his fingers into the crack. I squirmed and pulled against my bonds, tried to make some kind of noise—to shout for help, even though I knew no one would hear me. I lived upstairs from an accountant's office, and they would be long gone for the day. Besides, I couldn't make a sound—this bastard had gagged me with several of my own dirty socks. And I most certainly couldn't move.

☛

People always said that surprising a burglar in your house was the best way to get yourself killed—or worse. But I never thought it would happen to me or that the guy would let me get undressed first while he watched from under the bed. Or that a guy would be able to overpower me like this.

I had put up a fight—that was for sure. My shitty little apartment was in a shambles and there was a cut above my right eye and dried blood on my face. I had put up a fight—but he had subdued me. He had held me down and tied my hands, ripped off my bathrobe and cut the remaining rags off with a knife. Now he had me on my side on the rug, naked except for my Jockey shorts. My ankles and wrists were tied together in front of me. I was doubled over, which meant my ass was exposed.

He went around the apartment, emptying out drawers and looking for valuables. He didn't find much, but he made a real show of trashing my apartment.

He got my wallet and looked through it.

"Not much money, Jacob. Or do you get called 'Jake'? Well, Jake it is. Jake. You're a poor boy. Not too much to sell. I'll have to take something else that you got. I think it'll do just fine."

He kept going through my drawers. I felt my stomach turning as he opened the drawer that held my...photos. He pulled out the brown envelopes and looked through them one by one, chuckling.

"That your girlfriend, Jake?" He whistled, as if in awe. "Man, she really can strut it. She likes to do things for the camera and make pretty pictures. Looks like she does chicks too, but maybe that's only if you're watching. Well, one cock up your ass ain't gonna make her too jealous." He rummaged some more. "Yeah! Lube. That's what we need, and lots of it. Your straight ass is probably pretty fucking tight. But that's the way I like them... Oh, more pictures! Mmm...she likes it in the ass too. You ever taken it up the ass, straight boy? Nah, I didn't think so. You fucking arty types are all chickenshit. How'd you get a dildo that big up her ass, anyway?"

I flushed red and hot.

"Well, now I know what your girlfriend can take, pal. But it's you I'm interested in. I want to see how much you can take. I'm pretty horny, and I need a good come. I think I'll put it inside your ass." He bent close to me.

"You and me are gonna get a little more acquainted, punk."

He roughly pulled down my Jockey shorts, exposing my ass, and wedged his hand in between my ass cheeks. I squirmed and choked as I felt his finger going into me.

"That's right," he growled. "You're gonna get a good ass fucking tonight, Jakey-wakey. You thought you were real tough, putting up a fight and all. But you're just a punk. And I'm gonna punk you real good tonight, straight boy."

He worked his finger in and out of my ass, chuckling with evil glee the whole time. I whimpered and shivered as he finger-fucked my dry ass.

"What the fuck do you care?" he said. "You like chicks who take it up the ass, from the looks of the pictures in that drawer. Take it up the ass from real big cocks. It'll be just like that, only you'll be the one getting it."

He jammed two fingers up my ass, squeezing my cheeks tight as he worked me up. He kept rubbing his prick through his jeans with his free hand, getting himself ready to fuck me. He wore a tight pair of work jeans and he filled them pretty well.

He backed off, grinning, and disappeared for a second. He came back with a coil of rope in one hand and a switchblade in the other.

"Come on, honey, let's go to bed. It's our honeymoon suite! I'm gonna pop your cherry, you fuckin' blushing bride!" He laughed like he thought that was the funniest thing in the world.

He slipped the switchblade into his pocket and hung the rope from his belt so he could use both hands on me. He pulled me up by my hair and my wrists, throwing me onto the bed. It smelled of sweat and sex. He got me onto my belly and used his knife to slash the ropes that tied my wrists.

"Don't fight, now, or I might have to hurt you! I did it once, I'll do it again, fucker!"

He wrestled me down, holding tight. He had me good. He got one wrist tied to the bedpost and I managed to get the other free, twisting away from him. I got to my knees and tried to pull the rope free.

He bellowed in rage and brought his knee between my legs to connect with my balls. The wind rushed out of me and pain shot through my body. I collapsed onto the bed. He crawled back on top of me.

"See? All it takes is a knee in the balls and you're real, real obedient. Don't try that again, punk; it'll be your face next time."

He got my other wrist tied and I started to struggle a bit, just a bit, as he moved down to my ankles.

"What did I tell you!" He reached down between my legs. He got hold of my balls, and my whole body spasmed in pain. I quieted down right away. He squeezed harder, and I howled through the gag.

"Keep still, now. Don't want to damage you for your fucking horny girlfriend. She'd never forgive me."

He tied both my ankles. I was careful to keep real, real still. He walked around to the side of the bed, inspecting me.

"Not bad," he said. "I think your ass can probably get me off."

He slipped off his clothes slowly, taking his time. As he got out of his Jockeys, I saw that his cock was fucking huge. He was a monster. I'd never seen a cock that big. I breathed hard.

"Like what you see?" he said. "It's gonna feel real, real good getting into you."

He used the knife to cut away my Jockey shorts. Then he settled down on top of me, letting his naked cock sink into the cleft of my ass. His hairy arms curved around me.

He clicked open the switchblade and took care of my gag. He held the knife close to my face.

"Way I figure it, asshole, by the time you could make enough noise for anyone at all to hear, I could make you very, very sorry that you did. Plus, this apartment is pretty damn far from anything. I think you could scream all you want and all you'd get is a real bad cut, maybe as bad as they get. Isn't that what you think? *Isn't it?*"

I nodded quickly, desperately. He was right. There was no way out.

He slipped the knife down, away from my face. He wedged his hand under my body and got hold of my balls, squeezing them hard so that my eyes watered. He wrestled me onto my side, just a little, so that he could get hold of my balls good. He squeezed until I didn't think I could take the pain. Then I felt the knife. He was stroking me with the edge of the blade, right at the tender under-side of my balls. Teasing me with the feel of the knife's edge. Telling me what was going to happen if I put up a fight or wouldn't do what he wanted.

He was talking real low, in an almost gentle growl. "I knew you'd understand. I'm gonna punk you real good, put it right up your ass and fuck you till I come in your chute. And if you don't go along with it, I'm gonna take your balls with me in my pocket. Doesn't matter to me. Your straight ass is tight, just the way I like it, whether or not you got balls on that puny cock of yours."

He rubbed the knife more firmly over my balls, shaving off some of the hair. I whimpered a little and squirmed against him. He pressed harder, the tip of the knife against the soft nut sac. I held still. Slowly he eased the knife up my body, letting me feel it sliding against my flesh. He held it up against my face, pressing the edge to my lips. He began to stroke my face with the edge of the knife, almost tenderly. Tears formed in my eyes.

"But I got a funny kink about straight guys. I like to hear 'em beg. Can you beg for me, Jacob?"

I choked back a sob.

"Do it, Jacob. It gets me so fucking hard. It'll make it so much better for me when I fuck your ass—if I can just hear you beg for it first. It'll make me happy. And when I'm not happy…"

He moved the knife again, getting it up against my balls. But I said nothing.

"All right, I wasn't making myself clear. I want to hear you say something, punk. Just once, I want to hear you say 'fuck me up the ass.' And you better say it with feeling. Can you say that for me or do I have to make your girlfriend buy you a strap-on dildo?"

I panicked. My heart raced. "Fuck me up the ass," I whimpered.

"You asshole. You can't get away with saying it like that. I guess your bitch gets fucked by a rubber dick from now on. 'Cause yours ain't gonna be doing much." He stroked my nuts with the edge of the blade.

"Fuck me up the ass!" I said it louder, harder, desperate with fear.

"Not quite good enough." He ran the tip of the blade slowly up my cock.

"Fuck me up the ass!" And he made me say it again and again, 30 or 40 times, chuckling every time he heard it, and threatening me. Finally I sobbed and panted and moaned it, "Fuck me up the ass!" Like all the women in the porn movies I'd seen. And then he was finally satisfied. He leaned back on his haunches and picked up the lube.

"Sure thing, loverboy. I guess you must want it pretty bad."

The ice-cold lube landed in my crack, and he began to work it in. I felt two fingers going into me. I gritted my teeth. He worked me up to three. I held my breath.

"Mmm…not as tight as I thought. Maybe she's the one with the strap-on?"

He lowered himself on top of me, and his long cock slid into my crack. He took hold of my hair and sank his teeth into the back of my neck, hard. He knew right where to put his cock; my asshole had been opened by his fingers. I groaned as I felt the head pushing its way in.

"Real easy, punk. Just take it and it'll feel a lot better. You're gonna love it."

He pushed in, and my ass clenched tight. He didn't give way but forced it deeper, stretching my ass open and pushing his cock home. He got it into my ass, just an inch or two, and I felt like I was going to explode. Just to hurt me, just to torment me, he held it there right at the entrance.

The edge of the knife touched my cheek.

"Say it again, punk. Just once. For me?"

Gasping, aching, straining: "Fuck me up the ass!"

"Oh, that's good. You say it like you mean it."

With that, he sank in another few inches, slowly, then gave it to me all the way. I squirmed against him as I took it. His balls slapped between my legs.

I felt invaded, dominated, humiliated. I had been entered, and my will was broken. Every tiny bit I moved made my ass ache and clench tighter. I tried to relax and just let him fuck me. I lay there, limp, as he did me good, opening me up, taking what he wanted out of my yielding, unresistant body.

"Good boy," he said. "Now just lay there while I do you. I never take too long. I'm not one of those tender, loving types. I do it fast. I'll try to make it real fast for you, since I know you can't wait for my come."

He pulled out a little, then shoved it back in hard so that I gasped.

He took his time, first going fast, then real slow, letting me feel every inch of it. He laughed as he took his time. He knew that every second I was being fucked was humiliation and agony for me. But I lay there and took his cock up my ass. Accepted it. Submitted to it. Sweat dripped down my back.

"That's right, that's right," he growled into my ear. He brought his hand down my side, stroking my flesh. His sweat dribbled onto the back of my head. He shoved his hands under me and took hold of my hips, giving himself leverage as he went on fucking me. He seemed to enjoy every second of it.

I tried to give up my asshole to him. I gave myself over to his cock. It seemed to relax, and his lubed cock slid in and out much easier. But I could feel every inch of his flesh as he reamed me.

It started to feel better as he fucked me. But it stretched on, minute after minute, until I lost count of the thrusts. I couldn't believe his control. I could never be in a pussy that long without shooting my load. I realized that he was holding back, just to see me endure the ass fucking as long as possible. The sweat burned into my eyes. The bells in the church outside struck midnight, then 1. My ass was open wide, fucked open until it was nothing but a sheath for his cock. It was beginning to hurt like hell, my bowels filled with lube and shit and agony.

Finally, he growled into my ear: "You just don't get it, do you? You gotta beg for me to come. Say it."

It took me a long time and a few slaps across the face and a couple of strokes of the knife across my balls before I could croak desperately: "Come in my asshole!"

Then he told me it wasn't good enough, he was going to have to… finally, after I'd said it 30 times or more, he laughed and started pounding into my ass. I gasped in agony. He was finally going to do it.

"Oh yeah," he grunted as his cock shot long, thick streams of come into me. I could feel it squirting in and dripping out my asshole. He took a long time to come, and my ass felt like I'd just gotten a hot enema.

"That's good," he said. "Real good. Now I've got a few things to do before I finish up."

After he put his clothes on, he went into the other room and came back with several large brown envelopes: the photos from my drawer. Nude photos. He tucked them into one of my gym bags, along with my few valuables: a watch, a gold picture frame, one of her bracelets, a couple of other things. He zipped up the bag and got on top of me again.

"Now, I don't think you're in any condition to struggle," he told me. "But in case you are: don't. That offer still goes, if you want to try life as a girl."

He cut the ropes on my wrists and ankles, still holding me down. The long ass fucking had left me helpless. I didn't even squirm as he dragged me onto the floor and tied me on my side with my wrists and ankles together in front of me. I could feel his come smeared across my cheeks, dribbling down my thighs and onto the carpet. He gagged me with rope this time.

"Way I figure it," he said, "you can get out of those things in about 15 minutes. That's enough time for me to vanish like the wind. Now I didn't take anything worth much, so if I were you, I wouldn't think about calling the police once you get loose. Or I might have to come back with a couple of my buddies, some time when you're not alone. Got it?"

I nodded, and he smiled, patting my slick ass.

"Just remember, Jake. I can always come back. Your ass is mine, any time I want. Keep it open wide for me, OK? And do yourself a favor and get that bitch to use that dildo on you sometime."

The door slammed. He left it unlocked.

✍

It took me 10 minutes, not 15. I crouched on the floor among the remains of the ropes, found a pack of matches and my smokes. I lit a cigarette. I finished the first and smoked four or five more, until I felt vaguely sick.

The door opened again, and Micky came in. The gym bag was gone. He grinned.

"Jacob! Don't you make a fetching sight," he said, coming over to me. He bent down and kissed me, sliding his hand down my bare, sticky chest. "How was work?"

I cracked, and started to sob, and Micky picked me up and carried me to the bed, holding me, asking me many, many times what was wrong. He thought the scene had gone sour.

But it wasn't sour: I just had to cry, to close the scene, to complete the exercise and follow the night to its conclusion.

Like the other, it was just an act. It wasn't long before I stopped sobbing and started moaning, and Micky soothed me with tender violence.

✍

"What did you do with the pictures?"

"I burned them in the alley," he said.

I took a drag from my cigarette, dabbing come from my lips onto the butt.

"Nice touch."

"I thought so."

"And the bracelet?"

"In the river."

"Like a true artist."

The clock in the church struck 3.

Junkie

By M. Christian

My name is Chris, and I'm a writer. I have it bad.

You'll hear a lot of different reasons why people write in this book—from a sexual journey to empowerment or a way of making a living, to a way of saying what otherwise couldn't be said—but I think I'm unique. My name is Chris, and I'm a writing junkie.

Bad doesn't describe how bad I have it either, and it certainly doesn't describe how badly it has me.

It wasn't always this way. I've always been imaginative, always living several lives at once, only one of them "real." Stories and fantasy have always been a big part of my life. I remember deciding in the fourth grade to be a science fiction writer. I had never written a word, but I knew that's what I wanted to be. What could be better? Sitting around and dreaming up robots, aliens, weird tales, twisted stories, all day long—it was what I was doing anyway.

I started to think seriously about it in high school, and that's when I first tried to write. God, those first stories were awful (and in my darker moments I see my new stuff just as critically): a big dash of Ellison, a hefty sprinkle of Bester, some Lafferty, some Zelazny, and very little of me. I remember my fantasies around writing quite distinctly. I was holding a book with my pseudonym sprawled across the cover in gothic boldness and a stark, dramatic image such as a screaming face or an eclipsed sun or a crystal starship.

So I began and found out very quickly that it was much harder than I thought. The ideas were there, but the language just wouldn't cooperate. I had a poor grasp of grammar, an even worse comprehension of spelling, and I was dyslexic. I also suffered from an unreasonable need to be clever and to avoid simple language. Somewhere

I read Bradbury's idea that if you wrote a short story a week, one or two would have to be good, just by sheer probability. So I did just that. I wrote a story a week for years and years, religiously, pathologically, and every last one of them completely, absolutely sucked.

Now, of course, I know that all those wasted nights did me some good. They taught me discipline, gave me a sense of pride in that while so many of my friends were wishing and waiting, I was at least trying to achieve my goals. It also gave me a good part of my writer's "voice," the tone you hear reading this.

But writing then wasn't really love or even lust. It was work. Hard, miserable work. Yes, sometimes the magic was there and something sprang from my fingers that made tears run down my cheeks because *I* had written it. But most of the time it was as much fun as pushing a boulder up an endless steep hill.

Sex changed all that, but not in the way you think. Years and years and years later, and married, I was exposed to two special things: the wide wonderful world of sexuality and the idea that science fiction wasn't the only market for my writing. I knew both of these things before, of course. I've always been very sexual (even if it was just with myself), and I knew about other forms of writing, but I didn't really have access to either realm.

On a lark, my wife signed me up for a class taught by Lisa Palac, who was then editor of the *FutureSex* magazine. I'd tried months before that to write sex stories for women (or, at least at the time, I'd hoped they were women) I'd met on the infant Internet. I passed one of these to Lisa at the end of the class, and she bought it. Then Susie Bright picked it up for her *Best American Erotica* series.

Just like that I was a real, dyed-in-the-wool writer. A pornographer, yes, but still a writer. Slowly, here and there, I started to sell more and more stories. With my best friend Thomas Roche's help and support I recognized that all writing is writing and that a well-written smut story can be just as marvelous as anything in *The New Yorker*. For the first time people not only wanted to read what I wrote but were willing to pay me for it. It was incredible; it was fantastic; it was a dream come true.

As I write this, eight or so years after that first sale, I have a résumé that could choke a horse: 100-plus published short stories, a collection from Alyson (*Dirty Words*), editorship of seven anthologies, five monthly columns, and some very nice accolades. I've also written about three dozen well-received science fiction and fantasy stories.

But something has changed. Unlike that first sale that made me a professional, this transformation is harder to pinpoint. I can't look back and say, "There, that's when the bug bit, when the disease took hold." Perhaps it was when writing first stopped being work and started being fun or maybe when putting the words down began to be more enjoyable than the possible sale. All I know is I'm not the person I was when I started out. I can see this in the way I view what I do: The rock is gone; the hill has vanished. It's not work anymore; it's pure lust, a wonderful drug, my new religion—and I've got it bad.

✍

Allow me to really mix my metaphors for a moment. Writing is a sex drug, a literary Viagra, a literary nirvana. It's a genital thrill as well as a cerebral explosion, a religious high—and I love it. Sometimes.

When I teach writing I wax poetic about the magic of storytelling. We are magicians, the people in this book and other folks who feel the need to write. We create wonders out of nothing—no clay, no brush, no camera; just words, our own consciousness—and we create things that live longer than any pot, any picture, any movie. By ourselves, we create miracles with only our minds and dreams. This is not hyperbole; it's how I feel.

People ask me about my spirituality. Is "M. Christian" Christian, Pagan, Buddhist, Jewish, or none of the above? Answer: I'm a writer; that's my faith, my God. The same people ask about my sex life. Is "M. Christian" straight, gay, bi, a masochist, a sadist, or some mad combination of them all? I smile and say that I'm politically gay, socially bi, and physically straight, but my real lust is for writing. I've sampled a lot of drugs in my time, the hardest being speed and coke, the lightest being chocolate, but there is no drug more powerful than writing.

I really think I see the world differently. I walk down the street and everything I look at becomes words, a short string of description, the fragment of a story. When I talk, I often see what I and other people are saying as lines of dialogue. When I dream, I "write" my dreams, changing the outcome to suit dramatic structure.

When I look at people I can't help but wonder about them: what their lives are like, what they think, what their daydreams might be. When I'm in an erotic mood (i.e., have a deadline), I wonder what they might look like naked, like to do in bed, their first time, their last time. What do their orgasms sound like? What does their come taste like? I don't really get aroused by these thoughts, but I do get a kind of spiritual hard-on by coming up with what I think is a fuckin' dynamite story, when I just can't wait to get back to my machine and start to write.

Ah...for me, there is nothing better than when a story is going well, when everything just...clicks; when, from conception to completion, it's what I wanted to say, and I said it well. God, sex, drugs all fall aside when compared to the powerful magic of writing. God is in heaven and doesn't really care about us; sex is a messy joy that lasts for a minute, if you're lucky; and drugs make you feel like a wad of used gum the day after. But a story and the joy of the words—that can last for days, for weeks, sometimes even for years. I have characters that have stayed with me longer than lovers, stories that are more real in my mind than the time I lost my virginity or when my father died.

I have it bad, and it's glorious. Sometimes.

When it's good, I bathe in arrogance. I can do something you can't. I have stories that will outlive me, and I don't have to share the acclaim with anyone. I, and I alone, sat down and pounded it out of nothing but my own thoughts and soul. No actors, no instruments, no team, just me. Sex doesn't compare, drugs are weak, and even God is small and distant compared to the joy that suffuses me when I write it down just right.

The fact that I write about girls with ravenous cunts, butt-fucking bikers, leather-clad dykes, or bottoms with steak-tartare asses doesn't change a thing. I'm a writer, and that's all that matters. But since this is a book on sex writing, I'd like to focus on that.

I have a great little story. I usually write everything under the same pseudonym (out of a combination of a need for privacy and a mischievous joy in being able to recreate myself on the page), but sometimes I have to pull another one out of my hat. For example, if an editor has me in a book more than twice or the editor has a thing about a boy being in an all-girl book...whatever the reason, sometimes I pull out "Alice." Alice (to protect certain publications, I won't give her last name here) has sold about a dozen or so stories, sometimes with quite a bit of recognition.

So there I was at this party. Writing comes up. Someone says he has a story in the current issue of this certain magazine. I run the title and month through my mind and realize that I too have a story in the same issue and mention it. Curious, this guy asks me for the title. I tell him, then explain that I had to use my other name for that story. His jaw drops, falling right there on the floor—skidding across the linoleum until it rests against the fridge in the nearby kitchen. "I masturbated to that story," he squeaks, shocked and confused that the lesbian sex story he read and that got him off was written by a 40-year-old man.

I smiled. Damn, sometimes this job is so-o-o good.

In the back of my mind I have a file of stories like that and memories of conversations, letters, E-mails, book titles, and good reviews. I pull them out all the time and roll around in them. Yes, writing can be a burning hot drug and a damned powerful faith, but when it's good it's the best sex you've ever had. Stories like that make my dick throb, steel-strong, bobbing with strength. Rock. Hard.

When I finish a story it's like a great fuck. When I sell a story it's like an orgasm that rattles your back teeth. When I get in a book with "Best" in the title it's like a come that is God giving you the thumbs-up. When I sell a book, it's like the *petite morte* that shows you the glories of heaven: I am the sexiest man alive, my penis is great and powerful, my semen boils with genius, and my orgasms destroy buildings in Anchorage, Alaska.

Sometimes.

If you are not a writer, you can't understand. How could you? If you can't understand the glorious power of when it's good, then how can you ever understand how terrible it is when it goes bad?

When you write, it's just you. There's no one else to share the credit. When you fail, there's no one else to share the failure. It's just you, in the dark, by yourself.

There's something else you should know about me, to put this next part in perspective. Yes, failure is hard, but for me the good is rare and the bad is common: I'm a chronic depressive. My therapist, my ex-wife, and my lover all say the same thing: "You've picked a hard life for yourself," meaning that writing is not exactly the best choice for someone with self-esteem issues. I always explain that I didn't choose to be an obsessive writer; it's bigger than my religion, my hunger for caffeine, and my lust all put together. I didn't choose writing, writing chose me.

When it's bad it's very bad. Jesus on his chromium throne, it can be bad. Writing something that I know is just shit is like not having a date for the ball; getting a rejection letter is like getting stood up; getting turned down for a "Best of" book is like someone pointing at my dick and laughing; and getting a book rejected is like someone saying "You want to do what?" with disgust in their voice. More often than I mentally pull out those glowing reviews and wonderful sales, I moan and roll around in agony over the sales that didn't happen, the nasty rejection slips, the editors and friends who don't return my E-mails. I've never attempted suicide, but I've wished many times for death or at least discontinuance.

So where does that leave me? Right now my depression and anxiety feel like they're pushing me toward a point where nothing about my writing will make me happy—that all my negative feelings will wash away the successes, the inherent joy I used to feel about telling stories.

That is the fear, part of the depression. There's also something else that I try to remember when the pit yawns beneath my feet: There is a solution. A religious man would pray; an addict would either get clean or go on a bender; a sex fiend would get laid. But I'm not really any of those, and so my solution is different.

I'm a writer. I'll write.

I know that might sound simplistic, but lately I've been allowing myself to write simply for the joy of it: to play with words and stories, exorcise demons, and celebrate the ecstasy of creation. I've been trying to let go of the competitive, business side of writing and to remember why I do it.

When I teach, I say something like this, but I've been really trying to put it into practice: "Celebrate the story and not the sale." It's hard to remember that when some editor points at your wang (like I said, that's how it feels) and laughs his or her head clean off, but try I do. I've been trying to revel in creativity, to stay in that wonderful ecstasy of writing, to keep playing with language and words.

Happy ending? Not yet. But this story is a work in progress. It's hard to say for certain, but I think I'll be smiling at the end.

After all, I'm writing, and there's really nothing that's better than that.

COUNTING
By M. Christian

Overheated from the humid kitchen, the front windows fogged with condensation then streaked with clarity where drops raced down. The café wasn't exactly a place to show restraint, to bottle a smile, a smirk, a loud laugh. The place was safe, after all; the Militia were cracking heads in the Tenderloin, but this was the Castro/Mission— a world away. Still, Tubal was calm when I told him. No excitement. No pleasure. Not angry that *I* was telling *him* about it.

This was our space, not theirs.

"Cut his balls off, stuck 'em in his mouth," I said, "and sewed it shut. Don't know if he was still kicking when they did it, but he probably was. Hell, why go through the work if he was dead?"

Even the papers called it "an atrocity," a "brutal and senseless act of cruelty" in halting, official English. Hundreds dead in a food riot, "necessary means," secret raids, friends missing, "keeping the public order."

One civil servant accused of child rape—in whispers at bus stops, on illegal networks, in the endless lines for bread or clean water. Found with cock and balls stuffed in his mouth, stitched up.

"Number 7," I said. "In his blood on the wall."

The only thing Tubal said was "I wonder how high it'll go."

✍

I was lucky. I was safe because I was a necessity. My covert peccadilloes were overlooked because I was a system hack, the guy who kept the local Citicore network from delivering Sanskrit instead of the analyzed and digitized results of the Tokyo exchange.

I had acquired my skill because my father had managed to keep me in a Militia school until I was old enough to read and because when he was gone my street friends had opened some doors and shown me where the old info was kept.

Masoqui, the taciturn and finely sculpted Serb who ran the local Citicore office, knew I was gay—worse than dirt. He could've, should've turned me in. After all, he was a devout New Muslim. Rules were rules, God was in his heaven, and the police squeal line was a speed dial on his personal phone.

Unless, of course, you knew how to keep the machines working.

So I stayed in the dark, with bundles of stiff fiber-optic cable and humming junction boxes smelling faintly of ozone and cooking plastic. I worked my magic, stayed hidden in the walls, and survived.

✍

I had been going through one of the old burned-out wrecks in the Mission. The info I'd scammed had said it used to be an auxiliary trunk line for the old telephone company, before the Militia had rolled down Folsom and blown it as a makeshift firebreak—a little stronghold against the scattered potshots of the old Munipolice.

The building's upper stories were a gap-toothed shell, the lower floors buried under complex bergs of broken concrete and twisted steel. In the days before the Crazy, the navigable floors would've housed dozens of families. Now it was empty.

I found a hall that was bare, cleaned of broken concrete and smelling of brackish water and, faintly—the ghost of gaunt children with bloated bellies—urine.

One end was blocked by a solid steel door. Scratches and dents showed where the desperate had tried to force their way inside. The desperate, though, had starved or been killed before they could succeed.

Even with the power-arm I'd checked out of the tool library, it took me two hours to pry the door open. Then another two to clear away the rubble from the main junction boxes. It was worth it, though. Like bales of glassy hair, bundles of fiber and fine wire packed the lower level. Enough to keep the San Francisco Citicore running for a long time.

I had just started with the company back then, drawn purely by the hatred and desperation in the eyes of the old Serb, Masoqui. "You fix, I pay you," was all he said after showing me the cracked casings of the interlink junctions and the stained, frayed, and bent fibers. I said I would. "In two day," he said. I'd agreed. The only alternative was another week in the Unemployed Shelter, then soon to the heavy fighting in the Northern Wilds—I had been two weeks from military conscription.

It was getting dark as I finally made my way out with my treasure of lost technology, the sunset powerful and dull orange against the saw-toothed skyline. I remembered people talking about when the city had been tall and gleaming. State of the art, back when there was art. But all I'd ever known was the jumble of five-story buildings, rooftops jagged where the Militia had sheered them off. Not enough power for lifts, not enough food for the inhabitants—so make the city smaller. Or so the Militia had decided.

I could just make out the Citicore building, one of a half dozen buildings that still managed some precarious sky-scraping. Wet feet in shoes two sizes too big, stomach beyond hungry and now slightly distended, bundles of fiber wrapped around my shoulders, my waist, I pushed and pulled myself out. My thoughts were alive with little dreams (the only kind anyone could really afford, back then): clean food, maybe medicine, reasonable clothes, a room somewhere. Maybe even enough for wine rather than turpentine.

Guns: one of the first things the Militia had stripped from the city, then the state. Only the Militia produced them now, used them now—on criminals and deviants too slow to hide. The gun was a fear symbol: A stylized pistol on a square of red against a field of pure, unblemished white hung from the stones of City Hall.

The first time I saw it, I thought it was an old pipe. Then the realization came. I sat down, lowered my eyes, and stitched my fingers together behind my head: baser reflexes, familiar voices at food riots when I was a boy, and now food riots when I'm much older, screaming, "Sit or die."

"What are you doing here?"

I tensed, expecting a bullet.

He repeated himself, crunching over to me on the broken stone. I shook, rustling the bundles of fibers.

"Scavenging? That's all you're doing. Shit." the expletive carried the sound of release, and I felt the barrel of the pistol, the hot dot of his aim, fall from my head. "You could get killed for that, you know."

"I know. It's for a job. Parts to fix a fiber-optical telecom link." My words were crisp, stuttering, explaining way too much.

He hauled me along by grabbing one of the loops of line. "Come on, you can't hang around here."

I looked at him, Tubal, for the first time. My height, but stocky and well-formed. I could see his muscles even through his gray Maintenance jumpsuit. Bald. A salt-and-pepper mustache, bristly and stiff. His eyes, I found later, were so blue as to be closer to steel. His teeth, also later, weren't jagged tombstones on an eroding hill-side for once. Only a single wayward incisor, leaning backward. His breath smelled of lemons, and I thought instantly of money and the exotic things it could buy.

Too frightened to do anything but follow, hauling the power-arm and the cables that would help me fix Mr. Masoqui's fiber-optical telecom link station, Tubal led me out of Old Town, up to Mission. At the Militia checkpoint, he smiled and showed that nearly perfect smile to the young Militia men. Offering them slim black sticks of their intense tobacco, he made small talk with them—keeping me under his arm, protected. I was numb from the pistol and heard ringing in my ears—the bullet that was never fired. It was a zombie he escorted through the battery sellers, the water filterers, the drug markets. A zombie spared from death.

Days later, in my dark corner of Mr. Masoqui's building, I realized I'd been hard as a rock the whole time.

✍

The fibers did the job—enough at least to make the stone of Mr. Masoqui's face smile tightly with satisfied self-interest. My niche was won. Still, I didn't move from the alley at 16th and Guerrero, from the old blue Americom shipping crate, for nearly a month. All the cash Masoqui slipped me went into more fiber; ancient, corroded connectors; and water-stained and nearly illegible ancient manuals from before the Militia, the Reformed Western States, and New Muslim.

When I did move, my possessions in a canvas shopping bag, it was to a tiny room in an old Victorian: ancient plaster walls run with moisture, stained yellow, brown, and black from the candles and lanterns of previous tenants. My landlord was Chinese, an elusive figure who descended from his iron-barred fortress on the third floor only to extract the weekly rent. Everyone was in their rooms on Fridays, waiting for the soft knock of Mr. Sung. Failure to be present or not have the required 300 Sols would mean a visit from the Militia.

Of me, Sung had no concern or opinion, except that I was always there on Fridays with my money. I could've been collecting the genitals of children for all he cared. I was for him what I was for Masoqui: a resource. Everything else was immaterial.

My first month, I was caught outside in a riot. I hadn't been there long enough to recognize the neighborhood's telltales, the rhythm of the block: when the stores would be allowed to open, when the local Militia had to make its quota, when the insane would be released from their camps to clean and scour the streets of anything valuable or edible.

I was walking back from work, head lost in a maze of junctions, cross-connectors, light-boosts, and mirror boxes, trying to deduce a ghost echo in the inner-office trunk lines. I was too full of Mr. Masoqui's system to notice the closed windows or the quiet. Then… running people. Seeing them sprint past, chests rising, breath fogging the cool evening, looking behind as they ran, I turned as well.

A wave rounded Market—a panicked sea of old Militia coats flapping, feet wrapped in threadbare carpets, eyes red and desperate. A thousand, probably more, screaming and crying as people do only when they've tasted panic. I got no more than 20 feet before the wave broke over me.

A man, black and scarred from a fire so now a ghost of himself, struck at me as he passed. From behind, a woman, cradling a ruined arm, pushed me. I didn't have their momentum, hadn't seen what they'd seen, what had triggered their panic. I was treading water, doomed to drown.

A pack of wild children, a tribe drawn out of the alleys and shadows by the smell of opportunity, suddenly surrounded me. Hungry eyes appraising my clean clothes, my worth, the contents of my worker's bag as I ran and they chased. A cramp in my side came on so suddenly I thought for a fraction of a scream that one had knifed me with a piece of glass or a rusty sliver of iron or steel. Meat for the Dark Markets, old clothes for the camps. My breath was glass knives. My eyes were tiny and windburned from the cool night. My feet smashed, broke with each clawing stride.

They were jaguars. They were leopards. They were animals born and bred on the streets. And I was the sick member of the herd that day. I went for the alley. Stupid. So stupid. I moved, like drying clay, so slow, and they were there, blocking me in to bring me down and slice my throat.

The alley's mouth was fast approaching. Onto the sidewalk, around the stump of a telephone pole, my heart hammered in my head. I rounded the corner hard, driving an elbow hard into the chest and head of the girl? boy? I cut off. Behind me, I heard the spill, the scrambling on the hard asphalt, the tumble as the pack tripped and spilled. I'd bought seconds, but no more.

Then the boy who'd caught me was hit from behind, a sudden force—very loud—slapped him down. He was naked save for canvas work pants five sizes too big, torn and filthy, tied around his waist and ankles with colorful wire. In one breath the boy had been there, turning to impale me with his knife—a rusty triangle of iron—and then he wasn't; he became a tumbling pile of arms and legs.

I didn't know the sound, couldn't recognize it.

I tripped and collided with the hard street. I waited for the knives, the teeth, the nails. But…nothing. Turning quick, I saw the alley, saw the cool darkness of the deep city, the running and cries of the riot far behind. Tubal stood between the riot and me, the bodies of three wild children a jumble of meat and blood streaks on the asphalt. He was breathing hard, holding the pistol to his chest.

✍

"This is horrible," he said, pushing something vaguely purple with his fork. It was the winter of '12, six months later, and most of the city was cold and starving.

Carved out of old industrial, the ceiling was low, framed by useless lead and copper wire, painted with thousands of coats of thick black. The place smelled of being rushed. An underground meeting place, a secret café in a starving and freezing world.

"Amazing what you can do with garbage and camp rations," I said, trying to be cheerful. A riot the day before had been bad. Very bad. I couldn't wear or look at the shirt I'd been wearing. It wasn't my blood, but it was still blood. From somewhere. Shots, screams. I had begged Tubal to leave the pistol at home, to not take it with us when we went for our share of rations. The pistol made me nervous. He was angry with me, said maybe having it could have saved someone. I was angry in return: It could have gotten him killed. Or me.

"You need news?" said Geraldine. She was rare, and that made her special. Somehow she had managed to live in the nearby wilds and survive. Survive, gain weight, and dye her rat's nest purple. Too damned lucky, too damned informed, too damned exuberant. But she'd been around for years, and no one around her had vanished. Not many could say that.

"Give us the news, Gerry," Tubal said, pushing his plate of horrible purple improvisation aside and taking a long pull from the rotgut we were sharing. The polished tin can flashed and dazzled, distracting me from Geraldine pulling up an ancient folding metal chair.

I was the one who held the money. Funny how couples fall into their duties, their stations. I handed her a five, all crisp and unblemished, straight from Masoqui.

"Number 2. Written in his blood," she said in her practiced storyteller's tone, tracking back and forth between us to catch our attention. "A pipsqueak manager down at the docks, but brother and son to the uppers. Dad's the district superintendent, bro's the Militia chief. Liked 'em young, street said. Chicken hawk. Made visits to the camps with his bro. Two go in, half a dozen leave. Liked his German rubber and his special machines a lot. Got good enough, streets say, to make some of 'em last the night. Good, but not good enough. Goes to the camp once a week. Once a week and six get the good life for a while, until the next itch comes."

Tubal pushed his tin can over to her. She took a quick swallow, put it back down, and smiled at him. "Was all lined up to take over. Seems bro was on the way up to New Jerusalem and they was goin' to make him deputy Militia, maybe city superintendent.

"Took him a while to die. Gagged, cuffed, and hung up high. Slit his ankles, deep enough to drain. Hung there all night, most of the day. Drip, drip, drip. Servants knew to not interrupt his pleasures, to let him alone. Didn't interrupt this either."

I gave her another crisp five. Good news was rare, worthy of reward. "Bless Bourbaki," she said, giving the smile now to me, showing cracked and yellowed picket-fence teeth.

"God bless," I returned.

Tubal took his cup back, finished the rotgut, said, "I wonder how high it'll go."

✍

Tubal didn't seem rough. It didn't seem to be in him; he was more polished, buffed, restrained. Seeing him, you'd think he'd be a cool steel sword in bed, gleaming and strong.

And he was, some of the time. But other times he wasn't what you might expect, and certainly not what I'd expected.

At first he was that sword, and his hands were strong and immaculate on my body: grabbing my ass in a tense grip, hand locked firm around my cock, mouth up and down on my dick like a well-balanced machine.

He seemed to pose in bed. Not prance, and certainly not preen. Pose, like a statue, like a carved marble edifice, cool and strong. I remember…was it the first time, the second? Hard to say. The date

is gone, but even now the night burns in my memory. I'd been sucking him, teasing his long, muscular cock with the back of my throat.
With a muscled arm like a piece of well-maintained machinery, he
scooped me up, hauled me to my feet like I was a cheap trinket. For
a moment, our cocks battled between us, hard-ons smacking
together as we kissed.

Then he lifted me—a doll, a plaything—breathed steamy breaths
on my chest. Then down, forcefully parting my thighs with a pair of
quick, bruising slaps to my legs. I swallowed his throbbing cock with
my ass. Drank him. The whole time, every moment of our fuck, his
face remained frozen, immobile in control and determination.

He was like that most of the time. Not always—sometimes he got
rough. I liked that too, of course. For a long time.

✍

Number 3: The Militia scurried into their holes and pulled the
lids tight.

The newsletters, cranked out on some blotchy ink-jet system,
flapped loose and free down the quiet street. Looking down from our
second-story apartment window, I saw someone actually handing
them out. Plain as day, bold as the brave. A smiling Aryan with a
bone in his nose dressed in a new-looking Militia jumpsuit. *Cojones.*
You could feel the Militia's hot eyes on him like a panicked tension
in the air. He may have been found dead, later, but standing on
Castro and Market, then, he was alive.

*Our little birdie says that he won't be playing ball for a while, and in
fact might be off the team. Hard to return a vicious volley when you
have a handicap like that. No hands. No feet. We offer our sincere persecuted and murdered condolences to the Power and Water District
manager and for the young victims of his reign, whose bodies are still
being found in the Hunter's Point Wastes—and we applaud Bourbaki.*

It was a Saturday. I know it was a Saturday because I wasn't at
work, and Tubal would go out on long afternoon walks on Sundays.
I remember my hands hurt from work, from twisting leads and jam-
ming stubborn cables together. I had dozens of tiny cuts. I remem-

ber that we hadn't had sex for several nights because of my hands or maybe because of the periodic chatter of gunfire that echoed down the streets from Civic Center.

"I wish they'd do something," I'd said, staring out the window. The city was hot, blasted by light, wavering in heat. The man with the fliers had wandered off.

"Who are you talking about?"

I can't remember what he was wearing or doing. I just remember the words, and the baking cement outside.

"I don't know—the Militia, Bourbaki. I don't know. I wish Bourbaki would cut all their damned balls off, castrate them, make them fucking all go away. I wish the Militia would kill him—kill us all."

"Just wish something would happen?"

"I just hate waiting, trying to expect everything. I'm tired of being surprised, is all."

"I don't know. Sometimes surprises can be good things."

"These days? Come on, we get a little, they take it back—and then some. Kill them or kill us. I'm just so tired."

"It's the heat. It can only get better."

"I wish it would just get...*something*."

"It'll get better." He touched me then, on my shoulder. I glanced back at him. He seemed so collected: not hot, not bored, not frightened. I remember looking away, suddenly angry with his smile, his constant relaxation.

"It'll get better."

"I just hate waiting. It reminds me of hospitals. Waiting rooms. Like when my father had his heart attack. Waiting to see if he was alive or dead. Now *we're* waiting to see if we're going to live or die."

Sometime that afternoon he told me. His family had a tiny bit of land near the Oregon border. He'd kept the place going, kept his father going, after his mother was raped and killed. The half-mad Militia had cut off her hands, cut off her breasts, and left her to die in the pigpen. He told me quietly, calmly, one word pushed slowly out of his mouth by another, how his father had changed after seeing his wife's blood mixed with pig shit, of the midnight visits paid to his 12-year-old son.

One winter he'd left. Not angry, not frightened. He just started walking. He left his father to die in the cold or from his own hand. He hitched a ride with a grain caravan, made his way to the city, to me.

"Things will always get better," he said. And even though there was something secret, something with blood in it, that he wasn't telling me, I believed him.

✍

When he was rough…

On summer nights I'd dread the growl, for it meant having to wear long sleeves the next day. In winter the marks didn't matter so much; what warm clothes I had covered a multitude of sins. But winter had a cold edge to it, and a shortage of power and heating oil meant that every slap, bite, or punch hurt 10 times worse.

Well, maybe not always, and sometimes it was a spice. Then other times, when we kissed, when his hands went to my cock and mine to his, when his lips touched my cock or mine touched his, the fear went beyond excitement, beyond adding blood to my dick. I'd shake, the fear rising in me. I'd shiver. In the winter sometimes he'd…sometimes stop, thinking I was too cold. Sometimes.

Other times his growl would build, swelling inside him as if tied directly to his throbbing dick. That growl signaled his ferocity. A kiss became a bite, the copper taste of my blood stoking his furnace. He'd grip me so hard I would groan more from the crushing of his hands than the thought of his bobbing dick.

The first blow would come, quick as lightning, with a practiced accuracy that would bend me over. Gagging, vomit surging up my throat, I'd bend—forced by pain rather than want. His cock would enter my throat with a lip-rending thrust, mixing his salty precome with acidic bile.

Or my asshole would take him, forced if it didn't open with enough speed; opening, then swelling in a great rectal swallow. I became a tube for him, a fuck hole for his thick cock. Lubricated with slime, spit, or blood, he didn't care.

I didn't know what to call it. It always made me hard. Even though it was rough, fast, and painful, and sometimes I didn't want it, I was always hard.

It wasn't until much later that I actually became afraid.

✍

Another day—a Sunday (because Tubal wasn't there) in that summer of more vanishings, more numbered murders—someone called for him.

It was a rare occasion. I knew Tubal made calls, because sometimes he'd leave, right after dinner, right after sex, and go out "to make a call." I imagined him standing in the dark, in the rain, making whispered arrangements to agents and provocateurs. He would go out even though we had a telephone, a ridiculous luxury Mr. Masoqui had managed to acquire for me. Phones were pretty rare, and making and receiving calls even rarer. A voice out of the air was unique. All I ever used it for was to call Citicore to check the system.

On this day it rang. "Is Peters there?"

"Don't know him. Have you got the right number?" The voice was nondescript but not official. It lacked the practiced English and slapping timbre of Militia.

He recited it back. It was our number. "Tan, bald, mustache?"

"I don't know who you are. I don't know your voice."

"It's OK. Just tell him it's planted. Got that? It's real important. It's planted."

"I don't know what you're talking about."

"That's OK, just tell him. Planted, right? It's planted."

"I got the message, but I think you've got the wrong person."

"I don't think so. You just tell your pal."

"I'll tell him."

"Good. He enjoys his work. He'll enjoy this."

"I don't know what you mean."

"He gets a kick out of this, doesn't he? Your pal? He'll really like this. Makes him hard as a rock. I know, man. I know him from way back."

"Look, there isn't any Peters."

I still don't know what he was saying, telling me: a warning or a gloat. "He's always been like this. Been doing it since he was 9. Just worked his way up to bigger critters. More style, more flair. The man does love his work. Like his first one, stayed hard for weeks after. Couldn't wait to do number 2. What's he up to now, anyway? Seven? Eight? More power to him. Man's found his niche."

I hung up on him.

✍

Then it was winter. Time and our hero, Bourbaki, had given us names. Before, there was just *a place* where people might meet. In those days names could be used against us, so they weren't used. Now we could go to a little café called the Quiet Man, a little place with steamed windows.

It was days after the call, days to think and let it simmer. Dreams of guns, dreams of smiles, and the sound of shots. That morning in that street-side café: condensation running down glass, *me* telling *him* about it.

Numbers 4 and 5 bought us room and time. Six had shoved the Militia down deep into themselves, into their fortified complexes high on the hills. Now they only came down to kill in the Tenderloin, in a firecracker pistol assault on the only area left to them. Stories circulated about foaming Militia shooting in impotent fury at old, already bullet-riddled buildings.

I told him of number 7 and all he said was, "I wonder how high it'll go."

✍

He vanished after that night in the café. I had looked at him and seen something I wasn't supposed to see.

So now I sit, drinking bootleg that is almost drinkable. Things have gotten that good. I sit in a café run and frequented by copies of myself. The Militia knows we are here but won't risk the mutilations, the deaths, that Bourbaki would visit on them for one shot, one flaming bomb. Life is that good.

It's been two years since stumbling out of that ruin with yards of cable. Tubal was first a companion, then a hero. Now? Now I sit in the Quiet Man.

I have numbers to call, if I want. I could pick up one of the public phones, punch in a number and inform. Everyone knows Bourbaki, named after some mathematicians who tried to solve every paradox with numbers, with counting. They took the name of a French general and failed.

I knew what *our* Bourbaki looks like, talks like—the man trying to solve our problems with his own numbers. I know what he smells like, the sounds he makes, his deep-down laugh, and whom he might even love.

I might get shot for it, in revenge or as a reward. I might get a medal. Things might go back to the way they were. Things might go back to the fear of the gun, to bodies burning on the beaches, to friends vanishing like short dreams on waking, before a madman started killing all the right people.

I sit in the Quiet Man while people speak with laugher and joy about the doings of their hero. I sit with potato booze and try to decide to inform and betray and maybe live. Or stay quiet and let him kill his secret with me.

As I sit here, I wonder: *Am I still alive because he loved me, loves me? Or because I'm not worth counting?*

Contributor Biographies

Laura Antoniou is well-known in the alternative writing community, particularly for her *Marketplace* series (*The Marketplace, The Slave, The Trainer,* and *The Academy*), regarded as the S/M fiction of choice among pansexuals by the editor of *S/M Classics*. She is currently working on the next two books in the series. Antoniou has also had great success as an editor, creating the groundbreaking *Leatherwomen* anthologies and many others. Antoniou presents on various S/M relationship topics throughout the United States and Canada.

Scott Brassart is the editor of numerous anthologies, including, under his given name, the Lambda Literary Award–nominated *Wilma Loves Betty, Bar Stories,* and *The Ghost of Carmen Miranda.* Under his pen name, Jesse Grant, he is the editor of Alyson Books' annual *Friction: Best Gay Erotic Fiction* series, and the anthology *Men For All Seasons.* He lives and works in Los Angeles.

Patrick Califia-Rice is the author of several fiction and nonfiction books about radical sexuality, most of which were published under the name Pat Califia. At the time when this was written, he had just begun the process of changing his social gender from female to male. He lives in San Francisco with his partner, Matt Rice, and their son. He is also in private practice as a therapist and is an ordained member of the pagan clergy.

M. Christian has been called "one of the finest living writers of erotica" by Pat Califia and "today's premiere erotic shape-shifter" by Carol Queen. He is the author of *Dirty Words.* In addition, he has over 100 published short stories. His work can be found in *Friction, Best Gay Erotica, Best American Erotica, Best Lesbian Erotica, Set in*

Stone, *Men for All Seasons,* and many other books and magazines. He is also the editor of numerous anthologies, including *Best S/M Erotica* and *Rough Stuff* (with Simon Sheppard). He thinks *way* too much about sex.

WWW.JACKFRITSCHER.COM "invented the SoMa prose style" —*Bay Area Reporter.* Gay literary pioneer: 43 years of published writing; 4,000 pages (plus 1,000 photographs) in 30 magazines (founding editor in chief, *Drummer, Man2Man*); 16 books, including *Some Dance to Remember, Titanic,* plus biomemoir of life with his scandalous lover, *Mapplethorpe: Assault with a Deadly Camera*; photographer/director, 120 features: www.PalmDriveVideo.com. Burning history: www.JackFritscher.com.

R. J. MARCH, also known as Robert Warwick, lives in Reading, Pa. His collection of erotica, *Looking for Trouble,* was published in the spring of 1999. He has published work in *The Mississippi Review, The Literary Review, Men, Freshman, Torso,* and *The James White Review.* His journal pages, *Beer and Boys,* can be found on the Web site ARTelevision.com, and he is a featured author at Nightcharm.com.

LESLÉA NEWMAN has published over 30 books, including *The Little Butch Book, The Femme Mystique, Girls Will Be Girls, Out of the Closet and Nothing to Wear, Pillow Talk: Lesbian Stories Between the Covers,* and *My Lover is a Woman: Contemporary Lesbian Love Poems.* She lives with the butch of her dreams in Lesbianville, USA. Visit her Web site at www.lesleanewman.com.

FELICE PICANO is a best-selling author of fiction, poetry, memoirs, and other nonfiction. A member of the legendary Violet Quill Club, Picano founded the Sea Horse Press. He coauthored *The New Joy of Gay Sex* and wrote the award-winning novel *Like People in History* and *The Book of Lies,* a Lambda Literary Award finalist.

CAROL QUEEN (www.carolqueen.com) is the author of *Real Live*

Nude Girl, The Leather Daddy and the Femme, Exhibitionism for the Shy, and coeditor of the Lambda Literary Award winner, *PoMoSexuals* (with Lawrence Schimel) as well as *Switch Hitters* (with Lawrence Schimel), *Sex Spoken Here* (with Jack Davis), and *Best Bisexual Erotica* (with Bill Brent).

SHAR REDNOUR is a video producer-director-scriptwriter with her partner, Jackie Strano, for their company SIR Video (www.sirvideo.com). She likes her heels high and her champagne glasses sugar-rimmed. She's currently awaiting Diva-fine enlightenment for what book will follow *The Femme's Guide to the Universe* and *Starf*cker: A Twisted Collection of Superstar Fantasies.*

THOMAS S. ROCHE (www.thomasroche.com) is a fiction writer, journalist, spoken-word performer, and best-selling anthologist. He is the editor of the Noirotica series, *Sons of Darkness, Brothers of the Night, In the Shadow of the Gargoyle,* and *Graven Images,* and the author of *Dark Matter.* He is currently working on a series of crime novels and an omnibus collection of his horror and crime-noir fiction. E-mail thomasroche-announce-subscribe@onelist.com to subscribe to his free newsletter, "Razorblade Valentines."

SIMON SHEPPARD is the author of *Hotter Than Hell and Other Stories* and coeditor with M. Christian of *Rough Stuff: Tales of Gay Men, Sex, and Power.* His short fiction has appeared in several editions of the *Friction* and *Best American Erotica* series as well as in numerous other anthologies and magazines. His nonfiction column, Sex Talk, appears in gay papers nationwide. He lives in San Francisco.

CECILIA TAN is the author of *Black Feathers: Erotic Dreams* and the editor of over 30 anthologies of erotic science fiction, including *Sextopia, Fetish Fantastic,* and *Sexcrime.* Her stories have appeared in *Best American Erotica, Best Lesbian Erotica, Ms. Magazine, Penthouse,* and tons of other places. She's currently at work on an erotic novel titled *The Book of Want.*

LUCY TAYLOR is the author of the short story collections *Close to the Bone, Unnatural Acts and Other Stories,* and *Painted in Blood* as well as the Stoker Award–winning novel, *The Safety of Unknown Cities.* Other of her novels include *Nailed* and *Dancing With Demons.*